GODS OF ENERGY

THE FIRST IN A STUNNING NEW SCI-FI TRILOGY

GODS OF ENERGY

A.T. SOUTHORN

Copyright © 2021 by A.T. Southorn

The right of A.T. Southorn to be identified as the author of this work has been asserted.

All rights reserved.

No part of this book may be reproduced, stored in a retrieval system, or transmitted, in any form, or by any means (electronic, mechanical, photocopying, recording or otherwise) without the prior written permission of the author, except in cases of brief quotations embodied in reviews or articles. It may not be edited amended, lent, resold, hired out, distributed or otherwise circulated without the publisher's written permission.

Permission can be obtained from www.godsofenergy.com

This book is a work of fiction. Names, characters, places, and incidents either are products of the author's imagination or are used fictitiously.
Any resemblance to actual persons, living or dead, events, or locales is entirely coincidental.

Published by A.T. Southorn

ISBN: 978-1-3999001-8-8

Cover design & interior formatting:
Mark Thomas / Coverness.com

*When order reigns, time remains,
but order is inconstant.*

CHAPTER ONE

THE PRISONER

Being a prisoner had its perks. Arun sat unattended in the middle of a rotting hut, sturdy enough to shield him from the rain, thunder, and cold winds that plagued the longlight months. He twiddled his naked thumbs on a creaking wooden chair, mindful that his captors had taken his gloves along with his books and pocket scope. His scope would have once peered into the sun and the stars—mythical bodies hidden beyond the clouds. It was now resigned to spotting rival scavengers from afar; not much use in a windowless hut.

A door stood closed, straight ahead, only brought to light by dim rays spread through the hut from the slits high in the slatted walls. To Arun's right: a mountain of unlit candles, symmetrically arranged. To his left: a bed. It'd been years since he'd last seen one, let alone lay in one. His ears could only capture the same sound he'd heard since waking—rain pattering against the hut and dripping through a crack in the corner. He was surely far from any town and anyone he knew.

Arun couldn't remember a single face from his last moments as a free man wandering the fields. There were no chains nor rope around him, but scavengers would always bind, so the hut must have belonged to reclusive Hillfolk or fearless Hunters—bone-crunching cannibals that strayed in and out of town. Either way, it wouldn't be a fair fight, and a wry smile lifted on one side of Arun's face.

Knock, knock, knock—and the peace was shattered.

Arun's thoughts dispersed. Three knocks broke the spitting rain, echoing through the hut with no time in between. Showtime. He crunched his knuckles and fingers back and readied himself for yet another fight. Living life as a lone scavenger didn't teach him much, but it certainly taught him how to defend himself.

The door opened as Arun remained seated, never the aggressor, never the first to throw a fist. Muted daylight made its way past two cloaked figures standing beyond the doorway as rain fell around them—one tall, one small. Arun's pupils needed little time to adjust, but the sharp, cold breeze brought a shiver as it glided past his neck.

'So, this is him,' croaked a deep voice. 'I am a little underwhelmed, I must say.'

'The feeling's mutual,' said Arun, clenching his fists on his lap. He peered into the shadows, attempting to recognise a face. 'Who are you?'

'I am who lives here,' replied the tall, shadowy figure. 'This hook is where I hang my cloak. That bed is where I lay my head. So, who do you suppose you are? One of Aerkin's men? Or just a petty thief?'

Ah, *thief*, the word thrown at Arun whenever he found himself held hostage. 'Humour me. What did I take? Some of your precious candles?'

'You know precisely what you have stolen.' The floorboards creaked and cracked as the figures made their way inside. The small captor wore a hood and stood to the side, and the tall one stepped further forward, revealing a grey beard and wavy, long, receding hair to match—a man, an older man, hunching slightly underneath his black cloak. His middle finger on his left hand twitched, and his nose pinched, sniffing the damp air. It was both a charm and a curse for Arun to notice every minor element of a person's detail. The man wouldn't put up much of a fight dressed like that.

The realisation then hit him. Long, black cloaks. These *were* the Hillfolk: marauders and meddlers of the west. He'd never come across one in the flesh, but he'd heard the stories of torment and torture. That must be why they kept him here; they wanted to convert him. His body pinched with the same tingle he felt hearing footsteps at night, his heart beating through his chest. He rose from the chair, topping his adrenaline with a spike of headrush. He took in every second of this feeling. He loved it. 'I think it's time I left. Which one of you is gonna try and stop me?'

A chuckle escaped the man's lips along with a warm, misty breath that the incoming cold air quickly absorbed. 'You would leave without your gloves?'

'I only need my books and my scope. Keep the gloves. Something to remember me by.'

The two mysterious figures looked at each other, the man's fingers making a flurry of signals by his side.

'Kate…' The man nodded to her before turning back to Arun with his hands behind his back. 'I happen to be a glover, a career that rather handed itself to me in this new world. As you can imagine out here, I do not have much to work with but with what I do have I do extremely well.'

Arun was left confused by the man's winding words, but his eyes were instantly drawn to the second figure, presumably named Kate, stepping forward alongside her companion. Her shaded hand slowly unfurled to reveal a tiny yet bright blue light nestling in the centre of her gloved palm. Arun's eyes were fixated. The only brightness he'd ever known came from a human-made flame or the dulled daylight from the skies. How was she doing that? He'd never seen a glow like this before, clattering the wooden walls with a glistening blue. Yet somehow, it looked familiar. He stared deeper, noticing its radiance materialise bolder and brighter, sparkling in circles.

The man continued, 'My gloves are dear to me. Years of my life have gone into making a material so precious that even a single, loose thread curses me with sleepless nights.'

A faint humming noise vibrated the hairs in Arun's ears as the light continued to fizz in his eyes. It shook, horrifyingly beautiful, taking the shape of the hand of which it was born.

The man orbited Arun at a distance, eclipsing the blue light for a moment.

'So imagine my horror these last few years knowing a pair had gone missing. So tell us—'

'Where is she, and when did you steal the gloves?' Kate's sharp, deep voice cut the air for the first time. The blue light brought a glisten to her face. Pale brown mud and dark brown hair covered her cheeks and forehead, but her pupils shone the same blue as the light.

Arun fell back onto the chair wide-eyed, snapping out of his daze. These light tricks must be how they converted people. Don't panic, Arun. 'Where's who? And I didn't steal them. I found them; under some rocks near where I live.'

'Tell us the truth.' Kate approached as the man continued his orbit behind Arun. The vibrating hum of light cupped Arun's ears; it'd breached his confident, cocky defences. His chest bounced with the roaring beat of his heart. Why couldn't they have just been simple Hunters?

'What's that light?' mumbled Arun, fighting the torment of the glow.

'We're asking the questions,' said Kate.

'Perhaps we are dealing with an ignorant scavenger, after all,' said the man. 'His face is straining as if he might relieve himself. I would rather that not occur in my abode.'

The blue light softly dissipated in Kate's palm. 'Scavengers can't hold the light. I saw it, Nicholas, with my own eyes. He used it to block his weight in falling rubble—he'd be dead otherwise. He's not telling us something.'

Falling rubble. Emerging light. Arun remembered: searching the rubble of an old building, finding a boy, bricks collapsing from above, crashing down as a wave of solid matter, only to be broken in its fall by that same blue light spread across his hands akin to a shield. His gloves must have created that light and saved his life. But how? Did he cause the light to appear? That's the last thing he remembered before waking up on the splintered floorboards of the hut.

Arun took a moment to process his memory. Without a touch of subtlety, he lifted his hand to the tip of his forehead. Ouch! Damnit—his skin mimicked a volcano unearthed from his skull, throbbing with a small, open wound swelling in the centre. A moment's flinch gave way. 'Wait. How'd you find me? Were you following me?'

Kate crossed her arms. 'Never let your enemies out of your sight.'

'Enemy? I don't know you! Just keep the damn gloves. I'm leaving.' Arun stood once more.

Kate turned to glance at Nicholas, Nicholas stared back, and Arun's eyes darted each way as he awaited a response before heading for the door. Stalemate. Seconds passed without a word.

Nicholas approached Arun's right shoulder, now within reach. The slight shine from outside brought one side of his face to light, one eye gleaming light-blue. A deep, piercing stare emanated from his bushy beard and scruffy hair. He ran his open palm over and down his beard, pulling his sleeve back slightly to reveal a dimmed reflection on a circular, slick glass surface with three lines and twelve numbers, ticking intermittently. Arun had never seen one of these working before; there seemed no reason to need one.

'How old are you?' asked Nicholas, meeting Arun's gormless gaze.

Arun's fists clenched a light coat of sweat, still awaiting his moment to strike back. 'Twenty. Why? You like them young?'

The muscles in Nicholas's face relaxed. 'So you were born in the year 0 ADE. That is a first.' He turned to the mound of candles, pensive. 'So be it. If you feel you must leave, then try. Let us see how far you make it.' Nicholas held his palm out towards the door.

Arun's shoulders pinched together. Without saying a word, he ambled to the door between the two Hillfolk as if he were walking a tightrope. Their sour sweat shot through his nose to the back of his throat, almost tripping his stride. He walked through the open door staring back at the two, wary of a trap, but they didn't move a muscle.

Freedom, hopefully. Taking no more than two steps outside, Arun brought himself to an immediate halt. He opened his eyes wide as his short hair wiggled in the external wind. The greenest, long, flowing grass swayed down a hill's steep slope in front of him, flickering in the rain. Vibrant shades on the trees emerged from the ground into the faraway hills. Knee-high walls of stone partitioned the land, with abundant, multi-coloured crops surrounding the perimeter.

Small, basic huts and sheds scattered around a cottage, entirely untouched by the devastation of time. Arun couldn't remember the last time he'd seen a building from the old era standing in one piece. Had the endless quakes not reached this far? The fresh air brushed his nostrils, and a slight, crisp gale carried the only familiarity: the songs of waves of birds ringing in Arun's ears, migrating from branch to branch as the drops of late-afternoon rain fell from the leaves. This hill appeared more beautiful than any place he'd ever graced—a truly peaceful land.

Footsteps grew ever-present, thumping the sound of the songbirds away. Nicholas stepped out alongside Arun as high-pitched voices trickled from the edge of the hill. To the right, two children ran, escaping from the crowd of trees as if in slow motion, laughing with one another: life emerging from the dark. Arun could count on one hand the number of young children he'd seen before, aside from his younger self. There were only two elder women in his town, but even if there were more, the idea of bringing up a child in this world seemed bleak to him at best. The children on the hill bounced and bustled, kicking a chestnut towards another couple of figures emerging from the hut. The couple embraced the children tight in their arms, sealing their eyes shut with genuine expressions of joy. He'd never seen this before; he'd never seen a family.

What was this place?

'I know what you are thinking—it looks a little bit different to your Toss, I would imagine.' Nicholas used the term Toss: an acronym for town-of-sorts, largely heard from the mouths of lonesome farmers scattered far around the outskirts. Or Loners, as Arun called them. Nicholas must have been wary that a scavenger would take offence to the less than pleasant duality of the word. 'I assume that is where you live.'

Arun stepped away from Nicholas with caution, wary of any menacing tricks his cloak may hide. Those back home would have Arun believe the

Hillfolk lived in mudholes, kidnapping and torturing even the most innocent of people, not giggling across fields of glorious green. Had he been lied to? All this time?

Arun's mind dwelled on the vision he usually encountered upon leaving his lone shelter. Sliding the sheet of metal that acted as a door, every blink of an eye would bring something frozen in despair: a crumbled wall, a pile of broken glass, or scattered metal from old vehicles. There would always be a constant, harrowing reminder of the society that descended to their end despite having riches beyond any imagination. A time where survival was merely an afterthought, never mind the purpose of each passing day. It had never made sense to him, and he felt it never would. Yet for one lasting moment, as he stared across the hill, he'd seen how life could be as peaceful as in the books he collected. 'It's so beautiful here. It's how I always pictured life once was. I don't understand—where am I?'

'Home,' replied Nicholas. 'There are no bees to buzz, nor fragrance from flowers, but the absence of time rids us minutes and hours.' Nicholas spoke to a tune, a lighter tone than in the hut, with a sly grin to one cheek. 'If you believe in miracles, this is where they belong—at Berkley Hill. A place where forgotten time stood still.'

'I thought nobody kept track of time anymore.'

Nicholas's head darted. 'The horses are hungry.' He hummed to himself. 'You must be an impressive fighter to have made it this far as a scavenger without any significant disfigurement or facial wounds. Though your hands could do with a touch more care.'

'I got lucky, I suppose,' replied Arun in a daze, wary of Nicholas's senseless sentiments. 'Why d'you say I wouldn't make it far? Just be straight with me— am I your prisoner, or am I free to leave?'

'You are as free as you are allowed to be.' Nicholas breathed in a lungful of fresh air through his impressively large nose. 'But what reason would one have for not escaping their prison, with no lock on the door? You may wish to pretend it was the warmth from the cold or the roof from the rain, or even to play prisoner to excite yourself for a fight. But your arms were not tied, and a flimsy door would not stop you. We took what we needed from you: our gloves, yet you did not escape. You do not want to return home. You travelled the fields with all your possessions, not looking back once.' With a slow tone and a deep voice, he turned to Arun and uttered, 'I wonder why.'

Arun's jaw clenched. Nicholas could see right through him. The thrill of theft and a well-crafted storyline were the only comforts Arun enjoyed amongst the scavengers with whom he shared nothing in common. No friends or family awaited him back home. He'd ventured away with no intention of turning back, searching for a better life, never knowing where he'd end up. But never in his wildest dreams did he dream he'd end up here. 'Why treat me like a prisoner if you're so certain about me? That woman acted like she wanted to kill me.'

'Oh, she does. Her worries are not with the gloves as such but with the person who wore them. And I still believe you to be a thief, hence why we brought you here, but a crime is not what interests me now. You interest me. I wanted to test a scavenger's character.'

Nicholas held his hands behind his back and tilted his chin to the sky. 'You will have to forgive Kate. Those gloves you stole—'

'Found.'

'Yes. *Found*. They are very dear to her heart, and we have not seen them in years. Then you waltz through the Moorlands wearing them, using their power seemingly without prior knowledge, running from a home that's barely a home. You can hardly feel surprised at our suspicion.'

Arun caught Kate leaning against the door, listening in. Her eyes pierced through his.

'That brings me to now,' said Nicholas. 'We are always in need of help, and you are seeking new pastures. What others would call fate is simply a coincidence, one that benefits us both. Wouldn't you agree, nameless one?'

'Arun. Arun Owondo.' Arun was used to being the smartest of the scavengers but found himself searching for words here. 'What d'you need help with?'

'It is a pleasure to be a part of your story, Arun. I am Nicholas, and we need help fighting a fight far bigger than that of any scavenger squabble. Perhaps a fight that transcends this physical world.'

A fight that…what? An aged smile etched over Nicholas's face as if he found pleasure in Arun's blank expression. The gaze of all cognitive abandonment. Brain cells jumping ship into a black void. Arun still had no idea what Nicholas spoke of, and his nerves hadn't settled. '*Yeeeah*…I dunno. What makes you so confident I'll choose to stay and fight your fight?'

Nicholas laughed. 'You have consciously chosen to have no choice. That is the beauty of *dark energy*, from the very first moment you lay eyes on it. Now, there is much to discuss. I will leave you with Kate, as I have a quick matter to attend to.' Nicholas turned to his hut.

'Dark what? Is she gonna try and kill me?' asked Arun frantically, directing his eyes anywhere other than towards Kate.

'Perhaps. If it turns out you are indeed lying.' Nicholas smiled. Arun scorned. 'But if I know anything about a scavenger, it is that they would much rather fight their way out of a situation than waste timeless time with lie after lie. And you seem no different.' A calm look of contentment replaced his grin as he returned to his humble hut. He lent a loud whisper to Kate before disappearing. 'Be nice to him.'

As the drizzle continued to dampen Arun's hair, a silence filled the air. Kate remained motionless and speechless: a mannequin in disguise.

Arun cleared his throat to deepen his voice. 'Hi…so…that's some nice mud you're wearing.'

'Don't play games.'

'I'm not. I'm just trying to figure out why I'm here and what that light is and what I'm getting out of any of this.'

'What you're getting? Two things. And you've been wearing them on your hands until now.' Kate brushed past Arun and walked the meandering path down the hillside. She left Arun with no choice. He didn't even know where north or south was, let alone which way led to safe passage. Arun breathed in and shrugged his shoulders.

'What's dark energy?' he shouted.

'Won't find out if you don't follow me.' Kate didn't break her stride.

Bugger.

CHAPTER TWO

DARK ENERGY

Firelight flickered in the cottage windows where the hillside path led Kate and a now scampering Arun. The smell of oaky smoke filled Arun's nose as a small trickle of cloud rose from the chimney, whilst uncontrolled laughter and chatter heightened in his ears. This was a far cry from the stories he'd heard growing up. 'Don't go near the Hillfolk; they'll bring nothing but trouble,' 'they're fanatics, fantasists,' 'they drove this world into the ground.' Nobody had ever seen where they lived, though, and if they had, perhaps they wouldn't be saying such things.

Arun's eyes searched for the bottom of Berkley Hill; a fence stood open with a path leading away. Bingo. Why did he have the feeling he couldn't leave, though? One hundred or so steps. That's all it would take. Away from the Hillfolk and back towards abnormal normality. Arun stepped forward. Ninety-nine steps to go. So why did he stop? His left leg was rooted like a tree. He deliberated.

Arun eventually reached his destination: the open door of the cottage. A while longer here wouldn't harm him. Kate looked silently smug before storming in and weaving through the seated crowd towards an empty table near the back of the open-plan room. Arun peeked his head in as chatter and laughter drowned out the sound of the wind and the birds. The room of tables became instantly silent as if a Hunter had walked in. Arun turned all heads towards him and counted twenty-five, maybe thirty in his head. All were looking directly at him, equally flummoxed by the new arrival. The faces were of hardened fighters: some men, some women, some bearded, some shaved.

'He's a scavenger,' said Kate.

Bodies tensed, fists clenched, and stares turned to frowns—what a pleasant welcome.

'He *was* a scavenger,' reassured Kate.

After a slight pause, the muscles in all the room's faces reversed into a cheery smile. Clink—glasses raised, and general well-wishes spewed Arun's way. Still cautious, Arun pulled together the fakest of fake, clenched smiles to cover his tremble walking towards Kate. She'd chosen the table closest to the fireplace, flickering away beside a window. Dim shadows danced across the footprint-stained white floors and even whiter walls. A fragrance, sweeter than any he'd smelt before, must have arisen from the multitude of coloured fruits scattered from table to table.

'Sit,' Kate insisted. She pinched her nostrils, frowning as she did.

'Dinner!' shouted the voice of an incoming, ecstatic, curly-haired woman stampeding her way into the room as Arun sat. 'So, this is the thief. Is he staying?'

Kate nodded. The woman carried a tray full of slices of bread, carrots, an oddly shaped red vegetable, sliced meat, and a steaming bowl of liquid. Arun had never seen a meal so plentiful. The woman placed it under his nose. The thick, earthy, mushroom scent from the bowl flared his nostrils as the gentle heat from the fireplace stroked the outside of his right leg. Food and warmth—this was all too comfortable.

'Why 'ello, sausage. I'm Cole. I'm a little tied up at the minute, lots of mouths to feed, but I'll send my dearly betrothed over in a minute to greet you. Glad you're joining us.'

Before Arun could object, Cole slapped her hand on Arun's damp shoulder before taking leave. He winced. 'This is all a bit much. I don't meet new people that often—not ones that talk.'

Kate picked a handful of loose raspberries from the tray. She leant one arm back on the chair, and without her head moving a muscle, threw a berry into her mouth. 'Anyway. Going to tell me how you used the gloves?'

'I…uh…put them on my hands.'

Kate, pausing not for the first time, took a large sip of water from the tray and looked back at Arun. She smiled, albeit briefly, and swallowed the water resting in her cheeks in one gulp before examining him. He knew what she'd see—a clean face, bar the volcanic wound, sat beneath roughly chopped dark hair, some strands far longer than others. He bore plenty of thin, white scars on his hands, and his fingers were oddly smaller than one would expect and in a wrecked state, unsurprising for the usual scavenger fighting through rock and rubble each day. However, scavenging did have the advantage of strengthening one's arms, and fighting had given his knuckles padded extensions. For all the damage his hands retained, his radiant skin and clean-cut teeth gave the false impression he hadn't struggled a day. Rugged, but unlike the other scavengers back home.

Kate's lips twitched. 'Okay, how about this. Looks like you're doing a lot of heavy thinking. And I have to be nice, for now. So, I'll talk first. These are private grounds. We don't let many, recently any, strangers in. We go on our way and conduct our business in peace, and we most definitely don't put spells on people. I've heard the rumours.'

Arun avoided eye contact.

'The gloves we wear are Nicholas's creation. Most pairs are made unique to the person wearing them, based on their skill and physical strengths.' Kate let her eyes wander for a second. 'You're already familiar with Iris's gloves. She was my…best friend. She disappeared several years ago when a meeting went sour, and we hadn't seen the gloves, or her, since. That's where you come in.'

Arun didn't mention that the gloves fit, well, like a glove, to hide his slender fingers. He pulled his hands slowly back from the tray and clenched his lumpy fists, retaining a slim hope of masculinity.

'Anyway, Nicholas is probably right. I don't believe anyone as harmless as you would have done anything other than stumble upon them. Doubt you're using them as intended, either. So I think I'm right in saying you only use them to keep warm and to stop your hands getting sticky whilst you're eating plums?'

Harmless? How dare she. Kate was one hundred per cent correct about the plums, though. The gloves provided a perfect foil for the menacing fruit, absorbing juice perfectly whilst drying quickly, not to soak through. The gloves were primarily white but somehow didn't stain—the perfect material.

Arun began to relax, slumping in his chair, despite his reluctance and the hundreds of questions still darting around his head. 'I hardly wore the gloves.' A harmless lie. 'The first time I saw that glowing blue light was today with the bricks.' A harmless truth. 'I think it was today. It was today, right? How'd you create that light?'

'One question at a time.' Kate reached into her cloak and pulled out Iris's gloves. The dark lines and circles on the white material seemed mysterious now, despite Arun never giving them more than a moment's attention. She lay them out on the table, face up. 'The light you saw is dark energy.'

'But it's not dark?'

'Yeah…bear with me. I'm more an expert on the practical side of things, not the explaining. But let's give it a try anyway.' Kate took a deep breath. 'First of all, it's a—'

'It's a physical cosmic energy, to be precise,' exclaimed a voice from behind Arun. Great, another new face. A squinting, dark-bearded man took shape alongside the seated duo with a stool in hand, perching in a spot closest to the tray. He was the tallest man Arun had ever seen. If there were a brightness to this world, he'd be shadowing above them, curving the light with his delicately round belly, though his arms were thin as twigs.

Without hesitation, he leant close enough to kiss Arun's tray of food, squinting to a strain, before smashing together a mix of ingredients into a hastily built sandwich. 'It was the greatest discovery of the Age of Technology, twenty years ago. Before the Worldshift, or apocalypse, whatever your people call it. It's a binding force in our universe that can now be held and manipulated to our will—the most common energy source in all universes, of course. This power belongs in the cosmos, moving galaxies, and accelerating all matter. To have that power in the palm of one's hand…is to be playing God.'

The man, interrupting his own sentence, took a gaping bite of his roughly assembled sandwich. Arun, best off avoiding watching the crumbs falling from his chin, instead chose to stare longingly, with fixated eyes, into the palms of the gloves; they lay lifeless on the table. Intrigue engulfed his thoughts. What kind of energy could they wield, and how would it feel to hold so much power?

'If you were to believe my theory,' continued the man, 'it even connects us all to a higher consciousness.'

'Tej, don't start that nonsense,' said Kate.

'What? Just because you haven't experienced something doesn't make it unreal. In fact—'

'Last time I checked, you'd experienced nothing either. You just want to believe everything Nicholas says.'

Arun slouched into his chair, watching the two bicker, continuing to feel at ease when the sudden realisation of being away from normality refreshed his thoughts and broke his staring gaze. As intriguing as this had all been, Arun felt out of his comfort zone. It was all too much, all too soon.

'How far am I from the nearest town?' asked Arun blindly.

Kate and Tej fell silent, mouths half-open. 'Quite far,' replied Tej. 'Where are you from?'

'New Carterton.'

'New Carterton? That old Toss? It's full of no-good, rotten garbage dwellers. The lowest of the low.'

'We prefer to be called *human*,' replied Arun with a distinct blank stare.

'Ah, sarcasm! Of course, humanity's lost form of whimsy. Probably for the better. Sorry, I didn't mean *everyone*.' Tej took another bite with juice joining the crumbs in spilling out of his mouth. Arun could just about hear him through his munching. 'New Carterton is quite a while away. How did you find us?'

'Found him in the Moorlands,' said Kate.

'What were you doing there? That's barren swampland. It feels like that whole land has been flooded for years. Mudholes every—'

'It doesn't matter,' interrupted Arun. 'I suppose now you have your gloves, I'll be outta here. Can you show me the way?'

'Yes…of course,' said the man. 'Thank you for returning the gloves. You needn't.'

'Tej, he's staying here,' said Kate. 'I saw him use the light.'

Tej stopped, mouth wide open in anticipation of another bite, before placing what little remained of his sandwich back on the tray. The skin around his lips wrinkled around as his tongue wiped over his teeth.

'So be it.' Tej finished his welcome by wiping his stubbled mouth with the back of his thumb and directing his sharp line of conversation to Arun. 'I hope you know what you're getting yourself into.'

Tej stood and dragged his screeching stool, ending his brief introduction without hesitation. Before storming off, he took one final, squinting look at Arun slumped in his seat.

'What's his problem?' asked Arun, feeling his confidence returning to battle his nerves. He sat straight and maintained eye contact with Kate. 'And why does everyone keep saying I'm staying here? You can't just kidnap me and act like that's normal. I don't know how to do that light thing, and I didn't agree to anything. I have…important places to be.'

'That pile of rubble I found you under didn't seem important,' said Kate. 'Listen. I get it. You're on edge because you don't know what's going on, knowledge is comfort and all that, but we need more people. Good people. Talented people. And if you haven't lied to us, and you're strong enough, then we'll need *you*. Many people have been brought here over the years, but not everyone has wielded the light. Look around you. This is all we have.

'I know Nicholas says you can leave, and that's true to an extent. You're not a prisoner, but we can't just let raw, untapped talent go when it's so hard to find.'

Talent? What talent? Arun didn't have much to show for himself; a collection of books, a scope, and a strained relationship with cretinous thieves. Yet, he found himself in the unusual situation of feeling wanted for once in his life. Those across the room glanced in his direction, sending friendly nods and smiles his way. Unnervingly rare.

Arun rested his elbows, uncomfortably copying others he observed. So, this was what *normal* felt like? He felt a bubbling inside him; the same bubbles he felt stumbling across a new-old book. He knew this feeling, for it was excitement, laced with the usual doses of fear and fragility.

'Okay…so what're you doing with all this "talent"?' asked Arun.

Kate glanced around the room at the others. 'You probably think we live here reclusively because we don't like people, but that's not true at all. Well, except for Hunters.'

Arun nodded understandably.

'We want to help people. We're only hard on scavengers because we've had a few of you sniffing around here before.'

'Excuse us for wanting to eat.'

'No, it's not about what we have; it's about where we are. We're hiding. Hiding from someone who wouldn't just put us in danger, but everyone between them and us too. We keep to ourselves and only let in people who are strong enough to help us. That way, no more people are needlessly at risk.'

Arun zoned in on one word. *Danger.* It was precisely the thing he was running away from in the first place. 'Wait…what kinda danger are we talking? Look, I don't wanna—'

'It's fine, we're fine.' Kate chopped his words short. 'And the Hill has been fine for as long as you've been alive. We won't be in danger as long as we don't do anything stupid and keep hold of these….' Kate held the gloves out. 'Put them back on. They won't be perfect, but they'll do for now until Nicholas makes a pair for you.'

Arun's hands hovered over the table, cautiously picking up the gloves whilst the word *danger* still floated in his head. He'd worn the gloves plenty of times before without care nor concern, but paying closer attention this time, he ran his hand along the coarse fabric, his fingertips sailing along hundreds of tiny rough balls scattered across the surface. Black stripes ran down the fingers and palm, indenting slightly in the material and reaching a centre point in the middle; a small black circle, smoother yet still grainy. He'd never before stopped to think these were more than strange aesthetic patterns with a useful grip.

'Just to be clear—you don't torture people?' asked Arun, conscious of the rumours still.

'No,' said Kate. 'We live in peace here.'

The cottage quietened once more, others noticing that Arun held the gloves. His right hand entered one, snug from wrist to tips, and his left followed. He patiently examined the gloves front-to-back before tilting his head back towards Kate.

'These gloves can be as much a part of you as your eyes,' said Kate. 'But pay attention; I'll only say this one more time. We've tried to train others before, and sometimes we fail. So if you don't listen to us, you're going to wind up back at that Toss, where you so obviously don't want to be. And another thing, those gloves belonged to someone incredible. Don't even think about using them to eat plums.' Kate concluded her warning with sternly raised eyebrows.

Arun respectfully nodded as raindrops raced down the window beside them. Imitating the rain, the others in the cottage trickled over to the seated pair, eager to issue well wishes. Still bemused by the previous events, Arun returned aimless handshakes and dispatched smiles and nods; he didn't know where to look or what to think. He had a home, but it never felt like he belonged anywhere. But now that a glimpse of belonging presented itself, he couldn't feel more queasily excited.

He looked into his open hands once more, now mesmerised by the pattern he'd previously disregarded. Arun's lips moved, raising at each end. An unusual feeling overcame him. He was happy.

'So, you ready to begin?' asked one of the Hillfolk.

'You're not going to make it far with small hands like that,' said another.

'Thanks,' murmured Arun. 'I'm ready. What exactly am I ready for?'

'We've been training for years to restore the world to free land,' said Kate, 'to be able to rebuild humanity, for what it's worth. It's a cause we've dedicated our lives to.'

'Rebuild humanity?' Arun raised an eyebrow. He looked around at the room full of scruffy, rough Hillfolk, one with a half-broken glass of milk in hand, another looking exhausted from standing. They couldn't be serious. 'Okay, sure. How? By hiding?'

'It's not for the light-hearted.' Kate remained straight-faced. 'When Tej said holding dark energy in your hands is like playing God, he meant it. The only way we can be truly free is to rid ourselves of the vermin that destroyed everything in the first place. We'll start tomorrow as evening is encroaching, so eat up, get some rest, and be ready in the morning.'

'Hold on. That kinda…definitely doesn't answer my question.'

'You want to know how?' Without a glimmer of emotion, Kate answered. 'The day will come for us to stop hiding. We'll need to fight. First, the followers, and then the disciples. Then all that's left to kill is God himself.'

Kate turned away to the others as they continued to talk amongst themselves. Arun stood still, his lower jaw slouched, staring into nothingness.

CHAPTER THREE

SLEEP

'The rain on which my head collects,
is sent here from the south.
It forces me to look above,
and sample in my mouth.
It raises from the stormy seas,
and brings upon the land.
Turn newborn seed to planted tree,
Turn rock to stone to sand.'

Arun would always sing the same song to calm himself whenever the rains fell late at night. He'd been relocated by Cole to a new hut, warm from the storm, hovering his chin over a naked candle flame atop a small, dusty table. Unlike where he first awoke, this hut contained a window, allowing him to glance outside as raindrops danced down the reflection of his face. Arun paid no attention to his appearance. Why would he need to? Nobody cared.

It wasn't uncommon for multiple bolts of electricity to strike down upon the stretch of land he dwelt on. As the saying goes, lightning always strikes twice. Seven bolts in instant succession filled the distant clouds, scattering and joining with the others to create one almighty bolt from above; it would have decimated anything below.

Arun balanced for comfort on a chair with both front legs missing, using his own legs to complete the seat. Occasionally, he tilted too far back, each jolt prodding him awake whilst he batted between various thoughts. God. Family. The light. He glared into his gloved palms, the candlelight bringing their patterns to life.

It'd been dark for many hours, and there would not be many more, with Arun's troubles finally beginning to ease as he grew tired. Not that the unsympathetic crickets minded, chirping into the howling winds. Annoying little twerps. It could be worse, though—they were a far cry from the rattling metal and constant shouting back in town.

A table with a candle, a bed, and a basket were all Arun could see as he looked around, and yet he felt he'd stumbled upon golden treasures. All he needed was to remember to ask for his books and scope back, and it would perhaps be a proper home with things to call his own. *His* table. *His* bed. Not only a mattress but a creaky frame too. It looked to be the most comfortable sleep he'd ever have, and he didn't want to rush the moment. He stood and walked over, imagining the soft touch of the off-white sheet in his mind before his fingers could verify.

Arun pulled the sheet back, but the excitement drained from his face. It felt alien to him, thin and coarse. He pressed down on the mattress to find an unbalanced and unsteady surface springing back. Perhaps another time. Arun walked to the opposite corner of the hut and hunched down. Ah, perfect.

Knock, knock, knock. Those three knocks again.

'Te-lue,' shouted a voice through the rain. 'Ready?'

Arun froze. Had sleep deprivation finally consumed him? It was too late into the night for anyone to be awake. 'Te-what?'

Kate opened the door, which took hold of its movements and swung open, wind and rain crashing into the hut. The still and peaceful air now twisted in chaos, blowing the candle out and ripping the bedsheet off on an adventure.

'Te-lue,' said Kate. 'It's a greeting. Means I come in peace.'

'Doesn't feel very peaceful,' wailed Arun, fighting the wind as Kate stood stiff.

'Come on. The others are waiting.'

'You said to be ready in the morning.'

'It's close enough. Follow me.' Kate disappeared into the night.

Arun groaned, dragging his feet towards the door whilst covering his eyes from the marauding weather. One look outside brought him nothing but darkness and pins of darting water attacking his eyes. His eyelashes performed as valiantly as a row of headless horses.

Faint light flickered from across the other side of the Hill. That must have been the destination. With one quick, longing glance back at the bed, Arun turned, pulled his buttonless shirt up to cover his neck, and briskly headed out.

'Hurry up!' shouted a distant voice. Arun broke into a jog, losing balance running against the Hill's grain and the forceful push of the wind. He could hear the thunder in the distance, which brought a glimpse of light to help him on his way. Rain pelted down on him relentlessly, each drop adding weight to the hair on his head.

To Arun's left stood a lone blue-leafed tree the same height as he. It was the only tree he could see in the dark, as long streaks of shimmering blue ran down the disproportionately thick trunk. The leaves, in turn, emitted a gentle reflection of blue light. Odd.

As the skies punished from above, the ground rumbled beneath the huts for a moment. Arun crouched, with his arms out wide for balance. Minor earthquakes were common, but the occasional major rupturing of the ground below was a daily concern. Unfortunately, one could never tell which it would be.

With a touch of luck and an unfazed mind, Arun managed to make it across without falling, reducing his pace to a cautioned walk as he reached an open door of a hut at least thrice bigger than the others. He shook his hair like a dog, bringing his second-hand rainfall indoors and over the few standing figures he'd yet to greet.

'Welcome to the study hut,' said Nicholas, greeting Arun at the door. 'I trust you are well-rested now.'

'Yeah, the bed looked lovely,' replied Arun, dropping his shoulders and rolling his eyes. 'I'm. So. Tired.'

'If you did not sleep, then you did not have a productive day. You should always end a day feeling tired. Boredom leaves those awake at night.'

Arun shrugged. 'Yeah. Being captured was extremely productive, thanks.' He turned to Kate, noticing a face now clear and clean of mud. He felt a strange tingle in his body, rising from his gut. He'd rarely come across women with skin young like his. A mole in the centre of her chin was the only mark he could find. He floundered dealing with these instinctive emotions, but as far as he could understand, she looked…intriguing. Just as he began to turn away, she caught him staring at her.

Nicholas turned his back and strolled towards the front of the room. It was a much larger hut than his, one without a bed. Several scattered chairs surrounded a large, round table in the middle, which held nothing more than a roughly drawn map and two candles. Arun, Kate, and two dwellers from the group in the cottage stood opposite Nicholas.

'Kate tells me you saved a boy's life,' said Nicholas. 'You pushed him from falling rubble, leaving yourself in harm's way, is that correct?'

'I think so, yeah,' said Arun. He'd been focusing on the Hillfolk until now and hadn't taken time to remember his accident or how he ended up here. Did it even matter? Hopefully, the boy he'd saved on his journey was okay, but the Hillfolk didn't need to hear the story. 'It was nothing. He's just a kid.'

'It was everything!' exclaimed Nicholas. 'One can only be truly selfless when their actions benefit none but others. Sandwiches.'

'Did you just say sandwiches?'

'Yes, there are sandwiches in my bag if you get hungry. Oh, I do apologise. You see, whenever a thought drops into my head, I need to get it out. Rather that than be reticent.'

'Same. I could be in bed right now. What're we doing here, exactly? Figuring out how to fight a God? I'll save you the time: you don't. Goodbye.' Arun turned to leave.

'Now, now. Sit. You seem to have a thing for running away.' Nicholas shook his head as Arun turned back. 'I suppose it is understandable. So far, we have given you words with no surrounding context. All wick and no wax. You have gloves, and you have been able to use them. That is, funnily enough, the final step for those lucky enough to stay here. Usually, our recruitment is far more organised without long-lost gloves and thievery—forgive us.'

'I didn't steal—never mind.'

'We need to return to the first step. The reason you are here. Please, sit.'

Nicholas's words piqued Arun's ears. As Kate handed him a cloak, he pulled up a rotting chair, shaking off water from his clothes. He hovered halfway between sitting and standing, observing Nicholas. Eventually, he dropped down.

'Why are you a scavenger?' asked Nicholas. 'Or should I ask: what purpose do you hold?'

Arun glanced at those in the hut, all watching him intently. 'I...I don't know. There's not much to do other than survive. I guess we all thought you Hillfolk had something to do with this all.'

Nicholas chuckled. 'The irony in humanity is that it is the world's greatest creation and also its most destructive. So as part of humanity, we all take some blame.'

Arun straightened his spine and squinted one side of his face. 'So it *is* your fault?'

Nicholas chuckled again before clearing his throat. 'Not quite. Interestingly though, we are approaching a rather significant milestone. It has been twenty years, almost to the day, since we discovered dark energy. Twenty years of this destiny, credited to our love of insanity.'

'What does that mean?'

'It means there used to be billions and billions of us before then, earlier, in the twenty-first century. You'd walk some paths and struggle not to bump into others. Now you can wander days without seeing a face. I would be surprised if there were more than a million of us left, judging by what I have seen.' Nicholas paced the curve of the table. 'Look at us. Only two people on this Hill still have their parents with them, and they are just children born into this world. Otherwise, our families are long gone, and I assume yours are too.'

Arun scratched his stubble, unsure how to feel. 'I never knew mine.'

'Some say it is better to have loved and lost than never to have loved at all. Judging by the burden I bear and the gormless look on your face, I am not so sure. Did you want a sandwich or not?'

'Weren't you supposed to be telling me how this all happened?'

'Yes, apologies! Where do I even begin to begin? Do you understand the concept of money? Of greed? Of those that were made to believe wealth defined the value of their life?'

'I read about rich people…and kings. Great kings who ruled the land with gold.'

'Close enough. Let me put it this way: there were those who reached the top with a king's feast, who realised it was better to give away a half-eaten carrot than nothing at all. The rest of the people would chase the other half of the carrot, believing that chase would lead them to a seat at the table.

'Some people had several empty beds to sleep in, and others had none. Those in power could act above the law with impunity, yet those under it would feel its full force. A society with no balance.' Nicholas raised one hand to rub the curls of his beard and the other to twiddle a toothpick by his side. His hands were bare, although everyone else's were gloved.

Arun's strained frown filled the room. He couldn't comprehend any of this. His books had never said. 'But I thought everything was so…developed. Why wasn't everyone equal?'

'I could talk all day about how and why. Selfishness. Ego. Pride. Take your pick. Human nature and our desire for power is a fascinating thing; a feeling you will have never felt before, raging from a stagnant evolution that fuelled our lust for *more*.

'However, the hows and whys of getting to that point do not concern us right now. Let me ask you a question: in the unbalanced world I just described, what would become of humanity if one person, on the wrong end of the scale, discovered a power beyond the means of those at the top? A power greater than money and strength.'

Scavengers weren't the smartest, but Arun's books gave him the intelligence needed to understand Nicholas's point without reply.

'The person I speak of is Dr Richard Aerkin,' said Nicholas. 'A penniless physicist who felt failed by our civilisation. His team's discovery of dark energy, and the harnessing of such power, brought upon "The Great Balance", or so he wanted to call it. We on the Hill call it the Worldshift. Call it what you like. The sixth mass extinction of Earth would be most literal.'

'How's that true?' asked Arun. 'How's that even possible? One man... destroyed everything...because he was poor? I have nothing, and I don't wanna destroy everything even if I could.'

'Having nothing when everyone around you shares your pain differs from having nothing whilst seeing those around you bathe in luxury. That and... other, more personal reasons.' Nicholas turned around, deep in thought, mumbling something to himself.

Nicholas's words filled Arun's lungs. His mouth lay open, pondering the legitimacy of what he'd heard. 'I always imagined a past world full of wonder. All the books I read showed the beauty in life; incredible cities, wonderful nature, and the good in humanity. Why would someone do that? I don't believe it. Why would—'

At that moment, Arun learnt that a glance into the palm of his hand would calm his thoughts. Did the gloves make him feel strong, or was it the fact that he'd been given something special for the first time in his life? Perhaps it was even the feeling of the material clinging to his skin, holding his hand in comfort. No matter, it worked, and Arun's heart rate levelled. 'Why should I believe you?'

'What better explanation do you propose?'

'I...don't know. I haven't seen much outside town. Is it like this everywhere?'

'As far as I know.' Nicholas looked down, slow in reply. 'This entire planet has suffered greatly. Land and sky. Fauna and flora. There may be a preserved place like our Hill here and there, but I have yet to lay eyes.' Nicholas lowered his toothpick to the candle, igniting it. 'Twenty long years of suffering, since the last sunrise rose and the last sunset sank.' He blew the flame out.

'So the sun's real?' Arun froze as all eyes fixed on him. A moment passed. 'I knew it! But he covered it in cloud? How?' Arun shot to his feet, propelling the chair backwards. 'What's the plan then? How do we get the sun back? How do we get everything back?' Arun ambushed the Hillfolk in commanding fashion, instantly disregarding Nicholas's scathing reflection of the past era. As all scavengers do, they feel the need to fight when an enemy presents itself. Only one thing that made fighting a God even a bearable thought: a first glimpse of the sun shining down on the world. 'Is the sun as big as in the books? What does it look like?'

'It's round,' laughed one of the Hillfolk.

Nicholas stood motionless with an ethereal smile. 'So we have finally found your inspiration! You are searching for something beyond the towns, the hills, and the altostratus sky?'

'I just want it all to be true,' said Arun. 'The sun, the way I pictured life was. If we can get things back to how they used to be...we can make it better? Give everyone a bed? No more king's tables? The cities, the stars. Everyone equal?'

'That is precisely what we want, despite your enthusiasm being a little misplaced. There is still quite a bit to go over, but exploring dark energy is our best use of time. That is where you must start and begin to understand its significance. It is one of the four parts of any universe, along with ordinary matter, dark matter, and unknown energy.'

'Okay, uh, dark matter, and—' Arun stuttered, attempting to keep up with all Nicholas threw his way, half his brain still picturing what the sun would look like.

'It bears a name derived from its mystery, an invisible property filling space, once unable to interact with the electromagnetic spectrum, with light. We experimented with the Earth and the stars for answers, yet the patterns and wonders of our own living nature, deep in the deepest of oceans, was the key in bringing it to light.

'It is our creation, or so the most popular theory became. Everything around you. The trigger that sparked the last Big Bang, the fuel for all life. The resulting energy, dark and unknown alike, retreats to the Eternal Point after billions of years of acceleration and deceleration, working against gravity, pushing matter in the opposite direction as it passes through. And once all energy returns to the Eternal Point and all matter is expunged, the universe is created again. It is everlasting. Infinite.'

Arun examined the pattern in his gloves, head down, allowing Nicholas's words to pass over him. Arun pictured the beautiful, blue glow once more.

'Despite your undoubted interest in theoretical physics, I must wrap up. Understand one thing, Arun. We live by the rule: the darkness must die. It means we fight for the sun, but also for the day that we can cast these weapons back to the depths from which they came. Harnessing dark energy was the greatest, catastrophic mistake humanity could have made, but for now continuing to harness it is the only way we can save the planet and rid it of Aerkin. As long as he wields it, nobody is safe, and nobody can rebuild. He could destroy everything all over again. The future will remain as bleak as the present. A cycle of destruction. Do not take this responsibility lightly. The darkness must die.'

Nicholas turned his attention to Kate. 'Kate will be the one to train you up to speed physically. Listen carefully to her. I would give my life for her, and she knows it. She has become our strongest warrior, far more fearsome than even myself.'

Arun had perhaps underestimated Kate. He turned to her, watching her gaze at Nicholas with a look of complete respect and appreciation. So these weren't just Hill dwellers; they were supposedly warriors. Were they *that* good? Could they fight a God?

'The sky will soon be as light as can be,' said Nicholas, picking up his ripped, worn-down brown bag from the floor. 'I need to make way, but I wanted to catch you early to make sure you understood the significance of the situation you find yourself in. Aerkin is the root of our decay. Any destruction you've ever witnessed, the reason you spend your days hunting for food, the way the clouds flood the Earth. It's all him.' Nicholas walked towards the door.

'So, why are you hiding?' asked Arun. 'Why aren't you searching for him?'

Nicholas scoffed, resting his hand on the square, wooden door handle. 'Oh, we don't need to search. We know precisely where he spends his days. He sits atop his throne in a temple in the Mainland mountains playing God. The reason we have not already stormed it is simple: we need to get it right. There are no second chances for us or anyone else if we reveal ourselves and fail. It has to be perfect.

'I feel that moment is nearing, but until then, we hide. He knows we have gloves and that I possess a suit woven with the same material. These are the only things that can dispute his omnipotence, and it pains him. If he were to find us and kill us, he would truly have everything.'

Nicholas opened the door but paused. 'Good luck with your first lesson. And remember, a good glove should never go unworn.' He concluded with a wink, taking leave as the two nameless dwellers followed him. The winds howled for a second before the door slammed shut. A moment of silence followed. Arun stared at the door, repeating Nicholas's words in his head.

'Don't worry about Aerkin for now,' said Kate. 'We need to train. Hard. I need your full concentration, Arun. There's nothing supernatural about this. Have to use your strength and awareness, and need your instinct to work with the gloves too. Most important part of all…is your muscles.'

Arun tilted his head at Kate's arms. Although toned, she showed no mountainous muscle to match Nicholas's fountain of praise. She wore a white sleeveless top and ripped dark-blue trousers without her cloak for cover. Arun's attention was fixed on her arms, noticing that her gloves stretched to her elbows, and Arun's gloves stopped at the wrist. Envy crept in.

'Didn't mean how big your biceps are,' said Kate, folding her arms. 'The muscles in your arms work together with your gloves if you can control them. Though it does help if you've spent your life doing manual labour.' Kate pulled up a chair in front of Arun, grabbed his arms, extended his hands towards hers, and faced his palms to the ceiling. 'Tense your hands.'

'Okay,' replied Arun, staring into her eyes briefly. 'How long were you following me for?'

'Focus and tense,' said Kate.

'And where are my books and my scope?'

'Arun!' Kate's raised voice jolted Arun, a gentle reminder to never piss her off. Her voice softened again. 'Please. Try and feel every muscle in your fingers. This could be tricky, but you've done it once before, so I know those muscles are already activated.'

Arun focused. He tensed. He felt his fingers and the top of his wrist tighten. Nothing too abnormal, though, as he strained as hard as possible.

'Don't think about how hard you can do it,' said Kate. 'Think about being consistent. Have control over your muscles. Once you feel the gloves answering back, then you can use your strength.'

Arun loosened up, and the skin of his palms smoothed out, lightly shaking and tensed. He sensed the material of the glove nibbling at his nerve-endings. It felt like static, but without shock, dotting into him like pins and needles.

'Can you feel it?' asked Kate. 'The energy will try to connect you with the gloves.'

'What?' trembled Arun. 'It feels tingly.' He kept constant tense pressure on his muscles, wondering if the gloves would begin to brighten. The static feeling enhanced, entrancing him, tightening his muscles further, as if the gloves were wearing him. As he grimaced, Kate gripped his forearms, nearly defeating his concentration.

'Focus,' said Kate. 'Keep tensing. It's going to hurt a little, but you'll be fine.'

'Hurt?' bellowed Arun, fighting to regain his concentration as a burning sensation unleashed throughout his veins. His muscles ached, the static covering wrist to fingertip. Kate's fingers dug into his arms, pressing his veins to his muscle, stemming the flow of pain momentarily. A grimace turned into a moan, and the heat of a flame's core rose within; the sharpest pain yet ripped through his palm, causing his jaw to detach in an agonising scream.'

'I'm with you!' yelled Kate.

Arun stared into his palms. He couldn't take any more. He screamed again, swinging his arms back from Kate's grip. He fell over his chair, his head rolling against the floor, sweeping the dust with him. He scurried back along the floorboards towards the wall, rubbing the gloves against his legs before squeezing his fists shut.

'I shouldn't have pushed you,' said Kate, rushing over apologetically. 'That's my fault. I thought…I don't know what I thought.'

Arun took deep breaths, composing himself, doing well not to take off the gloves. He looked at Kate in awe as she bent down to check on him.

'It was only a second, but I saw it,' said Arun pacing his breath. 'Blue, pulsing, shimmering light.'

'Really?' Kate collapsed to the wall alongside Arun, with her hand back on his forearm. She laughed, although it sounded more like a panic attack. The two looked at each other, proud and relieved. 'That's amazing! I've never seen anyone do that first time. I guess you had practice with your little accident.'

'Little? Saving a life, and my own, was pretty heroic,' said Arun.

'Yeah. Not bad. I'd never thought of scavengers as considerate or kind. Funny, that. You thought we were devils, and we thought you were cretins. Turns out we're not too different.'

Arun fell silent for a few seconds, looking back down into his hands, not used to hearing semi-complimentary words. 'That feeling. It was magical.'

'Nicholas doesn't like that word. He prefers to say "scientific". It really does feel magical, though: the energy inside everything, inside your hand and the glove.'

'I wanna try again! Does it ever run out?'

'You can get tired and sore, but the light doesn't run out. Far more of it than there is air. Nicholas says it can't run out because it creates itself.'

Arun's intrigue entered overdrive. What else could it do? Could it grow? Could it move? His questions thundered like the lightning of the shortlight months. But the past few minutes of magic gradually made way to the past few years of thought.

'Arun?' whispered Kate.

'I often think about how the world used to be,' said Arun. 'I suppose everyone does. I imagined peaceful times with no war, no hunger, no suffering. Children running and playing everywhere. Everyone had a place to live and a place to work. Was the world really how he made it out to be?'

'Yup,' said Kate abruptly, leaving no hope for Arun to hold onto. 'People are still selfish now, but it sounded worse back then.'

'How could people have so much and leave others with so little?' asked Arun.

A pensive Kate stared into a shrouded corner of the room.

'I don't know. I don't remember how people were before then, but the fact we drove ourselves to that point shows you how truly awful it must have been. We just have to make sure we learn from our mistakes.'

Refusing to believe these harsh realities over his imagined utopia, Arun dragged his legs in and held his head low, rising to his feet. He grabbed the cloak that Kate had earlier given him and headed for the door.

'Where are you going?' asked Kate. 'We're just getting started.'

Arun turned to her, with his eyes strained. 'Sleep.' He opened the door, and with the sky waking the songbirds and the wind retreating, he headed out back to his hut. His cloaked silhouette faded into a mass of fog that crossed the grassy plane.

Arun reached his hut, finding he'd left the door open, and a barrage of rain had soaked the floor. Clunk—Arun kicked his shoes to the wall and closed the door behind him this time. He made his way to the corner and slid down the wall. But something was bothering him. He looked over to the bed. How could these objects of desire have remained empty when so many slept on the floor?

Nobody should be made to accept that their place was beneath others. He sighed. If that's the world he wanted to help build, that would be the first step.

Arun walked over to the bed, grabbing the sheet that had blown to the wall. He laid his body down on the mattress. Awkwardly soft at first, it formed a caressing hold around his body. A little bumpy in places, but generally quite comfortable. Interesting. Very interesting. He readjusted his position to get used to the comfort, and before he knew it, his eyes had crept shut.

CHAPTER FOUR

THE TWIN DAGGERS

Twilight signified another day on the Hill, and with that day, a familiar routine. Kate would be training by now if it weren't for Arun's hasty departure from the study hut; she hadn't moved much since. Filling her stomach would be a suitable alternative, though, as her stomach barraged her with demands. Kate stood and headed for the cottage.

As routine would have it, Kate barged through the cottage doors and followed her day-old footprints step-by-step to her seat by the fireplace.

'Morning!' said Cole, ever the morning person, ever the opposite of Kate, making her voice heard before she was seen, as usual. The voice came from the kitchen in the back. 'Nicholas around?'

'At a river meeting,' replied Kate. 'Still thinks if he brings me, I'll end up the same as Iris.' Kate sat, crossed her legs, leant one arm back, and tapped a tune with her fingernails on the table. Another monotonous day, another handful of tiny fruit, launching into her grateful mouth. 'I can take care of myself.'

'Don't worry. You know he loves playing the protective father. Those meetings sound dull as dirt anyway.' Cole entered the room, bringing over a tray of various fresh foods. Tej followed the tray with his nose as the two sat at Kate's table. 'And where's our new superstar?'

'Needs some alone time,' replied Kate, grabbing a handful of firm, tiny pinkberries with her bare hands. Lack of sun, lack of sizeable sustenance.

They were the nearest item on the tray, next to the bananaberries. Kate didn't remember much before the Worldshift, but a plastic tub of strawberries was always on the table in her room. The banaberries were similar—mutated strawberries that grew longer, curved, and never quite reached the radiant red of their ancestor.

On the other hand, Cole's slices of smoked meat had never enticed Kate, nor had the smell of fresh bread. It was far from the bread she remembered surviving off in her early days without her parents. She wasn't even sure if this could technically be called bread, as she watched Tej chew into a slice as if he were biting through leather.

'It's not too late to take the gloves back and continue our search,' mumbled Tej, pulling the memory of Iris into the forefront of Kate's mind again.

'You gave up searching long before I did,' said Kate mid-munch, her bottom lip laced with juice. 'Had a change of heart suddenly?'

'I simply meant—'

'No,' Kate interjected. 'I know what you meant. Hope you realise the only thing worse than losing someone you love is losing them and not knowing where they lay.'

'I'm sorry. I just don't see why we need to resort to Tossers. If that's our only option, then we might as well go back to looking for Iris.'

'Tehjin!' reprimanded Cole. 'He doesn't mean any of that, dear; he's had a tough morning figuring out how to put his trousers on the right way round.'

Tej sat straight, attentive as always whenever Cole called his full name. 'No, no. I meant no ill will to Iris. I just mean the boy could be dangerous, that's all. At least our last attempts at recruitment were Indies—you know, *honest* farmers, *peaceful* recluses. Tossers are dirty city rats.'

'Tehjin!' Cole reprimanded once more as she swiped away the bread in his hand, in-flight towards his gaping jaw. 'If we show him a bit of love and care, then who knows what he can do. The poor sausage has nothing to lose.'

'Those with nothing to lose are reckless,' said Tej.

'I have nothing more to lose,' said Kate. 'Think I'm reckless?'

Cole glanced at Tej with her eyes nudging forward.

Tej gulped. 'No, of course not, I—'

'I know how it feels to scavenge and be alone. Doesn't make Arun reckless. Makes him strong. Made me strong.' Kate stared into her gloveless palms to avoid snapping at Tej. It was a retained habit. Although wearing her gloves gave her power and confidence, she'd always had mountains of each before she'd ever witnessed dark energy.

'I'll try him again,' said Kate, sliding away from her seat. 'Thanks for breakfast, Cole.' As she stood, a lumpy paste of crushed bananaberries fell to the table from her clenched hand.

'You can clean that up, love,' smirked Cole, promptly following Kate with Tej's bread in hand. Kate grabbed the bread from Cole and took a gaping bite from the middle, handing it back, leaving berry-juice fingerprints on the bread that remained. Nope—still as disgusting as she remembered and not worth curing the rumbling stomach.

'Is the wedding still on?' asked Tej.

Kate left the cottage in a hurry, spitting out chewed up bread, and crossed the Hill towards Arun's hut. Halfway, a whistling Nicholas caught her attention, meandering up the steep slope. It seemed cruel for the weakest knees on the Hill to have the steepest climb to their quarters, but Nicholas had never displayed a desire to move.

'A fruitless meeting in more ways than one,' said Nicholas. 'Our local Indie friends seemed disinterested again. Perhaps their land is becoming far more arable and they no longer feel the need to rely on our produce. Or far worse, our network has been broken. We cannot keep having weeks go by without news from the Mainland.'

'How many weeks is that now?' asked Kate.

'Far too many. And many months more since we have had word on Aerkin's Knights. They are far too dangerous to be let out of our sights.'

'Maybe they've left the shores and gone south?' asked Kate.

'No. You know their task. They want our scent and are waiting to catch a trace—vile men. The further north, the better for them.'

'They could be trying a new tactic. Hiding and waiting, like us.'

'I highly doubt they are known for their tactical nous. They remind me of many I once knew, worshipping the more fortunate and powerful to the detriment and stagnation of their own lives. Except back then, the power came in the slightly milder form of fame and fortune. These Knights are nothing but followers. To anticipate where they are is to anticipate where Aerkin wants them to be.'

Nicholas wouldn't always make sense to Kate, but she appreciated his passion for keeping the Hill safe. She softly grabbed the back of Nicholas's hair with her clean hand and looked him deep in the eyes. 'Don't worry. Nothing's ever gotten past you to get here. And it never will.'

Nicholas rested his hand on Kate's outstretched arm. A brief smile turned back to a concerned expression. 'I fear someone or something is arriving. It could be those vicious Knights, or it could be something else, but I can only be certain it will not bring us any good. We have not gone this long without news since I first connected with the Mainland. I am most unsettled, my dear Kate.'

'Never known you to worry. What happened to "what good does it do anyone?".'

Nicholas chuckled. 'It is far easier to hand out advice than to follow your own.' As he spoke, Kate glanced towards Arun's hut. 'Struggling with your scavenger?'

'Oh, it's a lot for him to take in,' replied Kate. 'Think he's more interested in what's behind him rather than what's in front.'

'Are you sure? A man running away from home would be struggling to find a purposeful path forward. Remember, those without purpose....'

'...wander the surface.'

Nicholas smiled. 'He will warm to us. With purpose comes joy. Perhaps too much information does not suit a simple scavenger. If he wishes the world to be a better place, perhaps he needs to see how he can help instead of being told.

I believe he would be more interested in learning if he saw the Twin Daggers.' He gave her a suggestive smirk.

Kate nodded and gifted Nicholas a soft slap on the cheek. She'd always rely on Nicholas's speed to a solution.

She wiped her hand clean of the sticky bananaberries against the blades of wet grass and slid her gloves on, carrying on her path. She reached the door and barged in without knocking, closing the door behind her. 'Te-lue,' she muttered, noticing Arun had left the candle burning. The lumps in his bedsheets gave no motion apart from the slow rhythmic pulse around his chest. Kate had little sympathy for his lack of rest so far and filled her lungs with air.

'Arun!' shouted Kate, echoing against the narrow wooden walls as if a crowd had screamed his name. Arun lifted and turned his head in a daze. Kate noticed his scavenger reflexes kicking in, clenching his fists close to his chest. She wasted little time. 'Lesson one of three. Pay close attention.'

'I'm trying to sleep,' muttered Arun, falling headfirst into his pillow. Kate could barely hear him as he mumbled into the bed. 'You're the one that should be paying. My attention's valuable.'

Kate's boots squeaked against the floorboards. 'Why's the floor so wet?'

'Ugh.' Arun turned his head again, eyes closed. 'I left the door open this morning when you dragged me away.'

'Try not to treat this place like a scavenger shelter, please.' Kate walked across to the window and pulled over the sheet draped beside it, blocking whatever little natural light crept in. The sole candle now remained as light's only origin. Her footsteps squeaked back to the centre of the room with plenty of space around her. 'Look at me.'

Arun rolled around in his bed, still glued to his pillow and scant-eyed, facing Kate. With her arms by her side, she opened her palms towards Arun. He didn't seem as enthused as he did earlier, presumably expecting to see a small, blue glow.

Kate could wait no longer. She took a deep breath. And another. She closed her eyes and inhaled, waited a few seconds, then exhaled with her eyes fixated on Arun. The wind grew silent from its howl, and the candle's slight flicker turned to a still, motionless flame. Kate raised her hands, her palms directed down, feeling all ten fingertips pressed against each other, pinching to a point in front of her stomach.

Her arms shot out, with deep blue light taking the shape of two daggers. She leant out with the right side of her body, with one tip of a dagger piercing the candle's flame, extinguishing it. She turned back, raising the left blade to protect her face, and the right blade held out towards Arun. The entire hut turned a rich shade of blue, jumping each time she thrust her arms about her body as if the soul of lightning had crept indoors. One fighting stance quickly displaced another as Kate moved swiftly, beating out short breaths, as sharp as the blades she bore. A slight silence followed the wisped sound of the daggers slicing through the air. They appeared to have no handle, as she grasped the blades bare with her hands, with the light not piercing glove nor skin. She knew Arun wouldn't take his eyes off her for a second, not even to blink.

Kate finished her demonstration by slicing through the air with one hand and piercing the other down into the floor. She stopped the blade just as it touched the floorboard, splintering and shimmering. Kate let out a final exhale of breath. A look of contentment suffused her, as it often did whenever she yielded her blades. She waited for calm to return to the air and turned to Arun, who was more out of breath than her.

'The light defines who you'll become,' said Kate, rising sloth-like to her feet whilst the dimming light reduced her to the shadows. 'If you let it, it can consume you. It can never let you go. Troubles can mould to sins. Dark energy doesn't just rest in your palms; it rests in your mind. But if you control it, you can truly find peace.'

Kate closed her palms, sealing the light and returning the room to absolute darkness. She turned, leaving Arun with the sound of footsteps and the sight of her silhouette as she opened the door before disappearing to the outside world.

Kate looked ahead at the Hill running up to the left and down to the right. Forest sat behind, and the cottage and huts lay in front, yet all directions seemed the same. The chatter of Hillfolk leaving their huts brought the Hill to life for another day. Another monotonous day.

As rain began to drizzle, Kate raised her head to the sky to freshen her face. A walk into the open fields beyond the top of the Hill would bring a peaceful solace despite the gloomy weather. She walked up; she walked down. At last, beautiful, open fields and no thoughts to accompany her. The wind swept the grass beneath her feet whilst the clouds flowed fast above her head. It was as if the world turned without her.

CHAPTER FIVE

THE DOOR

'How comes lightning never strikes the Hill?' Arun asked Kate, standing with an open field ahead of him. 'The huts, the cottage, the trees, they all seem fine.'

A day had passed, and Arun ventured outside for the first time since Kate's display, joining her watchful gaze over the training Hillfolk. The day brought a familiar dull, overcast sky, but the absence of rain made physical activity less of a chore. His eyesight jumped across the numerous Hillfolk scattered across the field practising their fighting techniques. The trees in the distance covering the horizon imitated small hedges; such was the distance, and occasionally a startled deer would poke its head up, else one could mistake them for more vegetation. Closer infield, some warriors chose to engage in combat, whilst others had set up targets around them. Sparks of blue light from two-dozen pairs of hands brought the greenery to life where flowers would have once stood.

'Hello?' repeated Arun. 'Earth to Kate?'

'Sorry,' said Kate, shaking her head awake. 'Lightning? Don't know. Think it's just drawn away by all the material in the Toss's nearby.'

'You're welcome,' said Arun. 'I'm glad we serve a purpose after all. So, what about the quakes? How's the cottage still standing?'

'That I don't know. Guess that's just luck. Wasn't here during the first year of the Worldshift and the never-ending quakes.' Kate appeared to be watching the fields, but her eyes were glazed over.

'Right. You know, what you said yesterday got me thinking....'

Arun paused, watching Kate's eyes disappear under her clenched eyelids for a moment. She rubbed the sleep from her eyes as a yawn to end all yawns escaped her mouth.

'New guy!' breached a voice through the wind. Out of breath, three figures approached from the field, wiping the sweat from their various body parts.

'Jordan, Serr, Matuu,' said Kate, introducing the figures as they came within reach. She turned to Arun. 'Lesson two. Know your strengths.'

'The big boy with Iris's gloves,' said Jordan. 'You must be an expert to have them.' He rested his arms on his waist, forcing his muscles to attempt an escape from the cotton shackles of his shirt. His perfect, white teeth shimmered against his tidy stubble, brighter than the whitest cloud as he smiled, and his long pale hair danced symmetrically in the wind. He was the epitome of a storybook hero from one of Arun's books.

'Arun, this is Jordan,' said Kate. 'He's extremely strong, built like a tree, but not the quickest mover.' Jordan scoffed. 'You'll have noticed he can propel light, almost bullet-like, a great speed and distance. Look at his right glove. The black parts, the ridge, are raised mostly on the outside. They reach a point in the middle where the elemental material, the mantle, is exposed. This concentrates the light so he can propel it. Got that?'

Mantle, what now? Arun looked at his gloves, trying to work out what the pattern meant on his, though with his head bowed, his eyes couldn't help but be drawn to Jordan. How are his arms so big?

Without warning, Jordan threw an arm out to the side. Bang—a small bolt of light shot into a tree not so far away, blasting a hole through the centre of it, faster than a blink. His eyes never left Arun.

Arun took a defensive stance, backing away from Jordan's cocky smirk. Showoff.

Kate continued, 'Serr's the opposite—quick but slight. She doesn't propel light as she's not as muscular as Jordan, so Nicholas made her gloves to suit a different skill set. Got it? The back of her gloves are all overflowing ridge, and the front is mantle. This creates a large surface from her palms that can shield the area in front of her. Given enough time, she could shield others and form a wall. Not a bad close-combat fighter, either. You'll find the soles of her shoes are mantle too.'

Serr smiled and bowed her head, not displaying any power nor uttering a single word from her pressed lips. Her black fringe blocked much of her eyes. Could she even see Arun? She wore something resembling a poncho with a hood but draped down to her knees. Patches of varying materials and colours from other clothes were stitched into the black base material. Arun had witnessed her training moments prior. Her stances bore a striking resemblance to the art of Tai Chi from one of his books.

'Matuu eats a lot,' said Kate, looking increasingly tired of talking. 'That narrowed his movement options. Ironically his light is light, by weight, I mean, and sparse enough to spread a great distance. It's more like air than light and can do great damage.'

'I wouldn't dare. You'd all die,' said Matuu. Arun couldn't read Matuu's deadpan expression to see if he was joking or not. His cheeks fell onto his jaw and his jaw to his chin. Scars marred the hairless skin around his face, but Arun assumed this must be an insistence on shaving with blunted materials. Although extremely large, his movement wasn't that limited, at least keeping up with Jordan's striding pace. His right hand gently circled in the air beside his waist.

'So, show us what you've got, mate,' smirked Jordan. 'Do we need to stand back and peek behind our fingers?'

The pressure piled upon Arun now, with all four Hillfolk staring through him. He hadn't tried his luck with the light since his first attempt yesterday. Surely it had to hurt less. Right? He nodded to himself, turned to face away from the group, and took a deep breath. He held out his arms, facing the trees rather than the open field, spreading his fingers, his teeth gritted.

Arun tensed his hands and grimaced, trying to goad the muscle memory from his hands and let them do the work. After half a minute of grimacing, he heard a rising sound: Jordan sniggering, bringing a sharp whisper of 'shut up!' from Kate. Arun paid attention to the distraction and lost his concentration, releasing the hold on his arms and letting out a heavy winded sigh.

Kate pitched alongside Arun, grabbing his arms and returning them to the air. 'No. Don't give up.' She lent him a dented smile and a nod of confirmation before moving back. That's better. He relaxed his body as if he were back in the hut with her.

'Pity.' Jordan posed, arms akimbo. 'Came to say we're doing an attack drill soon. Whenever you're ready, Kate.' He turned to walk away. Serr's footsteps followed, then Matuu's.

Arun shut his eyes. Concentrate. He murmured to himself. 'Be consistent. Have control over your muscles.' Arun opened his eyes, feeling the heat in his fingers, to the light now emanating from his palms once more.

'Keep going,' urged Kate softly, as a tapered tube of light, no wider than an old penny, slowly emerged from Arun's hands, not too dissimilar to Kate's daggers. The tubular light raged in its emergence, sharding and crackling, unstable and serrated. It stretched out and curved upwards, reaching a sharp point. He grimaced. He groaned. He tried to curl his fingers—a step too far, as the light shattered into thousands of tiny little rays shooting off in different directions. Luckily the shards didn't make it a metre before melting into the air. Arun, managing to stay grounded, turned to Kate as his angst gave way to a wide, beaming grin. He turned to the other three who'd witnessed his feat.

'That was incredible,' acknowledged Jordan after a nod of approval. 'So if we ever go to the Mainland, I'll be sure not to get in your way. There'll be no stopping your immense power!' A jolting elbow towards Serr and a high-pitched laugh followed. Impossible—someone far more sarcastic and confident than Arun. Is this what he sounded like to other people? Oh, no.

'I'm joking,' continued Jordan. 'Once we're all out there, I'll have your back, mate. Just like I've got everyone else's.' He saluted Arun before leading the other two back to the field.

'Ignore him.' Kate laughed under her breath. 'You did good. Didn't fall over this time—that's impressive.'

'I'll save falling over just for you,' replied Arun. 'What was that curved tube of light coming out of my hands?'

'It's what Iris used to call her Linai. I remember her saying it meant "Light Shinai". They're similar to training sticks she used before the Worldshift.'

Excitement and intrigue—the feelings of wielding weapons of light. Arun had to contain himself from jumping with limp limbs into the air. The only weapons he'd ever held were heavy and hindering, but the light in his hands was a feather. 'So…are my daggers are bigger than yours?'

Kate rolled her eyes. She yanked his palms in a stiff upward motion. 'Look here. The mantle lines in your palms direct the energy. When you capture dark energy, it concentrates along the ridge, with the ridge slanted in the direction the light travels. You can see yours end up in a circle in the middle of your palm, so the energy reaches a point, condenses, and is pushed forward. The ridge is raised slightly on one side of the circle, so the captured energy protrudes in a curve. Just how Iris wanted it.'

'Yeah, yeah, yeah. So how do I hold it longer? And swing it? And fight like you lot?'

'Remember what I said about one question at a time?' Kate released her grip and stepped back. 'We haven't been training for a day or two. It takes time to feel comfortable in the gloves, years of working together building trust and confidence in each other.' She turned to the field and raised her voice so that the clouds could hear. 'Zachenne! New guy wants to see what years of training looks like!'

The heads across the field darted. A man, slightly taller than the others, responded with a distant shout, 'Defense formation. Three lines, shield Nicholas.' With the sound of his final syllable, the scattered warriors came together in a sprint, locking together like puzzle pieces, each knowing their place in the newly-formed grid. Jordan, Serr and Matuu arrived to complete the front row. 'Arms!' came another cry, resulting in a synchronised charge of light that ignited from two-dozen sets of palms, all raised to the horizon. The glow of each hand merged, turning the entire unit light blue, like rows of human ice crystals. The lone man paced around the grid to the rear, the only movement amongst the shimmering, frozen bodies. 'At ease,' came the final call, to which shoulders dropped, light faded, and bodies returned to their previous activity.

Arun's first glimpse into an organised unit left him speechless bar a puff of air that escaped the back of his throat. The only scavenger tactic employed back home was 'you take that one, I'll take this one'. But here...their movements, their connection; it was a togetherness he'd never seen before.

'Any more questions?' asked Kate.

'Nope.' replied Arun, staring blindly into the field. 'I'm good.'

'Great!' Kate patted Arun on the back. 'You should head back to the cottage. The others will be finishing up soon and will join you. I've got to head somewhere for a bit, but I'll be back before dark. Can you handle yourself for now?'

Arun turned to Kate. He needn't reply, for 'yes' was the only acceptable response. Instead, the two smiled a smile that belonged to a different age.

*

Arun sat alone in the cottage, unable to take his eyes off the pattern of his gloved hands. The cup of hot water beside him had soon lost all steam, and the berries to his other side lay untouched. His stomach would take a while getting used to the rate of eating that the Hillfolk enjoyed.

A sputter of voices grew from outside, and it wasn't long before the cottage erupted in laughter. The Hillfolk warriors stampeded through the door, webbed together with arms around shoulders, and piggybacks. It was hard to believe these were the same people who lined up in stringent formation.

'Newbie,' said one of the Hillfolk, her shirt covered in sweat and mud, 'mind if we join you?' She didn't leave Arun a second to answer before sitting beside him as the others followed around the surrounding tables.

'What about that show where the guy cooked meth?' said a man crashing into his chair.

'Are you sure that wasn't you?' replied another to a chorus of laughs.

'We're just talking about the things we miss most,' said the woman next to Arun, 'as always, it seems. Never found one thing we all agree on. You'd think it'd be music or a hot power shower, but there's always one, isn't there, Zachenne?'

'Always, Viv. Cold showers were better for your body. It's a hill I'll die on.' Zachenne sat straight, his posture held high. He was the only other of the Hillfolk Arun had seen with aged hair like Nicholas's, albeit shorter, with a silver shine and more youthfully styled.

'Oh, I got it!' announced Jordan, jumping out of his chair. 'I think I've finally got it.' All eyes turned to Jordan as he took a deep breath. 'Okay. A fresh pair of socks, straight from the dryer, on a cold winter's day.'

Heads nodded, eyebrows raised, and agreeable hums passed across the tables.

'Hmm...nah. I prefer bare feet in winter,' said Matuu.

'No, you don't!' shouted Jordan, pointing at Matuu. 'You damn well don't! Liar! You couldn't let me win, could you?'

'It's like a woolly jail for feet. Ugh.' Matuu lifted his feet to the table and crossed them, complete with socks under his boots, and placed his hands behind his head. 'Anyway, I still say it's the toilet. One flush, and the shame is off to another world. What's not to love?'

'What about you?' asked Zachenne, turning to Arun. 'Are you old enough to remember anything before the Worldshift?'

Arun had struggled to keep up with the fast-flowing conversation between the group and now felt the weight of the eyes staring at him patiently. 'No. Being a scavenger's all I know.'

'Oof,' was the assembled sound of various voices. 'Poor lad,' 'that's rough.'

'Is it?' asked Jordan. 'Didn't we all take everything for granted, anyway?

Before the cities crumbled, people didn't know what to do when electricity stopped working and water stopped running. People ended their own lives when they couldn't handle a life beyond technology and all that social media stuff.'

'Imagine that,' said Zachenne. 'Being as afraid of irrelevance as death itself.'

'Exactly. My brother couldn't cope with that....' Jordan's lips pinched together. 'Well, anyway, Arun here's built for the *real* world.'

Zachenne folded his arms. 'Until he gets an infection and dies without medication like Jonboy.'

'Jonboy liked playing with fire. Literally. It's his own fault.'

Arun glanced from left to right as the Hillfolk joked amongst themselves. His shoulders relaxed as a soft chuckle emerged despite not feeling a part of the conversation. Why would anyone play with fire? Good to know the level of intelligence here varied. He continued to listen but tilted his head towards his gloves once more.

'I feel I should say a quick word,' said Zachenne, standing up opposite Arun, speaking in a dull, stern tone. 'It's a tough world. Tougher than it's ever been, and that's coming from an ex-military man. So, anyone who's made it this far has already earned my respect. I'd like to offer—' He froze and stared at Arun, his mouth half-open.

'Arun,' came a whisper behind him.

'Arun! My sincerest welcome to your new home on the Hill, and to everyone else I say: welcome the newest Hillfolk warrior.'

A roar of cheers assaulted the cottage walls, and fists bashed the tables. Those beside Arun scruffed his hair and slapped the wind from the back of his lungs, before another pair of hands grasped the back of his shoulders, digging into his muscle. Arun felt far from being any sort of warrior, but the warm feeling of being embraced and cheered for was exhilarating. He didn't shy away from the faces as he did on his first day in the cottage. He laughed with joy, taking in each pair of eyes as they looked his way.

As time continued, the cottage voices grew louder, laughing the roof off with jokes Arun was too new to understand. He released a long rasping yawn, a sign that it would be best to head back to his hut, being devoid of energy without his midday nap. He stood, gave a few nods to anyone looking his way, and strolled to the door.

'Newbie!' came a voice. 'Give Kate a kiss for us!'

Arun laughed but continued on. That was a joke, right? There could be some weird rituals he didn't know about yet. He left the cottage and cut across the Hill slope, stomping the clean, dewy grass into the mud. He stopped to take another moment to breathe in the fresh air away from the cottage smoke. Ahh. Refreshing. Opening his eyes, the imposing figure of a cloaked Nicholas, standing by his own hut, waved Arun over with a joyful expression through the evening umbra. With little hesitation and a pinch of intrigue, he changed his course and headed in Nicholas's direction as rain trickled down once more.

'I have been waiting for a moment with you,' said Nicholas, showing Arun the door. 'After you.' His hut, full of candlelight to negate the lacking windows, was coloured ablaze. 'The burning is much and perhaps is my crutch, for I cannot stand fire, but it fuels me as such.'

'What are you talking about?' asked Arun bluntly.

'Oh, it is a twist on an old poem I found lying around. It does make me ponder. One's mind can be pervaded in the quest of erasing images from their past, but for most, erasing those memories is not possible, so perhaps it would be wiser to embrace them. Hence the candles.'

'Got it.' Arun wasn't sure what that meant. Nicholas closed the door and slid the wooden handle to the left, ensuring it stayed shut. He took a few paces before sitting on the floor, where he'd placed a steaming pot and two cups. Arun, first hesitant, brought himself down to Nicholas's level.

'I apologise that I have not been able to lend you my attention,' said Nicholas. 'I asked Kate to train you because it might be of a similar benefit to her as it is to you. After all, no relationship works one way. And if it does, it is not a relationship worth having.'

'No problem. But…what could she get from me?'

'Whenever the Hill gains a recruit, I try to see if they have the right spirit to help rekindle her passion—her excitement. But I am still waiting for someone or something to bring her back.' Nicholas poured a cup of strangely dark, warm water for himself and Arun. Odourless—a good sign. 'She was not always so stern, but I have noticed something different in her around you. So thank you.'

'Why—what happened? Something to do with Iris?'

Nicholas hummed and whispered to himself. 'Have a drink!'

'I guess we're off on another tangent then,' uttered Arun. A stern look dawned upon him as he sipped the warm liquid. His taste buds retracted, and his face imploded. The water tasted utterly earthy as if it had sat brewing in a puddle of mud for a hundred years. Arun had only ever drunk plain rainwater, and his senses weren't ready for unusual tastes. He held his nose and swallowed. 'Tasty. Thanks.' Arun winced, placing the cup back down far from comfortable reach. He wiped his gloves clean.

'Falkeworms,' said Nicholas. 'Amazing creatures. Over ten thousand metres deep in the ocean, you will find them. What I would do to get my hands on some.'

'Uh. Great.'

'Your gloves—Falkeworms are to thank. Hydrophobic cocoon fibres called Falkum render the gloves almost anti-absorbent. The peculiarities of this seabed slitherer do not end there, however. Place your hands together but leave a small gap between.'

Arun followed the only part of Nicholas's rambling that he understood, placing his palms together. A slight force pulled them together. He fought against it, but it continued to pull as if Nicholas was moving Arun's hands with his mind. Could he...no. Right? Arun pulled his hands apart in a panic.

'Biomagnetism. I tell you, one Falkeworm puts all other creatures to shame. Best of all, they are rather cute when they crawl.' Nicholas chortled. 'Magnificent little things.'

Arun continued with caution. 'So, you had some worms...and Aerkin had worms too?'

Nicholas released a heavy-winded sigh that misplaced his smile. 'Only one organisation had the resources and the needs to bring Falkeworms up from the deep ocean floor; it was far more expensive than you could imagine and is impossible to get to now. A team of specialist divers retrieved them, drivers transported them, and then eventually they ended up on the worktops of thirteen individuals. I was one of those individuals, and so was he.' Nicholas pulled a toothpick from behind his ear to twiddle. 'We were not friends, just colleagues. He stole some of the Falkum when he turned to insanity, but as the project lead, I had the key to the department stores and took the rest for safe-keeping. We are the only two that possess this material.'

'Oh. So...what's he like?'

'Sorry, I do not know much about Aerkin on a personal level, nor do I wish to.' Nicholas's hand froze, the toothpick suspended, and a smile returned to his face. 'How did your training go?'

As intriguing as the gloves' origin was, Arun always took the opportunity to talk about himself. 'Training went well. Sorta.' He glanced into his gloved palms and briefly pictured worms crawling along his fingers. 'Sorta not, actually. Everyone's going crazy with this light, like lighting a candle, but I struggle to create it and can't even hold it for more than a few seconds without it hurting. It's too much pressure. A couple of days ago, I didn't even know this all existed.'

'Exactly!' Nicholas leaned forward. 'It has not been long. It took humans four and a half billion years to awaken on this rock, so I think you can grant yourself a few more days. Thinking positive thoughts of yourself will only help improve you further.' Nicholas yanked Arun's hands forward without grace.

'You people like yanking arms, don't you?'

'All that scavenging over the years must have helped strengthen these muscles in your hands. I have a tip to help you deal with the pain. Massage your palms and fingers for a while before you start. Think of it as a warm-up for your hands. Soon enough, you will naturally get used to it and will have no trouble reaching expectations.'

'Thanks, I'll try that. Not sure what expectations I'm supposed to reach, though.'

Nicholas returned his poise and sipped his drink. His reaction couldn't be further from Arun's, with his nostrils flared open to consume every puff of steam and a light moan of pleasure escaping his lips. 'For now, let us not think of what we need of you but rather what you need of yourself. Tell me about your best quality, and I will see if I can help with your own expectations.'

Feeling a slight twist in his stomach, Arun thought about his usual routine. 'Well, I steal, fight, and dig mostly. I once did all three at the same time.' It wasn't exactly a resume to be proud of. However, it dawned on him that those daily chores had helped his hands find new purpose in his gloves. It gave him optimism. How unusual, this feeling of positivity.

'I also read,' said Arun. 'I make time for reading whatever book or magazine I can recover. I build as well. I usually have to rebuild my shelter back home as the weather wrecks it. Not sure if that just makes me a lousy builder, though. But I get better each time.

'I explore with my scope, I protect our group, I—'

'No, do not search too far for one thought,' said Nicholas. 'Clear your head and focus on the one thing that comes to mind when you think of yourself.'

'I...' Arun paused for a while. 'I'm unhinged. Like a thunderstorm.'

Nicholas tilted his head back, breathing deep through his nose as if taking in the remnants of tea that were caught in his nostril hair. 'A brutal assessment, but honest. Tell me what makes you unhinged. If you feel the need to open up, do not fight it. In fact, you might feel yourself being nudged in the right direction by the mushroom tea.'

Mushroom tea? That relaxing feeling, flocking all of a sudden. It was slight but noticeable, with the weight of his arms disappearing as they took flight within.

'Unlock your consciousness,' said Nicholas. 'Have you always been unhinged?'

'Uh, no, not always,' replied a contemplative Arun, looking into his hands.

Wow—the realisation of the lines in Nicholas's fingers. Would the wrinkles exist if he never closed his hands?

'Being unhinged could be beneficial to you. Would you believe me if I told you you had a second consciousness? A dormant mind, waiting to be unlocked.'

Nicholas squinted, leaning a hand on Arun's shoulder, his face revealing itself through the overgrowth of his hair. His eyes were tired and weathered, with waves of wrinkles riding down from his eyes to his cheeks, and his pupils were misty over the tinted blue. The things he'd seen must have taken their toll. The ends of his lips turned, gifting Arun a smile, followed by a dented laugh. Arun laughed louder in return.

'Why are we laughing?' giggled Arun.

'The tea,' replied Nicholas. 'It is quite exquisite.'

Nicholas must have been an experienced tea drinker, holding his poise together, but Arun lost control of his laughter, ignited further by a tune sung merrily by Nicholas.

'Mushroom tea is good for me,

It makes me laugh and makes me pee.

But should I drink a touch too much,

I'd wake up curled up in a hutch.'

'I don't know what a hutch is.' Arun continued to laugh, millimetres from collapsing back. His eyes stretched open, attempting to focus on Nicholas.

Nicholas slowly flattened his grin as the last huff of laughter left his mouth. 'Laughter releases endorphins and stimulates your heart and mind. Can you feel it yet? Your mind is seeking a connection, Arun.' Nicholas leant forward and placed his hand on Arun's knee, gripping firm with his fingertips. 'I know the feeling. Your thoughts and memories are not enough. Your mind is seeking the Central Door. All it needs is to be opened, by someone, from somewhere. And then we will all be unlocked. It could be the key to defeating Aerkin.

'Help me open the door, Arun. Help me find the secrets that dark energy holds. This could be the purpose you have so longingly searched for.'

Arun's eyes began to dart left and right, losing Nicholas's face, rapidly searching beyond his control. The fizzing blur of Nicholas's head drew larger.

'Tell me what you see,' whispered Nicholas, his strong, woody breath now spreading across Arun's face. 'Do you see the door? The orbs of omniscience? The cosmic web of the beyond? I know it is there—I have seen it. Take me there. Unhinge it for me. Find it, Arun. Find it. Find the—'

'Nicholas!' a voice cried. It carried from outside. Nicholas broke from Arun's gaze and shot up before storming out of his hut, leaving Arun to reset his vision and wobble to his feet. What just happened? Arun stumbled and peered outside to see the Hill flooded with folk, directed at a stranger standing still at the bottom of the Hill, his coat surfing the winds. Nicholas wasted no time marching down but bore no gloves or visible weapons—just a man huddled in his cloak. However, there appeared to be two or three Nicholas's striding forward. The stranger stood motionless as the group of Nicholas's arrived in his presence, with a blurry Cole muttering within earshot.

Arun's focus fluttered in and out; he tried his best to make out the conversation, but the voices merged into one. He stumbled back, resting an arm on Nicholas's bed. His memory became faded, with his eyes now shut and gravity pulling his head towards the mattress. The tea had taken him.

CHAPTER SIX

DIVERGING FATES

Kate departed the fields late in the afternoon to make her way back to the Hill—hunger had consumed her. She'd roamed down to the Moorlands, a mile north, a usual retreat for her when seeking solace. It was here that a bench with a crack through the middle sat facing the moors, and it was here that she and Iris used to sit watching the reflections in the still, murky water of the birds overhead.

Returning over the hilltop mound behind Nicholas's hut, Kate heard a raft of voices crashing against each other from below. She switched from a stroll to a jog to head towards the commotion, where Cole stood beside a stranger, halting him from proceeding further. To Kate's left, Nicholas made his way down from his hut.

'What's going on?' asked Kate, approaching Matuu.

'Stranger,' replied Matuu, pointing to the man, mid-munch of a sandwich—as unhelpful as ever. Kate carried on down to keep pace with Nicholas, minding the grass down the winding paths.

'This traveller only said one thing: "Nicholas Servington",' announced Cole.

Kate kept a few metres behind Nicholas, a lesson drilled in by him, always eager to protect her. She examined the stranger, wearing a long coat that covered all but his balding head, sat atop an unyielding look on his face. A gold chain with an unrecognisable emblem flashed from his neckline. He possessed a horse, standing tied to a tree a few steps behind, with half a saddle and more baggage than a lone man could need.

'I am Nicholas Servington. What is your business here?' asked Nicholas in a commanding tone of voice.

'I rode from the west,' drawled the man with an old city accent. 'I carry a message, a message for you. It reads Nicholas Servington: we await you in the west, in town south o' the river. We have the means to defeat Aerkin and weaponry to do so. We come from across the coast and have escaped his lands. Please hurry.'

'The west, by the river.' Nicholas twirled his beard. 'Which path? How did you find this place?'

'They told me, told me where to come, but it took a while in my old age. You must know what it's like?'

'Swine,' replied Nicholas. Kate knew this would irk him, being sensitive about his age. 'Nobody knows of this location, least of all Mainland messengers. I am afraid I do not find your account precise. You will find nothing more than hostility if you do not leave this—'

'Wait! The weapon is a glove. Yes, a glove. A glove he created before he turned the world sour. The messengers said I'd know it was you if you had the same gloves.'

Nicholas paced towards the man, towering over him as he fretted.

'You do!' the man exclaimed. 'I can see some of you have them. I'm telling the truth. The messengers said you'd understand. They said Iris sent them.'

'Iris!' Kate's face dropped with a gasp of air as the man's words grabbed her by the throat. She felt a surge of natural energy bubble inside her as she lowered herself to one knee. The joy, the anguish. The excitement, the pain. She burned with a bounty of conflicting emotions through hearing that name, hearing that she was alive.

Nicholas stood still, facing away from her. 'Everybody! To the cottage. Now.' He then directed his speech to the stranger. 'And you. Come, I will see that you find your path.' Nicholas placed his hands behind his back before leading the man and his horse away from the Hill. Still unable to find the right words, Kate turned to see Cole standing protective of the Hill with her arms akimbo, motionless until the two were out of sight.

Cole huffed and marched back up the hill. 'I'll put the kettle on.'

*

Kate sat silently in the cottage, thinking about where her lost friend was, where she'd been, and how she'd survived alone without her gloves. Almost all others on the Hill were inside the cottage arguing beside her, but she'd filtered out their voices before they'd even started talking. The gradual increase of rain began to knock on the cottage door as the sky turned dark.

Nicholas suddenly burst into the cottage, passing Kate in determined haste. 'We are leaving. Pack everything you have.' He strode to the front of the cottage and stood on a chair above the many heads below.

'Leaving for where?' replied Tej, pacing alongside Cole. Others began muttering, and muttering turned to expressive confusion. Kate allowed the Hillfolk voices to creep back into her ears as her vision of Iris subsided.

Nicholas raised his chin before speaking. 'We are leaving for the Mainland.'

'What?' shouted a voice from the back amongst the growing tone of mutters. 'Why now?'

'No good can come of this!' cried another.

'Now, now! My friends, the day has come and come it has too soon,' announced Nicholas above the voices. 'The timeless time for playing and planning has led us here, and the period we once called when is now. Grab all you need, prepare your steed, for tomorrow morning before the clouds can show, we will depart.'

Kate flung her head from side to side, assessing the reaction.

'Everyone? Really?' shrilled a voice. 'We need more,' 'this is insane,' 'this is a trap.' More voices joined the fray.

'Fellows, please. I had always expressed this day would be on our terms. Is it wrong to say you are not ready? For how long have you all been here, punching trees and kicking dirt? Tomorrow I will explain everything. For now, we prepare.'

'No!' shouted Jordan, with the wind from the open door crashing against the Hillfolk. 'Tell us now!'

This couldn't be a trap—they had to leave. If Kate missed her chance with Iris, she might never get another one. She glanced around the room again. Orphaned souls filled it, those who'd spent years under Nicholas's tutelage, trusting in him and his plan. They'd worked tirelessly for him in anticipation of this moment. Yet now it had arrived, it felt all too sudden. Kate put her head into her hands as the squabble continued.

'Quiet please,' said Nicholas to calm the chatter. 'Very well, Jordan. The stranger divulged more to me in a deeper message. The weapon in their possession would give us more hope against Aerkin than we have had until now. However, they will wait only a few nights before heading north and seeking solace in case they have been spotted, which is quite possible. Iris is supposedly in the Ruins of Rennes, a place not too far from the Mainland shore, but this place may soon fall into Aerkin's hands. We have to get to them now or never, or we may miss our moment.'

Ruins of Rennes? Kate knew nothing about this place, nor had anyone ever mentioned it before.

'We need more time to prepare,' said Matuu. 'What about food and…well, food?'

'We can each carry enough for several days, enough for the ride to the shore, via the west, and across the Channel. Our Mainland survival training will then come into play. Remember, if simple Mainland messengers can travel all the way here, together we should be more than able to do the same in reverse.'

'This is so sudden,' replied Jordan. 'Can't we get them to come here?'

'I am afraid not,' said Nicholas. 'We have only one option. Our chance has been handed to us, and our task is now clear. No more hiding. No more waiting. We must find this weapon and free this planet of its darkness.'

Whispers and chatter bounced between the walls before an argument broke out. Kate lifted her head and stared into Nicholas's eyes, more stringent than ever, with a gaze that pierced as if she stood nose to nose in front of him. He'd surely run out of convincing words to spread. Kate stood and took a deep breath.

'Okay!' she belted at the top of her voice before lowering it, pausing to let the echo escape. 'Tomorrow. We leave for the messengers and the Ruins of Rennes. The darkness must die—end of.' Kate brought the room to a freeze, the only movement from her as she lifted her hood and headed for the door.

A silence followed before Cole broke it, 'What will 'appen to the boy, Arun?'

'We leave him here and return to him with a better world,' said Nicholas. 'Now is not the time for babysitting.'

Kate stopped by the doorway. It would be harsh to leave Arun, but it didn't matter. All that mattered to her was Iris and finding her safe and sound. She turned her head to face the crowd gathered in the cottage one last time. Cole wrapped her arms tightly around Nicholas at the centre of the returning bounds of chatter, embracing him, though his eyes were fixed back on Kate's.

*

Night came without rain, but the sky maintained its usual dark and shrouded duvet over the Hill. Occasional moonlight illuminated the clouds, giving some wonder to the night sky and a subtle glisten of light to the land below.

Arun, waking up after his tea, opened his eyes wide, full of energy. He pondered if he'd been moved to his bed by Nicholas or if he'd wandered about by means of the tea and not his mind. He heard scurrying voices amongst the crickets as he woke. He jumped up and looked out of his window, noticing one by one a hut extinguishing its light until the last one faded.

He wrapped up warm and strolled uphill against the calm winds in no mood to stay inside. It was quiet; it must usually be like this during the nights on the Hill. He chose to return to the field where the others would train, hoping to find space to practice with his gloves.

As Arun strolled onto the field, he examined a single light glowing in the grass nearby. It took the shape of a hand, and although it could be anyone resting here in the dark, Arun knew it was Kate.

'Tello,' said Arun, forgetting Kate's greeting term.

'Te-lue,' she replied. 'Feeling any better? Saw Nicholas carrying you to your hut, I'm guessing mushroom tea?'

'Yeah. Horrible taste. It felt kinda nice, but then I fell asleep.'

'He shouldn't have done that to you. He's tried that with all of us. He's obsessed with drinking it and finding some sort of door. You can sit down, by the way.'

'Oh, yeah.' Arun collapsed to the ground, soaking his trousers on the wet grass without thought. 'Didn't mean to disturb your peace or…whatever it is you're doing.'

'I was just thinking. But to be honest, I could take a break from that. Never mind what dark energy can do—over-thinking can melt your mind.'

Arun looked at Kate's glowing hand, remembering how mesmerised he was when he first saw it. A ring of wet grass around it twinkled a pale shade of blue. 'What happens if I touch your light? I mean…just asking out of curiosity. I'm not going to. Well, I would, but I won't. I just meant—'

'Nothing much. Don't ever ask me to punch you, though.'

'Noted.' Arun smirked nervously. Kate's body stretched out across the ground, half highlighted by her glow. He laid down beside her with his eyes and palms facing the sky.

'You're the *strongest* warrior then, huh? How'd you all figure that one out?'

Arun received no reply for a moment, hearing a faint sigh from Kate's mouth before she spoke. 'It is what it is, I suppose. I can turn my light yellow if I concentrate hard enough, and nobody else here can. Nicholas says it's to do with the electromagnetic spectrum or something like that. Blue light scatters more than any other, so when dark energy reflects light, it displays how dense it is. It goes a shade of green, then yellow, then orange, and finally red, all across the spectrum.

'So that's why I wouldn't want to punch you. Because even if you did protect yourself with your light, I'd break straight through and kill you.'

Arun gulped and lay in silence. It was too dark to tell if Kate was smiling, though a slight chuckle soon after gave her away. He directed his attention back on his hands. Each time he'd created light, it'd been more straightforward than the last. With this in mind, he hoped trying again would bring at least less pain, although grimacing and gnarling wouldn't go well alongside Kate's tranquil state, nor would following Nicholas's advice of massaging himself. He instead laid in peace and stared into the dark abyss above.

'How did you survive?' asked Kate. 'You don't look or sound like other scavengers. Those I came across can barely string a coherent sentence together. Must be more to it.'

Arun searched his memories for something deep and insightful about finding his way in the world, but the truth was all he could conjure up. 'I don't remember much from when I was young apart from this one man who took shelter with me. He kept us away from trouble as much as we could, and the days were pretty uneventful other than him doing something for me. He'd feed me, read to me. He taught me how to use the scope. The scope! Where are my belongings?'

Kate let a moment pass without reply. 'Sorry, I left them where I found you. Didn't think to bring anything else.'

Arun feared that would've been the answer after many days of forgetting to ask, but it didn't take the sting away. That was everything he owned. Gone, unless he could find time to go back. 'D'you remember where you found me?'

'Sure. I'll—' Kate paused again. 'Just don't worry. Anyway, what about that man? Where is he now?'

'Your guess is as good as mine. One day I woke up and he was gone, and all his stuff too. All he left was a note, and I just had to carry on living that same life. I was so scared but I couldn't do anything else. And now I barely think about him anymore—that was a long time ago.'

The faint outlines of dark clouds gently pushed across the sky, merging and splitting as they often would.

'Didn't you look for him?' asked Kate.

'I looked for a while, but…it's hard. I was too young. I just got on with it and kept reading and kept surviving. Then I had to fight for myself. People twice the size of me would empty my shelter. Every time I'd try to stop them, and every time they'd beat me down. Until one day, they couldn't beat me down anymore. I just…never expected to be alone at that age.'

'That's nothing. I was on my own when I was about five.'

Arun released a short cough. 'Sorry—I didn't know we were playing "ultimate survivor".'

'Even if we were, I think we're both losers.' Kate turned onto her side, facing Arun. The glow of her hand now gently illuminated her face. She smiled and looked into his eyes, but her lips soon curled back. 'My first memory was of the blood-red sky, the smoke, and the burning. That was the first few days of the Worldshift. My building collapsed, but a neighbour brought me outside through a crowd of others running and crawling whilst my mum stayed behind and tried to save my dad from fallen brick. Think I waited and waited, just staring at the rubble long after anyone had escaped. Expected them to appear suddenly, and everything would be all right. That was the last time I saw them. Their faces are a blur now. I'd do anything to remember what they looked like.'

'That must have been scary.'

Kate turned back to face the sky. 'I guess. Like you—I was too young to fully get it. That neighbour looked after me for about a year and vanished too. Then I was scavenging and hunting. Then, when I was about seven, I found the Hill. And here I am now. I guess you've spent all this time trying to live in my shoes.'

Arun let out as much of a laugh as possible through his nose. His muscles were completely relaxed, his body sunk into the damp grass. 'Well, I've got your friend's gloves, so I must be doing something right.' Arun waited for a response, but the air whistled. 'Kate?' Still nothing.

Arun continued to search the clouds, wondering if he'd said something wrong, but his aimless stare into the sky brought a different answer. A patch of darkness began to push the clouds away, and a white dot twinkled in the middle. 'Hey! Look! D'you see that?'

'What?' huffed Kate.

'No, look, up there in the clouds. The dark patch. And the dot.'

The dot found solace with another fainter dot. Then another. As each second passed, another dot would be born in the sky. They grew in number outwards from the first in a jagged circle, some now exceptionally bright and sparkling through the freed atmosphere.

Arun gasped. 'Are they stars?'

'I…I don't believe it,' said Kate as they both lay motionless. 'The stars. They're so beautiful.'

Arun forgot to breathe. He'd never witnessed the stars in the sky, but the moonlit clouds had finally parted over the lands above his head for the very first time. The galaxy's glow filtered through the twinkling lights as more and more emerged from the cosmos. The light that had travelled far through space and time had finally broken through to reach a simple quartet of eyes.

Arun had read about the great beyond before. The mystical worlds of all materials, colours, and sizes. The billions of stars in each galaxy of billions more. He could never comprehend it until now. Although they were tiny white dots in the sky, the window to the universes had opened, and Arun felt both smaller and larger than he'd ever done.

As a layer of water welled in Arun's eyes, his gloved hand moved closer to Kate's, which had kept its light. His palm graced hers, and a heavier, deeper glow illuminated as if responding to the light sent from the sky. Their hands embraced, Arun's muscles tensed, and a comforting warmth grew in his palm as the two turned to one another to see the glow in each other's eyes. The light in their palms grew with intensity as if they were passing energy between them. The intense sensation ran up Arun's arm and through his body, and his heart beat with the vibrance of a slow, heavy bass. Clouds of hot air escaped their cold, dry lips, with gentle blue sparks dispersing their breath. Weightlessness followed with the pausing of time.

Before Arun could breathe in again, he felt a strong breeze and looked up. Kate followed. The stars faded fast and retreated behind the clouds; they did so before either of the two could say goodbye.

Arun found no words inside him. He snapped out of his light-headed gaze as Kate pulled her hand away and jumped up. Without a word, she marched back towards the Hill.

'Kate? Where are you going?' asked Arun, perplexed.

'It's late,' replied Kate as her words softened in the distance. 'I need sleep. Goodbye, Arun.'

Arun waved. He couldn't tell if she turned around to see, but even if she did, the darkness would have captured it. He turned to stare at the glove that had graced Kate's, and it held an opaque yellow glow that soon faded out, just as the stars had done.

CHAPTER SEVEN

THE GUARDIAN OF THE HILL

Arun's eyes peeled open to the sound of distant thunder the next day. The sky shone at its muted brightest, given Arun had been awake late and slept through most of the morning; he'd spent the night lost in examining and testing his gloves. Massaging his hands had a promising effect, gradually easing the pain that the surge of energy presented, allowing him to ignite and extinguish his gloves without a heavy, burning sensation. With nothing to concentrate on, he'd caught himself stopping to think about Kate every other minute. Yawn—he rubbed the sleep from his eyes and started the day by thinking up a morning routine that could accompany his new life on the Hill.

First, he got dressed, putting on his gloves before anything else. Secondly, he performed mild clenching exercises and massaged his hands once more. Lastly, given Kate's impressive display in his hut, it would be best to practice some stretches and stances. He rose from his rest, performed the first two steps of his new routine, and gave himself space in the middle of the hut. Deep breath. One. Two. Three.

Arun ignited his gloves after a brief struggle. He swung left and then right. In his mind, Arun transcended mortal combat with impressive turns, high kicks, and punches that any seasoned fighter would be proud of. Whack, slash—enemy after enemy falling at his blessed feet. Untouchable. Unbeatable. But deep down, he knew his intimidation could do with major improvements, as he stumbled and bumbled and grunted and groaned like a true scavenger fighter, without any of the grace that Kate displayed. Making it up as he went along, he finished with a final flurry, spinning multiple times and punching the wall.

'Argh!' wailed Arun, shuffling back in agony, holding his throbbing fist in the other palm. His fists had seen fair use over the years, but you could never get used to punching solid oak. The gloves didn't offer much help either, with light trapped in his palms, leaving his knuckles protected by only the thin material. Yet, despite the pain, the muscles in his hands didn't burn as sharply as before.

Arun collected the cold air through his teeth and drifted towards the door with a pinch of growing confidence. As he reached to grab his cloak, hanging on a lone hook beside the door, he paused. Odd that no one had burst through his door to wake him or yelled his name down the Hill. Perhaps the thunderstorms brought quieter mornings here. Never mind.

Arun wrapped up warm and headed out, noticing the only human-made light featured on the Hill emanated from the cottage. He briskly walked across, hearing no chitter-chatter from inside other huts nor roaring laughter from the cottage. Opening the creaking door, he found Cole and Tej sitting by a table in the middle of the room with only a tray of food for company.

'Why 'ello, sausage,' greeted Cole with a melancholic tone. 'Breakfast? Or perhaps lunch?'

'Sure,' replied Arun, walking over. 'You know what I was just thinking? What if I'm meant to be here?' Arun searched the tray for the healthiest breakfast option fit for a day of muscle-building.

'Umm…what do you mean?' Cole's expressionless face stared back—not the reaction Arun was hoping for.

'Well, it makes sense. I was born twenty years ago, just as they discovered dark energy. I don't know when my birthmonth is, but let's imagine it happened on the same day. And then I end up here, finding out I have to join the fight against Aerkin.'

'There's such a thing as coincidences, dear,' said Cole, followed by a soft, muted chuckle.

'And I'm finally starting to feel comfortable in the gloves, like I can feel their energy instead of just a burning pain. And then there's Kate. She's great. Great Kate! She's a real survivor like me. It sounds like she's also had a really hard time in the early years when—'

'They're gone,' interrupted Tej. 'Everyone's gone.'

Rude. Arun frowned and pulled up a chair but stood beside it. 'Gone? I knew I shouldn't have gotten up late. You know, I haven't had a proper sleep since I arrived. Are they practising?'

'Thank you, love,' warned Cole to Tej. 'I think you'd better grab our boy a tray of his own with some nibbles whilst I talk to him. Oh, and *the note*.' Tej, huffing audibly, stormed off to the back of the room and turned the corner, out of sight.

'Where are they?' asked Arun, growing suspicious.

'The thing is,' said Cole, tilting her head as if the words were etched on the ceiling, 'last night, Nicholas returned after meeting a messenger and ordered that everyone who could fight should leave at dawn. They're on their way now, far away, to the Mainland.'

'The Mainland?' exclaimed Arun, taking two steps back. 'Now? I have to help them fight! Where'd they go? Which direction?'

'Arun. You can't fight. They didn't take you.'

'I can fight! I have gloves. I always fight, I can fight, damnit.' Arun turned and turned around once more, animated and wild, beginning to wheeze as his lungs tried to keep up with his heart. He glanced out the window, back to Cole, then to Tej, whose head turned the corner. He continued to turn and twist as if his feet were at odds with each other.

'Sausage, you're staying 'ere with us,' said Cole. 'I'm so sorry, but you're safe 'ere.'

'Safe? I don't need to be safe. I'm a fighter. They're out there, Kate's out there, without me. They could be in trouble.' Arun paced. 'Oh no…trouble. I could help.'

Arun launched himself towards the door but rested both hands against the grain instead of opening it. His eyes swelled as he bit fiercely onto his lower lip to stop its quiver. This feeling: what was it? He replayed the cackling sound in his head of Nicholas's laughter and the beauty of the stars laying beside Kate. She must have known on the field they were leaving. How dare she not tell him.

Arun brought his eyebrows together in disbelief. Was it something he'd done? Perhaps he was seen as too weak. Or did they simply not like him?

'It's too late; they left on the 'orses,' whispered Cole, walking up to him and placing her hand gracefully on Arun's back.

Horses? What horses? What else didn't he know? Various thoughts swivelled and swished, each question overlapping the last as his eyes swept like a typewriter. But he settled on one realisation. He was simply not wanted—a feeling entwined with him. He turned around, brushing Cole's hand away from his body. His eyes were sore as he looked her in the eye. 'They abandoned me.'

'No, my dear, no. They went to fight for us,' reassured Cole. 'I know you're upset now, but it was the right thing to do.'

'I'm not upset. I'm…annoyed. I thought I wasn't just a scavenger to them.' A drop of salty water fell upon his lips as he searched his mind for the memory of faces—faces of the departers who began to show him the meaning of family.

'Come on, fella,' said Tej, bringing a tray of food towards the centre of the room. 'We're here, as are the Trellocks, of course. We're still a community.'

Tej placed the tray on the table and pulled away a seat meant for Arun. Once glorious in sight and smell, the Hill food now appeared stale and bland in Arun's mind. He held his head low in thought. A dawn departure on horseback would make it impossible for him to catch up, and he'd probably lose himself alone in the fields. Any lingering thoughts he had of running to find a horse and galloping after them vanished with the fact he'd never ridden before and wouldn't likely make it a step before falling.

Arun wiped his eyes and calmed his panting breath. Again...what was this feeling? Silly that he should feel these emotions, having been here only a matter of days. Composure, Arun. But it had been so magical, all of it, down to the simplicity of feeling tingly looking at a smile on a young woman's face. He couldn't help but feel a sense of loss.

'They're doing this for everyone, sausage,' said Cole. 'For every living thing, for our future. Our job now is to keep 'ome safe for their return. Come, sit down.'

Arun felt resigned to talking to the two cottage-dwellers instead of standing in the rain or retreating to the hut he'd not long ago awoken from; there was nowhere else to go. He arranged his feet which led him to the table. 'Why d'you both stay? Did they leave you too?'

'Leave us? No, I don't bother with that light mumbo-jumbo,' said Cole, walking alongside him. 'I was 'ere when Nicholas arrived, and I 'elped him and Ms Berkley build up this place. But fighting? I'd blow my own 'ead clean off.'

Arun bowed and rubbed his eyes with his gloved fingertips, in no mood for jokes. He turned to Tej.

'Me? I'm just here.' Tej reached into his pocket with one hand, holding a slice of bread with the other. He pulled out a scrap of stained and wrinkled paper and placed it beside the tray. 'This is for you.'

Arun's legs collapsed into the seat. There it sat, a note with the name *Nicholas* at the bottom. He dragged it towards him to find his name scribbled at the top.

> *Dear young Arun,*
> *You will be as frustrated reading as I am writing.*
> *We had only just begun our turbulent journey together, and I believe you would have succeeded far beyond our expectations. You now have a new journey to undertake. Although you will not have the tutelage that others have had, nor did I and I did not do too bad!*
> *Everything you need is with the key under my bed. It unlocks a room on the upstairs floor in the cottage. The equipment here will*

allow you to become the Guardian of the Hill, as I until this day have been. But use with caution. It will take as much of you as it gives.

Protect our home, protect our people, but most importantly, it will be up to you to take back our world from Aerkin should I fail on my journey. Every choice you make from this moment on could decide the fate of humanity.

Remember this, Arun. You did not find the gloves to follow in mine or anyone else's footprints. You were meant to forge your own path and choose the doors you walk through.

Nicholas

P.S. Take good care of my tree

'What does it say, sausage?' asked Cole.

There were no words to be said, only thoughts to be thought. The overwhelming burden of Nicholas's words piled on Arun's already fragile state of mind. The fate of humanity? Arun only knew of the word 'responsibility' in written form; he could barely keep a collection of books and his scope safe, let alone humanity. At least one feeling subsided with the letter: the feeling of not being good enough.

It was as if Cole and Tej disappeared from the room, and all that existed were Arun and the note. Even the scent of food sent itself astray. A faint hum rolled through the air, which must have been Cole calling his name, but Arun didn't listen. He blindly strolled out of the cottage instead.

Arun wandered the Hill and the fields, unsure if he'd walked for minutes or hours. A lone deer brought life to an otherwise still field ahead. It aimlessly strolled, smelling the grass, perhaps looking for a trace of its herd. The following field led Arun to a small but wide, wooden structure to the left, nestled between two smaller huts. He had no thoughts about what it could be, still trapped in his head, roaming towards it. The smell of the building was apparent as he strolled closer; only one thing could be so fragrant and fresh yet disgustingly throat-tingling: manure. Not a scent he often came across in the towns but one he instinctively knew.

Lovely.

Walking inside with a scrunched up nose, Arun found himself in an empty stable, looking around at the open gates and equipment, dormant and scattered on the floor. Short rays of light peered in from broken slats. He'd never stepped foot in here, but he could feel the rush and scurry of twenty-odd horses being led from their stalls. He couldn't believe his foolishness sleeping through the morning, but also how selfish the group were to have left without a wave goodbye for the one possibly responsible for the 'fate of humanity'. Deep down, he wouldn't have allowed them to go if he knew. He'd have followed them by foot if necessary.

Arun crossed into the Hill and headed to Nicholas's hut. Inside, it was dark and lifeless, with all candles and sheets removed as if nobody had lived here for years. Arun wasted little time reaching for the key, sleeping on the dusty floorboards. Great hiding place. A browny-gold colour dressed the key; it was long, sturdy, and ringed at the end. This would be the first time Arun held a key that would lead somewhere.

He steamed down the Hill towards the cottage, with Cole and Tej now nowhere to be seen. A creaking, twisting wooden staircase led the way to the top floor for the first time to a far creakier wooden floor. A narrow hallway greeted him, with the walls covered with ripped strips of hanging patterned paper and old electrical lamps that remained fixed in place. Arun ran his fingers along the wires leading from the lights into the wall. He could only imagine what kind of shine they would have once produced from underneath the curved glass surface.

Arun tiptoed across a dirty rug, checking one door handle and another before casting his eyes on a door with a faint glow at the end of the hall, bearing a strange golden handle in the shape of a lion's head. He recognised the impressive mane from a nature book he'd read.

Arun slid the key into the lock and tweaked his wrist right and left; such a pleasantly straightforward contraption. The door creaked open, granting access to a dark, misty, and gloomy room full of boxes and chests of drawers, a complete and utter mess.

With a lifetime to spare, Arun followed a path created by constant footprints in the dust, leading to a row of open boxes. A dim glow of light spread through the sole dirty window in the centre of the front wall. The first box contained old clothes with no exciting or exceptional material. Digging through, Arun discovered a grey, stained shirt at the bottom, folded over, bearing an illustration of a yellow semi-circle. He opened it up, watching the circle as it transcended into the sun; Arun witnessed his first ever sunrise. Oh, how magical it must feel to see a real one.

The next box looked far more interesting, with a pile of books stacked high above the fold. Uh—on closer inspection through the dust, these were science books and magazines Arun would have no chance understanding. *ParticlUS Issue 108 March 30 2068: Falkum's Fallacy—Wonder or Weapon?*

As Arun reached for the third box, he noticed two clothes stands in the corner. One stood bare, but the other drew Arun's gaze. Partly hidden by a stack of boxes, a mostly white suit of armour hung from the stand. He moved closer, observing the unquestionable material of the white mantle of his gloves. No way. It couldn't be, could it? He pushed the boxes aside and gazed upon its full glory. The occasional black and gold lines along the seams were the only ridge breaking the sparkling white shine, and the suit split into three parts: the torso and sleeves, the legs, and the boots. Arun's mind emptied of doubt; he'd found the equipment Nicholas had left for him.

Arun unhooked the torso of the suit and held it in his arms. It draped over his hands like a simple yet slightly heavier and firmer shirt. He slid the garment over his top, fitting him surprisingly well, stretching elastic-like to match his shape. It didn't quite reach his wrists, leaving a frustrating gap between that and his gloves, but the tight grip made him feel protected. He basked in wonder at every inch of material. He should show Kate…oh, that's right. Never mind.

With the boots and leggings completing Arun's new look, he walked to the side of the room and sat against the stone-cold wall, choosing a cleaner spot than the surrounding dusty floor. It was as if this spot had been sat in many times before. Arun's eyes scouted the room once more before noticing a floorboard ajar to the left. In a world of debris and decay, this brought no suspicion. The fingerprints around the edges, however, did.

Arun stretched and pushed the board up, revealing a black book peeking up at him, clean, bearing no sign of dust or damage. It was rare to find a book in such good condition after all these years. He picked it up and ran his hand over its coarse front cover before opening it to find a scribbled message on the inside: *Never forget. It's all for them.* At the bottom: *Nicholas.* As he turned the first page, it became clear that Arun had gained possession of a diary. Nicholas's diary.

CHAPTER EIGHT

THE GROUP OF TWENTY-SOMETHING

*T*he Known Timeless Timeline by Nicholas Servington. A compilation of experience and information.

Residents at Berkley Hill track timeless time (TT) using the new Gregorian calendar. TT has been reset, beginning ADE 0 (After Dark Energy). This follows the Gregorian calendar except for the eradication of time as a constant measurement, meaning hours, minutes, and below have ceased to exist except in common parlance. Anything before ADE 0 is written as BDE with no following number. This is also referred to as forgotten time (FT).

ADE 0—The partitioned year of destruction begins with Richard Aerkin's 'Great Balance'. Civilians watch in horror as the skies turn red in one moment in time. Those on the old European continent experience devastation, likened to a nuclear explosion, with a blast radius of hundreds of kilometres. Anyone who witnessed how he did this is instantly killed.

I escape Europe to the Home Isles and go into hiding.

Clouds cover the Earth in the following days, with such density that daylight is all but eliminated. Tremors in the Earth are heard throughout the globe, with news reports blaming worldwide military action or climate change. Word of a world war begins to spread. The east points at the west. The west points at the east. Governments seek to blame. People seek to be safe.

The sky gradually turns brighter, but tremors turn to earthquakes (quakes). The unstable Earth enters a new age as quakes begin a daily cycle, with some lasting full days or more. Quakes range from minor tremors to city-demolishing catastrophes. Each day brings an indeterminate outcome.

Reports of the end of the world end as fast as they begin, with electricity failing in most areas. Chasms open across the globe, and new mountain ranges and volcanoes burst into the sky. Lands move and reshape as the Earth's tectonic plates reform below. A significant amount of all life is wiped out within this first year. Hoarding food and sleeping rough is the new normality.

I eventually discover Roman remains upon a hill and take refuge. Only two people reside, the caretaker and a member of museum staff, but their cottage remains intact despite the quakes. Finally, a place to make plans.

*

Sat atop his horse with a gracious grin, Nicholas read through his timeless timeline, a small notebook that detailed the years gone by, from ADE 0 to the current year of ADE 20. The remaining pages were scanty, so the upcoming weeks would perhaps require their own notebook. In his bag sat the two remaining empty pads that he owned, alongside the Glove Directory and the Language of the Mainland, though he found himself rueing his forgetfulness over the one notebook he valued above all: his personal one, hidden at home.

He had spent the previous moments mumbling additional sentiments that he had not noted in the previous years, simultaneously whistling a tune, keeping his brain busy as always. A procrastinating mind births unhealthy thoughts: an old age mantra for the new world.

Old concrete roads with weeded decay paved the way southwest, but Nicholas opted to lead the group of twenty-four Hillfolk through the silent fields and mires. This created a more direct route and kept the group away from unwanted attention seekers.

The group rode silently at a trotting pace under calmer mid-noon skies. A storm had passed, leaving the horses to walk on waterlogged greens between the broken trees of lightning's visit, one still smoking from a split trunk. The group could see the city's outskirts far ahead, where narrow towers of smoke emerged in the sky. The bigger the city, the bigger the scavenger population. Yet, not all scavengers could be labelled the same in these cities, as most were simply survivors, sheltering and hiding in the debris for years and years.

'Think there are more Tossers like Arun around?' asked one of the younger group members from behind. 'Or just scumbags?'

'I would not go as far as to call them scumbags,' replied Nicholas. 'When the world cried foul, they took to cities for dry shelter, materials, and companions. They were bred in a society addicted to entertainment, and barren lands do not present such.'

'So we're some sort of anti-entertainment rebels?'

'That makes sense,' came another voice through the trotting hooves. 'I can name a few names.'

'No, no,' said Nicholas. 'Those like us simply looked to these hills for solace and natural foods. We explored a different path to them, and differences are not automatically a bad thing.' A wonderfully executed sentiment, Nicholas.

The riders formed an impenetrable unit, led by Nicholas, with Kate riding diagonally behind. Eight Marshals followed: fighters more comfortable with close combat. The contingent of Jordan, Serr, and Matuu rode ahead of five Guards at the back: slow but powerful defensive fighters who would take position in battle beside the Marshals. The remaining six flanking the sides were Tarios, whose gloves all possessed a strong elastic fibre cuff joined at two seams. These could be pulled back and fired, projecting light an impressive distance, though slightly slower than Jordan's muscular lightning bullet. The Tarios leader and Nicholas's tactician, Zachenne, rode furthest forward.

'Defence formation, third combat?' Zachenne rode with perfect military posture, head held high to display his strong bone structure and a serious demeanour causing intimidation in anyone conversing with him. His voice rarely strayed from a monotonous and emotionless tone.

'Not yet,' replied Nicholas. 'We are still unsure of the kindness of our welcome, should we be welcomed at all.'

'The last time I was here, they hurled rocks at me from behind every wall. I've never understood being blamed for something I didn't do.'

'I would not worry, friend. You know you are in the presence of ignorance when others seek to blame rather than query.'

Some had spent the best part of fifteen years together; others had only been around as early as two years, but Nicholas and Zachenne ensured the Hillfolk all knew the different formations, and they all knew their role. After all, the Hill could only provide three main activities: eating, talking, and training.

'How much further till we're there?' a voice from behind uttered. A moment passed without reply.

'Until we're there. Until we're home?' replied another.

A small smirk escaped Kate's face after accepting a glance from Nicholas. 'I need to know how long I'll roam,' she sang in return.

Nicholas, stone-faced and focused on the task, faced forward towards the city. It would take a while to reach the centre and perhaps another half-while before finding the travellers. The others fell silent again. The group's only delight was to watch the scenery pass, though perhaps they did warrant a slight pick-me-up.

'Before I see my love,' declared Nicholas after a long pause, to a raucous reception. Most did not waste a moment before joining the song in unison, though Nicholas and Kate listened on.

'How much further till we're there?
Until we're there. Until we're home?
I need to know how long I'll roam,
Before I see my love.
One more time.'

'Been a while since I've heard Matuu's roaming song,' said Kate to Nicholas as the others sang on repeat.

'I wouldn't mind it being a while longer', replied Nicholas. 'We should be remaining quiet and incognito out here.'

'You're too cautious. Who here would dare challenge us, especially with you wearing your suit. Relax.' Kate returned to the song mid-chorus.

Nicholas chuckled to himself. With his usual cloak over him, Nicholas did have one difference in attire this morning as he grasped the horse's lead: his gloves. His right glove was the only one on the Hill with no black ridge on it; it was entirely white.

'None of us lonely fools have loves waiting for our return; only our universe knows why that melody makes them merry,' remarked Nicholas.

Nicholas turned to Kate, whose eyes focused on the distant land, deep in thought. He knew her better than any, but journeying far away from the Hill was treading new ground for all. He began to wonder if anything was bothering her but stopped himself. He quickly buried his thoughts and returned his lips to a whistling tune, turning his attention back to the path. The entering of a city would often spell at least a little trouble.

'Think we're heading for a trap?' asked Kate.

'The feeling of unease will always linger with messages of anonymity,' said Nicholas. 'Anyone could have sent this message. A child. A murderer. But if it is a trap, I cannot wait to get caught.' He winked at Kate, an expression that would always keep her calm and confident. 'Do promise me one thing, though. Do not speak of Iris until her name is mentioned first. We must be wary of the words that leave our mouths now we have left the comforts of home.'

Kate nodded, but Nicholas felt a reluctance.

Not long after the reverberated voices had stopped singing, the group had reached the fallen concrete jungle, striding atop their horses from the fields. Like travelling from one form of civilisation into the remains of another, they emerged from the old Middle Ages into the new. The grey rubble, orange rusted steel, and natural greens of grass and weeds battled one another for supremacy, and puddles collected wherever the ground dipped, devoid of reflection. The old decay of flesh that once pained Nicholas's nose amongst sleeping towns had become a rarer occurrence nowadays, though turning a wrong corner could bring a return of the putrid scent.

'I never feel comfortable in the setting of a Toss.' Nicholas's eyes searched the debris.

'What's the name of this place?' asked Kate.

'I am not sure, and not sure it matters either. We only name things to be closer and more familiar to them. I do not have that urge here. Perhaps there is an old signpost somewhere if you still feel the urge.' Nicholas sent another glance to Kate, who still seemed pensive. 'I forget: do you remember much of the quakes before you came to me?'

'Not really,' replied Kate. 'Remember the tornadoes and hurricanes more. Felt like they'd never end.'

'Ah, indeed. I had word from a friend who had witnessed hailstorms that felt like a thousand—'

'A thousand bowling balls crashing down on them. I know.'

Nicholas's reminiscent smirk relaxed. 'Quite. I often talk with Cole about how we made it this far. How that cottage still stands is truly a miracle should miracles exist.' Nicholas glanced along the sea of rubble. 'To think of all those under these homes that have perished. So sad.'

'At least we're still here. What about dogs and other animals? Must have been so many more species. People can't help but feel that they suffered most, but everything's suffered.'

Nicholas pouted his lips and returned to whistling his wandering tune.

Vague outlines of the brick buildings that once stood began to engulf the group as they trotted further into the city centre. Low walls crumbled despite remaining intact, but these were few and far between and only served as climbing obstacles for the desperate, stretching flora. No structure stood larger than a couple of metres tall. The Earth was digesting cities, a bite or two more by every spin.

A cold metal head rested beside the arm of a fallen statue, caught within a crack in the Earth. Scraps of old cars were scattered around it, those that the sinkholes hadn't swallowed first. Joining the group, amongst the wreckage, were dozens of pondering eyes that slowly shut their makeshift doors and disappeared behind stubborn walls.

A scratching sound against rock interrupted the horses' trots. A man, skinny and rough, huddled far to the left, dragged a body through loose rubble. The body had one arm missing and bloodstains all over, the same red smeared all over the skinny man's mouth. He stared directly at the group, emotionless, shifting to the side and eventually disappearing from view.

'Greetings to you, too!' Jordan called out from the back.

'Now, now,' remarked Nicholas. 'We are nearly there. Why risk aggravating those with nothing to lose? Least of all, a Hunter.'

'They'll meet their death,' added Matuu. All were familiar and far from intimidated by Matuu's lack of sympathy.

'Ha! From you?' laughed Jordan, almost launching himself off his horse. 'I'm beating you twelve-two in sparring, remember? Sit back and let the pro handle things, mate.'

Matuu huffed. 'You'll cry for your mummy when the real fight starts.'

'And how do you suppose you're going to do when you're on the Mainland, and we're not on horseback? Or were you planning on losing a few kilos by then?'

'You'll lose all your kilos!'

A silence cut between the two, and Nicholas could only assume Serr had intersected between them, blocking their view of one another with that large flowing head of hair to end their squabble. Yet, it could also have been the calming air that brought the group's attention as they arrived in what would have been the city centre.

'Be on your guard,' announced Nicholas. 'And remember: steer clear of any who approach. I do not fancy contracting Dengtu.'

'I thought we couldn't get infected here?' asked a Marshal.

'Doesn't mean it can't be brought here,' said Kate.

The horses moved from trot to tread and turned their heads to the occasional rustling. A loose parchment parkoured across the wreckage as the horses found walking a straight line troublesome, their footing lost under unstable concrete. One by one, the group halted. Moments passed without movement from them nor the surroundings.

Nicholas dismounted and walked towards the side of the rubbled road where a laminated sheet began to wobble in the wind between two rocks before being caught in Nicholas's glove. It held a familiar design. He grabbed it and began to read, as memories from twenty years ago immediately flashed back into his mind. A menu. His favourite. Nicholas need not explain to the group that this was the town where he once grew up. He knew the name. He knew the streets and the paths and the shops. He knew the house that once stood two roads back. He discarded the menu, buried the memories, and returned to his horse.

'Silence,' said Nicholas. 'So often the sound of tranquillity, but not here.'

Before he could mount, Nicholas squinted his weary eyes to a wall in the near distance where two shadows caught his attention, dangling, attempting to climb over awkwardly. They wore torn, muddy, and hooded clothing, not much different to a scavenger's wardrobe. The figures released themselves to the ground, now in full view of the riders, and stopped in their tracks. They had frozen, and looked scruffy enough to be journeying messengers. Each group lay eyes upon the other, staring in anticipation.

'That must be them,' said Kate.

One of the men let out a howl, though it was unclear if he declared himself friend or foe.

'Viande!' the other cried as the howler continued screeching into the air. A horde of heads appeared over the rubble to greet the Hillfolk. Archaic shouts erupted. Arms raised, pumping and shaking in the air. They rushed towards the horses, spears and rocks in hand, bellowing out their lungs. 'Viande! Viande!'

'Viande…' uttered Nicholas. 'I believe that means "meat".'

'They want our meat?' asked Kate.

'Yes, but not the meat in our bags, but rather the meat on our bones.' Nicholas raised his voice and commanded, 'Zachenne, fourth combat.' Without a second's notice, the six Tarios archers split from the group and pushed forward, galloping ungracefully on the uneven earth. Their hands released their seize on the horse's leads as they reached full pelt, drawing their gloves with the hostiles in range. Compact balls of light transformed in their palms into thin bolts, preparing to fire into the onrushing enemies. Unlike arrows that arch in the air, these bolts projected a straight line, and once they had pierced through all in their reach, they would fade out into the air. Close-by they were almost always fatal, but further back, they could leave only lasting damage.

Nicholas mounted and rode behind, keeping safe distance. He watched on as, one by one, a bolt fired upon the rubble. Some hostiles leapt behind walls where they would have believed solid matter would save them. It would not. The first hostile fell as light passed through material, skin, and bone, then bone, skin, and material once more, shattering as it exited his body. Each zapping sound of light created a chaotic burst or bang from the material it passed through. Rocks and metal hurtled undirected through the air towards the Tarios, to no avail. The enemy were not hardened fighters; they were followers. Civilians, without a plan. This was not a fight but rather a hunting session, as if the Tarios were back on the Hill hunting deer.

All Tarios remained atop their horses, untouched, slaying all menaces ahead of them, some making their first kill. The cries of 'viande' quietened, and Nicholas noticed the Tarios lowering their hands solemnly, one by one, as the remaining enemies retreated into the shadows and disappeared into the distant debris. Zachenne, however, still fired his light as the others watched. These were far from his first kills. Seemingly unaffected, he held his posture perfectly high.

Two of the Tarios looked to each other, perhaps for support, perhaps for confirmation.

'To the left!' shouted Zachenne. Nicholas spotted a spear, launched at great speed towards the nearest rider. It met the rider's side and grazed past her, ripping her shirt and slicing her arm. As her arm pulled back, she strung her glove and shot a bolt straight through the hostile enemy peering beyond a gaping crack in a crumbled wall, instantaneously. There were none left in sight after the spear-wielder fell, apart from thirteen remaining figures, motionless on the ground.

'Never let your guard down,' said Zachenne. 'Even when the odds fight with you.'

Nicholas scanned the environment behind the Tarios line, and there appeared to be no attackers from the other sides. However, one small rock tumbled to the ground from a relatively close pile of wreckage to his right. With his eyes locked on the mound, Nicholas chose not to announce himself physically.

'If anyone should be hiding in that pile, speak now and walk freely,' announced Nicholas with an assertive authority.

'Don't hurt us,' a voice shrieked.

'We're messengers,' stuttered another voice.

'We're looking for Nicholas.'

'Old man, lots of hair, deluded.'

'That is enough, come out,' replied Nicholas. 'I am the one you are seeking. Let me see you.'

Two cautiously decorated figures side-stepped the rubble and made their way into view, with their hands held head high. The meat on their bones had all but withered, and short, scruffy hair sat above their scruffy skin; the two posed no threat.

'They lied; I think you look great,' one said.

'You look incredible,' added the other. 'Not a day over fifty.'

'Names, please,' snapped Nicholas before the two could add another word.

'That's Denis.'

'That's Emitai. Don't hurt us. We're innocent.'

'Innocence is best left to those with nothing to fight for.' Nicholas hummed. 'That accent is unmistakably one of many from the Mainland. Which continent?'

'North,' replied Denis.

'But originally south,' added Emitai.

'There's more than one continent?' asked Jordan. 'You said there was only one.'

'Not quite.' Nicholas tilted his head, one eye on the group, one eye on the travellers. 'The Mainland is a singular mass from the old continents of Europe and Africa. They shifted on their plates after Aerkin's rise, so far and fast that they merged into the now known singular mass of land.' Nicholas turned his attention back. 'One would presume these two have migrated.'

'We lived near where the border collided,' said Denis.

'The volcanoes and the purple mountains,' said Emitai. 'Near *him*.'

Denis and Emitai raised their chins in unison. 'Is it true? Do you know *him*?'

Nicholas returned his stern focus to the two. 'Never mind that. We are here for one reason. It seems you two hold a message. Knowledge of a weapon?'

Denis furiously nodded his head. 'Yes.'

'Can you show it to me?' asked Nicholas.

Denis's nodding turned sideways. Emitai sneezed before looking at his hands with disgust. He wiped his hand down his shirt, top to bottom.

Nicholas squinted. These buffoons weren't making life easy for him. He placed his arms on his seated hips and gestured to the two to come closer. Nervously looking at one another, they whispered before shuffling towards Nicholas's stern-faced horse.

Both young men looked to have encountered a rough journey. It would have taken over a week to reach the city from the shores of the Mainland. Their clothes were torn at the seams, their skin raw, and their shoes, if one could call them shoes, were made of scrap leather, wrapped and bound by rope. They stood close to one another, avoiding eye contact with anyone. They huddled, childlike in stance, matched by how they masked their fear in juvenile responses.

However, the small travellers were empty-handed, travelling together with no form of defence or attack in these times: an audacious feat, one Nicholas noticed under his blunt responses. The two had obtained a message and a mission to find a man in a foreign land. Instead of looking for a peaceful retreat, they chose to be brave and complete their task. Men of courage stood before the group, driven by hope. Nicholas huffed before smiling.

'The group of vermin had Mainland accents,' said Zachenne, as the Tarios and Hillfolk regrouped with Nicholas. 'They must have been following someone.'

'Just as I expected,' replied Nicholas before turning to the messengers sharply. 'You two would have me believe they followed you? Have you no stealth?'

'We took the long way!' insisted Emitai.

'There were no other boats,' added Denis.

'You...' Nicholas stuttered, for once unable to pull the right words from his brain. 'Alright. You best jump on. We are already prepared to journey to the Mainland, so you have ample timeless time to prove why you are of any use to us.' The two stepped forward. 'Wait! One of you sneezed. When was the last time you two coughed up blood? Any headaches? Fever? Swollen ears? Discoloured earwax?'

The two glanced at each other with an awkward suspicion. They held the back of their hands to each other's foreheads and checked their ears. 'No, we're fine,' they both uttered.

'Very well,' said Nicholas. The two did look virus-free despite their inverted stomachs and lacking hygiene. A sneeze was not a concerning symptom either. 'Chop, chop.'

They jumped aboard with Nicholas and Kate as Zachenne took the group's lead. They moved into a slow trot, heading towards the bodies of fallen Mainlanders.

Nicholas sensed the travellers looking across at one another. He thought to himself—no—no need for mindless thinking. Instead, Nicholas's busy brain mumbled a tune as the group rode towards the afternoon fields.

'So, first things first,' said Nicholas.

'Yes,' replied Emitai. 'Food. What have you got?'

'We're starving,' added Denis. 'We haven't eaten properly in days. We'll be happy with fruit, meat, vegetables, and anything else.'

Despite the incoming rainfall, Nicholas handed them a water container whilst the smell of bread escaped his bag, attracting the pairs' eyes.

'I know you can smell the bread,' said Nicholas. 'Enticing, I know, but keep your hands off. We are not limitless in supply. Now, this weapon. Explain.'

'So…' said Emitai as Denis guzzled an overflowing mouthful of water. 'This creature, Iris—'

'Iris!' interrupted Kate with her glaring eyes wide open. She would have been biting her lip until now to speak that name. 'Where's Iris?'

'We can discuss Iris later,' said Nicholas. 'We need to hear of this weapon.'

'Just tell me she's okay,' Kate desperately interjected again. 'She's in Rennes?'

'Kate.' Nicholas delivered one final reprimand, and he only had to glance at Kate to enforce it. Glancing behind her, he caught Denis bouncing his eyebrows, throwing his hand into the air, and catching a small roll of bread that his companion had swiped, giggling as he did so.

Nicholas locked eyes with Denis. 'Emi!' squealed Denis. 'That's rude of you. Put it back!' He threw the roll of bread back from where it came and tutted out loud.

'The weapon, Denis,' said Nicholas. 'Or Emitai.'

'So, this Iris. You said *she*? If you say so. She said they know where your old gloves are.'

'The ones you made with *him*,' added Denis.

'Who's him?' asked Kate, chiming in again. 'Aerkin? I thought you just worked in the same team. You didn't make gloves with him…did you?'

Nicholas kept quiet as Kate locked an intense stare on him. He noticed other riders glanced around subtly, also silent.

'No…or rather, not quite. My research was purely academic. My focus remained on detecting dark energy. I did not see our discovery as a weapon.' Nicholas reached for his ear but did not find his toothpick to twiddle, so only his beard could keep one hand busy. 'However, I do recall a prototype that I had a hand in. It was so long ago. What more were you told?'

'Let's see,' said Denis.

'Something about making a pair of gloves work,' said Emitai.

'And you need to find Iris.'

'She'll be in the Ruins of Rennes.'

'With someone named Hena.'

'Hurry, quick, before they come.'

'Also, look after the messengers.'

'It'll have been a long journey.'

'Feed them as much bread as they want.'

'That's enough,' said Nicholas, avoiding eye contact with Kate. 'Prototyping. Theorising. Those were good days. Experimenting instead of farming and maintaining stables. We find ourselves with less purpose in life now.' His ears twitched back, but no one else spoke a word to his tangent.

An unfortunate silence unfolded until Kate broke it. 'You made gloves with him….'

Nicholas shook his head. 'I know what you are thinking, but do not think of me as dually responsible for the state of the planet. The European dark energy project provided tangible results, and an entire team worked tirelessly for the betterment of humanity and not the comfort of a paycheque or the promise of power.'

One by one, the horses' hooves fell silent until the only ones clattered came from under Nicholas's perch. He turned his horse to face the group. Some eyes glanced, others pierced.

'Can I go over to their side?' whispered Emitai, stuck behind Nicholas.

'I vaguely remember when Aer—' continued Nicholas, stumbling at the mention of Aerkin's name. 'Richard first developed a pair of gloves. We discovered that the fibres from Falkeworm cocoons could detect, attract, and manipulate dark energy when powered by a small electrical current. Naturally, being a loosely flowing material, we thought we could form it around objects, even fingers and palms. Perhaps one day, we could make clothing or tools that powered our devices and equipment, needing little battery or charge. There was even talk of an improved age of space travel and the opportunity to explore other solar systems.'

Nicholas looked to the sky. He knew better than to expect the calming blues. 'And so it was, the current powered the material, and the material created natural light in the palms of our hands as if we were holding our own small replica of the sun.

'It was in time, when time did tick, that Richard discovered our muscle and natural energy could produce a similar result, and he did away with the electrical unit on the glove. It sounded preposterous, but he proved me wrong. That was the last time I saw Richard; he disappeared. It would be months before I saw what he had become: Aerkin.

'We are yet to understand dark energy in all its cosmic mystery fully. But somehow, I understand him far less.'

Nicholas concluded his speech as his calm voice full of disastrous discourse gave way to his horses' trotting. Soon, he heard other hooves following. No one said a word, though. Who knew what thoughts now plagued their minds as they traversed green fields, away from rubble once more. He needed them on his side, every single one of them.

'Did you boys come from the Mouth?' asked Nicholas, diverting the topic. He received confused mumbles as Kate caught up beside him, not offering him a look. 'Perhaps I should rephrase. Did you have to sail through a narrow passage to reach an old port?'

'Oh, yes,' answered Emitai.

'And did you find a man named Gorm?'

'Oh, yes,' answered Denis. 'He told us the way, and we left our boat with him.'

'Right,' said Nicholas. 'Then that is where we shall journey.'

'Wait.' Kate twisted her back to the new companion. 'Tell me about Iris. Is she okay? You said *creature*.'

'So, Iris, you're sure it's a she?' asked Emitai before hastily continuing. 'She was…okay. Until she took her hood off. Her face, you see, it was bad. There were scars everywhere, one big, long one up the side of one cheek. It went through her eye, and that eye was blood red.'

'Hair was cut clean off on that side, too,' said Denis. 'Ears like cauliflowers. Behind the damage, she looked like the people from the Far East. You know that bit already, I guess. Oh, her voice was deep and broken too, and she kept snivelling. And hunching. I thought she lived in a cave, to be honest.'

'Enough,' said Kate through an exhausted sigh. 'There anything good you can say?'

The air fell silent for a while. 'We saw her fight a couple of times,' said Emitai. 'Man, I didn't want to be those guys. I've never heard so many bones being broken in such a short time in my life. I'm glad we were on her side— she's scary'

Nicholas kept a watchful eye on Kate, eager to catch her expression.

'I see.' A reminiscent smile spread across her face. 'So, she's fine.'

Kicking their heels, the group sped up to continue their journey southwest towards the shore. The group of twenty-four had become the group of twenty-six.

CHAPTER NINE

NICHOLAS'S NOTEBOOK

Panic—Arun's head hurtled forward. A door slammed shut, waking him from Nicholas's secret cottage room; he must have fallen asleep. The sound came from beneath, from downstairs, as nobody stood in sight. The feeling of incurring a strange dream shook him; if only he could remember what happened.Stupid brain. He bore a sore neck from sleeping slouched but hurried to his feet. Dusting himself down, he heard Cole and Tej through the thin floorboards, talking and strolling around the cottage.

'So how do we go from feeding thirty to feeding five?' asked Cole, causing a loud thud that reached Arun upstairs, collapsing onto a chair with another couple of thuds, presumably putting her feet up one by one. 'The food will go all rotten.'

'I'll have cleared the kitchen in no time, love,' said Tej.

Arun dashed downstairs to greet the two, stopping Tej in his steps as he made his way to the kitchen. Arun stood still, posing by the crackling fireplace, fully dressed in his new, white, fabric armour. The mantle covered all apart from his head, wrists, and ankles. His eyes were drawn—the two had returned with freshly picked vegetables in the most oversized baskets he'd ever seen. Must. Eat.

'Oh, 'ello, sausage,' said Cole. 'You're looking sharp. How're you feeling?'

'Better,' replied Arun, resting his hands on his hips. 'There's not much I can do about it, is there? And there's not much point in sulking either. I guess I'll just strut around in my new suit.' Arun puffed his chest out.

'That's the spirit!'

'So, it fits,' said Tej dryly. Arun caught a sceptical gaze aimed towards his groin.

'Yeah, it's a bit tight,' said Arun. 'I feel like it's hugging me. Everywhere.'

'It fits perfectly,' cried Cole, running over towards Arun, grabbing him and dusting the back of the suit down. 'It's perfect. Nicholas 'asn't worn this in years. I thought he'd got rid.'

'I also found this,' said Arun, showing the notebook in his right hand. 'It's his diary, and there's a lot written in it.'

'Rather nosy to be reading other people's things, don't you think?' griped Tej.

Despite being well aware of his own thieving ways, Arun took offence. He caught Cole directing a look to Tej that he could only describe as Earth-shattering. 'Right, so what does that make inviting someone to your home and then disappearing forever?'

'Boys, sit!' snapped Cole before the two could argue further. Arun was dragged by his arm alongside Tej, feeling Cole's grip as she squeezed up and down his bicep. He caught her staring at him with that huge grin of hers. She pushed him and Tej down onto the chairs, where the three sat in silence for a few seconds glancing at each other.

'What are we waiting for? We 'ave to read it,' insisted Cole, grabbing the book and setting it to page one.

'I wouldn't bother,' said Arun. 'If you think his tangents when speaking are bad, you should try understanding this. "When science prevailed, it brought humanity to its knees, and here's my recipe for strawberry muffins." Good luck.'

'Oh, that's just Nicholas. Once you get past the—'

'*Got* past.' interrupted Arun.

Cole withdrew her lips into her mouth. 'Arun. Listen. Nicholas has travelled a path more crooked than all of ours. You'll get used to the tangents in the book. If you want to understand Nicholas and everything on the Hill, you'll need to understand the way he talks. And I know exactly where to start.'

Not a life story, please.

Cole continued. 'I remember trying to understand his tangents and derailed trains of thought a long, long time ago, when he first came 'ere. I thought he was a maniac at first, as they were worse back then. He'd witter on all sorts of nonsense throughout the day. But eventually, he explained it to me. On the day all this nasty destruction began, he woke up like any other day. Brushed his teeth, shaved his face. Oh yes, I know, a beardless Nicholas, he was delicious, believe me.'

Tej sat hunched in his chair, rolling his eyes.

'On that day, he went to leave his 'ouse and turned back to his wife and young daughter. He said he'd never seen two more beautiful things in his life as they played with each other. He didn't say anything to them, but he was 'appy and left for work. I think you know where I'm going with this.

'When he got to work, he saw smoke and fire rising from the building. He knew something was up. Fearing more for his family than 'imself, he turned around and went back 'ome.

'Now, I could never understand this next bit, but that monster was at his 'ouse. Aerkin, standing in front of the door. I don't know why he was there, but it's 'eartbreakin.' Cole raised her hand to her mouth, bowing her head. 'Tej...' she added, leaning back.

'The house was on fire,' said Tej bluntly. 'Nicholas said Aerkin just stood there waiting for him, not moving a muscle, staring directly at him. He tried to run inside, but the flames roared through the windows and doors. Then he tried every corner of the house but couldn't find a way in. All he could do was drop to his knees and watch as Aerkin walked away.

'Nicholas lost his family that day, but he said what stuck with him all these years is that he didn't speak his mind before leaving for work. You could suppose it became a reflex after, as if he doesn't speak, he just mumbles and whistles and waffles on. I've heard him say some ridiculous things, but you just have to let him say them. Because really, he's not saying it to you; he's saying it to them.'

Arun stared in silence at the open book. He didn't know of the relationship between Nicholas and Aerkin yet, but the book would surely give him everything he needed to know. Great job, Arun. He'd been busily preoccupied with his feelings and forgot to consider the motivation of others. This was a world in which all suffered in one way or another, yet he couldn't comprehend the pain Nicholas had experienced.

'You see, he didn't abandon you, sausage,' said Cole, her nose snivelling slightly. 'I've lived my quiet little life by my grandmother's teaching, and I believe it could 'elp you too: everything we enjoy, we should enjoy from the old generations, and everything we create, we should create for the new ones. Nicholas has got some things to take care of, for his sake, for ours, and for your future. And maybe one day you'll do the same for the next bunch.'

Arun rested his hand on the book's front page but closed it and moved it to his person. As usual, his burning questions bubbled inside. Light rain spattered once more, and he made himself comfortable, slumping into his seat for the time being. Cole patted him on the shoulder as she got up, taking the supermassive baskets of food to the kitchen. He swiped a bunch of berries before she disappeared.

'You two play nice,' said Cole, turning the corner. Arun and Tej smiled at each other. Given the Hill's uncomfortably scarce population, it would perhaps be best to behave in a less hostile manner. It wouldn't stop Arun thinking better of Tej, though; him and his annoyingly crumb-riddled beard.

'Let's start over,' insisted Tej. 'I'm not that difficult. I'm just harbouring a grudge, I suppose.'

'Against who?' asked Arun. 'Everyone?'

Tej's face fought a grimace. 'What, not who. I arrived here about fifteen years ago. Nicholas allowed me in to try and train me up. He was still in the process of building huts, choosing to stay here for as long as it took, sheltered by the trees and far from any city. But it wasn't the people or the mission that enticed me. I was fascinated by the science of it. The stunning radiance of the glow in his palm, capturing energy that had flowed from outer space. I used to watch all kinds of sci-fi shows when I was a kid. Spaceships and alien worlds. There was this mystical and foolish, romantic connection between us simple apes and our universe.'

Tej paused his story to stroll over to a cabinet by the side of the room. He pulled out two glass bottles, but they had a thick, frothy, brownish liquid inside instead of a clear substance. He gave one to Arun and opened the other.

'You ever had beer?' asked Tej. 'Made it myself. It'll make the days pass quicker until their return.'

Arun dipped his nose into the strong, pungent, fruity fragrance of homemade beer that closed his throat shut. 'I drink rain. And I've tried mushroom tea, so I'll pass trying anything else for now.'

'Doesn't make sense to me but suit yourself,' Tej took a swig and slammed the bottle on the table, grimacing. 'It's pretty horrible, but it serves its purpose well. So where was I?'

Arun paid more attention to the off-warm beer bottle in his hand. 'Apes in space?'

'Sure. So the light was incredible. I tried to train with him, Nicholas, of course. Berkley and the kid were tearing the house down with their sparring, and I couldn't even get more than a spark to fly. He seems to think I have arthritis.'

'Do you?'

'No! I'm sure I don't. I just…I don't know what it is. But all he wanted to do was train and fight. He didn't want to explore more uses for it. I thought we could build amazing new things. Renewable energy, powering tools and vehicles, carrying on his scientific research. Etcetera. He had the books and the materials. But no, it was all about gloves and fighting for him. Revenge. Oh, he planted a blue tree though, so good for him.'

Another swig of beer oiled Tej's throat. Arun could almost taste it just watching him.

'I don't blame him, though,' said Tej. 'Look at what he's been through; it's a shame, that's all. So, after a bit of time, he decided I wouldn't be able to use the gloves and fight.' Tej took a deep breath. '…And he took them away from me.'

'But you stayed? Why?'

'I came for the light, but I stayed for something far more beautiful.'

Cole returned with a tray of food as Arun clinked bottles with Tej; he'd still not mustered up the courage to try his.

'Wow, I should 'ave just left you two alone, to begin with,' chuckled Cole. 'Give us a beer too, love.'

'You can have mine,' urged Arun, grasping the book and rising to his feet. 'I'm gonna go for an evening walk. The smell of that beer is making me dizzy.'

Tej raised his bottle again. 'Told you. Serves its purpose.'

Cole handed Arun a sandwich as he got up. It was vast, with greens, leftover meats, tiny tomatoes, and a mushy plum sauce stacked high, twice the size of Arun's drooling mouth. Perhaps having fewer people around had its perks, more so than being a prisoner.

Arun left the cottage, retreating onto the drizzly, benighted Hill, leaving the lovestruck couple kissing behind him. On his way, Arun glanced towards Kate's hut on the opposite side of the cottage. Varying emotions were an unusual feeling for Arun, and there had been more in these few days than he could remember for years. A new creeping emotion climbed his stomach as he looked towards the hut—the feeling of wanting to see someone's face one more time.

*

A night, morning, and day had passed on the Hill, with Arun returning from a now-usual walk along the nearby stream. Before the early-evening rain could sweep him down the Hill, Arun reached his hut. He opened the door but looked to his right. A trodden path had formed from his hut to the cottage. He hadn't been sticking to the path; he'd been damaging the greens of the Hill. That's it. From now on, he had to stay off the grass. As the 'Guardian of the Hill', he should be keeping the splendour and not making things worse. With the door shut behind him, his cloak hanging, the candle lit, and his new boots kicked to the wall to dry, he jumped onto the bed and stared at the notebook at the foot of the mattress. He hadn't mustered up the urge to read it yet, afraid of what words awaited him. Perhaps now was the time.

Arun took a deep sniff of the air before reading a word. The downpour against the wood produced a magical aroma, one he did not think to appreciate until now. It was calming and constant. Rain shattering on metal shelter in the towns didn't have quite the same majesty.

Arun opened the book on page one as before, with an open mind this time.

Day one—Tuesday?

Fires in the double house at Croix-de-Rozon—arson or dark energy?

Remember the house—arched door, white walls, shutters.

Science prevailed—at what cost? Humanity brought to its knees on this day.

Remember strawberry muffin recipe—Claire's favourite.

75g strawberries.

250g flour (~~self-rai~~ plain).

Arun's eyes scanned the page as he'd never seen a recipe in his life; his cooking knowledge extended as far as mixing fruits and searing river fish. He might as well have been reading a manual on quantum physics.

Wait until golden brown or...was he at the house, looking for my work? Did he find it, or did it burn?

No matter how long it takes—don't give up.

Arun turned the page.

He disappeared. Where is he? Always talked about the mountains.

Kill him.

Kill him had been scribbled over each other multiple times, underlined, much larger than the words above. The sharp pen marks had pierced the page, and the page below displayed the same seven letters. Nicholas held himself as polite and charming, albeit intimidating to a newcomer like Arun. The man who scribbled those two words at the end of the page seemed a different man altogether. Arun continued, expecting to see a further dive into madness, but instead recalled more of the Nicholas he'd known.

The light I gift unto the world, will one day shine the brightest beam, to those behold conducted love, and share beyond the sun's full gleam. My true life's work I emphasise, for none contest my pure conceit, and to this light creates her own, the cycle of her life complete. My light. My Claire.

The elegance of Nicholas's words took the weight from Arun's chest as he lowered the book to his waist. Arun could not understand the emotions written before him, but he could sense the anguish that must follow Nicholas and drive his decisions. He stared into the splintered ceiling in a daze. Where were the others by now? How far from home must they be? He pondered Nicholas's state of mind but couldn't help envisioning Kate beside him. Her eyes, her face with those muddy cheeks that somehow still glowed. Arun lay peacefully in a dream-like state for many moments before turning another page, with each word now engrossing him more.

That is how it all started—a dream. A dream to show me the door to the beyond. A glimpse of the true possibilities that our science was not ready for. She used to speak to me. She used to guide my way. Now all I have is the material and my mind. Is it enough?

Achoo!—an explosive sound brought Arun back to life. This was not his sneeze, nor one from outside. This sneeze came from inside the hut. Arun lay motionless, confused and a little unnerved before searching the hut with his eyes as his head lay still. Candlelight flickered, and a shadowy figure danced in the corner. It swayed from side to side. Was this the returning mushroom tea, playing tricks on him? Or a manifestation of his gloves? 'Hello? Dark energy?'

Arun closed his eyes and pretended he didn't see anything. Achoo!—the same sound exploded again, this time higher-pitched and appearing to escape from under the bed. Arun opened his eyes. The figure in the corner was now a shadowed illusion. Arun leaned over and popped his head underneath the mattress.

'Hi!' said a young girl.

Arun yelped and jumped out from his bed, almost to the ceiling, cat-like, confused and rumbled. The stories he'd read of ghosts and ghouls under the bed came to mind. He scurried over to the wall to put his boots back on. Never mind the boots, just get out of there, Arun. As the girl shuffled forward, the candlelight shone on her face.

'Don't mind me,' said the girl. 'I was just tidying.'

Arun stopped, reaching for the door, and recognised the family girl from when he first arrived. 'You're the Trellock girl?'

'Yes. Malorie Trellock. And you're Arun Owon-dowo. The pleasure is all mine.'

'It's Owondo.'

Malorie spoke in a well-mannered yet mischievous way. She clambered to her feet and looked to Arun to be around eleven or twelve years old.

'Tidying what?' asked Arun. 'There's not much to tidy under there.'

Malorie dusted her clothes down. 'This hut is *naaasty*, and it's all wet. A pig would find peace here.'

'Get out,' said Arun, walking to the door and yanking it open. Malorie stood still, attempting what appeared to be puppy-dog eyes. The two stared each other down, not saying a word.

'What's this?' asked Malorie, grabbing the book from the floor and opening it to a random page.

'The door's still open whenever you're ready.'

'They've been spotted on the Mainland shore,' said Malorie, beginning to read. 'The Aerkin Knights, for lack of a better name. Five masked men who follow his religion. Ooh, this sounds interesting, Arun Owon-dowo.' Malorie cleared her throat. 'Their light shines red like his, riding the seas on an ancient ship. They slaughtered an entire town that did not bow to their will and bathed in their blood. Who are they? Are they searching for me? Recruiting?'

Arun closed the door to stop the intruding rain as Malorie jumped on the bed, engrossed in the diary's content. She wore an oversized hooded jumper.

The logo on the front had become worn and unrecognisable; not that one could find any logos easily nowadays. Her trousers were a ripped denim material but more brown than blue. Finding clothing from the past era in a usable condition was challenging, given the chaos and weather over the past twenty years.

'Storytime is over. I'm going to bed, goodnight.' Arun might be trapped unless he found a creative way to get her to scurry off.

'No, it's not late.' Malorie kept her eyes on the book and turned the page. 'The red light. How does it come to be?' Malorie propelled herself off the bed, away from Arun, as he reached to swipe the book from her grasp. 'Like the sky, our blue light scatters, but down at sunset, the red light is contained. Is the energy denser? What does denser mean?'

'Is that what the book says, or are you asking?'

'I wouldn't be staring at you if it was from the book.' How dare she use sass against him.

'Right. Denser is...thicker. Stronger, I think.'

'Okay. I'm bored.' Malorie closed the book. 'What can we do? Let me see. Shall we play conkers?'

Arun's eyelids pressed together. He'd never experienced this relentless persistence and excessive levels of high-pitched inquisition. 'Can't you go play with your brother?'

'No. He doesn't play much. He has anaemia, so we have to be careful with him.'

'A-what-now?'

'I don't remember what it is, but dad says his blood's not red enough. He gets a lot of headaches. I put him to sleep and got bored, so I came here.' Arun caught Malorie staring at him, head-to-toe. 'Your outfit is funny. I don't like it, but it suits you.'

Arun's squint turned to a frown, increasingly frustrated with Malorie, who seemed set on staying in his hut for as long as possible. He had one last option: grab her by the nape and toss her out into the rain. He pictured her rolling down the Hill and ending up splashing in a puddle of mud by the trees, with tears streaming. A smile rushed back to his face.

'Don't smile at me. It's creepy. Do you have any conkers?'

'I thought I'd heard the end of people going off on tangents,' replied Arun, reaching for his cloak. 'I'm going for a walk.'

'But you just got here? Wait! Good idea, actually. There are plenty of conkers in my treehouse. I built the treehouse myself. Let's go.'

'I'm going to the cottage…to get…something.'

'It's not going anywhere. Do it later. Come on!'

Arun huffed as loud as he could but secretly felt a little intrigued by the girl's suggestion. An avid builder himself, he wondered what she'd constructed. 'So…a treehouse? In the trees? A house?' Malorie nodded. He stepped out of the hut with her jumping in front, excitedly taking the lead. Sigh. It's not like he had anything else better to do.

*

Treading over fallen leaves and wet bush, Arun and Malorie journeyed into the hillside woodland that soon transitioned into a dense forest of living and dead trees. Arun could just about navigate the weeds and tree roots as Malorie had grabbed a cracked lantern from her hut to lead the way through the evening freeze.

'I always come out here,' said Malorie. 'I have a path of twigs that lead the way. I have to rebuild them often. Deer and all sorts come through here. They come quite close to home.'

'Fascinating.' Arun was doing his best to avoid their droppings whilst keeping an ear on the rustling bushes that softly broke the sharp grasshopper chirps. The occasional snap of a twig shuddered his shoulders. Though a brave scavenger, he'd rarely venture outside unprotected in the dark.

'I like your gloves,' said Malorie. 'My parents say they were using their gloves all the time. And then Mum got pregnant. And then she said she had to hang up her gloves. And then Dad decided he would too. I always see them looking at the gloves, though. I think they really miss using them.…'

Arun zoned out as Malorie continued to talk. He scanned the environment, taking a deep sniff of the damp wilderness. Shadowed tree branches formed monstrous arms of evil wooded creatures, leaning towards him, grabbing at him. He didn't like it one bit here.

'But I also think they're just objects,' continued Malorie. 'I wouldn't miss an object. I would only miss a person. Do your parents use gloves?'

'My parents are dead,' said Arun.

'Right. Most people, when I meet them, seem to say that. I suppose I'm lucky. My parents are the greatest people that ever existed. Even greater than Nicholas. In second place is my brother George. He doesn't talk much, but he has the most amazing smile. I try to take him hunting when he feels good. The stealthy stay healthy! That's what my dad taught me. Do you like talking? You don't seem to.'

Arun would never again take for granted the beautiful sound of silence. 'Maybe your brother doesn't talk because you do it for him.'

'He's five. I don't think you have much to say when you're five. Okay, this is the treehouse. Don't tell George I let you in. Dad says he's not allowed.'

Arun tilted his head up, then down again. 'I thought treehouses were supposed to be high up in the trees,' said Arun, noticing a mound of chipped trunks and branches leaning up from the ground. Sheets of tattered plastic were draped over the top to keep the treehouse, or small hut rather, sheltered from the rain. Arun's displeasure was beyond expression.

'It's a house made of trees. Why would it be in the air? Silly.' Malorie led Arun into the house and started picking conkers from the corner. Arun hunched, barely able to fit inside without his head scraping across the log beams. He glanced from side to side to see she'd hoarded magazines and books, scattered around, surprisingly well kept. It reminded him of the inside of his shelter he'd built back in town. Not how it looked, but how it felt.

Malorie had hung different materials on the sides to add colour, and bushy branches formed into a chair for her to sit and read. A wooden crossbow with a bag of bloodied, hand-crafted arrows rested in the corner. 'Do you like it? I spend a lot of time here. The hut on the Hill is more like my parents' place, but this is where I feel most comfortable. This is who I am.'

'Yeah, it's incredible. It's a bit like my home. Actually, it's a lot like my… home.' Arun's shelter felt a world away. Although he didn't have much before, what little was his took years of effort to collect. He always retreated to his books when he felt low or had been in a brutal fight, and his scope made him feel like an ancient explorer of the past. He'd become so swept away in his search for purpose, the beauty of the Hill, and the majesty of the light that he'd forgotten the small things he once enjoyed. It wasn't a perfect life, but it was his life.

'This is all I have,' said Malorie. 'My dad said that he used to have hundreds of toys when he was a kid. There were places you could go and get anything you wanted. He said I've had to grow up completely different than how he did. But I'm better and smarter for it.'

Arun examined a conker from the floor with a smiley face carved into it and a crack running down the middle. 'You're awfully perceptive for a twelve-year-old.' His eyes were drawn back to the forest, and Malorie's voice began to fade.

'I'm thirteen. I've had to grow up real fast, dad says. Right, pick up any conkers you can find. Some of these are a little broken already. I'm a great player, as you can—'

Arun rushed out without answering, his scurrying footsteps alerting Malorie to his escape. She called out for him, but her cries were lost to the trees as he headed for the Hill's dim, flickering lights. He tripped over loose tree roots and bumped into branches, carelessly fighting his way back. He could pretend it was all a dream, that he pinched himself on the day he arrived and woke up beside his books again. Forget about Nicholas, forget about Kate, just as they had done him. He could live on as he did. He'd made it twenty years already, so how could it be that bad? The faint cries from Malorie hollered in the background, but it was never going to stop him.

He stormed into his hut like thunder in the rain, darting left and right, preparing to grab anything that might be useful, but nothing in the hut belonged to him. He had everything he came here with, in addition to the suit he wore. The suit—it would be a great shame to lose it, given the power it could wield. He imagined what he could become if he were to practice; the fiercest scavenger in the land, or better, the fiercest warrior in the land. The danger back home wouldn't matter anymore. He could go find his books and scope, return home a free man, and take anything he wanted. He stared into the palms of his hands at the thought of others cowering beneath him, too scared to fight him ever again. His fists clenched.

No. It was a passing moment, driven by pure emotion. Calm down. His fists relaxed. This suit wouldn't help him; it would only change him. He needed to leave it all behind. He pulled off the boots muttering to himself, 'Wretched Hill. Wretched place.'

Arun stood bare-footed, remembering his soleless shoes were still in the cottage. Damn. Thinking for a moment, he eased the mantle boots back on; it was impractical to walk home otherwise. He stretched the glove mantle from each finger on his hand but realised he'd found these himself, and they now belonged to him; they were useful for eating plums. He reached over his head to take off the shirt but stopped. This he had no reason to stop, but he didn't need a reason. It was all or nothing. Having changed his mind, and without wasting a second more, he kept his suit intact, turned around, and walked away for good. At least this time, he closed the door behind him.

Storming down the Hill, Arun caught the cottage windows reflecting in his eyes. He didn't care much for Tej, but it would be disrespectful to Cole if he vanished. His scavenger lifestyle required little consideration for others, but he knew the right thing to do. He diverted towards the cottage in search of Cole.

Arun barged into a deserted downstairs area but could hear voices from upstairs. He climbed the cottage staircase with caution, unaware if he'd be walking in on anything unsavoury. He wasn't quite sure what unsavoury consisted of, but he'd read some interesting books on mating rituals. Reaching the top, a thin band of light escaped the door at the end of the corridor as voices fled with it. The floorboards were creaking, so he listened and peered through the gap instead of tiptoeing further.

'You'd think he'd be more generous,' said Tej, digging around the cardboard and finding the old science books. 'This is exactly the kind of thing I wanted to learn more about, and it's just been sitting here collecting dust all these years. Well, at least I have my gloves back.'

'I think he's been generous enough, love,' said Cole.

'Maybe if he kept to his books instead of his weapons, he could have created something to have ended this all sooner. It seems a little short-sighted.'

Cole opened a box of clothes that, at first glance, grabbed her interest. She lifted an outfit out. It looked far too small and would only fit a child. She glanced at the side of the box and dusted the front of it off with her foot. It must have said something unusual, as her fingers fell limp, and the dress floated back into the box it came.

'Here's something interesting,' said Tej. 'A knife.'

Cole, looking faintly distant, responded monotonously. 'Why's that?'

'It has dried blood on it. I know Nicholas had been training up a band of light-wielding super-soldiers, but...you know? I didn't exactly picture him ever stabbing anyone. Or fighting in general. He seemed like he would impart his knowledge, knit some gloves, and then one day walk off into the forest in search of that door he bangs on about.'

'You've always had such a way with words.'

Tej waltzed over to Cole with a look of love riddled with cheeky intent, grabbing her hand and removing all free space in her way. 'Indeed I do, Nicole Neso.' He swept her down into his arms and held her with a menacing grin on his face. 'We always said one day they'd leave, and we'd be here all alone to create our own mischief. Why waste any more time, my love?'

'You know I can't resist you, but please put that knife away, or you'll find my screams aren't the good kind.' Cole dragged herself back up by Tej's shoulders. 'And you know I don't like that name.'

Arun stepped forward to interrupt the pair. Wait—

'I feel sorry for the lad,' said Tej. 'Born to scavenge, scarce chance to reproduce, left behind by the others. Well, at least he's got his choice of huts now.'

'I think he'll leave soon,' said Cole. 'It's just not his 'ome. You can see how uncomfortable he is now they've gone. You can see it in his face.'

'What? No. Anyone who can harness the power in those gloves would never be able to let it go,' said Tej, walking towards the door. 'Plus, didn't you say he ran away from home in the first place? He'll stay.'

'But 'ome is 'ome, my love. No matter who you are. Besides, when 'ave I ever been wrong?'

Arun lent himself a sly smile at Cole's impressive reasoning. Before Tej could enter the hallway, Arun had made his way down the staircase and out into the dark. He meandered down the path carefully, not treading grass where he could see, and reached the bottom of the Hill. He didn't look back, for he felt Cole was watching. Turning to the path, he heard his name through the cry of a young girl. Not his problem. Arun walked on, determined, as his old life awaited.

CHAPTER TEN

GORM: PART I

ADE 1—*Heavy cloud returns, bringing the 'Cold Snap'. Quakes settle, but temperatures drop. Life continues to fall at an alarming rate, with food supplies dropping severely. Crops and natural foods diminish. Humans begin hunting, including cases of hunting other humans.*

The ground continues to heat from core activity, bringing heavy lightning storms. These mix with snow and hail storms to create frequent thunder-snowstorms. Life must be eradicated in areas with usual harsh winters. Famine is widespread, but hoarded foods and hunting still prevent global extinction.

I begin work with the remaining Falkum material. Need dark energy to protect the Hill in case Aerkin finds it.

ADE 2—*The Cold Snap ends. The 'Great Migration' begins as humans travel great distances across lands in search of safer pastures, hopeful that the grass is greener. Only the greater continents and Home Isles travel is recorded, and all cities and towns are rumoured to be demolished.*

A resurgence of major quakes occurs to halt any rebuilding attempts. Volcanic activity increases, but hail is replaced by heavy rain, severe flooding, and further thunderstorms.

Ocean life begins to thrive and becomes a significant food source spreading fast throughout the once scarce rivers. Hope, perhaps, at least to stem the flow of creeping insanity.

Two nights had passed since the group's departure from the Hill, and one more morning stood between them and the coast. Raindrops sprinkled overhead through the trees as the group of twenty-six made their final stop to eat and stretch on the grass beside a puddled path. The port known as the Mouth drew closer, for the group could see a faint line of ocean resting on the horizon between two hills.

Nicholas ran his fingers through his beard, looking ahead to the clouds steeped in white gradient to a blackened grey. Flashes of lightning filled the skies far ahead, although it would take a while for any thunderous explosions to reach their ears. Nicholas was the only one of the Hillfolk who had scars to show from occasional sea ventures, so as the others enjoyed their rest, he murmured to himself about the hard work ahead.

Denis and Emitai hovered in a squat to avoid the wet grass, filling their silences with blinks and twitches to each other. They took a bite of bread, almost in sync. Food was now half depleted. Emitai wiped his empty hand under his armpit before smelling it and didn't look too displeased. *That will be enough of watching those two today.* Nicholas turned to Kate for any kind of acknowledgement; she sat quietly, staring out into the drizzle.

'This is taking way longer than we took to get to you,' said Denis.

'Why are we taking the fields and not the roads?' asked Emitai.

'We are taking the incognito route,' said Nicholas. 'We will avoid trouble with intrigued strangers and are far less likely to be spotted or followed.' Nicholas aimed a couple of raised eyebrows towards the pair. 'Isn't that right, Denis and Emitai?' He climbed atop his horse and rallied the others into formation for the final journey down. Kate mounted her horse without looking towards him still.

The others rose, and all noticed Jordan and Serr approaching from nearby bushes, hair scruffed, buttoning up their shirts. Matuu audibly tutted in distaste towards the pair. The three readied themselves, and with all fifty-two legs on horseback, the group moved into a near-perfect formation. Kate, with

Emitai in tow, rode slightly further back than usual.

Nicholas led the way and uttered the first thing that came to mind to ignite new conversation for the final half-hour of riding. 'So, young traveller—'

'I think we need a bigger boat come to think of it,' interrupted Denis. 'Ours could only fit about ten. Unless you're okay with sitting on laps.'

'Seeing as you were followed, there might just be a few more boats conveniently waiting for us,' said Nicholas. 'Otherwise, Gorm will provide for us, providing he still possesses the guile I remember and is in one piece, no thanks to you. We may even have to stretch our horses' legs a touch further. We get closer to our desired destination and lose no time if we head west. Given half of Brittany has succumbed to the crumbling Earth, a cliff will prevent us disembarking for a lengthy stretch.'

'Are you sure you know where you're going?' asked Denis. 'Mainland is south.'

'Evasion is our aim, young one. How many times must I remind you fools that you were followed? The enemy might expect a return journey on the Mainland's north coast. We will head west and then south alongside the land, introducing ourselves on the west coast.'

Nicholas rolled out a map from his pocket. He, as always, kept a scribbled map of the new world with him. It would be more accurate to label it the map of two continents, given he had not travelled far since the lands moved, many of which he had omitted. It did, however, detail many old cities, rivers and disused railways through the Mainland. Nicholas deduced a journey from the west would be a touch safer but would mean longer at sea.

'Do you perhaps possess knowledge of what to expect in the Ruins of Rennes?' Nicholas asked of his tandem companion.

'No,' replied Denis. 'Although Iris made it seem urgent, to come before *they* come, so by that sense, nothing good.'

Nicholas chuckled. 'We thrive on nothing good.' He gave one last look at the word "Rennes" scribbled down on his map, running his finger along the contour of the Mainland before rolling it away.

'You two look alike,' said Kate, announcing herself ready to talk, without addressing Nicholas. Her horse skipped several steps, arriving closer to Nicholas and Denis.

'We're brothers,' said Emitai.

'If you hadn't guessed,' said Denis. 'That's how we both escaped. Emi came looking for me. He's three years younger than me, so always thought I'd be the one saving him.'

'Haven't been together this whole time?' asked Kate.

'No, it's a bit of a story,' said Denis.

Emitai's face blossomed. 'We love stories! Tell him, Denis.'

'Okay, Emi!' snapped Denis, leaving no room for Kate or others to interject into storytime. 'You know how a lot of people in the Mainland are captured or converted? We were no different.'

'We didn't complain, and they didn't kill us.'

'A fair deal. So we were split up quite soon after that. I think they chose me to be in their army as I'm stronger than—'

'Army?' asked Kate.

Nicholas glanced at Kate but hid his emotions. 'Army?' he mumbled to himself in surprise. Tension grew in the air.

'Yeah, huge,' said Denis. 'Don't get us wrong, we'd love to help you fight, but we'd die instantly. We're going to lay low for a while before finding our family. They're much further south. We—'

'Tell us about the army,' interrupted Kate.

'It's my story, but okay,' continued Denis. 'I'd say it's at least a few thousand strong from what I saw, but all I saw might not be all there was.'

A silence drowned out even the trotting horses.

'What do you mean thousands?' asked Kate. 'Thought there were just a few groups scattered across the land. Nicholas, is this true?'

Thousands, Nicholas. Nicholas mumbled to himself.

'They have groups everywhere, sure,' replied Denis. 'But the temple is where people flock to. They call it the "Domum Bia", in the mountains, where they say it don't look like Earth no more. Where there's snow and smoke, and thunder rising from volcanoes instead of falling. People come to praise him there but end up getting converted into soldiers.'

If a sixth sense existed, it would be alerting Nicholas to Hillfolk jaws dropping one by one behind him. In his twisting vision, heads turned as if they were blowing in the wind.

'He's a God, the warmongering sort,' continued Denis. 'They sing his name and everything.'

'Wait. You do know what you're in for, don't you?' asked Emitai. 'Iris said you were coming to kill them all. Aren't…you…' A glum look shattered his and Denis's earlier confident expressions.

The drizzle of rain turned to a heavier pour, and eyes turned to Nicholas, looking for his confidence. His gut twisted as he mumbled to himself. He needed strength in the right words. The journey couldn't end before it had begun. As his murmur turned to a hum, Denis broke the silence.

'But you must know of the Mainland uprising, right?' asked Denis with a hopeful inclination in his tone.

'All those recruited refugees secretly banding together,' said Emitai. 'I thought it was a rumour in the army, but Iris mentioned it—about them being in a place called the Caldeira and others in Rennes, so I knew it must be real. Is it true? Isn't that what you're coming for?'

'It has been known, yes.' Nicholas seized his opportunity, answering before his group had a chance to raise the tone of their sceptical murmurs. 'I do concede I did not anticipate their army to be as big as you say, and I would not have even called it an army as such. However, I would hear such stories of an uprising on my regular meetings by the river, and I believe this to be true—bands of fighters willing to join us and march together. With the heart of the free folk and the power by our light, we will be victorious. We will reclaim our lands and lay waste to the false God who consumes it.'

Nicholas could feel the group's ease in reaction to his words, which he summoned from his gut rather than his mind. Elegant, Nicholas—showing confidence as intrinsic to the group as the food they ate.

'Why didn't you mention the uprising sooner?' asked Kate.

Nicholas's soft smile diluted. 'My dear Kate. For now, we do not know the true extent of what lies ahead, and I did not think of troubling you all with rumours and things that may not come to pass. We have one objective, that is all.'

'That's easy to say. We deserve better than blissful ignorance. I know you, and you wouldn't lie, but keeping things from us is just as bad.'

'You do know me, and I know my words cannot blind you. But I need to lead a group, my dear Kate. I need to balance our hopes and confidence with reality. Should I indulge others in all that has worried and plagued me over these years? These are not your burdens. By being here by my side, you are already giving me more than I can ever show gratitude for. I am the leader. I am your sponge. All you need to do is fight. Allow me to absorb everything else.'

'But we should have—'

'I am sure Iris is taking care of everything,' concluded Nicholas before turning back to Denis and Emitai. 'It would be quite convenient if you two were to tell us everything you know about the army. After all, it appears you were best placed.'

Nicholas caught Kate shaking her head and tensing her brows before looking ahead.

'Yeah, sure,' said Denis. 'I can't tell you where. I haven't seen a map in years. South in the purple mountains is all I can say, and the rest I know is from what I saw. There were regular soldiers like me, a load of master soldiers, and then the one who commanded them; some called him Aerkin's Bastard. Others called him Bastilig; that's executioner to you. Aerkin made weapons of light for him and the masters.'

'Bastilig?' pondered Nicholas aloud, an alien name to him. He curled his beard. 'How many weapons of light are being made?'

'Just those, I think. Us regular soldiers—we just got scrap metal. Basic armour, rusty shields, some had spears, some had swords, and some had metal poles and sticks. We just had to dig through piles and find what was most useful. Those that disobeyed got sent *below*. Once they got sent below, they never came back.'

'By this "Bastilig"?'

'Yeah. He was pure evil, by rumour. I never got close. Regular soldiers had plenty of time to talk. They say Aerkin looked everywhere on the Mainland for someone. He wanted to find the tallest, strongest, and fastest person—a specimen of what remains of us all.

'So when Aerkin found him, he wanted to make him armour that used the light. The light didn't work with Bastilig that well, though. Aerkin mutilated him, so they say. Did nasty things to his skin and muscle; experimented on him, and something to do with the muscle reacting to the light, which I didn't understand.'

Nicholas writhed with an itching sensation that almost made him curl up.

Denis continued, 'There was even a celebration held for him. Some said it was like a festival. Drums. Dancing. The "Birth of the Bastard", they called it. But as it goes, Bastilig took his pain out on the masters when he finally wielded his armour, and they took it out on soldiers. They were beaten and bloodied, sometimes just for the fun of it. I was never beaten, luckily. But I guess that's it. That's the army you asked about. The aggressive, merciless army.'

'For someone who's been through so much, you seem to be generally optimistic,' said Kate. 'Not exactly aggressive or merciless.'

'I am when I'm forced to be….' Denis sent a look to Emitai, whose head lay bowed. 'Emi had it much worse, though; I don't know how he did it. I just want my revenge, but I don't let it get the better of me either. It definitely shouldn't be the death of me. Bastilig brought pain to many, but I guess he wasn't born that way. Nobody is. You can turn anyone into a monster if you have the power and the time.'

'Did you ever speak about revolting? Thousands of you against a few with light?'

'You wouldn't be asking that if you'd seen Domum Bia.'

None of the Hillfolk chose to reply, nor Emitai, who'd grown silent behind Nicholas the last few minutes.

'We've been through so much,' said Denis. 'It's hard to remember how it used to be. Playing with toys, safe with our family, and with a roof above our heads.'

'Although I find it fascinating that you have stopped stumbling over each other's sentences,' said Nicholas, 'we are just about concluding the first part of our journey. Be on your guard. And why is that, my two new friends?'

'We were followed,' replied Denis and Emitai in slow, monotonous unison.

The group trotted on, treading the remains of the port city. The chaotic remains resembled that of the previous city, but the cold breeze brought the raw, salty ocean scent, paining the noses of those who had not ventured this far before.

'Welcome to the most damaged areas in the lands: the coastline.' Nicholas halted his stride, overlooking the port from the ruins. 'Rising seas and crashing waves have decimated these shores, whilst the quakes decimated cliffs and coastline.'

'What's that smell?' asked Jordan.

'The smell of the sea, my friend, and a port to boot. The one built by man has made way for a new and natural creation that opens like a mouth drinking the ocean. Quite fitting, if you ask me, as its previous name was Ex-mouth.'

'What's the plan?' asked Emitai.

'We enter the Mouth.' Following a wink, Nicholas scouted the area as if his eyes could zoom like a pair of binoculars. 'Be on the lookout for a small, elderly, crab-like fellow. He usually stays hidden, although now and again comes out if he spots something unusual from his hideaway. One thing is certain, though; whenever I visit, it doesn't take too long before he appears.'

'Are you saying you're unusual?' asked Denis.

'Sounds about right,' said Emitai.

'Nicholas!' shouted a voice from the bushes behind.

'Gorm?' Nicholas spun his steed, almost throwing Denis to the ground. 'Is that you?'

Gorm stumbled out from nearby bushes and waddled past the formation. His stature paled in comparison to most, five feet tall and hunching slightly to make himself appear shorter still. His arms and torso were blocky and muscular, but his legs were twigs of balancing bones. The sparse hair on his head was grey where one could find it. As he made his way past the group, they could all see his face; his broken nose resembled a lightning bolt, his misaligned jaw hung from his cheeks, and his ears appeared non-existent.

'It seems this new world has truly made monsters of us all,' said Jordan as Gorm shuffled past him.

'I've always looked like this, cheeky sod!' Gorm fumed, proceeding in his determined steps. 'Nicholas, lad, you brought your pets, but where be you a few days ago? The port—it ain't mine no more!'

'What do you mean? You were always so crafty with your boats.' Nicholas jumped off his steed to greet Gorm with two giant hands grasping his cheeks, covering his face whole but for his nose. Kate followed.

'Mainlanders. Plenty. Too many for me. You gotta get rid of 'em.' Gorm raised a hand to Nicholas's horse. It neighed and showed its teeth, sending Gorm scurrying back.

'We were planning on partaking in a little sea adventure anyway,' said Nicholas. 'So, I guess those are our two birds; all we need now is a stone.'

Gorm laughed ferociously, throwing his arms back. 'I knew you'd come through, lad. Go get 'em. Oh, if you want a bigger boat, they brought a biggun. A ship. Rank lookin', like it's from the old ages, but big enough for all of yous.'

The breeze caught Nicholas's breath whole. 'A ship? Did you see…?'

'Aye,' replied Gorm softly. 'They're long gone, though. Two-ish days north.'

Nicholas snapped his neck towards Kate. 'The Aerkin Knights. They're here.'

Kate gasped. Her eyes widened. 'The Hill! We have to go back.' Kate turned to the group and paced to her horse. 'Arun. Cole and Tej. Come on. The Hill is in danger. Come on!'

'No…' said a concerned Nicholas, rubbing his hand over the hanging moustache hair in front of his mouth. 'We have to keep focus. Iris is waiting for us.'

'What's going on?' asked one of the Tarios from atop their horse.

Nicholas paused under Kate's gaze. He took a deep breath, fretting back and forth. 'The ship: it belongs to the Aerkin Knights. It means, or I suppose it means, they have followed our new friends here. And in following them, it would have led them in the direction of home. But this does not divert our path.'

'What about the Hill?' asked Kate. 'What about Arun? He can't defend them yet. We can't just leave them there. They'll die!'

Nicholas scowled but to reason rather than reprimand. 'We have a plan. The Hill has been safe for twenty years, and it will stand for twenty more. No one will find them. There is no use returning for a boy we have known for several days. Have faith in the Hill.'

'So why did we have to go the long way?' Kate's arms flung open. Nicholas knew she wouldn't let this go. 'We're strong. We could have stopped anyone in our way.' She pointed at Nicholas. 'You were scared.'

'Kate!' Nicholas retorted in a powerfully raised voice before lowering his tone. 'How long have you known me? Seventeen years. You know me inside out. I am not scared, nor am I careless in our approach. A needless fight on our lands could have cost us lives. My task is to get everyone there and back in one piece.'

'There won't be anything to go back to.'

Others in the group were beginning to mumble and groan. Jordan and Zachenne rode to the front of the group to intervene.

'Let's not get all emotional now,' said Jordan, riding alongside Kate.

'We've got work to do,' said Zachenne. 'These knights are behind us. Our way is forward. If you don't mind, Nicholas, I suggest we ride for attack and make use of their ship.' Zachenne turned back to the group after Nicholas signalled in agreement. 'Attack formation, seventh combat. Ride on!'

CHAPTER ELEVEN

GORM: PART II

Kate watched as the group rode down to the Mouth, taking new shape and galloping around the outside of herself, Nicholas, and Gorm; the three stood motionless. Denis and Emitai awkwardly clung to the two remaining horses.

'Good luck, lad,' said Gorm, leaving the two to talk. He departed back into the bushes.

After years of peacefully training and preparing to fight, Kate had already found the first few days more challenging than she'd ever imagined, and she hadn't raised a fist yet. She'd always felt prepared, but these past days had disturbed the belief in herself.

Merciless murderers were heading for the Hill, and the remaining Hillfolk were no match for the Aerkin Knights; if discovered, they'd be left with no chance to survive. Nicholas had told Kate all about them. They destroyed everything in their path, mutilating and torturing in the name of Aerkin. They'd be looking for Nicholas. He wouldn't dare turn back.

'We should not leave the group alone for too long,' said Nicholas. 'Let us ride on now.'

'I'll go back,' replied Kate.

Nicholas bowed his chin to his chest. 'Even if you did, it would not make a difference. I cannot let you go, and it pains me to insist. We are social animals. We stick together.'

'Try telling that to Arun.' Kate couldn't help but cast her mind to him, abandoned and untrained. The stories of the knights were horrific. He wouldn't last a second.

Nicholas pulled Kate into his arms in a light embrace. 'I first laid eyes on you when you were a young girl. I promised you I would not let anything harm you, and I intend on keeping that promise. Please trust me, Kate. Our only path is south.' Nicholas gripped her tighter, feeling her muscles loosen up. 'You know how safe the Hill is, and the chances that those knights stumble across it are beyond minimal. Every moment we waste is a moment Iris could slip through our fingers. We are in a race to get there. Come, please.'

Kate contemplated. Nicholas was right. The Hill was far too remote to be stumbled upon without direction. All she could do at this point was hope. Taking solace in her leader with the returning thought of seeing Iris, she huffed and muttered, 'Okay,' glancing back at the path they had travelled. She turned her back to home and mounted her horse alongside Nicholas.

'Sweet,' mumbled Denis.

Arriving at the Mouth, Kate could see precisely how it got its figurative name. The coastline raised high into thin cliff ridges that circled out to sea, declining and meeting in the middle. A gap split the rocks where the ocean filtered through for boats to enter if the waves allowed. Jagged rocks swarmed the perimeter, almost teeth-like, resembling the bottom of a monstrous, fossilised jawline. It looked to have been a volcano that failed to form, as the water bubbled sporadically in the centre with the heat from the Earth's raging core.

The group peered into the bay of The Mouth. The boats were only identifiable by their remains scattered across the water and rock. A dark, stained ship towered over the wreckage, with large flowing sails and a beheaded sculpture stretched across the blunted bowsprit. The waves gently swayed back to front, and the ship barely moved—the group dismounted by the rocky coastline with caution, anticipating hostility.

'Our boat,' said Denis.

'It's gone,' said Emitai.

Nicholas whispered, 'Never mind that. As it turns out, Denis and Emitai, if we can take this ship and leave the Aerkin Knights stranded, you may well make it into my good books.' He walked onto the ramp of the ship before igniting his vocal cords. 'Bolheil!' He yelled a foreign greeting that Mainlanders were beginning to use. They'd begun transitioning into a new language away from the "slurring English tongue". It consisted of a mix of old European languages, newly created vocabulary, and Aerkin's insistence on resurging "beautiful" Latin, so Nicholas says. Silence followed. 'Bolheil!' Nicholas yelled again, elongated at the top of his lungs.

A man appeared, scuttling at the top of the ramp, dressed in rags, filthy head to toe, and with a soaked towel in his hand. He looked to be a simple cleaner or crewman keeping watch. He'd do well to keep his distance.

'We are looking for safe passage,' said Nicholas. 'May we join on your journey?'

The man's body stood motionless whilst his eyes scanned the others. The group had hidden their hands and gloves under their cloaks and behind their backs, surely innocent enough.

'Beunfowl!' screamed the man, jumping for cover. Shouts and bangs echoed within the boat, leading Nicholas to step aside and flick his wrist towards the boat nonchalantly. The unhesitant close-combat Marshals stormed up the ramp, lead by Kate, as the lone crewman at the top attempted to kick the ramp away. The ramp shifted, leaving the Marshals shuffling to regain balance, and with a corner of the ramp resting on the boat's edge, Kate leapt aboard and stamped her boot down on the man, trapping his leg. She lifted the coward and launched him overboard.

She peered over the edge, watching the splash of the water before the man emerged, gasping and flailing. The result of years of training. Hundreds, if not thousands, of takedowns and tackles had preceded and embedded in Kate with the same ease as getting out of bed. Though away from home, it felt like the very first time. She snapped out of her gaze to catch the Tarios lined up along the dock, keeping aim, being cautious not to attack and risk destroying any of the ship's details.

'Stay behind the Marshals!' shouted Nicholas, ever protective of Kate. 'Formation!'

As the Marshals filled the deck ahead of Kate, a swarm of soldiers overflowed on the opposite side with metal spears and armour, though they were more rusty bronze than sparkling silver. War cries bellowed from their bellies, and they cautiously approached as the gloves of the Marshals shone a bright blue. Kate looked on, scouting the boat with her gloves bearing no light. This would do perfectly for a journey to the Mainland.

The boat's soldiers prodded their spears in the Marshals' direction to intimidate them, but the Marshals glanced at one another, unmoved. One brave but careless soldier could wait no longer. He thrust his spear forward, only for it to be stopped in a Marshal's hand; the spear would have pierced straight through if it wasn't for the glow of his glove. He wrapped his fingers around the spearhead as the glow expanded, turning the arrowhead orange, with the rest of the soldiers looking on in fear. The Marshal then snapped the arrowhead clean off.

The soldiers trembled, but they must have come from a fear far more intimidating than this: Aerkin. They must have had no other choice. They rushed the Marshals in number, screaming to release their fear as the groups brawled. The spears were useless, being grabbed and tossed aside. But some of these angered warriors ran in with bare fists. They punched any body part in reach but were hit back ten times harder from the power of the energised Marshal hands. A soldier struck one Marshal to the ground, but another Marshal tackled the soldier away and punched his metal helmet. The fist full of energy held so much power that it broke the helmet inwards, crushing the soldier's skull. The Marshal froze, his fist glued to the metal. His eyes widened.

Kate stepped over the backs of brawling men and strode to the steps leading below deck, keen to snuff out any unseen danger. She arrived below to find one crewman standing still, panicked and shaking. In his right hand: a bottle shoved with a flaming cloth. In his left: a note, or a letter. His teeth chattered in his grimaced jaw, allowing incoherent wails to escape. His eyes were fixed upon Kate.

'Whoa, whoa, whoa,' said Kate, approaching with both palms held open. 'Let's talk.'

'You…you'll never…stop him,' muttered the crewman in angst.

'Ignite!' shouted a soldier from above. Kate knew this word. Everyone knew this word. She looked on in a panic as the crewman threw the bottle at a pile of rags. Before Kate could even reach the flame, it had spread across the rags to a barrel in the corner. The fire began to spread with fury.

'Prellundis Aerkin.' The soldier stood in the middle, surrounded by his flames. He looked at Kate and screeched before his chattering jaw gave way to a menacing grin. He screamed again, laughing at the top of his lungs as the fire engulfed him. 'Prellundis Aerkin! Save me!' Others rushed down, but they fumbled in front of the flame, offering no idea how to help Kate stop the spread.

'Marshals, retreat!' shouted Kate as the deck glowed orange. The onboard group escaped down the ramp in a hurry, turning around to see flames igniting the surface.

'Is that it?' panicked Jordan. 'We let it burn?'

'Yes,' replied Nicholas, in a tranquil state as the others faltered beside him. 'Funny. For all this otherworldly might of cosmic energy, we are powerless to stop the grounded flame.'

The group watched as the orange glow spread across the ship like a swarm of blazing insects. The sailcloth burnt away, the timbers split, and the sabotaged ship left the group without passage. Zachenne stood on the edge of the dock and picked off any remaining soldiers he could see splashing in the waters below with bolts of light. Kate watched as the arrows of frustration illuminated the bodies and the surrounding water.

'Is that necessary?' asked Kate.

'Yes,' huffed Zachenne, still raining his light. 'War is without sympathy.'

'Well then,' said Nicholas, 'it would perhaps ease our conscience if we called them monsters rather than soldiers.' He joined Kate in staring into the chaos below as parts of the burning ship collapsed into the bay to join the bodies. 'They chose death over surrender. I wonder why?'

'Does it matter why?' asked Jordan.

'It always matters why. It is the one word that separates us from the animals.'

'I'm pretty sure every single word separates us.'

The fire raged on in the heart of the Mouth as the group returned to their steeds. All except for Kate. She chose to examine the wreckage a while longer. Her eyes turned orange, and the heat caressed her skin as if she were back home in front of the cottage fireplace. But as the fire incited, her vision transcended to memories of her first home. She heard the calls and screams of her neighbours as her building burnt down.

Staring into fire would often bring unease to Kate, but the thought wisped away. She brushed the flicked ash from her skin and turned to carry on with the others.

'Are they gone?' Gorm scurried and flailed down the rock to meet the group, having witnessed the commotion.

'Kissing the ocean floor,' replied Matuu, pursing his lips together before blowing a kiss to Gorm.

'Suppose that's kinda what I meant,' said Gorm, scurrying as far away from Matuu as possible. He peered around Kate's body to see the boat engulfed in flames. 'Nicholas! The ship! You mad or what?'

'My dear friend,' replied Nicholas, 'we were witness, that is all. However, now is no timeless time to mope and whine. We require a new vessel to vanish upon.' Nicholas put his arm around Gorm's shoulders. 'We saw a falcon on our way down. Sorry, fleeting thought.'

'You never change, lad.' Gorm sighed. 'Alright. Let that rotten ship burn if yer sure. Best be followin' me then to hidden boats,' he said, giddy in his step to have his port back. 'You ain't gonna like it much, that ship were far better for yous all. This one I got, thrice smaller and thrice cosier. I hope yous all know each other well, 'cos you will after this. Oh, and leave them horses; they won't get far climbin' over rock.'

'I didn't understand half of that,' muttered Jordan. 'What's wrong with your speech?'

'Yous what? This is just how I talk.'

'I wish it wasn't.'

Gorm stormed off in a huff, leaving the group to pack their belongings in a hurry and follow him west. It didn't take long to reach him; Gorm was a waddling bottleneck, and the sharp wet rock slowed him further. The effects of the hidden moon could still be witnessed as the previously gliding waves began crashing into the rocks. The rocks grew steeper across the shore as the group followed on, ascending into more of a cliff climb than a walk.

'Is this really necessary, hermit?' asked Jordan. 'Can't we go around?'

'Someone tell pretty boy that it ain't called a hiding place if it ain't hidden.' Despite Gorm's slow and meagre walking pace, he climbed up the rocks at great speed, propelling himself only with the strength of his arms as the cliff steepened: a two-armed spider. One by one, the group attempted to keep pace, looking to their left to see nothing but a steep fall to the bubbling bay, and to the right, a rocky roll to the ruins below. Gorm reached the top and turned to wait for the struggling warriors.

'How much further would you have an aged body climb?' asked Nicholas, falling to the top where the rocks flattened out. Kate and Jordan soon followed, as did the rest, one by one.

'Relax. We're 'ere,' replied Gorm, pushing a boulder to one side with little effort. It revealed a thick, rolled-up rope tethered to an unsettlingly rusty hook. He swung it out beside him and allowed it to fall far down the side of the cliff until it yanked tight to the hook. With a smile upon his face, Gorm wrapped part of the rope two times around one arm and two times around the other. 'Yous all got gloves, yeah? Good. No more than three at a time, and don't look down.'

Gorm slapped his crusty hands together, leapt backwards and slid down the rope, swinging around and guiding himself down, safe from harm as the rock protruded inwards. Kate peered over the edge to see him slide further away before stopping himself three-quarters of the way. He swung, back and forth, back and forth, inching closer to the cliffside as he did. He eventually came within an arm's reach and launched himself from the rope, grabbing a rock, instantly disappearing into the wall shouting, 'Woohoo!'

'You're joking,' said Jordan, peering beside Kate, distressed. 'There's no way we're doing that.'

Serr walked in front of the others towards the rope, turned her head to Jordan, and uttered the word, 'chikin.' Jordan, nor anyone else, spoke her language, but Kate knew precisely her intent. She jumped over the edge without holding onto the rope, disappearing in an instant.

'Serr!' shouted Jordan. Kate leaned over to notice Serr grabbing onto the rope, zipping down. Jordan swirled his head around. 'She's insane. This is insane. I didn't sign up for this.'

'Brave Jordon of the Hill,' said Kate. 'Are you afraid of heights?'

'No, of course not. I'm afraid of this…ridiculous…half-arsed setup. A rope on a rusty hook? The hermit has lost his mind!'

'The hermit, as you so elegantly call him, is our only hope,' said Nicholas, holding the rope out. Emitai grabbed hold in an instant, fearlessly leaning far over the edge before crawling off, leaving a trail of breadcrumbs scattered behind him.

'Oh, you…' Nicholas mumbled on.

The group wasted no time grabbing the rope and letting it guide them down, one after the other. As they approached the bottom, they were pulled forward to a gap in the wall utilising a thick stick that Gorm extended. He pulled each group member in until three remained at the top.

'Are you sure this is safe?' asked Jordan, with the rope now wrapped around his body.

'It's my famous knot,' added Kate. 'I give you my life. Just ease yourself down, and you'll be fine.' Kate slapped him on the chest as Nicholas chuckled on.

'Okay. Come on, Jordan. You can do this. You're incredible. You're the greatest.' Jordan edged his heels to the break of the cliff, taking a final deep breath. 'Or. I could—' Kate's hand had swiped across his chest, pushing him back, throwing him into gravity's reach. He screamed, jolting up from his waist as the rope dangled him in mid-air.

'Leaving our shores for the first time…this is where it truly begins,' said Nicholas. 'I could not be prouder of you, and I hope you hold yourself with the same pride. I trust you, my dear Kate, though it has been a rough start. We will only succeed if we stick together.'

Nicholas lay his hand on Kate's shoulder as she nodded, not speaking a word. Before taking the rope, she turned back to look across the land towards the direction of home. She remained hopeful that the Aerkin Knights would find nothing but failure, satisfied in the feeling Arun would be safe on his way to becoming the Guardian of the Hill.

Kate grabbed the rope and descended beyond Nicholas's view, not far behind a slowly inching Jordan. The rocks near the bottom were dry as Gorm pulled them both in, and the footing was level and steadier, thankfully, as the light wouldn't reach all corners. A narrow rock path led Kate down, revealing a large, dark cavern. Dim light filtered in from a small gap where the water flowed out to the windy seas, allowing Kate to see three boats floating on a shallow pool of water.

With all the group now beside the water after Nicholas's arrival, Gorm led them to the boat on the far side. It didn't overshadow the other two before it, but it could undoubtedly hold more Hillfolk, the trade-off being it was far worse for wear in condition. The white paint had chipped to the point that the colour could hardly be seen, and the heavily dented hull made it challenging to spot which parts remained in their original position. Windows that once had glass panels were now open to the elements, but it stayed afloat, and that's all that mattered.

'Let's take all three, just to be sure,' said Jordan, rubbing his aching waist at both sides.

'No 'eck, yous all get one boat and one boat only,' snarled Gorm. 'The first is mine, and the second is me wife's.'

'You don't have a wife,' said Nicholas.

'Yet,' said Gorm, throwing his finger into the air. 'Middle one needs repair anyway. Yous can only take third. And that's final. There're two cabins down below and old dirty cutlery too if yous all feeling fancy. She might look knackered, but the mast and mainsail ain't half decent. No rudder, so oars are on deck if yous need; makeshift riggers and locks on side. Yous'll have to kneel if rowing. Old engine removed and replaced with…can't remember. Don't suppose them gloves can make oil magically appear anyway. Good luck. Godspeed. Sayonara.' Gorm untied the boat and readied it for sail. 'Climb on!'

The group hurried on and bunched together on deck as Nicholas walked beside Gorm to say goodbye. Kate stayed with Nicholas, eager not to miss out on important conversations.

'You going to fight him then, lad?' said Gorm.

'Yes, our moment is now,' said Nicholas. 'This will probably be the last timeless time I get to see that gormless face of yours.'

Gorm chuckled, 'Name and nature lad. I'm betting on yous all sailing back, even pretty boy.'

'You must have seen the ship sail in, right?' Kate interrupted the joyful tone of the two friends. 'What did you see when the ship arrived?'

'I saw 'em. All five of 'em, a group of others ahead of 'em. They took same path as 'em Mainland boys, walking, no horses. I know you told me 'bout 'em before, lad, but I never imagined what I saw. They looked…evil, y'know? Their weapons too. Think I stopped breathin' for a minute as they marched on.'

'Yes, Gorm, I know,' said Nicholas. 'They will not find the Hill, though. Just take care of yourself for when they return here and find no ship to sail.'

'Nobody catches me. I catches them!'

Nicholas grinned before hugging Gorm. 'Goodbye, old friend.' Kate couldn't understand how they could be hugging and grinning with news like this.

Kate marched back to the departing boat with Nicholas following. The impractical physical rowing of a large boat would make taking twenty-six men and women on a day-long trip seem unbearable. But the journey began well, at least, with the boat moving in the right direction; they headed for the small gap in the cavern. The waves didn't hit hard in the passageway, but they could see the dark clouds had drawn closer through the opening. The thunder thudded louder, and the lightning burst brighter.

With all twenty-six sardined on deck, Nicholas shuffled to the front of the boat, and a prolonged cough brought the chatter to a halt. 'Folk of the Hill. I have one last message to share before the open sea, if you would lend me a moment. Be not afraid—that is something I cannot force of you. Be not wilted—that is something I cannot hold to you. For across the sea lies a land of unknown, not the smells or the sights or creatures that roam. The comforts of home and what you've left behind are gone, and gone they stay, and only through this journey can you find your true way. No. I will not ask much of you. The only thing I can ask is that you remember. For our memories are what make us who we are.'

Matuu nudged Kate's arm. 'I heard him practising that in the bushes yesterday.'

The boat coasted in silence, only the sound of waves against the hull adding to Nicholas's sentiments. The group made their way through the gap, and the light blinded their eyes momentarily as the seas opened up before them. All eight Marshals had grabbed an oar without knowledge of sailing to guide them. It took great strength to row the boat out, but their gloves lit up gently, testing the light's energy in adding force to their strokes, careful not to melt the carbon fibre handle. It would help push through the waves and fight the winds, perhaps for hours and hours of rowing unless the sea breeze aided them.

Kate folded her arms and leaned overboard, watching the ocean waves for the first time in her life. The boat shifted her balance, causing a fluttering unease in her stomach. It didn't matter—the shimmering water's beauty had captivated her.

The boat made it over its first small wave, but many more would come and many bigger. Kate raised her head to the clouded sky as a raindrop landed on her bottom lip. The weather of the destroyed sky was turning already, and the crossing of the Channel had begun.

CHAPTER TWELVE

A SCAVENGER'S STORY: PART I

Arun stirred late into the morning, having wandered through the night after leaving the Hill without the slightest idea how to navigate the dark. On occasion, the slight light in his hands would only help show the bushes around him and the cracks beneath his feet, ending with him exhausting himself into a bush by the side of the path, hidden beneath the overarching trees. He had that feeling yet again, just now, waking from a strange dream without remembering a thing.

Arun turned his nose towards an acrid smell to his left, finding a scattering of fresh animal droppings on a flat patch of mud. Charming. The drops of water falling from the trees above provided the only movement, and the splash as they hit the leaves below provided the only sound. Before he could move a muscle, the peace retreated, and a moving shadow shot Arun's senses into overdrive.

'There you are, silly sausage,' said Cole stumbling excitedly into view, shrieking sounds of joy and smelling of freshly toasted bread. 'I'm glad to see you're okay!'

'What are you doing all the way out here?' Arun rubbed his eyes and rolled out from the overgrowth, tiptoeing over the gifts from the wildlife.

'All what way? We're about five minutes from 'ome. Don't tell me you wandered about all night now?'

Arun looked up and down the road, alarmed and confused. 'No, we can't be. I took the path east, then the road south, turning east, and then, I think north.' Arun paused and let a huge sigh of disappointment flow through him. 'Then back west, I guess. I lost my direction in the pitch black, and the paths are winding, okay?'

Cole's cackle vibrated through the air, bringing the dangling dew crashing down upon Arun. 'I had a feeling you wouldn't make it far, no offence, sausage. I brought you some bread to keep you going and all in case I spotted you.' She offered a small half-loaf to Arun. Her sparkling bright teeth sat in her grin, beaming through his waking eyes. This is what it must have felt like waking up to sunshine.

'I'm not coming back, Cole, I'm sorry,' said Arun, stretching his arms, legs, and mouth wide open.

'I wouldn't ask you to. You 'ave your own way to go and your own reasons. But know one thing, if you ever get 'ungry or ever want to try some truly nasty beer, we'll be 'ere for you. Oh, and do take care of that suit, if not for yourself, then for Nicholas.' Cole hugged Arun tight, squeezing what little air he had out of him. 'Now go south, but don't turn east until you've no path in front of you. North-east will lead to some familiarity, I'm sure.' Cole turned, then turned again. 'I don't know what you're running from, sausage, but I 'ope you find where you're running to.'

Arun watched as Cole returned up the road. He'd forgotten to ask which direction was south. Opposite to her, right? It'd be weird to start following her. He brushed the loose leaf off his body and set off, with something bothering his mind. What was it? It only hit him a few minutes down the path. Thank you—a term rarely heard in town. Arun couldn't remember the last time he'd uttered these words. Cole was too far gone now, but it would have been nice to say it. Never mind.

Walking the winding paths of the west brought a peaceful joy as one could get lost in the fairytale-like scenery. Shades of green burst to life through the copious cracks in the old roads, and the untrimmed weeds and foliage spread beside them. Given the lack of direct sunlight, one would not feel too ambushed by the bush overgrowth, but it grew enough to surround and create natural tunnels of greenery and vegetation. If lucky, one could encounter a rare falcon swooping through the trees as Arun had once seen. As he walked the tunnel path, he named the roads the Rainforest Roads. Anything to keep him from thinking about the potential danger that awaited him back home. His gloves helped restore his confidence.

As Arun approached a crossroad not long on his walk, he noticed something a little unusual splattered on a bush under the trees. A suspiciously placed dark red substance. Blood. It had to be. He'd spilt plenty in his time. He leant down, taking a glove off, and ran his thumb over one of the splatters. If the rain hadn't washed it all away by now, then perhaps the blood had yet to overstay its visit.

Arun stared closer at the bush, as more splatters appeared resembling small berries, and a lopsided bush lay ahead with a suspicious amount of broken twigs to one side. Interesting. As his nature dictated, Arun stepped into the dense wilderness to investigate, unafraid of taking a chance in the daylight.

At first glance, nothing unusual stood out, but further in, a large collection of decaying mushrooms grew to one side, some bigger than Arun himself. Was this what Nicholas made him drink? Ugh, Arun gagged. Behind them, a collapsed tree lay on its side, with another plant growing from the underside of the trunk. Where there's death, there's life. Or so Arun thought…

After a few further paces, Arun spotted two bare feet emerging from the overgrowth. His stomach turned, not knowing if this would be a familiar face from the Hill or not. Nicholas? Kate? He snapped out of a vacant stare and rushed over, pulling the body out by its legs. A man lay motionless; Arun found him simultaneously recognisable and unrecognisable. He had no hair, but the man's skin still had colour. This body hadn't been here long.

Horse hoofprints scattered around the body heading off into the woods. This man may have been on horseback and suffered an attack. Arun played the chase out in his head. Yes. He must have run into the forest and fallen into the overgrowth. No missing limbs—so not the work of Hunters. Couldn't be scavengers either, as the man's possessions weren't sought; a gold chain with a dragon emblem clung to his neck. Strange. Gold and silver carried no value, but many chose to steal and scavenge these items to keep as ornaments and decorations. The only things of exchangeable value were, and always had been to Arun, food or books.

Arun opened the long black coat on the man, although it rather peeled away, to find multiple wounds expressing a pungent and rotten smell that threw Arun's head back; these looked clean-cut by a sharp blade or knife. The Hill stood barely ten minutes away by straight path, so the man must have been riding there or perhaps riding out.

Arun took the gold chain. He held it in his hand, opening his pocket with the other. Wait. Was he innocent? Did he deserve his fate? What was this feeling preventing Arun from dropping the chain in his pocket? Perhaps the past few days on the Hill had started to challenge him. Nah. Arun shook his head and dropped the chain in his pocket. But before he turned to return to the road, he glanced back into the bush. An odd colour caught his eye, off white, in the shape of several twigs. Only these weren't twigs. They were bones—a human hand resting in the bush, reaching out from a skeleton. Two bodies in the same place but from different times. Was this a den? A trap?

No thanks.

Arun rushed to scamper away but suddenly paused. He heard something—a whisper. Or did the wind carry a coincidental tune? *Where is she?* The voice spoke again, clearly a woman's voice, from a direction and distance he couldn't detect. It was almost as if the voice resonated deep in his mind. He glanced at the skeleton once more, but it would be foolish to stay. He hurried back, unwilling to unearth more treasures, unwilling to risk falling to the same fate.

*

Hours passed, and Arun still thought of the bodies he'd found. Arun had seen death before, but not like this, not in the calm of peaceful greens. Here it stuck out like a winged horse. Lost in his mind and with the wind carrying the songbirds away, a strange rustling sound in the bush brought Arun's silent stroll to a halt. Too small to be a deer, too large to be a rodent. Arun's head darted around, almost detaching from his shoulders. No natural predators roamed these lands apart from humans themselves, so a stranger may have followed. Had the murderer stalked him to add to his collection? Arun tried not to panic. Wearing the suit gave a true sense of security, and being a scavenger came with a bag of tricks.

Arun continued, pretending not to care. He walked close to the bush on his right side to measure the change in sound and detect which side of the road it originated. Again, a slight rustle of a bush followed by light footprints. Arun's confidence grew. His fine-tuned ears deduced the sound came from two trees behind to his right, gifting him the upper hand. A momentary glance. Nothing. He stopped to take a deep breath, pretending to look far ahead, before turning sharply and sprinting into the bush. He jumped and leapt forward, reaching the tree and…nothing. Not a sound. He checked the ground to see if an animal raced by but could see nothing but leaves and conkers. He looked around, and another conker appeared, but this one hurtled past his head, narrowly missing.

A giggle echoed from the trees. 'I see you.'

'Girl?' barked Arun, still frantically searching but unable to find a single sign of life. What's her name? Was it Marjorie? Mandy? No…Malorie? That's probably it, but *girl* will do just fine.

'Over here.' Malorie jumped down from a tree to reveal a face covered in bush and arms camouflaged in mud, with a small bag hanging from her back. How long had she been following Arun undetected? Impressive. She stood, gleaming, wearing a strikingly red woolly hat, loose threads falling from all sides. 'I told you I was good at hunting! And I caught myself a human. So that means you're mine to keep now.'

'Thanks, girl, but you really shouldn't be out here so far from home. Bugger off now.' Arun stepped back out to the road and continued walking.

'But I came to give you your book.' Malorie joined Arun on the road; he heard her soft footsteps chasing after him. She jumped ahead of him, intercepting his path. 'Here.' She handed the book over.

'I don't want it,' replied Arun, brushing past her, knocking the book to the floor. 'It doesn't belong to me.'

Malorie's footsteps chased again. 'It's really interesting, though. I asked Cole, and she said it was yours. Like that suit. So if you took the suit, why won't you take the book?'

Arun stopped, missing the calming silence that had protected his ears throughout the day. He closed his eyes to count to five and opened them to find her standing ahead of him. Two small hands held the book up again, assertively.

'I thought you liked books?' asked Malorie. 'That's what Cole said.'

Arun squinted. 'If I take the book, will you go home and never, ever annoy me ever, ever again?'

'Yes!' Malorie beamed brighter than a gloved palm. 'Another successful mission.'

Arun grabbed the book, and at the same time, stepped forward around Malorie and walked onwards. Within an instant, he started to question himself and if his conscience allowed him to leave a young girl alone on the road. She'd brought herself here, so it wasn't his fault nor his responsibility to return to such a cause. Feeling confident, he walked on. He stopped, then walked on again. Eventually, Arun stopped without hesitation. He pulled the gold chain from his pocket and examined it. Would hanging it on a pile of metal in his shelter serve any purpose? Would leaving a girl all alone in the middle of nowhere not play on his mind? Maybe these past few days had taught him to think better of himself and others. He turned his day around to head back to Malorie.

'Hi,' said Malorie, just as Arun swivelled around.

'I thought I told you to go home.'

'You didn't say when. My dad says you should always be clear with your words. What's that in your hands? I've never seen that colour before.'

Arun gritted his teeth. He pondered a polite response but shied away from admitting to someone, let alone a child, that he'd ripped the chain from a corpse. 'Here, you take it. It's obnoxious looking, like you.'

'What does that word mean?' asked Malorie, snatching the chain from Arun's hand. 'It's so shiny. I wonder what this animal is. It's quite mean. I imagine this is what Aerkin looks like. What does this thing even do?'

'Nothing. I read that people would buy these things and wear them.'

'Buy? Like goodbye?'

Arun scratched his head and released a stretching sigh. 'No. Well, I think there were these tokens that you would earn for working, and then you could buy food and things like this. Does it matter?'

Malorie looked clueless. 'Why wouldn't people just give things to other people? Why did you need tokens?'

'I dunno, fairness?' Arun surveyed the environment as Malorie examined the necklace. 'Nicholas told me money and things like this were what defined a person, what people strived to have. It's what caused so much death.'

'That's dumb. I value my family. If this is what it does to people, then I don't want it.' Malorie held out her arm to Arun, the necklace hanging between her fingers.

Arun thought for a second. 'Nah. Throw it.' He looked behind Malorie, down the road he'd walked so far. It hadn't been a long journey, but a few hours back and a few hours forth again was the last thing he wanted. It would be dark before he made it back to his town—a waste of a day. It would be best to head back to the Hill and wait for the morning. 'Come on. I'm taking you back.'

'We can't go back. Cole said you were going to a Toss. I want to see a Toss!'

'Are you insane, girl? It'll be hours before we get there. You're not going all that way without your parents.' Arun stepped to the side and pointed back with both hands, his insistence evident. Why would anybody want to come to a Toss? He kept a keen eye locked on her.

'My parents said I could come. There's a lot for me to learn there.'

Arun hummed. 'There's no way any parents would say that. Well, at least I don't think they would.' *Do parents do that?*

'Yes, they did,' replied Malorie as she flung the bag from her shoulder and reached into her bag. 'I'm old enough. They gave me bread, some water, some extra clothes to wear, a compass thingy, and a stabby-stabby.' Malorie pulled out a rusty penknife to Arun's bemusement. She thrust it forward and back, throwing him off balance.

'Careful!' Arun pressed his palms to his forehead. How do parents deal with this? His mind wandered, picturing her tied up and thrown over his shoulder, with rope covering her mouth as he carried her back to the Hill. No. She'd squirm and kick the whole way. Not worth it. Shaking the thought and aware it would be undoubtedly impossible to stop her following him, he huffed in defeat, once again by the mighty Malorie.

'Okay then.' Arun turned, paused, and turned again. 'Wait. There's one small problem. I'm in a little bit of trouble, nothing much, just kinda-sorta-maybe got people looking for me. I can't guarantee that it's safe.'

'What kind of trouble?' asked Malorie, smiling.

'The bad kind.'

Malorie's smile grew bigger.

Ugh. Arun couldn't dissuade her, her heart was set on coming. He looked at his gloves, knowing even the glow would be enough to scare off challengers and keep them both safe. Hopefully. 'Okay. They're freeloaders, called the Freeloaders. They think I stole something from them.'

'Did you?'

'No questions. They don't live in my town, but they obviously know where I live, so please just try to keep your voice down. And no running off. In fact, try to move as little as possible. I'm serious, girl. They're not looking for a chit-chat; they're looking to hurt me.'

'Oh.' Malorie's smile dropped away. 'I'll be good.'

'Come on then.' Arun turned around and continued, leaving her to hurriedly return her belongings to the bag. Ching—the sound of the gold necklace, thrown to the floor, folding in on itself.

*

Hours passed, and the two travellers made one final stop before reaching Arun's shelter. They sat beneath trees, with the sky's light fading within the heavy rain clouds. The evening would soon bring a darkness that would leave them stranded. Arun's muscles ached, including his ears.

'So, can you use the gloves?' asked Malorie.

Arun nodded as he brushed breadcrumbs off his gloves before holding his right arm out. With the usual grimace, he brought the light to his palm. As it grew brighter, it concentrated in the middle. Sparks of light flew out as the sharp, curving bar emerged. It shook, as unstable as each time he'd tried before, but this time it didn't dissipate; he could hold it for longer, still bearing the light's pain. He attempted to grasp the light with a clench of his fist, but it shattered as he did. He glanced at an unusually silent Malorie, staring in wonder.

'I need more practice,' said Arun. 'Kate told me I could hold these swords of light called "Linai", but I haven't figured out how yet. But check this out: I figured something out last night when I got lost….'

Arun sat with his knees up. He clenched both fists, his eyes, and then his entire body. His head started shaking, almost in vibration, as his legs shook side to side. Disgruntled noises escaped from Malorie beside him, but that didn't put him off. His body ignited. The suit lit a faint blue, evenly distributing the energy, igniting him like a vast, blue, human firefly. Only his uncovered head and his feet were dull, despite his boots being mantle material; Arun hadn't managed to get them working yet.

Arun closed his eyes, not to the darkness of his eyelids but a sky brimming with heat and fire. 'Kate,' cried a woman's voice. Again, and again, it cried. He couldn't turn his head. All he could do was watch as the burning clouds swept the sky.

Feeling a punishing and burning sensation in his entire body, Arun released the pressure on himself and crumbled backwards. He stared up into the crying trees whilst his muscles pulsed and contracted. His body felt like stone, trying to contain his spirit from escaping. Gasping for air and with no energy left in his limbs, he turned to Malorie, speechless, with her jaw collapsed.

'How long was I out?' asked Arun.

'Like a second,' stammered Malorie. 'It happened so fast.'

Arun lay in discomfort. Was she telling the truth? It felt like a minute or two, not a second. He regained his breath, still glued to the ground. 'A second? Impossible.' Arun's mind must be playing tricks on him. He rubbed his aching eyes, almost pushing them back into his head.

'I thought you were going to explode,' said Malorie. 'How'd you do that?'

'I'm still working that out,' said Arun. 'I thought yesterday I could light up and lead myself in the dark for a few hours. I collapsed after a second and woke up a while later. I think so, anyway, it made my memory a little hazy.'

'Wow. So that's what that looks like. I read about it in Nicholas's notebook. I wouldn't worry. It says it takes a lot of energy, but you get used to it. However…' Malorie turned her head as if she didn't wish to continue.

'What?' asked Arun.

'Oh…nothing.' She turned back to Arun, less excited in her tone. 'It's a weird book. You should read it.'

Arun grimaced in rising to a seated position, coming back to life. 'Right… so how about you read it to me then? You get to talk, and I get to learn, so we're both winners.'

'Sure. I'll need to finish it, though. I also need to re-read it to make sure I don't make any mistakes. I really don't want you to explode.'

'Me neither.'

'I'll read as we walk, or it'll get dark. Shall we go?'

Arun stumbled somewhat but returned to his feet. 'I'm not sure you thought this through, arriving in a town for the first time during dusk.'

'Of course I thought it through,' replied Malorie. 'You'll be there to protect me.' She giggled, skipping away. With an eyebrow raised, Arun followed.

Arun and Malorie arrived in New Carterton's decimated ruins as the sky fell dark, nearing Arun's old shelter with the rain now streaming down. The two struggled for footing in the twilight along the broken road, with streams of water running down piles of rubble on either side. Arun prepared himself to shield Malorie from a rude scavenger welcoming; however, none could be seen or heard. He instead basked in the silence that came with Malorie's darting head, watching her examining the wrecked cars and fallen buildings, exactly how he must have looked when he first laid eyes on the Hill. Whatever made her happy.

CHAPTER THIRTEEN

A SCAVENGER'S STORY: PART II

'This is it,' whispered Arun, leading Malorie across a broken brick path towards a car's cold metal body, the door of which had *Arun* scratched into the side. A sign reading 'V.I.P' stood bent on the other side of the entrance. Victory In Practice—Arun's best guess. He'd arrived home, although he didn't recognise it at first without all his books.

Hunched, Arun picked up one remaining ripped page from a book. The shelter was just an empty shell, a shell that didn't feel like his anymore. The walls and roof didn't matter; it was the books and his scope that were truly his. Though it didn't matter too much for now, as Arun's only concern was keeping Malorie calm. She shook from the cold, sitting beside a wall he had primarily constructed from scrap metal against loose brick. He sat beside her, shoulder to shoulder.

'What's that?' asked Malorie, examining the page Arun held.

'It was from a book about motorcycles,' replied Arun. 'I've always wanted to ride one. They had two wheels, and you sat on it, like a horse I guess, but you could travel ten times faster.'

'Horses are beautiful. Why would sitting on a pile of cold metal be better?'

'Are you saying the Revolution X2 Turbo Delta is...*not* beautiful?'

Malorie stared at Arun with her mouth slightly open. A small burst of air escaped, but nothing more. She lifted her knees to her stomach and rested her chin on them. She seemed absorbed all of a sudden.

'Why are you really here?' asked Arun.

'To explore!' exclaimed Malorie, without moving her head. Arun waited.

'Well...' said Malorie, 'that, and I don't know anyone like me. I love my brother, but he can't go exploring with me. And my mum stays home to look after him. Dad does a lot with me, but he's really strict. I just want to have some friends and explore with them.'

'Just get some rest, and we'll do some exploring in the morning.'

'I'll try. This isn't how I imagined a Toss. You're not how I imagined a Tosser either.'

'It's *scavenger* to you.' Arun glanced at the footprints around the ripped tarp floor, not his nor Malorie's. No surprise there. 'Anyway, your imagination's right. I'm different. The others all seem to be fine with how things are. They just accept it. "It is what it is," they say. But I dunno how you can accept it when you look around and see how much better the past was.'

'I don't know much about the past.'

'I'll show you my books if I ever find them. The past is fascinating. I've always wanted to learn more about it. Nobody else here reads or cares about learning, and it shows.' Arun yawned and slid down the metal sheet, leaving his neck rested on the wall. 'I never truly belonged here amongst these people. I don't belong anywhere. I don't even know what a proper home is or what the purpose of all this is. It'd be nice to belong somewhere, I guess. I thought I finally found that place but...never mind.'

'Nicholas always says we belong somewhere else,' said Malorie after a period of silence. 'He talks about finding a door. A door to open the mind. Whatever that means. He says once we find it, we will all go to a place beyond. Free of Aerkin and all of this. But my dad says he's wrong; he says con-scious-ness is a con. There's lots more to discover here first. And there's good to the world too. It's not all bad. Is it? I've always wondered—'

Malorie's ramblings were soon lost to the roaring skies as thunder terrorised the town. Arun felt her trembles beside him whilst howls from scavenging foxes and, according to her, other mysterious creatures raged on in the distance. Heavy rain created a stream of tiny drummers across the car roof as metal clattered in the wind, although the loudest bangs seemed to be by human hand. A powerful strike of multiple strands of lightning from the sky lit their tiny shelter as if a sky of flickering lightbulbs had returned to the world. Arun eventually fell asleep with Malorie clung to his arm like a leech through the night.

*

Morning came as Arun, who barely slept, stared blankly out to the soaked ruins. A small stream of water flowed down the cracks of an old street carrying loose debris and foliage. Arun would typically hear one or two scavengers by this time, laughing or fighting, depending on the amount of sleep they'd had the prior night. This morning, however, was unusually quiet.

Malorie had now awoken. Although, in reality, she probably didn't sleep a second either.

'How'd you sleep?' asked Arun.

Malorie grumbled and rubbed her eyes. 'Can we go back to the Hill today?'

'Don't be too hasty,' said Arun, standing and preparing to leave, scouting the area one last time for any sign of the Freeloaders. 'I thought you wanted to explore. I need to get some water from the bucket-hide first.'

'Wait for me,' said Malorie, scampering to her feet. 'Don't leave me.' She belted out of his shelter and followed, almost joined to his leg. 'Did you always sleep like that?'

'Yeah. You get used to it. I can't actually remember not being used to it. The truth is, I found the Hill weirdly quiet, and I had better nights here than I did there. The only noise back there without rain was the crickets, and you focus in on them, and they become a constant pounding in your eardrums as if a million were in bed with you. And they never stop. They even talk more than you, girl.'

'Hey!'

'Here, though, there're too many things to focus on. And eventually, you learn that you're safe at night, and nobody dares to come and steal from you in the dark because they can't see a thing either. It's the day that's dangerous.'

The two arrived to collect water from an old contraption of buckets Arun had set up a while back. He'd perched a car wheel above a shallow hole in the ground, with the tyre mostly shredded and a metal pole resting through the rim to keep it suspended. The contraption consisted of a rope twisted around the wheel with both ends tied to one bucket each, one resting above ground to store cold rainwater, and the other submerged in a deep, narrow hole to hold warm water that the Earth had heated. The wheel turned, the bucket raised, and was swapped over if needed. Arun would soak his feet with the warm water and, for everything else, use the cold, providing the previous user hadn't sabotaged it through anger or stupidity.

The two sat against a decrepit concrete wall to drink from the overflowing cold bucket.

'What's wrong with that man?' asked Malorie out of the blue. Arun turned to spot a limping man walking towards them in the distance, with his hands in his pockets, losing balance constantly on the rubble. He wore a ripped yellow raincoat, still coated in dry blood from the famous "Carterton Civil War".

'It looks like he's had it quite bad.' Arun recognised the man from his scavenger group nicknamed Shark. Arun didn't feel like divulging his name; he liked to bite people in fights. But that was the least of his concerns. 'He looks worse than bad, actually. I think the Freeloaders are here. Okay, girl, it's not safe for me anymore. I need to get out of here.' Arun rose but Malorie was in no rush.

'Can we talk to him?' she said. 'Maybe he can tell us where they are?'

Arun's urgency fought with him, but she was right. He sighed and nodded. The two jogged over, Arun hunching to Malorie's height to remain unspotted and assess the damage, but Shark collapsed to his knees as they reached him, releasing a piercing wail that crumbled the walls around him. Anyone near would have heard. His mouth stretched open wide, revealing each of his teeth taking their own direction in life.

'Hey, who clocked you?' asked Arun hurriedly. 'The Freeloaders?'

'Yer not dead,' replied Shark in a broken, croaky voice either side of an agonising moan. 'Neither's old Shark. It's only a matter of time, though.' The blood on his face made him almost unrecognisable, and beneath his eyes his tears mixed with blood. Arun looked down at Shark's bloodied hands. His fingers ended where they began.

'Ahh!' squirmed Arun. 'What the hell happened to you?'

'Same old Arun. Clueless and two days late to the party.' Shark laughed and spat out a mouthful of blood before looking up at his former gang member. 'Why weren't yer here? Hang on.' Shark looked up and down Arun's body. 'Ya...Ya ain't working with them now, are ya?'

Arun and Malorie stepped back in confusion as Shark scurried in retreat, twisting his ankle on debris. He released another piercing wail.

'Get gone! Don't hurt me. Please! I dunno any more,' Shark cried and curled into a foetal ball. 'Please. Don't hurt me. Please don't hurt me. Please.'

'It's me. Arun. It's okay.' Arun inched towards Shark and leant down, placing his arm around him, causing him to flinch. Sniffling, wheezing—all manner of bodily fluids now drowned his mouth and nose. Arun made eye contact with him; his breaths began to return to a normal pace.

'What'd I do wrong?' mumbled Shark.

'Nothing. Where are the Freeloaders? I'll take care of them.'

Shark shut his eyes in a panic and curled as far as his muscles allowed. 'Not Freeloaders. Five. Five wearing black and grey. With those red weapons. Yesterday. They did this. They did this, and I dunno why. They did this. They did this. They did this.'

Arun returned to a straight posture as Shark continued to falter beneath him. He felt Malorie huddled next to him, searching her bag before pulling out the book; she must have remembered something. Before she could get the chance to find the page, Arun had launched himself onto rubble to scout the area.

'We have to be wary and find others,' said Arun.

'What about him?' said Malorie.

'His time was due.'

Arun headed uphill along the street, hurrying Malorie along with him. He searched behind walls and under shelters in a flurry, fast becoming lost in his hometown. Typical. The one time he wanted to see another scavenger, he couldn't. With a sharp turn of his head, he spotted a wrinkly forehead sitting upon a pair of eyes, peering around a corner. Arun rushed over as the head vanished but was found again with ease, quivering atop a motionless man hunched in a corner.

'What happened here?' Arun asked the stranger.

'Come here, little lady. I'll look after you.' The man held his hand out in Malorie's direction with a menacing smile through rotten teeth. He licked his lips. Arun stepped between them after spotting Malorie reaching for her penknife, which she'd moved to her pocket during the night.

Arun towered over the man. 'Look at me. What happened here?' He raised his tone.

'You wanna know how many people begged for death?' The man's head rotated. 'Or how many had their wish granted?'

Arun turned to scan the environment once more. 'Girl, the book. Let's get out of here and learn as much as possible about them.'

The man lunged around Arun and tried to grab Malorie by the arm, but Arun pushed him back against the wall. 'You'll beg for death too!' The man screamed in her face.

Arun grabbed the man by the throat, almost growling, locking him against the wall. He analysed the eyes of this monstrous man, ignoring the fishy breath spewing from his mouth. His hand tightened around the scavenger's throat, choking him with the intent to scald rather than harm. Though he wasn't just choking the man. His hand shone blue with a vast glow of energy, far greater than he had managed to train himself to do prior. This felt different, this time instinctive. His hands were out of control, burning, and shaking with power.

Arun released the tension in his face and the grip in his muscle, causing the light to simmer away into the air. The man released a hollow gasp. As Arun removed his hand, a hole in the man's throat appeared, a curved tunnel running straight through his neck. Blood trickled out around the parts of flesh that weren't burnt, his eyes fixed in place as his body collapsed to the floor. Oh, no. No, no, no. Arun sharply turned to Malorie, speechless, trembling, her hands covering her mouth.

'I didn't. I didn't mean to kill him. I…I just…' Arun frantically stammered before losing his words completely. He ripped the gloves off and threw them to the ground. The young pair looked down upon them, silently waiting for the other to speak.

'We need to go,' said Arun, looking at Malorie's face, faded of colour. He cautiously lifted the gloves and stared at them—loose material flailing in the harsh breeze. He knew these were weapons, but seeing them crumpled up after taking life without much effort troubled Arun. They were, after all, part of the reckoning of this world. Sliding them in his pocket, he walked on. He turned back to check on Malorie; she began to follow, but not even her footsteps made a sound now.

The two stayed quiet as Malorie read the book to herself and Arun navigated the wasteland. They came to the outskirts and looked out to the fields heading north. A line of smoke drifted to the sky from the remnants of a fire. That's when Arun spotted them. Five figures head-to-toe in grey and black in a straight line, walking through the furthest field away on a gentle slope, away from the smoke. He couldn't see much detail, apart from the dark outlines of what appeared to be the weapons Shark mentioned. The feeling of fear replaced the feeling of solemnity.

'It's them,' said Arun, nudging Malorie. 'It's got to be them. From Nicholas's book—the Aerkin Knights. Where are they going?' Arun found his bearings by the fields he could recognise. 'The Hill is west, and they're heading…north. We're okay. Don't they have horses?'

Arun turned to Malorie. She had her eyes set on the fields, watching intently, looking as worse for wear as Arun felt.

'Girl,' said Arun. 'Did you find anything else in the book?'

'Yeah,' said Malorie, with a reluctance in her voice. She turned a handful of pages and cleared her throat. 'I've witnessed these knights and heard from others of their displays. Aerkin moved further towards religious autonomy, a Godlike belief in himself. He does not follow the sacred structure of religion, but I use it for lack of a better term. These men are willing followers, rewarded for their strength with weapons of light. They have trapped the powerful red variant of dark energy, see page fourteen. Unsure how he has trapped the light in weapons.' Malorie paused to sniffle her nose and clear her throat again. 'They seem to be able to switch weapons on and off. Perhaps a contraption. Magnetised? No success in experimental replication.'

Malorie stumbled as she read, not knowing some of the words. She turned the page, and another short pause followed. 'Side note. Armour made of iron. Weakness? Their trapped light can't be fired or projected. Must be attached to a weapon. Best course of action is to attack them from afar, not hide and let them get close. Train more Tarios.' She closed the book softly and held it to her side. 'Did that help?'

'No,' replied Arun, drawn back to the fields as the figures inched forward. The tenseness in his body began to release. 'Strange how the further away something is, the less intimidating it feels, right?'

'Can we go back to the Hill?' asked Malorie. 'I want my family.'

Arun scouted the area further. 'If they're heading north, we won't need to worry. We can search for stuff they might have dropped.' Arun turned. Malorie's head was bowed, offering nothing back. 'Okay. Or...we should keep an eye on them. Make sure they don't find the Hill. How about that?' He scouted again, spotting a couple of bodies scattered around the debris. 'I have an idea. Come.' He signalled Malorie to follow him and hurried back with her slowly in tow to his bucket-hide

'Shark,' said Arun, arriving by the seated scavenger and kneeling beside him. 'I have a message.' Shark wilted with his body collapsed against a wall. He made no acknowledgement of the return of the two. 'Okay, well, if you can hear me, scavengers are in more danger if they stay here. Tell anyone remaining to head to a village of huts in the hills. It's north-west deep into the fields. Take the west road out and keep steering north uphill. Don't go downhill at any point, else you'll get lost. It's about six to eight hours walking, but you'll notice the greens getting greener. Follow these deep greens until you find it on your left.'

Shark, still motionless, blinked to show he had body and mind about him.

Arun needn't care about his old gang's lives, but he chose to offer them the same luck that life had granted him. He understood that home was here for all and him as well, but to stay here risked life and sanity just to keep comfort in a familiar setting. It wasn't worth it. Nicholas might have had good reason for not letting many people on the Hill, but Arun couldn't follow those ways. A safer life on the Hill awaited all.

He stood, looking down on Shark. 'Everyone has something to fight for, even you.' He turned to walk away.

'Just go,' said Shark, vaguely audible. 'How many times have you run away now? Nine? Ten? Just go and don't come back no more.'

Arun had no reply. He left north in pursuit of the Aerkin Knights. Malorie followed head down, close by.

CHAPTER FOURTEEN

EARTH'S FURY

*A*DE 3 to 4—Weather remains volatile but unchanged for this year and next. Thunderstorms increase and decimate the ruins of towns and cities further. Many die when finding shelter here, most likely due to poorly constructed shelter or touching exposed metal.

I finish work on a suit that works like Aerkin's. It has its limitations, damaging my skin and muscle when I exhaust myself with it. The plan to heal the world begins.

The Hill discovers a lone girl named Kate. She has stayed alone since ADE 1 and somehow managed to survive. She hunts for herself. She eventually trusts us and stays permanently at the Hill. She reminds me of what could have been.

ADE 5—The 'Greatest Depression' is upon us. Many strive to survive but cannot reach the highs awarded to us in the previous era. They are lost. I predict the young moulded by this world don't face such tortures.

I finish work on Kate's first pair of gloves. She is brilliant. She loves the glow of ignited dark energy and takes to wielding it like a natural. A three-band ex-military group discovers the Hill. We begin to build huts to build a group of warriors.

Future revision to ADE 5—The Great Migration ends here as far as I know, as humans look to settle whenever convenient. No land could be untouched by devastation. The joining of the Mainland continents ends with the formation *of the Immanis Mons mountain range. A vast land of purple mountains and volcanic activity. It begins near the event epicentre, stretching east to the pre-existing Alps mountain range—Aerkin's new home.*

*

The steady, solid rock of the land no longer lay beneath, as the oceans swept restless Hillfolk feet away by the will of the waves. As the sky turned dim, the whites turned grey and the blues black. Night crept closer, and the group would have to travel through it to survive. The line of land they could once see had now vanished, and the sea flowed up as if it met the sky.

Barrages of misty, salted water ambushed the sailboat at every bump, though it felt as if the waves were crashing against one's stomach. As soon as one wave would pass, another would announce itself. These hurdles of the land's tears were not overwhelming in size but constant in number, thundering into the boat and rendering the distant thunderstorm pale in comparison. The group persisted and took turns rowing and navigating, although their efforts would not make much difference if the waves won the battle.

The sky above soon released waves of its own, with thick streams of rain pelting the boat at all angles. Cyclonic winds made it almost impossible to stand still at any given moment, though through all this, the boat had managed to stay afloat. It was beaten, battered, smashed, and lashed but all in one piece.

Sat below deck on a bus-stop-like bench, Nicholas whistled a pensive tune to himself as his aged body raged side to side between Emitai and Serr. Standing or sitting wherever space was available, those cramped around them held firmer but visibly more unsettled. Jordan sprinted to the back with his hand over his mouth, consumed by seasickness. 'Where is Kate?' mumbled Nicholas to himself.

Kate opened the cabin door, right on cue, bringing the chaos of the waves and rains with her below deck. The winds were so strong they carried her words off to sea unless she yelled. 'Got an hour of light left!' Holding onto whatever she could get her hands on, Kate clambered through the crowd to reach Nicholas. Matuu shut the swinging cabin door and locked the winds away behind her.

'Wonderful,' replied Nicholas.

'Not the word I had in mind,' said Kate. 'Not the journey I had in mind either. Not going to die, are we?'

Nicholas released a familiar chuckle to himself. 'We are in one piece, are we not? I knew Gorm would not let us down, and indeed he has not.' Nicholas searched the cabin for faces but found mostly the crowns of bowed heads. 'Do not worry, my friends; the night will be calm, as the Channel needs to sleep, too. It rages evening and morning but settles night and day. We will be fine.'

'Unless we crash into the rocks and die a horribly painful death,' said Matuu.

Nicholas was the only one to return a chuckle. 'Thankfully for us, the Mainlanders light the shores like beacons so we can take advantage of their misdirected hospitality.'

Kate let out a sigh of relief, stretching her legs after hours on deck.

'Never shying away from manual work, even off land, my dear Kate,' said Nicholas. 'You are an example to us all. But you should rest during the remaining journey.'

'Exactly what I plan on doing.' She closed her eyes and leaned her head back.

Silence passed for seconds as the waves slowly settled. The group had grown tired of holding the sways in their stomachs. A lone candle, held by Nicholas, was the only source of light as the sky fell asleep.

'This silence is worse than the seasickness,' said a returning Jordan. 'Nicholas, I don't suppose you have any sea stories to put us to sleep?'

'Stories?' asked Denis.

'We love stories,' mumbled Emitai, his head swaying, looking far more downtrodden than he did on land. An explosive sneeze without his hand blocking his mouth brought those around him to shuffle away.

'Anything apart from that damn door in your dreams again,' said Matuu.

'What about this glove?' asked Kate. 'Remember anything special about it?'

The glove. The one that started everything. Various thoughts came flowing into Nicholas's head, thoughts that he'd buried for many, many years.

'Yes, the glove.' Nicholas knew he carried a calming voice, and his voice filtered out the soundwaves of the tilting tides as he spoke. 'You have all become more aware, since we left, of the extent of my work with Richard Aerkin. I would like to be more precise with my words now that we are not reliant on timeless time. Richard and Aerkin are two very different entities to me. We all speak of Aerkin, as you know, but I speak very little of Richard. I find it easier to use that name to speak of him before all the events that plague us.'

'Does it matter?' asked Matuu. 'Same spiteful, worthless monster.'

'Yes, it matters. The man I call by his first name was hard-working and brilliant—a genius. Far more intelligent than me, but I was his superior in work terms. He loved science with such pride and passion, and became overjoyed when picked to work on the dark energy research project. Dark energy had its theories, and another team of physicists thought they had proven its existence before I realised they made a fundamental mistake. I amended the theory using a recently discovered species of marine worm, the Falkeworm and its cocoon, as the substance to detect dark energy passing through. The idea was to work alongside the team at the nearby particle acceleration facility to create a machine that attempted to follow the laws of black holes and suspend dark energy inside it. Buoyed by this life-changing experiment and the chance of having his name written in history, Richard jumped straight in.'

The heads facing Nicholas bobbed side to side in the swaying vessel with their eyes stabilised in place.

Nicholas continued. 'I suppose our real turbulence began when he felt he surpassed my knowledge of dark energy and wanted to lead the project. He became censorious, uncaring of our methods, budgets, and restrictions; he just wanted to build and create. And so he did, sometimes without my knowledge. Late nights, insomnia, and stealing equipment were all in the name of science and defiance of the company's structure.

'As it was, and as it was everywhere, you clash with those closest to you, but you always maintain your respect for them. I stuck to my methods within the bounds of conventional science whilst his theories ventured into the realm of metaphysical dimensions. As always, conventional science prevailed, succeeding with a cryocooled ribbed plate of Falkum with an electrical current passed through it. It was the only material that would work under those conditions. Better yet, the material could be harvested. Humans of the past thrived on a good harvest.'

'More glove, less science,' interrupted Jordan. '...please.'

'I am reaching my conclusion. We collected the results and finished writing the paper. It would be the most significant announcement in human history; it would change the world. But before we did, I made the biggest mistake I would ever make. You see, Richard came to me with a glove he'd created that required no power source, no cryocooling, no particle acceleration, but instead relied exclusively on the human body. I dismissed it. To believe dark energy could be held in a room, let alone reflect light, was beyond anything we had worked on. He had taken our research and tried to make a mockery of it, I thought. I lacked the imagination I should have had as a physicist. In dismissing it, I dismissed him.

'I remember it vividly. He slid this loosely stitched glove on, made from our precious material he had stolen, clenched his hand, and started screaming. But nothing happened. I thought his insomnia had devoured him. He tried and tried, screaming and shouting. "I created light! I created light!" I lost respect for him that night. That night I lost *him*.'

Nicholas ran his fingers through his coarse beard. The group sat wide-eyed.

'There is absolutely no doubt in my mind that Richard would have followed down this path no matter what I said or did. His real quarrels were with companies, rich folk, and the natural order of the fabricated human existence we once lived, trapped chasing gold for pleasure, creating a pool of destitution for the unfortunate ones below. He always spoke to me of geniuses who gave everything to the world but died with no riches to their name. A great injustice and imbalance, he said. He refused to fall into that same fate.'

'Why didn't you tell us any of this sooner?' asked Kate.

'In the beginning, I said nothing. I feared what I knew would get me in trouble. You must all understand that I trust you, but my history with him still leaves me in self-doubt, let alone how it must sound to others. And it would not make a helpful difference either. In fact, it might even do the opposite in bringing humanity to a man that denounced the very same thing.'

'It's not like we'd feel sorry for him after what he did. Richard, Aerkin, whatever. He is who he is.'

Nicholas took a short pause to consider his next words, for he had never before spoken so freely about this. Twenty years of silence—broken. 'You know…I do wish I could have believed him. Not because it would have changed his path, for as you say, he is who he is. But because it would have changed mine. I would be sat in the hills, drinking tea with my wife and daughter, far from where he resided. Instead, this world fills me with a gut-wrenching vengeance that never leaves my side. Their faces abide wherever I go. The bountiful healing of timeless time will never be a friend of mine.'

Nicholas sat stone-faced, eyes fixed on the floor. 'I can only hope that the original glove may prove to be of any use. I do not know how, but as we always used to say: we must look for answers, for that is the only way we move forward.' Denis took the candle from Nicholas to rest his hand, and with all other eyes wide open, Nicholas closed his.

A young blonde girl, seen through the smashed window where smoke poured out and fire chased after. The cries of 'daddy' through exhausted tears, with a motionless body crumbled at her feet.

'Daddy, help. Daddy, please.'

Only an outstretched arm replied, helpless.

She soon collapsed when the coughing stopped, joining her mother's eternal sleep. It was in this state, where the void of light replaced Nicholas's vision, that he would relive the suffering in their demise, as always.

*

Hours had passed into the night, and Nicholas woke to a loud crashing thud against the boat. The howling winds attempted to burst through the hull, and the shattering rain pummeled the deck above.

'Everybody up!' shouted a voice from the deck. Nicholas attempted to stand, but the boat jolted to its side. It threw all in the cabin into a pile against the wall.

'Sea sleeps through the night, does it?' screamed Kate towards Nicholas, fighting to open the cabin door. A lucky grab prevented Nicholas from falling to the other side as the boat jolted again. Kate opened the door, with the others climbing and crawling behind.

Nicholas arrived on deck to see Matuu holding Serr steady at the front of the boat an arm's length away. In desperation, Serr generated a broad wall of light curved around the front, forming a shield she struggled to hold. Matuu held Serr with one arm to prevent her from slipping and losing the boat's protection, and with his other, he vigorously held onto the railing. The shield stretched over four metres tall, high over the others like a giant, glowing front sail, lighting the entire boat and the rains around it. It was the only light in an otherwise dark, frightening, and truly alive environment. The struggling humans were bright and brave but ultimately a speck in the violent ocean.

Nicholas commanded the others at the top of his lungs. 'Everyone, hold on! Do not let go of anything! Do what you can to fight the waves or stay back down for cover if you cannot!' The group heeded his words as another wave came crashing into the boat. Another wall of water exploded across Serr's shield. Some Tarios had attempted to fire bolts at the waves, but they shot straight through and had no effect.

Nicholas attempted to make his way to Serr and solidify the defence, fighting against the weather as he did, unable to keep his footing. However, before he could get anywhere close, he looked above the shield to witness the Earth's ultimate power: a wave more immense than any mountain he had seen emerging from the dark. The wave was subtly brought to life by the boat's intense light but emerged brighter as it hurtled its might towards the group. Their light could not reach the top of the wave, though, and it appeared as if this wall of water had no end. The group stood no chance; the wave would swallow the boat whole—the journey over before it began.

The tumultuous storm drenched their eyes. Kate attempted to hold onto Nicholas as they struggled to keep steady, but they slipped and collapsed into the railing behind them. Amongst the screams and shouts, Nicholas put his hands together, ignited his gloves, and unleashed a furious beam of dark blue circular light, as wide as himself, straight through Serr's shield and into the body of the wave. The shield shattered, and the others could see into the full might of the ocean now, as it came crashing down either side of the boat, illuminated by the ungodly beam.

The beam broke through the middle of the wave, but not in its entirety. Through the wave's gap, the boat launched over the remaining water and surfed over the crest, crashing down to the sea, bringing the sound of a thousand thunderstorms. Water now enveloped the deck and leaked below. No energy beam could fix this, and the group panicked, grabbing whatever they could or just their hands to sweep the invading liquid and throw it overboard.

Nicholas braced himself as Serr built up her shield again to protect the boat. She pushed her hands out wide, light growing from her palms, frost expanding on a pane of glass. Matuu held her still as she curved around the railing. However, the boat took a forceful hit, and Serr fell backwards, breaking and extinguishing her light. The group identified another huge wave as the Tarios shot light ahead, the only illumination available.

Two Tarios brought Nicholas forward, holding him steady as he reached the front of the boat. Again, he unleashed his beam upon the Earth's fury as the battle between humans and nature raged on. He cut from left to right with his beam, collapsing the wave, though not defeating the wave entirely as it imploded, crashing down in a crumbling wall to form great pools of rapids, spewing and swallowing water.

The waves threw the boat from side to side, trapping it in a spinning pinball machine, churning the group on the flowing floor before spitting them out. Nicholas continued to fire smaller aimless beams ahead with each curved hand, but these waves would not settle. He looked forward, flanked by his warriors, wondering how far back the waves would stretch. He summoned all the strength and muscle remaining in his body, hoping to generate a beam of light that would travel as far back as the horizon. It would be impossible, but he would never give up.

'Nicholas!' screamed Kate.

Nicholas released the beam from his hands as Kate lunged her grasp to his arms from behind, grabbing hold of him. She screamed into his ears. Her gloves ignited, flowing energy into his own. The beam grew in size, unleashing a far more powerful stream of light upon the world; the ocean lit up as if the sun had returned to the seas. Kate's hands had transfigured from blue to yellow, and the beam grew faster and turned yellow in return. Both were now screaming, and Nicholas's hands were almost burning. They collapsed to the floor, and with them, the energy dissolved to the misty rain and the air.

Nicholas. You're fading, Nicholas. Get up.

*

'Kate!' Nicholas shouted; he woke on the boat for the second time, although a dull sheen had replaced the darkness around the cabin. He lay crumpled on the floor, next to a sleeping Kate and a stirring Jordan. The boat still rocked from side to side, but more peacefully, along the sleeping sea and beside the squawking seagulls. Despite Nicholas's weather predictions being in complete disarray, the boat had survived the night. Nicholas looked at Kate and sighed with a thankful grin before noticing her eyes displaying the most severe rapid eye movement he had ever seen. It was as if her eyes were trying to escape their lids.

'Viv's gone,' said Jordan, acknowledging his leader's waking presence with the news.

'Viv?' Nicholas shook his palms of the scorching burn from his overpowered beam. Viv was a Marshal, one of the most recent Hill recruits. 'Have we—'

'You've been out for a while. We did what we could, but she's gone. She drowned in the rapids.'

Nicholas bowed his head. He had failed one of his own already, on his own plan, on his own route. Death was nothing new to a man who had lost everything, but somehow the feeling had never changed. That same rise of the stomach; it grabbed him whole. 'I am responsible.'

'At least you did something. I don't know how, but you and Kate calmed the weather. I just wish I could have helped. I felt so ill, and I was useless…I'm sorry.'

He knew at that moment, hearing Jordan's first ever apology, that he would have to push his stomach back down and continue to act as a leader. For as sorry as Jordan seemed, the Marshals would be ten times worse. *Be strong, Nicholas.* A sorry leader would be their downfall.

Nicholas took on the challenge of encouraging Jordan's ego. 'Be kinder to yourself. Once we have stopped jumping off cliffs and sailing seas, that is when we require your best, and that is when you will come through. The real fight is against people, not nature.'

Jordan was unmoved. Suddenly, Kate awoke in a panic, shooting up with a deep gasp of breath.

For the worries Nicholas held over Viv's loss, they would never compare to the fears of Kate coming to harm. 'My dear Kate! Your eyes were fluttering faster than I have ever seen. Was it the usual nightmare?'

Kate swept the sweat away from her forehead. 'Where are we?'

Before Nicholas could answer, Kate threw herself to her feet and made her way outside. Nicholas followed as she did, checking her posture and strides for any sign of injury.

The grey morning greeted them on deck, complete with a light morning drizzle. Land appeared close by to the left: the Mainland. To the right, nothing but whipped water with lines of white bubbles flowing with the breeze. The calm waters had brought the freshest air to the group's noses, the smell of salty citrus: natural purity. It seemed almost insulting for the sea to do so.

All seven Marshals were rowing, silently tilting back and forth, with Matuu taking over the eighth position. He struggled to keep up the pace. Anyone would. A glance from one of the Marshals towards Nicholas was all they could muster. They didn't need a pep talk; they needed to be off the boat as quick as humanly possible.

Nicholas turned to Kate and watched closely as she looked out over the deck at the bubbles settling on a darkened patch of the sea surface. Her jaw dropped. A towering burst of water erupted from the ocean, spraying mist high into the air as if the rain had turned upside down. The dark patch grew to a monstrous size, and the large grey body of a sea creature emerged above, a creature the likes of which she would have never seen. She stopped breathing, mouth wide open, as the size of the beast continued to grow. Nicholas kept his eyes on Kate, preferring the wonder in her face to the spectacle overboard.

'They are whales,' said Nicholas with a muted tone. 'The largest creatures alive.' He spotted smaller, jumping creatures surfacing in his peripheral, bouncing alongside the whale, seemingly singing to each other. 'Dolphins. Extremely intelligent.'

'They're so big,' said Kate, looking engrossed.

'The bigger the pond, the bigger the fish. Welcome to the ocean.'

The creatures swam in synchronised majesty, flowing through the sea. They were a dull grey, with indiscernible features, but the way they graced the water with such carefree joy brought life and beauty to the waves. Nicholas watched Kate, unable to keep her eyes off them, smiling and following each jump. The whale's body started to go under, but its massive tail swung into the air as if to greet the passengers. As the tail slowly dropped and sank into the depths below, the dolphins disappeared with it, leaving the boat to go on its way. Two tears trickled down Kate's cheeks.

'There is much to be thankful for in this cruel world,' said Nicholas, moving an arm to Kate's back, choosing to focus on what the ocean gives rather than takes. 'I never knew of many creatures in the Channel before, but they now swim in abundance. I feel there are now more whales on this planet than there are humans.' Nicholas left Kate to her tears as Zachenne approached him, avoiding Emitai and Denis, who were busy trying to lure seagulls in with scraps of food, perhaps hunting for a bigger meal than the scraps Nicholas awarded them.

'The winds have pushed us well,' said Zachenne. 'A little too well. We've reached the west coast, too close to shore. They might spot us.' Zachenne paused. 'I trust you heard—'

'Yes. Viv. I need to focus on getting us to land safely without another incident.' Something caught Nicholas's eye behind the boat, breaking the horizon. It may have been a small island they had sailed past, but it appeared to be bobbing on the waves. 'Keep an eye on that object behind. The whales may not be the only ones wishing to greet us.'

As Nicholas attempted to return below, Kate shouted out from the side of the boat. 'Why don't you have your suit?'

Nicholas paused for a second. He looked down to spot a ripped opening in his cloak, revealing a simple white shirt beneath. He hummed to himself for a moment.

'Nicholas?' Kate called out again.

Nicholas curled his beard. 'I chose a better fate for it.'

He caught Kate's forceful stare before she placed her hands behind her head. She stood silently, waiting for him to speak again.

'You have always required me to be blunt and direct with you, my dear Kate.' Nicholas sighed to himself and turned. 'I left it with Arun.'

'Arun? Why?' Kate raised her voice. 'What use is it with him?'

'Far greater than it is with me. We might not return this journey, and in that boy, we have a young fighter with spirit and the ability to create light. The only things missing were the material and the knowledge, and I left both to him.'

'We needed it to fight! Might as well leave all our gloves behind if that's your thinking.'

The voices of others simmered down, and Jordan made a rare appearance up top, presumably hearing the two raised voices. Even several Marshals turned their heads as an audience gathered.

'You should never make plan A without considering a plan B, my dear Kate,' asserted Nicholas. 'We must not think of just ourselves; we must think of a life beyond our own.'

Kate's arms flew apart, animated against Nicholas's words. 'I *always* think about life beyond our own. What about the lives of those abundant dolphin creatures or all the wild animals roaming free back home? Isn't that the wonder of life? Isn't that part of what we're fighting for? In fact—when's the last time you watched a deer without hunting it or actually fed the horses instead of just remembering to do so? You only seem to care about humanity, finding a stupid door in your head that doesn't exist, and your revenge!'

Nicholas stepped forwards with a commanding tone. 'Do not accuse me of such things. I have lived through both times, and I have taken little and given back my all. I hunt so we can eat, and I work hard so we can sleep in peace. A leader's duty is to lead, so leave me be about my ways. I am simply here to help you all see the sun one day. All I wish to see is where my family awaits me.' Nicholas inhaled the sea's fresh air to regain his composure. 'And if there is no such afterlife, I will see nothing.'

'But…' Kate stuttered, her eyes still tensed. 'No! The suit was so important to us, Nicholas. It always has been. Made us all feel protected, unbeatable. It feels like there's so much you're keeping from us, and I don't know why.' Kate's glaring eyes relaxed, with her shoulders resigning to a slouch. 'You need to communicate. Tell us, what's our plan without it? What's plan A? Get this weapon, then run in there, screaming and throwing light, hoping for the best?'

'Do you remember how I first described Aerkin to you? The two words I used?'

'Yes.' Kate's blink lasted a moment, above a deep breath. 'Immortal. Invincible. How could I forget?'

'Precisely.' Nicholas walked towards the front of the boat to address the larger audience of the group. 'Aerkin's ability to conceal himself in his entirety with energy is, for lack of a more elegant word, unbeatable. The glow of his light is so dense that it turns a deep shade of red, the reddest red there is. Watching his power as it shatters and splinters is a genuinely chaotic sight—as if he had stolen fire from a deeper pit than Hell. Our light is not strong enough for this. The suit back home would not be strong enough for this. The gloves with Iris may not be strong enough for this. But now is the best chance we have before I grow too old. I am running out of timeless time and mind.'

The eyes of the Hillfolk danced around at each other.

Nicholas continued, 'I have thought about this for long, with or without the suit or this new weapon. These materials do not hold bearing over my fate. I am the sacrifice we must make. Aerkin will see me, he will torment me, and he will want my end. This is the only way I can imagine to get him to let his guard down. If he sees anyone else but me, he will crush them like insects.

'This is why I divulge only the information I need to. My goal is set, my outcome obstinate, and I do not wish for any of you to attempt to change my mind or change the greater plan, even though it will bring my end. I have grown fond of you all. That is my greatest weakness. I bury a pit inside me this morning so we can move forwards.'

'You're using yourself as bait?' asked Kate. 'As a sacrifice? You've always known this, and you never thought to tell me.' Kate's head sunk to her chest briefly. 'What makes you think he'll see you unarmed and let his guard down for a—'

'Contrary to what—'

'Nicholas!' Zachenne called out from the back of the boat before Nicholas could finalise his retort above Kate's voice. 'Come, someone is tracking us.'

Nicholas rushed to the back in a panic, not before taking one last glance at the fury that fell upon Kate's face. Reaching the back, followed by the others, Nicholas observed the small object in clearer view. A boat bounced on the waves, similar in size to theirs.

'They're not heading for the shore; they're heading for us,' said Jordan.

'Finally, a challenge,' said Matuu.

Small, shadowy figures moved on the boat. It was still a hefty distance away, too far for Nicholas and the Tarios to fire on and too unsteady for Jordan to attack accurately. The same could not be said for the other boat, though, as a loud ping of metal against metal threw the group into surprise.

'Down!' shouted Nicholas. All ducked out of sight in unison. Nicholas looked overboard to see a fresh hole in the hull. 'They have a gun!'

'A sniper rifle,' said Zachenne calmly. 'Stay down.'

'Where'd they find a gun?' asked Jordan. 'I thought you said guns didn't exist anymore?'

'Excellent question.' Nicholas crouched back beside the rails. 'Serr, shield. Marshals, forward. Who knows what other tricks they possess.'

'I'll introduce myself,' said Matuu. Nicholas followed Matuu's gaze as he looked up to the sky. The rain turned from drizzle to downpour. 'The ocean's in my ancestry, and they're trespassing.' He and Serr stayed at the back of the boat, and Serr again created a barrier of light to protect the boat and stave off the attacks.

Think, Nicholas. *Think.* 'Ah! Old weapons have one major weakness: ammunition. It is unlikely they are stocked. We can withstand this. Just stay behind the shield.' He clenched his hands, still feeling yesterday's burn.

Kate knelt beside Nicholas on the left side of the boat, the side closest to land. The boat fast approached a peninsula, and the land stretched out to greet them. The two looked to the land and spotted the figures of Mainland scouts in the distance as another gunshot fired and pierced the boat's hull again.

Nicholas peered over the edge. 'On second thoughts, we may not be able to wait. We cannot let them pierce beneath the water level.'

'Scouts on the land!' shouted Kate.

Nicholas turned to see a group of figures on the cliffside beginning to move. They were indiscernible in appearance but were hurriedly packing their belongings. Nicholas considered igniting his beam, but two scouts had already disappeared from view, too far away to stop.

'They are going to send word,' faltered Nicholas, batting his head between both problems, both still too far away for the Tarios to solve, but they tried anyway to no avail, their light fading into the air. 'We have no way to stop them. This is a disaster.'

Nicholas checked the back of the boat to find Matuu whirling his right hand wildly in horizontal circles above his left hand. Faint blue light seeped from his palm like a mist of tenuous cloud collecting in the hand beneath. He held the energy until it expanded near his chest before releasing it into the wind. He pulled his left hand away, and with his right, continued to whirl a stream of energy into the ocean that took the shape of a thin, swirling tornado of light. Nicholas hadn't seen his creation in the wild to this extent. His eyes lit up in wondrous blue.

The edge of the peninsula now reached as close to the boat as possible.

'I'll stop them!' shouted Kate, between two rowing Marshals. 'I'm fast. I'll follow signs and meet you.'

Nicholas turned back. 'No! I cannot let you leave.'

'I have to.'

Nicholas panicked. 'We have to stick together!' He paced over to Kate as fast as his aged knees would allow. 'Remember, I cannot lose you.'

'And remember, he can't know we're here.' Kate offered nothing in expression. 'Ruins of Rennes. I won't be long—the darkness must die.'

'Kate!' shouted Nicholas with an outstretched arm as his fingertips reached her skin to no avail. Kate leapt off the side of the boat and swam towards the peninsula.

'Overboard!' shouted Nicholas. 'Kate is gone! Stop rowing!'

'Let her go,' insisted Zachenne. 'We can't push the boat to the rocks. We need to continue south to find a shore.'

'We need Kate!'

'You'll crash this boat and take us all down with you!' Zachenne shouted, surely so his voice could carry over the chaos.

If Kate had made way on land, Nicholas would have kept her in his sight. But in the seas, his aged body prevented chase. The rocky coastline stretched as far as he could see, with boat-high waves crashing into steep rocks at all angles. All he could do was watch as his strongest warrior dwindled from his sight. He searched his thoughts for an idea, anything to retrieve her. *She's gone, Nicholas.*

A rasping scream came from the back of the boat. Nicholas turned to see Matuu struggling to contain a thickening tornado from his glove. He forced it further out with each strong swipe of his arm, but the punishing winds and rain were spiralling the tornado out of control. Water spiralled up to match the wind's shape as another gunshot rattled the boat. A splash of water erupted into the air, meaning the bullet had passed into the hull below the sealine.

'Get below deck and find the hole,' said Zachenne calmly to the others. 'They're too accurate. That's not possible from an untrained arm at that distance.'

Nicholas helplessly watched the chaos unfold. Zachenne tried once more to send a bolt of light their way, but it faded out beside Matuu's tornado. Jordan ran off, preferring to be below deck, and the Marshals continued to row as fast as they could. Nicholas had lost track of where to go and who to help.

Another bullet hit below as a shout roared from the cabin. Nicholas took one last look at his swimming companion before scurrying and slipping across the wet deck. Heading down with two Marshals, they found Jordan writhing in agony on the cabin floor. He held his right bicep to contain a stream of blood as two gushes of water poured into the boat.

'Tend to him and block the holes,' said Nicholas. One of the Marshals hesitated at first, meeting Nicholas's concerned frown, but took to her role by blocking the cabin holes with her hands. Her body pressed up against the wall; another bullet could kill her. The other Marshal tended to Jordan. Another shout, back on deck.

Breathing heavily, Nicholas returned to see Matuu's tornado picking up speed and stretching further into the ocean, now much wider than the boat. The sky transformed to a misty cloud of light, rain, and gales; the only thing missing from the mayhem was lightning. The other boat soon disappeared beyond the shroud, with Matuu wilting despite his arms still in motion.

Nicholas stumbled to the back beside Matuu and fell to his knees. He stared out between the railings. The energised tornado finally reached where the opposing boat should have been, and Matuu fell to his knees, meeting Nicholas's level. Matuu held his arm out firm above the railing to control his energy and keep the tornado of light from collapsing. He let out a final scream and released his arm from his created storm. As he did, the hostile boat appeared again, launched into the sky by the tornado. Bodies and loose objects came hurtling out as the wreckage spread across the water, along with the tornado that had lost its energy and collapsed, cascading into the sea.

Serr sprinted to comfort Matuu on the floor; he had held on for too long, and Nicholas knew he would need a while to recover. Wheezing and unable to communicate with his compatriot, he offered a thumbs up before passing out.

Nicholas sat, pensive, as Matuu collapsed into his lap. With Kate traversing the ocean and Jordan and two Marshals below deck, Zachenne appeared in front of Nicholas and took the chance to serve orders to the rest of the group. 'Serr, search the boat for damage. I'll check below deck, and we need to keep a lookout for any other boats. Everyone else—we are still hours away, so rest.' He squatted down to Nicholas's eye line. 'Are you okay, Nicholas?'

Nicholas stumbled to the railing, pushing Matuu into Serr's arms. 'Yes. I am...fine.' He walked around the side of the boat and leaned over to look out towards the shore, seeing Kate had nearly reached land. The waves were starting to pick up again as the volume of rain increased. He watched on as a pang of guilt rumbled in his stomach. His thoughts attempted to escape his mind once more, but he pushed them back to their depths. Nicholas clamped his eyes shut and clenched his hands to the railing whilst a faint blue glow emanated from his burnt hands.

CHAPTER FIFTEEN

HUNTING IN CIRCLES

Arun and Malorie sat resting their aching bodies on a crumbled wall in the late afternoon. Arun stared into a field with the encircled knights still in view, swamped with thoughts of his new friends and where they'd be on their journey by now. Had they reached the Mainland yet? Were they safe? Malorie caught the corner of his eye, running loose string through the conkers she'd brought with her. A strangely calm afternoon fell upon the two.

Malorie hadn't spoken in a while, and a deep worry befell Arun. How do people cheer up a child?

'So…you wanna play conkers?' asked Arun.

'Sure,' said Malorie, dangling a conker by its attached string, but the usual exuberance in her voice had fallen. 'This is how you play. We each have a conker. I go first, as that's the will of the conkers. I pull my conker up towards me and then swing it back down to hit yours. I have to try to do as much damage as possible, and then it's your turn. The winner is the last conker standing. My game name is the Conqueror of Conkers. What's yours?'

'Are you okay?' asked Arun.

'Yeah. Are you?'

Arun knew his truthful answer wouldn't help her. 'My game name is Arun.'

'Would the conkers please make their way to the stage?' Malorie's tone continued to drawl despite the playfulness of her words. 'Conqueror of Conkers, are you ready? Yes. Arun, are you ready?'

'Yeah,' said Arun, now entirely focused on movements from the knights. Malorie's conker vibrated his hand, and within the split second that he looked down and up again, the knights had formed a straight line. They moved forward without warning and were quickly out of view, beyond the protection of trees that Arun and Malorie sat under. 'You win; let's go.' Arun jumped off the wall and threw his conker to the ground.

'That's not how it works,' replied Malorie, now pursuing him. 'But I accept your resignation. One-nil.'

'They're turning slightly west—that's not good. There's another town that way, but the main road from there will head directly west. I think. Which way is west again?'

'One moment,' Malorie searched her bag and pulled out her compass; the glass on the front had cracked. 'I need a new compass.'

Arun sighed. 'Great. We'll pick one up at the store on the way back.'

'I think it's still working. Yeah, they're going north-west.'

After having tracked the knights for most of the day, Arun had grown exhausted, wary that the skies would soon darken. Malorie, a small bundle of energy, walked on with ease.

'I think we have a few hours of sunlight left,' said Arun. 'Let's follow them until they stop again and then find a place to rest.'

Malorie's forehead squeezed into wrinkles. 'They won't travel through the night? What about their weapons and the red light? They might use that to find their way.'

'We all need rest; they're only human. Right?'

*

Another hour of tracking had passed. Now and again, Arun and Malorie would lose sight of the knights, as they kept a healthy distance, but would eventually regain sight by Malorie's guile. Rain refreshed them at various times throughout the day, and as the young stalkers would walk under the trees and through bush, the knights maintained a straight line losing no pace in their haste.

The lands fell asleep. Arun and Malorie stopped near a row of bushes upon a hill, looking down on the town the knights duly arrived at.

'It's too wet and cold here,' said Malorie. 'Can we go into the forest?'

'No. I wanna see what happens. This is where the Freeloaders live.' Arun watched on whilst starting to feel the tips of his fingers kissing the evening frost. He looked down at his cold, soaked hands and put his gloves back on. As he slid one hand in, he envisioned the scavenger he held by his throat and what had happened. He closed his eyes and put the other on hurriedly.

'Look!' said Malorie, pointing to the town as a gloomy grey mist clouded Arun's view. Red light ignited behind the fog as distant thunder transformed the atmosphere into a blistering rage. The red lights marched forwards, in and out of view behind the knights and the rubble. They weren't clear enough to examine; the shapes took many different forms. Some light held a small straight line, another held a line but wisped and flowed at greater length. Another took the shape of a ball of red flames floating through the air: a mystical orb.

Arun's muscles in his face dropped. He knew what would come. And although the mist and the thunder would eclipse any other sound headed their way, Arun could almost imagine the shouting and screaming of those below. The light flowed faster, launching, prodding, and swiping. They were red symphony conductors of a silent orchestra. A straight ray of red light hurled forward and half disappeared as if it were entering a wall, or perhaps a body.

Flurries of lightning woke the land for just a second, enough time for Arun to see the figures in the darkness holding their weapons of light, ambushing and slaying others in the dark. The weapons would leave an intense burning colour where they struck, painting the victim with a burning ember. The idea of the Freeloaders falling to dust might have once sparked joy, but It was perhaps settling for him that he heard no screams.

Despite Arun and Malorie standing soaked in the rain, they couldn't move. The motion of red entranced them. One by one, each weapon of light slowly returned to a still but didn't fade away. Another flurry of lightning brought them to light once more. They stood in a circle, motionless.

'What're they doing?' asked Arun.

Malorie put her bag over her head to shield her from soaking. 'I don't know. I don't think they can do much. It's too dark now. Maybe they're cold?'

'Sure, that's it,' said Arun, smirking. 'They're asking who forgot to bring the blankets.' He spotted two red lights continuing through into the ruins whilst other lights reversed back the way they had come. 'They're splitting up. I wonder if some of them are going back? Heading for shelter?'

'What if they head back to your Toss?'

'No. That wouldn't make sense.'

Arun led Malorie into overgrowth beneath a group of trees. Malorie shook the water off her jumper and removed her hood.

'It does make sense,' said Malorie. 'I would always double-check places. Just because a rabbit wasn't there in the morning doesn't mean it won't be there in the evening. That's what my dad taught me.' Malorie seemed to be returning to her talkative ways.

Arun thought for a moment. 'Nah, they wouldn't waste a whole day going back. They have to have a plan.'

'They were…killing…those people so quickly. That didn't feel like it had a plan or a purpose.'

'There's always a purpose.' Arun walked through the overgrowth to scout each direction, planning their next move. No ideas came to an empty mind.

'I don't eat pig meat,' said Malorie.

Did she just say she didn't eat pig meat? 'Right. Useful. Thanks, girl.'

'I remember the first time Cole gave it to me, and I saw my dad try some. He screwed his face up and spat it out. Said it was nasty and foul. So then I didn't want to try it. I get given some now and again. I still don't eat it, though, and I don't really know why. It must be nice if they offer it. I just don't because my dad didn't. So maybe these people just do what they saw Aerkin do. Maybe they don't know why.'

Arun looked back out across the field they had ventured from and followed the red lights with his eyes, continuing further south along the exact route they had come.

'If they go back,' said Malorie, 'they might find that sad man. And you told the sad man where the Hill was. And then they'll find the Hill. I was going to say something at the time but—'

'No.' Arun's eyes creased together as he looked aimlessly into the ground. His heart weakened. Could that happen? Had he foolishly set a trap for the Hill? He paced side to side. 'No. They won't. They couldn't. I…I didn't think about that. I couldn't leave them there defenceless. That's the only way I could get them to move. You saw the state Shark was in—no, they won't find them. Will they? We didn't deserve to hide unharmed in the Hill whilst they crawled without their fingers. Or worse—'

Arun placed his hands over his mouth and nose to end his rambling. He took a moment to think about his next move. After deliberating with himself in Malorie's returning silence, he could only think of one option.

'Let's go,' urged Arun, finding west by his bearings.

'Go where?' replied Malorie. 'We need to rest. It's dark and cold.'

'We'll find something.' Arun skipped out from the overgrowth but stopped. He turned back to Malorie to see her shivering, soaked from head to toe. She didn't even have a cloak to cover her clothes from the rain. Arun felt a lump in his throat. He opened his mouth to speak—

'Have you killed anyone before?' said Malorie.

Arun didn't know what to say as his shoulders shuddered. He shook his head, waited a moment, and returned to the overgrowth and knelt in front of her. 'I didn't mean to. I messed up. It doesn't feel good, but…we have to move on.'

Malorie nodded slowly, but it didn't seem genuine.

'Listen, girl, I normally do what's best for me, and that way, I can only blame myself. So maybe we can…I don't know. Talk about it instead? D'you really wanna stay here?' Arun removed his cloak and placed it around her shoulders.

The cloak dragged along the muddy ground behind her, but she pinched it around her neckline and let a soft smile escape her face.

Malorie looked up, followed by Arun, and although the top of the trees couldn't be seen, the odd raindrop filtered through to their hands. Surely she wouldn't want to stay here. Please. She huffed and lifted the bottom of the cloak, and without a second more passing, uttered the word, 'Onwards.'

Arun scruffed her hood before leading the way, his gloves glowing bright. He ran across the fields westwards with his little, hooded companion keeping pace. The smell of farmyard fields in the rain covered the air. He could hear horses galloping away in the surroundings to find shelter in between the howling thunders. Arun fought the winds in a soaked-through shirt, with his hands now burning from the prolonged captured energy. Before he could rest his hands, he reached the outline of a wooden structure. He slowed to a halt as Malorie charged into the back of his legs like a stampeding goat.

'I think I see shelter!' shouted Arun over the rain. He walked around, feeling for an opening or a door. The structure stood tall and broad, or long, as the two walked beside it. Still fighting to hold the energy in his hands, Arun arrived at a door that towered and stretched, similar in size to the stable doors back on the Hill. A chain rested over the handles, so Arun thought to grab hold of it with his energised gloves in the hopes of breaking or cutting through it.

'Hurry!' shouted Malorie against the ever-growing gales.

Arun felt his hands start to burn as if dipped into a pot of boiling water. He writhed in agony, squeezing the chain as hard as he could, turning it bright orange. He pulled his hands away from each other as hard as he could, at the end of his pain threshold. The energy from his hands basked the door in light, illuminating a sign. The chain stretched, twisting and elongating. With one final pull, the chain broke and fell away, throwing Arun onto his back.

'No humans.' Malorie helped Arun up and led him hunched into the shelter. 'That's what the sign said.'

'That's great news. I didn't know animals could open doors,' quipped Arun, still holding his burning hands. Malorie took his gloves off and threw them to the floor, and Arun was left to witness no damage. The throbbing and burning sensation resided in his muscles, leaving his skin perfectly fine. He looked around as Malorie tended to his hands, although it was almost impossible for him to see. 'It's okay. My hands will be fine.'

'It smells like we're in a stable, or a—' A neighing horse interrupted Malorie. 'Never mind.'

'Okay, this is good, unless the horses are aggressive, or we're stepping in some horse muck, or it's someone pretending to be a horse. Hello?'

'Maybe an Indie lives here.'

'Indie?'

'Yeah, it's what we call people that live alone around old farms and fields. Nicholas says most of them are nice. He gives them food, and they give us information.'

'Ah, yeah, Loners. I've come across the not so nice ones. Don't ask why.'

A glimmer of light flashed through the stable. It grew more prominent, dancing from side to side as it did. Arun's arm was squeezed tight by Malorie. Shouldn't she be reaching for her penknife?

Arun bent down to lift his gloves slowly, to not make a peep, although the roaring thunder drowned all other sounds out. He slid them back on his sorely aching hands. Bang—the stable door yanked wide open, and a lantern shone from the sturdy arm of a messy-haired woman. The lantern sent sharp spikes of candlelight across her face, and her thick frame of her glasses battled the shadows. Nobody spoke, although she couldn't be that threatening. Could she?

A threat then announced itself in the form of a whistle to end the silence. The woman's whistle brought a couple of soft-sounding, ringing bells, which erupted into the menacing barks of two enormous dogs. The dogs appeared on either side of the woman, sitting instantly and awaiting instruction. They looked to be rottweilers, although Arun only knew of breeds by pictures in a book.

'Good day,' faltered Arun. 'We're only looking for shelter. We'll leave you be. Sorry.'

The woman held the lantern towards the youngsters. Standing a few metres away from the two, she brought her other arm into focus, revealing a large meat cleaver.

'You didn't read the sign, thieves.' The woman spoke in a broken and croaky manner, with a slight pause between each word. 'That leaves me no choice.'

'Can people stop calling me a thief when I haven't stolen anything?'

The woman took one step forward, one step too far. Arun's instinct brought the light to his fisted hands, despite still aching, and his suit glowed just as bright. The entire stable sparked into blue bolts of shadowed light, bringing three horses up on their hind legs, neighing in screams against the rabid barks of the dogs. The woman joined with the cries of the animals, yelping and dropping the cleaver. Arun stood grimacing in burning blue.

'You're one of them Hillfolk,' croaked the woman, hunching beside the door. She'd be wise to consider her actions. The woman lowered her lantern, serving no purpose against Arun's light. 'Come inside then. You'll freeze out here.'

Arun collapsed forward, drained of energy, but maintained an intimidating stare set on the woman, forcing her to leave the stable with her dogs frantically following.

'I don't like this,' said Malorie, holding onto Arun's shirt as he knelt.

'Just stay close. She's more scared of us.' Arun attempted to sound confident in his words to ease Malorie despite the dubious feeling, and she nodded. He led her by the lantern light up ahead, which crossed a short field and reached a small house, which looked to have been patchworked with whatever loose material the woman must have found.

Keeping cautiously aware, Arun stepped into the house, Malorie still holding on. They made their way into the living area, where the woman had laid the lantern on a table surrounded by chairs, with other candles dotted around. Old strips of wallpaper curled off on the one standing original wall. Otherwise, the room consisted of a mismatch of metal, wood, and brick. A bent and broken chandelier hung from the ceiling, albeit held by a rope for a questionably artistic purpose. A fireplace, unlit, stood in its original state—a beautifully horrid room.

'Take a seat, little ones.' The woman sent the dogs away into the adjacent room. She sat, now unguarded and without weaponry, which settled the nerves of Arun. 'What do you want from me?' she asked, still croaky and pausing intermittently.

'Just shelter,' replied Arun, 'and…to borrow a horse maybe.'

The woman raised her finger through her mucky hair and into her ear, slowly rotating it back and forth before removing it. 'I must be hard of hearing.'

'It's urgent. There's a group of men walking around killing people in the towns. We need to stop them. We need a horse. Please.'

'I see,' drawled the woman. 'A group of men. Walking around. Killing people.' She leaned closer towards Arun, almost entirely over the small glass table separating their seats, with her face illuminated above the lantern. 'And you think my horse can stop them?'

'What? No, no. We'll ride the horse.'

The woman's glasses held no glass, just the front of a frame and white bandages wrapped around the sides holding a string in place around her head. She sat back in her chair.

'What's your name?' asked Malorie. A couple of rats scampered across the floorboards. 'My mum taught me it's rude to talk to people without knowing their name.'

The woman turned her head to face Malorie. 'I lost my name a long time ago. Just call me what you will.'

'Georgina,' replied Malorie instantly. 'I like the name Georgina.'

'I like it too. I will rename my dogs that.'

Arun rolled his eyes. 'Look, can we stay the night? We'll be gone before you wake.'

'I suppose,' replied the newly named Georgina. 'I could do with the company. One tends to turn a little crazy when all alone, year, on year, on year, on year.' Her cackle echoed through the empty halls.

'Thank you. And what about the horse?'

'They're perfectly sane, don't worry.'

Arun looked on with squinted eyes. The amount of time it took her to utter each baffled sentence was exasperating.

'Okay. Well, can you show us to a room? We'll be out of your way. We have food also, so you won't know we're here.'

'I'm afraid you're mistaken, young one. I do know you're here.'

That was enough. Arun stood and urged Malorie to follow. He explored to find solace, hopeful the doors would have locks. The dogs sat together, staring at Arun as he peeked into their room. He looked back. 'Girl, come on.'

'You have a pretty face, Georgina,' said Malorie. 'Despite the hair. What does your smile look like?'

'No sunshine, no serotonin. No serotonin, no smile,' informed Georgina, smiling creepily afterwards.

'Forget I asked.' Malorie swiped a candle and finally followed Arun's insistence. He led her around the decrepit house. A couch in one room had no cushions, and a bin opposite overflowed with mounds of decomposing food, with the stench of year-old rotting meat. At least the swarming flies found joy here. The two finally made their way into a small room with the door wide open and nothing inside. A lock was fixed to the door to Arun's delight. However, predictably, the part of the wall it would bolt into was missing. Perfect. Another rat scampered across the room.

'I feel at home already,' said Arun. The two made themselves comfortable, with Arun leaving his boots by the door as a half-hearted lock, which would hopefully keep the flies out, at least.

'I don't think I'll sleep well,' said Malorie.

Arun took a moment to think of the best way to comfort a small girl for the second time that day. He still troubled himself with the vision of the man he'd killed, and he imagined Malorie might be too, but focusing on soothing her at least helped to subside this vision. 'I can protect us from dogs, don't worry.'

'How so?'

'Well, although I can't use the suit for too long, it does give me strength. I'm a good fighter too. I can handle ten dogs, let alone two small ones.'

'There are dogs bigger than that?' Malorie gasped, looking as if she hung onto every one of Arun's confident words.

'Sure. These guys are nothing. I'm a warrior. Here, watch this. Try to hit me.'

'What?' Malorie seemed confused at first, but Arun kneeled to her height and coaxed her towards him. He caught her looking at his hands, hesitant. He took his gloves off and tossed them aside.

'Hit me,' insisted Arun.

'Okay, so, just a punch? In your face?' Malorie took up a fighting stance.

'Yeah, but more than one, and keep trying.'

Malorie clenched her fist, frowning at the request, and launched towards Arun. He dipped his head away. She tried again—he ducked. Again and again, Arun kept avoiding her. He flicked her nose, causing her to growl. She launched at him with a bombardment of attacks that were now turning into slaps. He avoided most and blocked others, flicking her again. In reality, Arun may not have been the most intelligent fighter, but he knew how to dodge a punch.

Malorie huffed and hunched. Arun had proven his point. He looked at her frustratedly panting, but the two then laughed. He assumed she must be feeling comfortable around him again. Result.

'Okay. Let me read you some more of the book,' suggested Malorie. 'I've marked some pages related to those knights. Do you think we should just take the horse in the morning?' she ended in a whisper.

'Sure,' said Arun, sitting down. 'Or I could piggyback you and neigh all the way.'

'No thanks.' Malorie fetched the book and opened a page towards the end. Her eyes scanned the page before reading aloud, 'The Aerkin Knights are now based on the north shore. The Sword Knight, the Scourge Knight, the Mace Knight, the Axe Knight, and the Unknown Knight. All but one name is self-explanatory. Their teams will monitor any boats that arrive or leave. We may soon lose our connection to the Mainland if our eyes can't find safe passage.

Another route required, ideally west. If messengers from the north shore arrive, knights will follow. I fear they seek to capture me and bring me before Aerkin.

'They are commissioning a statue to be built on the north shore: Aerkin. They are establishing the one true religion. Aerkin is now a God and has initiated prayer rituals towards him. The knights are known on the Mainland as the Aerkin Disciples, but I reject this definition, for their leader is no teacher. Ironic how the scientist who questioned religion has created his own, though I wish I could call it a cult. He used to say he and I were the "Gods of energy". I will never acknowledge this.'

Malorie paused. 'And then there's a line scribbled out. That's the end of that page.' She started to flick through previous pages to find another extract.

'Wait.' Arun placed his hand on the book to stop the pages turning. 'The previous bit: messengers arriving would mean the knights would follow. That's exactly what happened. And we were left behind.'

'Nicholas knew they would come…but didn't tell us?'

'Yeah. Exactly.' Arun stood and held his head deep in thought. It was one thing to be abandoned, but being abandoned in the knowledge that danger headed their way left Arun sore-hearted. How dare he. Did Cole and Tej know? Arun paced around the room, trying to piece together the reasons for all these decisions that ultimately left him feeling they never cared for him on the Hill. He needed to know more. 'Why? Why didn't Nicholas mention it in his letter? Is there anything after that? Is there anything about them leaving?'

Malorie searched the last few pages. 'There's a note to someone named Claire and a drawing of a journey.' She turned to the last page. 'There's a message at the end, but it's called 'A Crown for the Queen'. Shall I read it?'

Arun nodded, still pacing.

'Days are numbered. No word for a while, and without information, we are vulnerable; a herd of headless deer. Kate is reaching her potential. I will need to take her to Aerkin and end him once and for all. She will be our saviour. Then I can be in peace. Must feed the horses. Title: Plan B. Find and select someone new to create a new group of warriors to defeat Aerkin should we fail. Should perhaps right my wrongs, be driven by a strong heart and good moral intention rather than revenge. Leave suit with them, and hope for a better future. This is the final page, and fittingly, the final message.'

Plan B? Arun considered the meaning of these notes intently. He couldn't shake the feeling of annoyance at not having been told these details before their departure. 'I'm starting to think these Hillfolk are a group of heartless warmongerers rather than honest friends. I mean, I didn't even know them that long, so why am I surprised?'

'Maybe they didn't tell you because it would change what you did. Nicholas is really, really smart.' Malorie closed the book. 'We are honest. At least, I think we are. I am.' The roles had momentarily reversed in their relationship. Arun returned to a seated position, head down, lost.

'It doesn't change what you have to do,' said Malorie. 'We're here now. And tomorrow we're going home. Nothing in the book will change that. So we just keep going on our way.'

'But it's just strange. Telling me all this would only have made me better prepared. We'd be safer. I just worry there's more I don't know.'

'You shouldn't worry about things you can't change.'

'Easier said than done.' Arun paused, then chuffed. 'You're quite smart, huh.'

'I know, I have to be,' replied Malorie, curling up on the floorboards. She turned away and rested her head on her hands. 'Everyone on the Hill was always really nice to me. I'm sure they were just as nice to you too.' Malorie left the candle to burn on a broken plate. 'Goodnight, Arun.'

Arun closed his eyes, but tiredness didn't sweep him. He sat, deep in thought, awaiting another sunless morning.

*

That night, the thunder roared more intensely than it ever had, and the lightning only ever stopped to take a deep breath, striking the lands with ferocious consistency. Arun's sleep was disturbed, not just by the weather, the hard floorboards, nor even the friendly rats; to a scavenger, they had no choice but to be friends with the ravenous rodents.

But it was in this sleep, Arun found himself, without warning, capsized deep into an endless pit of water. It soon seeped away, and he found his footing on a boat. Wind and water crashed with chaotic force, and the seas were unforgiving. Hanging on to a railing, he looked ahead and noticed Matuu holding Serr. She'd created a shield at the front of the boat, but a wave of water made its way around the shield and swarmed Arun, drenching his vision. Wiping the wet away, he opened his eyes to see Nicholas beside him, with a large beam of light leaving his hands, breaking through Serr's shield and separating a monstrous wave. He reached out his arm, though it wasn't his. It belonged to a woman. He knew these gloves, too, for they belonged to Kate.

'Arun. Wake up,' said Malorie. A nudge rocked Arun's arm.

Arun jolted into life, drawn to his hands, with his back fixed to the wall. The dream felt so real that he struggled to adjust his bearings for a few seconds.

Malorie continued to try and snatch Arun's attention away from the dream. 'Arun. Come on. It's nearly morning. We should probably go.'

'Right. Yeah, of course,' stumbled Arun, searching the room. 'Hey, have you ever had a dream that you were someone else?'

'Let me see. I've had a dream that I was a princess, and I slayed the dragon on the Hill and saved everyone. It was still me, though. So no.' Great story. Arun dusted himself clean as Malorie draped her bag over her shoulder. 'Come on. We should probably go before she wakes up.'

The two made their way back into the stable by tiptoe as the calmer morning rain fell. The dogs were nowhere to be seen nor heard, and no candlelight reflected in the windows, so the path was clear. Malorie mentioned she'd ridden a horse many times before, so she took the lead as Arun uncomfortably joined behind her. He could just about see over her head, making the perfect seat for a scouting passenger. However, the lumpy saddle looked to have been repaired a thousand times before and left Arun feeling an embarrassing discomfort between his legs. How did people do this all the time?

'Hold your horses,' Malorie giggled. She tapped the horse, and it trotted out through the open stable doors.

Leaving the stable, Arun looked to the house one last time. His heart froze. Three figures stood by the door, only twenty metres away: three of the Aerkin Knights. They stood rigid, tall, draped in black cloaks, dull grey armour, and holding menacing unlit weapons. They wore dark masks, each slightly different in shape from the other, and they all stared directly back at the two sitting atop the horse. Arun could almost feel them. Their clenching fists. Their tilting heads. To them, Arun and Malorie must have looked like innocent farmers going for a ride. But there was no time to be wasted and no caution to withhold. They needed to flee.

'Go!' Arun instinctively kicked the horse into action as Malorie stayed speechless. He watched in fearsome awe as one of the knights turned back to kick the door from its hinges. The horse sped away, throwing Arun's head back forwards. He relied on his ears now, and all he could hear, as the sounds of galloping hooves and drizzling rain faded in his mind, was the sound of two protective, barking dogs and their wails as they were put to sleep. A scream soon followed, but the two were too far gone now, and they could barely hear it.

'Keep going. All the way west. Just go home. Don't stop. Just keep going. Just keep going.' Arun's choppy words were all he could say to a frightened Malorie and himself. He didn't know what else to say, nor did he fancy doing much more talking. The two stayed silent as the galloping hooves went on and on, ahead of a tower of smoke rising high behind them.

CHAPTER SIXTEEN

ALONE: PART I

On the fourth day from home, the first foot from the Hillfolk group arrived on the Mainland shore, or rather a rocky coastline with waves crashing into it; Kate had swum to the closest bit of land she could find. Wary that the scouts on land would be packing their belongings as fast as possible, Kate discarded her safety, energised her gloves, and latched onto the first rock the waves crashed into. Her shivering body spread against the hard rock like a crab, under heavy fire from the rain. She climbed the gradual incline, using her daggers to latch into steeper rock like a pair of pickaxes.

Unaware if the scouts had spotted her leaving the boat, Kate approached level ground, crouched with caution. There they stood, four men not more than thirty metres away, dismantling shredded and patched-up canvas tents, with three horses tied to poles further ahead.

Was splitting from the group a sane idea? Kate would always find clarity when alone, but that was in the safety of the hills back home. She didn't know what to expect out here, but neither did she around Nicholas and his growing list of confusing decisions. There was no time to think about turning back. Kate had only one immediate motive in her head: stop the scouts. But as her feet graced the Mainland, her stomach lifted with the feeling of being one step closer to seeing Iris.

Kate slowly approached as the men faced away, preoccupied with packing.

As she stalked within ten metres, the corner of her eye caught another man appearing from the right, tying up his trousers with some loose string. He spotted her and stopped. Kate stopped. Everyone stopped.

'Vilintrus!' shouted the man, a word unknown to Kate. She ignited her daggers instinctively and regained her posture. The other men, flailing, picked up whatever weapons were by their side. Metal poles, blunted knives, and rusty old tools were now held in the air aggressively pointed at her. Rain continued to smother the land. Kate's daggers illuminated the rain around her like two orbs of blue light, and her long, dark brown hair drenched across her face. She made the first move.

She ran to the man standing alone, who swung a pole wildly in her direction, keeping her at bay. Kate's approach showed overzealous naivety as she momentarily forgot her training, without the safety of the Hillfolk to fall back on. Her heart beat like the rain. Right foot, left—left foot, forward. The others moved to form a circle around her, but she backed away and gave herself space behind, almost cornered in all forward directions by these men of the Mainland. Attacking as an underdog would be foolish, so she defended and counter-attacked. Slowly stepping back towards the rocky coastline, and with the stormy seas behind her, she raised her daggers to her face, and the light bounced off her cursed eyes.

Kate dropped momentarily as the earth shook beneath the battle. An earthquake rumbled, the first she'd felt on foreign land. A glance back to the cliff edge brought caution as stone and rock collapsed from its perch.

'We'll skin you alive,' grunted one of the scouts. Kate gritted her teeth in reply, rising back to steady ground.

One scout leapt forward, swiping with a knife. Kate dodged the attack and sliced back, avoiding a pole stabbing her from the side. She swung her arm around and cut a quarter off the length of the pole. Another leapt forward, and she managed to slash the man's arm, but not before he had grazed hers with his blunted blade. Kate's first real fight had started against her plans.

The cautious battle continued as the rain fell: the third army. Nobody dared move out of turn, lest it be the end of them. Kate avoided attack after attack and drew slashes of blood from the men, but nothing fatal. A highly skilled warrior in training, her nerves at being on the Mainland and alone in a real fight were far too distracting. Battling along the small cliff edge and dancing on wet rock and patches of muddy grass, Kate finally took control, slicing the hand off a knife-wielder and cutting the metal pole down to the measly efficacy of a feather.

Adrenaline pumped through Kate's veins. The daggers she wielded turned a shade of yellow. She fuelled herself with confidence and gained strength as the battle continued, outnumbered but not overpowered by these simple scouts. A grimace turned to a grin. Roaring with a release of energy, she slashed a scout to the ground with a fatal swipe, and another soon followed. A solemn second was all the world could allow her, thinking about the lives she had just taken; the second and third time a human had its life ended at her hands. One solemn second. Any more, and she'd be next to follow them.

Two scouts remained, although one chose to flee to the horses leaving a single remaining scout to face Kate's full attention. He seemed to notice something in her face as she lunged forward. He narrowly avoided her and stabbed his tool through Kate's left shoulder. She screamed in agony at the incising pain of a wound for the first time. The pain was sharp and numbing, throbbing and blistering all simultaneously. The tool wasn't entirely in, but deep enough that the light in her arm on that side faded; Kate now relied on one dagger, and the scout was unarmed.

Enraged, Kate let out a monstrous scream as the rain pelted her eyes. She threw the tool to the floor and lunged again with no fear. The scout soon followed the same path as the tool he wielded, bloodied and motionless in the mud.

Kate had no time to check her wound as she chased after the last man who flailed anxiously in his attempts to untie his horse. As she reached him, he narrowly escaped her grasp on horseback, but a rope lay loose on the ground, still tied to the horse. She picked it up in a hurry as it unravelled, screaming in anguish towards the palm of her hand, turning it yellow. With all her energised might, she pulled back as hard as she could to send the horse stumbling to the ground. The rope in her hand was scorched. Letting go, she screamed through her throat, with her lips slammed shut, the pain doubling through her ignited hands.

Kate heard the scout's anguish and turned to see the man's legs bending in unnatural directions as he crawled to safety. She hurried over and stepped on one of his broken legs, producing an almighty scream. 'Don't want to have to kill an unarmed man, so tell me you won't go speaking of this to anyone.' Quite selflessly, in a time of chaos, she had given the enemy a chance to escape and change his ways. She wouldn't lower herself to their level.

The man turned with a grin, trying valiantly to hide his pain as Kate towered above him. 'I'll tell them all. Prellundis Aerkin. Prellundis Uma besin.'

The second half of his statement made no sense to Kate. She was unfamiliar with the Mainland language, but the name 'Aerkin' said everything she needed to know. This man looked proud to announce his intentions, and he also looked resigned to death. He left her with only one option—regrettably.

'So be it.' Kate closed her eyes and looked away. She cleared her mind of worries. The scout made one last incoherent statement before Kate cut his throat swiftly, giving him a quick death.

Kate gagged. She couldn't work out if her mind had tricked her or if the man's blood beneath her had the smell of burning rust. It was sickly, and Kate avoided looking down to see the fatal wound. She battled with herself, urging her to assess her damage and the lives she had just taken. "You'll endure a steep learning curve after your first battle," Nicholas would always say. However, she made her way back without gifting a look to the man as the injured horse trotted away in the opposite direction. She thought of an excuse. No use examining the dead; they posed no threat without a breath.

Upon untying the rope of a remaining horse, a cry escaped from the bushes. Kate steadily approached with a dagger of light in hand and noticed the scream belonged to a baby. Kate pulled back the bushes protecting the cries and saw a young couple cradling a baby, rocking back and forth, trying to hush its cries. The young woman looked up, with tears in her eyes, scared and helpless, as the man, muddied and unarmed, hunched his neck into his shoulders in trepidation.

Kate's light faded as she knelt to greet the family. The baby's gleaming eyes softened her racing heart, and the anger she retained from the fight started to drain. She looked to the man for answers. 'You speak my language?'

'Yes,' replied the man. 'We innocent. Don't hurt baby. Please'

'What's your intention here? Why are you with those scouts?'

'They burnt hut and kept us. We didn't know where to go. Please don't hurt baby. Please.'

The woman remained silent with fear in her eyes, cradling the baby tighter in her arms.

'Brave to bring a passenger on this ride.' Kate stood up, accepting their fear as truth. All these years of training to fight gave nothing in preparation for handling innocent people and children. Kate relied on her instinct to guide her and left the family alone, but she found some loose material from the scout camp and handed it to them.

Kate rode on horseback, passing by the bushes and the huddled family. The mother scampered for the material to wrap around herself and keep her child warm whilst the man did nothing.

As Kate trotted off away from the coast, she questioned how the woman had acted; the woman seemed fearful even of the supposed father and leant away from his comfort. She held her baby slightly to the side, away from him rather than between the two. Perhaps it was nothing, and Kate knew nothing of parenthood, but she took one last look back at the family to ease her concerns. She turned, noticing the woman pushing the man away. His eyes met with Kate's. In a hurry, he sprinted to untie the last horse. A scout, it must have been, hiding in innocence and awaiting his moment to escape.

Kate stormed back against the flow of wind and rain, catching up to the man just as he had jumped on the horse and kicked off. She chased, keeping close in tow, but her horse couldn't catch up far enough for her to reach the man with her dagger. She fixated on catching him, releasing a short shout of frustration, not towards him.

The rider rode east, past a tilted sign that pointed conveniently to Rennes. Frustrated in chase, she couldn't let this man go free. 'Stop!' she shouted, knowing her fruitless effort was the only other thing she could do. She checked the bag attached to the saddle to see if she could find a weapon to throw, but it contained nothing but fruit peel and, for reasons she needn't know, teeth. All Kate could do was ride on.

*

Much time had passed, and Kate had fallen further behind as the horses tired. Thanks to the rains passing and the air clearing, the man rode still in sight. Now and again, he would turn around to monitor their distance. A ruthless and aggressive stare replaced the cowering and lame face she had first seen.

The riders passed through a field of gigantic, fallen wind turbine structures smothered in weeds. Trees partitioned each small field, making it difficult to see too far ahead, but it would likely be more plain fields and rubble. They rode alongside bushes where the twigs carried little green, scarcer than any she'd ever seen, and the fields were far muddier. The old roads were worse off than back home, covered in more weeds and mud than concrete. Some sections were submerged completely. The Mainland seemed a much harsher land but not as decimated as Kate had imagined. Perhaps the decimation lay more inland.

Humans had also made their mark on this landscape. Kate witnessed large spikes of wood scattered around in the following field, emerging from the ground. Attached to these were bodies hanging upside down. Wire and rope held their legs together near the top, and their arms hung unbound at the bottom. There were no blood, wounds, nor scars. How awful her own species could be.

The warmest part of the day arrived later, though the difference in temperatures between night and day didn't vary much these days, certainly not enough to remove one's cloak. The horses reduced their canter to a trot, with the man now far in the distance. He was, however, leaving the muddy fields behind and entering collapsed walls and ruins. These ruins looked a lot smaller than any of the town-of-sorts Kate had seen closer to home. Large puddles of brown water dominated the green. Perhaps an old village once lay here. Some of the broken stone walls held unlit torches, and so life may have been present, but she could not risk letting the man escape, not even down dangerous paths.

A few minutes after, Kate had reached the same ruins by way of a single mud path that looked to run directly through to the other end of the ruins. She'd lost track of the rider but soon spotted the horse he rode tied to a broken fence; it had the same white and black pattern. Kate dismounted, wide-eyed, focused, and not bothering to tie her horse up. As she walked towards the man's horse, the stone and brick walls stood taller; some looked as if they had plastic and metal roofs. These makeshift buildings were clearly in use. Ahead were two more parallel paths; there must have been twenty to thirty decimated buildings in all.

Turning a corner, Kate ignited her right hand and attempted to ignite her left. A sharp pain ran up her arm at first, but she bore it and strained to force another blue glow into existence. She froze to listen for any movement and was rewarded with the sound of hurried footsteps running through puddles, ending in an audible splash. Kate set off in chase, turning into a small gap between broken walls. She found the man fallen, drenched in a deep puddle, removing a brick from the wall parallel. Rather than throw it as expected, he pulled out a metal container from the wall, which Kate presumed contained a weapon. He dropped the key he juggled in his scattered palms into the puddle. Congratulations, Mainlander, for hours spent riding here had now been rendered fruitless.

Kate approached the man as he scurried backwards in a crawl, forgoing the key and holding onto his ankle. She pinned his arms down as he tried to resist, his ears submerged in the puddle, but he couldn't match the strength of Kate's energised hands to push himself back up. Not too tight, else his arms would melt away.

'Where are we?' asked Kate.

'You're done for now.' The fallen man burst into hysterical laughter as his body splashed left to right under Kate's pressure. 'Dead! Dead, dead, dead. He'll cleanse your sins and burn your bones.'

Kate added a slight clench to her grip, which sent an immense burning pain into the man's arms, causing him to scream aloud.

'Tell me. Who else is here?' demanded Kate.

The man spat in her face and screeched, and in return, received a dagger of light into the side of his neck. Kate looked away as the man drew his last breath, clenching her teeth but not closing her eyes, as her light vanished still within his body. She placed the back of her wrist to her nose in anticipation of the smell.

Kate had forgone taking a breath since she pinned the man. She let out a massive sigh of anguish, still avoiding eye contact with the body. However, the day was fast becoming relentless for her. A child ran across the path ahead, leaving her no time to reflect nor rest. How many people were here? She hurried to her feet and ran to the end of the path. Turning left, she saw no child; nothing but village ruins.

CHAPTER SEVENTEEN

ALONE: PART II

Trudging along various paths through the ruins, Kate listened for any sign of movement. She found herself on an old road, concentrating on her footing amongst the cracks. One significant gap ran through the centre and opened up to the depths of the Earth.

A faint, intermittent humming rose from the silence in the distance ahead. Kate drew nearer, realising the hum carried the melody of a deep chant; it sounded as unclear as day, sung in a foreign language, but that didn't halt her tread.

'Medin. Entin. For Uma,
Medin. Entin. For health,
Medin. Entin. For dachi,
Medin. Entin. For nachi,
Sosinon i retnis, sosinon!'

The chant repeated, sedated bar the final line sung with a shout. Kate found herself in front of two doors, one slightly ajar, as the sound escaped from within. As with the other makeshift doors and walls scattered around, these were chipped and decaying, overgrown with weeds. Kate spotted the child, now far down the road to her right, looking at her, not moving a muscle. He seemed joyous, almost playful. He scampered behind a wall and out of view.

Kate turned her attention back to the door, pushing it open slightly, spotting men and women sitting on the floor, their chanting continuing. Although it was afternoon, heavy clouds dimmed the skies, and an abundance of torches brought light to the room. A dim ray of light glistened through, so Kate squeezed her head in rather than bring further attention to the outside light.

A man knelt towards the front of the room, wearing a gold and red robe. He faced the front, looking up upon a statue built of scrap material. Kate couldn't understand the chant but could undoubtedly see the word 'Aerkin' written on the statue's base. The chant stopped.

'Aerkin, show us light,' recited the man at the front. 'Show us warmth. Follow in your words, we will, and reward us with the returning sun. Sosinon i retnis. Prellundis Aerkin.'

'Prellundis Aerkin,' chanted the rest in repeat.

Kate watched on with a mix of fear and fascination. These people were genuinely misguided to believe Aerkin would bring the sun's return. Her fear ran dominant as the fleeing child appeared, running out at the front of the room to stand by the statue in plain view of the crowd. He pointed to Kate.

Kate didn't move, but the hairs on her body stood. The obedient crowd followed the man at the front in turning towards the back of the room. They stood one by one on the spot, waiting, perhaps for instruction.

'We have a visitor,' said the man in a welcoming manner. His words were calmly carried by the wind and left no harsh tone to Kate's ears. He looked to be middle-aged but with clean-shaven skin and even cleaner clothes. 'Are you a child of Aerkin?'

In trepidation, Kate retreated two steps to the outside path, leaving the door further ajar.

'No, no, no,' said the man. 'Do not fear. You *are* indeed a child of Aerkin, as are we all. Come all. Let's greet our new daughter.'

The crowd of thirty or so filtered outside from the room into the natural light, peacefully smiling at Kate. She found herself in the middle of the broken road with the crowd curved in front of her, leaving a gap for the man to announce himself in clearer vision. He ran his hand through his thick, silver hair, sweeping it back. His tilting smile and poised face were as welcoming as his words.

'Aerkinism can offer you so much,' said the man. 'Come, child, join me. I am Rillen, one of many eyes and ears, and this is our Shrinetown.' The man going by the name of Rillen held his hand out. As he did, so too the others, standing as if they were in a photograph.

Kate pondered the result of igniting her daggers and going to war with thirty people. They weren't armed, but they'd swarm her. It would be best to take her time and leave when the moment presented itself. None in the crowd looked to her hands, a likely sign they didn't know the power in her gloves. They stared into her eyes, rarely blinking, all smiling, some with bright red ears, some coughing. They didn't seem at all well.

'Come,' said Rillen, still holding his arm out. 'Listen to one of our sermons.'

'In a rush,' replied Kate. 'If you could remind me of which way is east, I'll be on my way.'

'Rush?' Rillen laughed. 'There is no rush in this world. We only seek the reborn light in the sky. Until then, we pray. There is no wait.'

'Sorry,' maintained Kate, beginning to back away. 'Not the praying sort.'

'I suppose you'd rather keep those gloves a secret,' shouted Rillen before returning to a calm state with a smile on his face. 'My child.'

Kate ignited her gloves reluctantly. Those in the crowd gasped and turned to one another. Their reaction was that of those who hadn't seen dark energy before, but Rillen looked as if he had. At first, he didn't say a word. He simply stared into the glow of the gloves. His eyes widened, and his bottom lip curled in beyond his pearly teeth.

'I see.' Rillen took a deep breath to think. 'So violence is your only retort? How primitive.' Rillen, with his soft tone, turned to speak to his followers. 'Relax, my children. This is precisely what Aerkinism prepares us for. Those who have stolen the light will seek to steal our land and forever steal the sun. We must be strong in our will. And show them a more peaceful way. Only then can we return the light to Aerkin. And he will return the light to our skies.'

'Prellundis Aerkin,' chanted the group again, reviving their focus and dedication.

'Stolen?' Kate, exasperated, clenched her daggers. If they were blades of steel, they would have cut her hands in two by now. Sharp pain from her wound brought discomfort, but for only a second. 'Nothing natural belongs to one man.'

'In the eyes of Aerkin, we are all his. So return us the light, and he will greatly reward you.'

'There's nothing you can give me, and the only thing I can give you is death,' replied Kate without remorse. Her frustration grew, rotating her left shoulder. Her body, in its entirety, ached from the day's events. Patience grew thin.

'Death. Yes.' Rillen put his hands behind his back and looked to the skies, walking forward. 'We are aware of the glorious death that awaits us. To live amongst the stars, become one with the light and energy, and join as an extension of Aerkin himself. There is only one higher reward. To bring Aerkin the gift of light, in this life rather than the next.' Rillen lowered his gaze back down to Kate. 'You will conform. Just as Iris did.' His blank stare slowly turned into a smile, with his lips pressed together.

'What did you say?' Kate's light grew stronger, turning yellow in her uninjured arm, as her frustration stepped aside for a fit of raging anger. Kate, before, would have given him a painless death.

Rillen stood in the centre of the road to match Kate, and his followers soon surrounded him, forming a barrier from wall to wall across the path. 'That is why you are here, is it not, my child? It is what Aerkin predicted would come to pass.'

'Have you taken her?' replied Kate, the anger now blunting her words.

'For that information, you must grant us the light. In the name of Aerkin.'

'Prellundis Aerkin,' chanted the group on cue.

Kate marched towards the group.

'Nuh, uh, uh,' cautioned Rillen. 'We can still offer you a genuine deal.'

'Where is she?' repeated Kate, pausing her advance. As she stopped, a man appeared behind her, leading the horse that the scout rode in on. He held a blunted knife to its throat.

'Don't concern yourself with that,' said Rillen, watching as Kate turned to the sound of the neighing horse. 'You won't escape without your horse. The deal is simple. Give us the gloves, and we'll give you Iris's hands.'

Kate ignited her daggers, turning back to Rillen. She stormed forward purposefully and without fear, causing the group to scurry.

'My children, don't panic,' announced Rillen, calm and assured. 'Aerkin's glory awaits.'

A few brave men and women edged forward before one ran towards Kate screaming. He left her with no time to think. She cut him down in an instant but didn't watch his body crumble under the loss of life. It was a slight and swift action, but it brought her to pant. She clenched her jaw to hide her tremble and made her way towards the others. Three more tried to attack without weapons, but Kate cut through their limbs like butter. They stumbled to the ground in agony, maimed without the glory of death they sought.

Kate's clenched jaw couldn't hold back her panting as her nose breathed heavily, but again she didn't look at the fallen bodies. Others in the group picked up objects and rocks from the debris around. They stood still. One man hurled a large rock, but Kate pressed her arms together in front of her face. Her long gloves, stretching down her forearms, ignited and protected her head and chest, breaking the rock on impact. She advanced once more.

The horse neighed wildly behind Kate, bringing half of her attention. The captor had lost control of the hostage animal, and as Kate turned her head, he ended its life with a blade to the throat. It let out a cry as it bled, stopping Kate in her steps and sending her into a spiralling rage. She sprinted towards the man as fast as she could. He trembled with his blade held out towards her but stumbled over backwards. She heard a shout from behind but ignored it and stood on the man's arm with her blade facing him.

'I said, stop!' cried Rillen. 'I will give you information, but you must stop. His life is not yours to take.' Kate turned to see the advancing Rillen, stepping over the bodies of his injured and fallen followers as if they were rocks, as the unharmed ones stayed put.

The man Kate stood above was worth something to Rillen, unlike his many perishable followers. This whinging man had faltered and rewarded Kate with the leverage she desperately needed for answers.

'I am only one of Aerkin's many senses,' said Rillen. 'So I can only give you so much. Remove your leg from him, please.'

Kate removed her foot but took the man's blade, throwing it far into the debris. She stared back at Rillen intensely as she stood above the fallen man. 'Speak.'

The calm in his voice had disappeared. He trembled. 'We've known of this Iris for a long time. Aerkin has long been interested in following her movements. He instructed us to never capture or interfere with her. I lied about having her hands. He let her be, let her build up her small sinful revolution. If she ever stepped onto our land, we would only follow every step she took. She was our key to everything. Aerkin knew she would unwittingly give up the location of those who stole the light from us one day. And now, here you are. That's all I know.'

Kate felt the energy drain from her body, depleting her of all anger and focus. All that remained was a singeing disappointment as her light faded. Iris. The uprising. All hope gone. A journey for nothing.

'Please, let him go,' said Rillen. 'He's my son. He doesn't know better. I've told you everything. We've done nothing wrong. This is everything we have lived for—the return of the light. One half of the Aerkin prophecy has come true. The end is near, and none of what you're doing will matter anyway.'

Kate's piercing stare ruptured the air between Rillen and herself. No tears dropped from her unrested and bloodshot eyes.

'We know there are more of you,' said Rillen. 'The one that first stole the light: Servington. I can only advise you all to hand over the gloves and go back in peace. Aerkin will show you mercy.'

'And if I don't?' replied Kate, defeated but still unable to bend to this man's will.

'Aerkin will be your conclusion. He is the new, one God. It's impossible to think otherwise.' The rest of Rillen's followers surrounded him once more. 'Step away. Please.'

'I just wanted to make you proud, Papa,' came the voice beneath Kate. 'I'm sorry, Papa.'

Kate wiped her eyes despite the dry tears. Her knees buckled on the brink of collapse with her teeth gritted. She couldn't let this stranger dictate her fate. She wouldn't accept Aerkin as her fate either, no matter how likely it now seemed. Rillen's words had done little to dissuade her. Her head began to shake, and her instinct pushed her to a place of pure rage. She lost control of her feelings. This was it. This truly was the end. And everyone was coming with her. She looked down to the man cowering beneath, ignited her gloves, and drove them through his heart.

'No!'

A scream of agony released from Rillen's whimpering mouth. Seven brave followers roared to a stampeding ambush. Kate turned to them with blades of blue and yellow in a flush of fury, forgetting the pain in her shoulder, wildly slicing at anything and anyone she could see approaching. Rocks and sticks pelted her, but her overwhelming anger pushed her into the oncoming attackers, cutting limb from limb. None of the followers restrained from their attack, throwing themselves at Kate. A woman threw a punch, blocked by Kate's glove, burning their hand. It would have felt like punching a wall of lava.

Kate kicked the woman back and swiped the others down, fraying their clothes and flaying their skin. Nothing but a handful of sacrificed lambs lay by her feet within seconds, writhing in pain. She spat to clear her mouth, standing sprayed in their blood.

The others in the group had seen enough. They dropped their debris and fled. Only one fanatic remained alive and standing tall. 'You will kneel before him!' screamed Rillen, finally losing control. 'You will beg for forgiveness, and he will give nothing in return.'

Kate stood gasping for air as her light faded. The pain in her shoulder returned, piercing through her adrenaline. She heard the cries of fallen foes around her but didn't look down. Instead, she walked over to Rillen and struck him to the ground with the back of her glove. She stood over him, not knowing herself what her next move would be, as he looked up at her, dazed.

'Prellundis Aerkin,' stuttered Rillen.

Kate knelt and grabbed him by his hair. 'Where…is…Iris?'

'You thieves thought you were going to meet her, didn't you?' Rillen's words came swift and slurred. 'She's long gone, on her way to Aerkin. He will pass his judgement. If you make it in time, she might still be in one piece.'

Kate ignited a dagger and held it close to Rillen's neck.

'No, no, no,' squirmed Rillen. 'Please don't kill me. No! I surrender. I don't want to die. Please.' The blade shook millimetres from his skin. 'Servington's sins have cost us all. They're now your sins. I'm defenceless. Please.'

All it took was a blade to his neck. A man who'd persuaded his followers to die for their cause had turned against it the second his life was threatened. There were no mentions of Aerkin—just a man showing his true self. He deserved a painful death.

'Don't do it, please. I'll help you. I won't tell anyone.' Rillen paused, mouth wide open. His eyes spoke next. He'd accepted his fate.

Kate cut Rillen's throat without debating the nature of his surrender. She didn't look away, eyes stretched, watching as his life ended. The sound of him trying to speak as the blood left his throat didn't break her. There'd been many deaths on this day; some attributed to nerves and others to skill. This was the first death Kate would attribute to satisfaction.

It was all over. As rain fell in full force, all that moved beneath were a handful of writhing bodies on the floor, and the unharmed child, running away into the distance with the top half of a teddy bear.

Kate stepped over bodies and roamed through the so-called Shrinetown. The dark sky had not yet started to set, but this day had already taken more than a full Earth's cycle from her. She stood alone and truly lost, in direction and her mind. Rain washed away the blood upon her; the only useful thing the world had provided to Kate on this day.

Kate sat in the middle of the road beside the crevice and stared into the distance. She contemplated Aerkin's intentions and intelligence seriously. Before, she had only Nicholas's words to base her thoughts on. He made Aerkin seem chaotic and the destroyer of a decaying world. However, Rillen had given Aerkin a sense of strategy, planning, and guile. This was no longer about merely igniting their gloves and attacking all in their way; this had become far more thought-provoking and tactical than Kate had mentally prepared for.

Her fingers drew the name 'Iris' in the dirt. Iris could be anywhere, and it was perhaps foolish to take one madman's word for it, but she couldn't shake the overwhelming sadness that had been plaguing her since the group left the Hill. The feeling Iris had walked back into her life only to have her taken back just as swiftly. Iris could be anywhere by now. Home or Mainland. Dead or alive. Not knowing was the worst feeling of all, bringing her eyes to water and her fingers clenching into a fist through the dirt. She loved Iris more than she could ever know.

Kate wiped the name from the dirt and looked left then right, wondering which direction to go. She could accept the group's fate and return home, perhaps arriving in time to save Arun and the Hill. Or she could accept home was no longer safe, and the only real journey led to the unknown Ruins of Rennes. She got up and wandered forward, for now, head down and in no particular direction, leaving the ruins behind.

Finding herself alone with her thoughts for the first time, Kate meandered, with no chatter surrounding her and no immediate threat to tackle. Only the open Mainland fields were ahead of her now. However, one distraction would appear in the form of a horse with a saddle, roaming free; it looked to be the horse Kate rode in on. It munched on a patch of grass beside a muddy tree, head down, with one eye wide open. Kate felt a glimmer of hope and cautiously approached the steed, stroking it and brushing its hair with the palm of her glove. Nature had saved her, not for the first time in her life. Mounting the horse, Kate set off at a slow trot in whichever direction the path took her.

Night arrived on the Mainland, and Kate had found shelter by a group of dense trees. She had to keep herself slightly aware, as two Mainland scavengers, although keeping to themselves, were nearby conversing; they occasionally looked over at Kate as they spoke. If only they spoke English. Thunder also plagued her ears, and she lay back against a cold, thick tree and fluttered her sleepy eyes.

Kate cast her mind to the night before—a dream on the boat she finally had time to think about. It wasn't her usual dream-turned-nightmare of burning buildings, but a dream where she imagined roaming in a room she'd never been, wearing gloves she'd never worn: Iris's gloves. Boxes filled the room, also containing Nicholas's suit. A coincidence, perhaps, considering Nicholas didn't have his suit when she awoke. Just a dream.

In her sleepless state, Kate spread her arms to her side and smeared them in the muddy grass before rubbing them across her cheeks and forehead. The two scavengers turned away, undoubtedly confused by her actions. She tilted her head back and whispered a song she would often sing whilst laying alone in the fields, looking to the night sky.

'I search beyond the moon glow,
I search beyond the cloud.
I fight against the city light, the atmospheric shroud.
To find the stars that wander,
To find aurora green,
But my reflection of this world is all I've ever seen.'

CHAPTER EIGHTEEN

THE WESTERN SHORE

*A*DE 6—*Daylight is back to normal under cloudy conditions. Direct sunlight is still blocked, but mild warmth can be felt on some days. Many summers have passed since the last pollinating insects were seen on the Hill.*

Rain starts to fall with consistency. Brown trout, water, and some rarely found fruits and vegetables are the only sources of sustenance. The remaining humans become weaker, most likely due to lack of nutrients from the ground and the sky.

Wild dogs begin to roam on their own. They are difficult to find despite evolved domestication. They are in constant fear of everything, including their former masters.

I design three pairs of gloves for the military group based on their archery request to test my Elast composition. This proves successful, and their leader, Zachenne, is tasked with training archers.

Future revision to ADE 6—The Mainland Temple begins construction in the mountains, consisting of a palace and an arena. He is revelling in a world devoid of modern comforts.

ADE 7 to 9—pages missing

*

The group of twenty-four approached the Mainland's western shore as the afternoon arrived. The weather had been tolerable since they moved south, although the winds were still heavy. Nicholas, searching his map for a route, indicated a beach bay up ahead would be the perfect landing spot. He and the others were rightly apprehensive after the journey they had endured, and the life that was lost at sea, but one man standing beside Nicholas, Zachenne, seemed calmer than any other.

'I have something to ask of you in Kate's absence,' said Nicholas to Zachenne. 'Your leadership traits have proven far more important than I anticipated throughout our journey. Away from the Hill, I do not possess the calmness under pressure and direct approach that you hold.'

'Your leadership is invaluable; you can ask anything of me,' said Zachenne.

'You care deeply for those in your subset and always take their best interests to heart, but you also know how to lead and demand more from them. I suppose what I am trying to say is that I would like your assistance in rallying the others, without my direction, especially in times of danger.'

'Whatever you ask. I'm honoured just to be fighting alongside you, friend.' Zachenne confirmed his new role by Nicholas's side with a handshake. Nicholas had never seen him raise a smile, nor did he now.

Nicholas looked back to the ocean as the boat pulled closer to the beach. He did not expect to see anything, certainly no other boats, a floating body, or Kate swimming back to rejoin the group, but he could not help but look. Zachenne nudged him to break his stare. He turned to see a man waving towards them on the beach, flailing his arms wildly as if welcoming long lost friends home.

'We should take caution,' said Zachenne, with Matuu joining Nicholas and Zachenne at the head of the boat. 'I fear no one is truly alone out here.'

'Agreed,' replied Nicholas, rearranging his meagre belongings in his bag for the journey ahead. 'Matuu, bring the Guards to the front of the boat. I will fetch Serr.'

Nicholas headed below deck and found Serr sitting beside Jordan, tending to his wound. They had spare cloth to use as bandages but nothing else. A sheet of metal melted by energised hands covered the holes in the hull.

'We need your presence up top,' said Nicholas.

Jordan, looking sorry for himself, began to stand.

'No, relax, Jordan. Stay here and rest. You will have to continue as you are, at the mercy of your body's natural healing.' Nicholas gestured to Serr and held the door open. Serr made her exit after a considered rub of Jordan's arm as Nicholas observed Jordan briefly. 'Your confidence seems as shot as your arm.'

'It had to be my right arm,' said Jordan. 'What if I can't shoot as well as I used to?'

'Your wound will heal if you take care of it.' Nicholas sat next to Jordan, who placed his head in his hands. 'Jordan, you are a brave part of this group. But do not let the past few days damage your belief. Perhaps it is a steep learning curve for you to find the balance between confidence and arrogance.'

Jordan said nothing in return.

'I expected as much,' said Nicholas. 'Take care of your ego, my friend.'

Jordan remained below deck, holding the same sorry posture. Nicholas returned to receive the Mainland's welcome.

The boat reached as far as it could, still a few metres from wet sand, and so the group disembarked one by one.

'Remember everyone,' announced Nicholas, his final words before touching foreign land. 'Mosquitoes could equal Dengtu. Dengtu could equal death.'

'So, everything here wants to kill us,' said Matuu. 'Easy. I've survived Australia.'

The beach stretched far left and right but not far deep, reaching a cliff edge covered in chalky white and brown rock as if the sands were climbing towards the sky. On leaving the boat, the group pulled their legs through the water, rushing to touch dry land a day after setting sail.

'I guess this is it, wise, old man,' said Denis. Nicholas frowned, hearing 'old'.

'Looks like you're heading inland, and we're taking the coast south,' said Emitai.

'Yes, my friends,' replied Nicholas. 'I would wish you luck, but you have already travelled these lands enough. I am sure you will return unscathed.'

'When this is over, you can all visit us!' said Emitai. 'Our ma makes a perfect barbeque. You won't ever have a better meal in your life.' Denis and Emitai winced.

'Uh. He means if you make it back,' said Denis. 'Not if, sorry, you will make it back.'

'Sorry, the whole sacrifice thing. Never mind.'

Nicholas smiled at the two. 'I will accept your words loosely, my friends. I do not doubt the great taste of your family food. Save a large plate for this belly.'

The man on the beach made his way to the waterfront to meet the tide that brought the overseas travellers. Removing his hood, he appeared ecstatic, with a grin that only Cole could match. 'Greetings!' he declared.

'Greetings indeed,' replied Nicholas. 'I was unaware we would be expecting a solo welcoming party.'

'I am a deliverer, a part of the Mainland uprising,' the strange man replied ecstatically, almost as instantly as Nicholas finished his sentence. 'I am to lead you to the base. We have been eagerly awaiting your arrival.'

Nicholas searched deep in the unmoved eyes of the man to judge his intentions. His long, unwashed hair flowed in the wind, and his nose and teeth all came to sharp points. His hands were twitching by his side. The tune Nicholas would whistle in his head disappeared as his heart started to beat a little faster. His suspicions grew. *Be wary, Nicholas.* 'I believe we came to this shore quite by chance. How did you know we would arrive here?'

The deliverer offered another quick-fire response. 'We were very precise. Please, follow me.'

Nicholas lowered two fingers from each fist beside him, consciously but naturally, to not draw suspicion. Zachenne and Serr, standing either side, were taught to be aware of this signal. With his boots still being washed by the tide, Nicholas offered a further query to the man. 'You mean to tell me, of all the many beaches on the Mainland, you chose to come here alone and wait for a group of strangers that may not have even been on their way?'

The man chuckled directly at Nicholas. He did not respond instantly this time, and the two stared at each other.

'I assume you are Nicholas Servington?' asked the deliverer.

'What else did Iris tell you?' said Nicholas, dropping another finger on each side, three in total now dangling.

'Not Iris.' The deliverer's smile and fake mask faded. 'You are kindly welcomed to the Mainland by my host: Aerkin.'

Every muscle in Nicholas's body tightened as the name grabbed hold of him.

'He wanted you to know one thing.' The deliverer leant forward and spoke a whisper. 'Enjoy your stay.' He reluctantly closed his eyes tight and lifted his right hand into the air. 'For his children.'

Nicholas dropped his little finger, and the signal was complete. Serr pulled in front of him and ignited her shield. The Guards pulled in on the left side and the Tarios on the right.

'Prellundis Aerkin,' whispered the deliverer through Serr's shield, his face barely visible.

The group saw a small line of flashes along the clifftop as a horde of bullets ambushed the group, followed by thundering gunshot blasts. Most hit Serr's shield, which had not fully covered the group yet. Nicholas turned. A Guard on the left side fell to the ground, and on the right side, Denis sank into the shallow sea. The deliverer, still whispering in prayer, was pierced by multiple bullets and fell into the shield. A splash of red lay on the shield before melting away, as the shield sparkled yellow with each shattering bullet.

'Denis!' screamed Emitai, tending to his brother and pulling him further in behind the shield, away from an expanding pool of red in the water.

'Link forward!' yelled Nicholas, instructing the group to link arms and move inland as one collective entity behind Serr's shield. The shield grew big enough to cover the group from the forward assault as Matuu raised Serr by the waist to ensure bullets couldn't reach over to the warriors trailing at the back. Matuu marched on, and with everyone linked, they pushed forward, passing over the deliverer's body. One of the Tarios held onto Emitai, who held onto Denis, pulling him up water and sand, with the fallen Guard dragging along the other side.

The bullets stalled in volume and dwindled to a halt as the shield remained unbreakable. The Tarios from the side leaned out and fired bolts of light to the cliff. One man suffered a direct hit and fell off the edge to the rocks on the beach perimeter. Back on her feet, Serr passed backwards through the group, shielding them from attacks above as they reached the bottom of the cliff. Nicholas spotted Jordan cowering at the rear, clinging onto others.

The silence after the barrage relaxed Nicholas, a sign their resources had already depleted. They would be easy to ambush without their ammunition once they could identify a path to the cliff edge.

'Where now?' Matuu asked Nicholas. 'We can't stay here.'

'Use your beam, Nicholas,' winced Jordan.

'That's too risky,' said a Guard. 'The cliff will collapse. 'Others began to throw questions in a panic.

'Somebody help! He's bleeding!' shouted Emitai aimlessly. His brother had been hit in the neck and was bleeding profusely; Emitai's hand could only prevent so much.

On the other side, the Guards tended to their fallen friend by attempting to safely cauterise the wound in his chest.

'I can see an incline and a gap over to the right,' said Zachenne. 'It's our only way up.'

An odd-sounding noise perked Nicholas's ears as if a large drop of water had dropped into a pool. A moving object whistled from above, followed by a split second of silence.

Suddenly, an explosion swarmed the top of the shield, bursting the groups' eardrums. Fire and smoke encapsulated them. Blinding sand blew in from the sides as they crouched for cover in unison.

Serr stood tall as the shield of dark energy held together with immense power, far beyond any human-made object. So powerful that the only effect from the explosion was for the shield to turn momentarily yellow on impact. Serr would not have felt as though anything had hit her hands, such was the strength of dark energy; she would have only suffered a slight warming sensation. She puffed her cheeks at Nicholas, easing his worries by a paper's width.

Nicholas shook his brain back into place. Various thoughts were swirling in his head, but he pushed them back to focus on a plan. 'To the right, link forward!' barked Nicholas, ordering his group along. The unit hurried right along the wall of the beach. No more gunshots were heard, but Emitai and a Marshal carried a motionless Denis forward whilst the injured Guard wheezed along on the other side.

Another deep, loud drop of water echoed. Not a second later, an explosion from behind the group propelled the ones at the rear forward, and a sandstorm unleashed itself under the shield. Emitai had to drag his brother from the floor, now uncovered, as the occasional bullet threw up the sand in an attempt to pick off any stragglers.

As the group moved forward, Serr's pace dropped, ensuring the shield could now cover the back of the group, too. They were almost domed, so the assault from above diminished once more.

'Halt,' ordered Nicholas as they reached the incline. He took a moment to check the rest of the group. Emitai had dropped to the floor, exhausted in anguish. The injured Guard took a seat to the right, holding above his left lung, coughing up blood.

'We should move up quickly,' said Zachenne from the front. 'Can the wounded walk?'

Emitai started to shout Denis's name in floods of tears. Others murmured.

Nicholas observed the panicked group as a ringing noise obscured his hearing. Screams somehow made their way above the noise into Nicholas's head. Serr held firm, her arms shaking, but stared into Nicholas's lips. Everyone awaited an order. Nicholas fretted, trying to keep his composure, but he could not; his heart raced at the idea of Aerkin being at the coastline. It would have meant the group's end if so, and such a thought ruptured Nicholas's state of mind. *Save them, Nicholas.* He kept Zachenne waiting and instead took back his focus with the only humane thing to do: he checked on his fallen Guard, whose face had now paled beyond his choking throat.

Emitai sat on the floor, trying to speak to his brother, as the Marshal carrying Denis caught Nicholas's glance and shook his head. Emitai couldn't hold back his tears as the others looked on. 'Please, Denis! Wake up! Please…'

Nicholas hurried over, devoid of thought and fraught with despair, as Emitai cried into his brother's chest. Nicholas didn't know where to turn. The Guards were now attempting to resuscitate their fallen companion after collapsing from his slump. Another barrage of gunshots belted against the shield.

'Denis,' cried Emitai. 'All this way. For nothing.'

'I am truly sorry young one,' consoled Nicholas for lack of words, his eyes scouting the cliff edge for danger. 'I promise you will suffer no same fate. I…we will get you home. But we must get going.'

Emitai crumbled on top of his brother. 'We travelled so far, Denis. Just us two. I refuse to let it be for nothing. I'll avenge you, Denis. They'll pay for this. I'll make them all pay!' Emitai slid from Denis's body in anguish and removed his resting hand from his brother's chest.

'Nicholas, this is no time to talk,' repeated Zachenne, urging motion. 'We need to move.'

Nicholas again checked Serr's expression to see her jawline strained. 'Group, we can mourn soon. We need to gain height. Tarios, take the edge of the path up. I will be behind.'

Jordan sped into action past Nicholas, ignoring his earlier advice of taking rest; he rushed forward with the Tarios. They approached the top of the cliff, each monitoring every direction in sight. Reaching the highest ground, they were greeted by men attempting to fire on them. A Tarios bolt pierced the heart of one, and the other found himself out of ammunition before fleeing; a bolt picked him off not long into his sprint for safety. Nicholas maintained his position at the back, looking on.

Green grass and bush covered the top of the cliff. The group could see far along the ridge as another man appeared from behind one of the bushes, holding what appeared to be a large pipe. The man raised it to rest on his shoulder. Before he made another move, a bolt of Tarios light struck him down.

Nicholas urged the others up as the Tarios finished removing the hostiles. Suddenly, another man rose from a nearby rosebush. Jordan raised his arm to power his glove but let out an agonising yell. Before Nicholas could intervene, a Tarios shot an unerringly accurate bolt of light on the turn, saving Jordan.

'Hostiles further up, out of range,' said Zachenne, watching further on down the cliff as distant figures fled from their hiding spots. 'We should give chase.'

'No,' said Nicholas. 'What would be the point? Aerkin knows we are coming.' Nicholas lost his calm demeanour for a moment as the others gazed at him for answers. He looked around in each direction, not quite knowing what it was he searched for. 'He has the upper hand. But how? He cannot be omnipresent in this world. It is impossible. Is there a spy amongst us?' Nicholas raised his voice. 'Someone who deems to plague me from within?'

'You can't be serious?' said Zachenne. 'How could we? We never leave the Hill.'

Nicholas's darting head subsided. Zachenne was right.

'Mind your emotions before suggesting we've already failed,' said Zachenne. 'Don't you trust us to succeed?'

'Yes. I do...sorry.' Nicholas watched a depleted Emitai trudge up the slope and felt a similar defeat in himself. He felt responsible. Again. 'We have no choice but to continue. We have roamed this far.'

'Are you well, Nicholas? You're not yourself.' Zachenne's suggestion would seem unempathetic to Nicholas, having minutes ago led the group to safety under assault. His heartbeat drummed against his chest.

Nicholas looked around. He realised the answers did not surround him; he was looking for something inside himself. The panic of Aerkin's awareness, Kate's departure, and the death of group members not long into their journey had shaken him. He breathed heavily in exhaustion and relief. Hillfolk had spent years clinging to his every word and viewing him as the most intelligent being in the land, but he now found them staring at him. Not an admirable stare, no. This was something else.

All Nicholas could offer in return was a damning verdict of his efforts so far. 'I would always use my confidence to protect myself and all of you. But I cannot find it in me this moment. It seems easy to lead an army of warriors from the comfort of your home, but in these unknown lands, I am afraid I am no wiser than you are.'

'Was this journey a mistake?' asked Zachenne as the group members looked at each other in search of Nicholas's misplaced confidence. 'That's what you offer us after just minutes on this land after years of preparation?'

Now, Nicholas's only option was to show Zachenne the same blunt honesty Zachenne lent his own team. 'Mistake or not, this is the only journey we have, my friends. Have I been the leader out here I had hoped I would be so far? Perhaps not. But it does not mean I will stop trying to return this world to all its inhabitants. Savages run this land we have come to. But those same savages have also come for the Hill. We either carry on together and fight together on our terms, or we can leave our fate to someone else.'

The Guards and Emitai looked over the cliff edge down to the beach. It had all happened so quick. Emitai fell to his knees, bowed his head, and wailed into the wind.

Nicholas reached for his bag under his cloak and pulled out his map. The next path would lead the group to the northern river heading east. He stood still, examining the route as the rest of the group murmuring to each other rattled his ears.

Nicholas put the map away and walked on with intent. The threat of Aerkin had passed, and his heartbeat returned to normal. He pushed his thoughts back into the cold, dark crevasse of his mind and began to whistle a tune in his head. He whispered under his breath, 'Hurry now; we must not lose any timeless time.'

CHAPTER NINETEEN

CAMARADERIE

*A*DE 10—This is it. There are not many left. Animals and humans alike are adapting, but many species are extinct. I estimate that 0.1—1% of humans remain, although I cannot receive word from distant continents. I fear humanity's end. If the world does not end me, my body surely will.

ADE 11—The cold touch of death brings peace. Beautiful, beautiful peace.

ADE 12—Warmth! Hope! The 'Natural Resurgence' begins during an unusually warm period. Fauna and flora are increasing noticeably for the first time on the new calendar. The hardy plants that bear no fruit now hold some. The fields lack direct sunlight. However, some wheat is seen to have grown in old fields but dies almost instantly. Perhaps the heated soils have acted as life support. Rejoice! Are plants adapting to lack of direct sunlight? They must still rely on photosynthesis. Who cares! What I thought was impossible is now only extremely unusual. Life. Beautiful, beautiful life.

*

That night, the group found shelter in a small yet dense woodland area beside a Mainland river, where two Marshals squatted, cleaning their boots of the hardened mud that had settled through the day. Rain poured down, bombarding the group as if they still stormed the beach, with the voluminous trees as their shield. They managed to light a well-kept fire despite water seeping through, staying warm through the night, and keeping full on the unripe fruits from the nearby bushes. The Mainland's blackberries lacked flavour but thankfully had not diminished in size with the lack of direct sunlight, whilst rosehips added variety for those who could stomach the pungent taste. Hopefully the river would provide a rich breakfast of fish.

Nicholas sat amongst three of the remaining four Guards as they paid a silent moment of respect to their fallen friend. They handed him their companion's gloves. He held them close to his heart. 'These gloves are far too precious to bury, and out of respect, we will not lend them to anyone else.' He walked over to his bag, folded them, and placed them inside. The faint, alarming buzz of an insect passed his ear as he did. He slapped the side of his neck and felt the rub of blood and bug solids on his fingertips. He feared the worst: a mosquito. He rubbed his fingers together, feeling more substance to the bug's body that resembled a small housefly.

Beside his bag, the other Guard—Mo, a Tarios—Olivia, and a Marshal—Shaw, sat in a triangle, solemnly discussing the days behind. These three were usually found together under brighter circumstances on the Hill.

'How did it feel?' asked Mo.

'I didn't feel much during the fight,' said Shaw. 'Just had to clear the ship as quickly as possible. There wasn't enough time to think about the deaths. Not looking into their eyes helped. I think. It was only on the boat when it hit me. I thought it was seasickness at first, but the sickness is still with me.'

'I felt the first death,' said Olivia. 'Back at the Toss. Helps that I hunt. In a weird way the body collapsed just like a deer. Like the bones turned soft.'

Nicholas caught Mo's eye. The Guards had not been called to fight as of yet, but perhaps waiting and watching was equally as frightful.

'Nicholas…' Mo looked confused and downtrodden, pausing for thought. 'We…we're the good side, right?'

'That depends.'

'On what?'

'On who wins.' The three heads looked at each other. Nicholas's unease since arriving on the Mainland showed in his answer; it wasn't a leader's response. He breathed in deep and attempted a calming response after the oxygen had filled his brain. 'If it eases your conscience, just remember one thing. We are killing because we have to. He kills because he wants to. The darkness must die.'

The triad nodded, seemingly reassured, but reassurance was a short-term drug.

'So,' said Jordan, shooting up and breaking the wider group's silence. 'Nicholas hasn't spoken a random thought in a while. Any reason?'

Nicholas froze for a second before glancing around at the heads that twisted in his direction. 'It appears to have been a rocket.' As usual, he left no moment to ponder his thoughts and blurted out the first thing that came to mind. 'The explosions on the beach, I mean. For those who do not know, armies of old used these weapons to inflict great damage. So much power in such a small object.' Nicholas glanced at his gloves. 'That man must have found one and not used it all these years. It would be a great surprise to see any more of these on our journey.'

'What if they're making more of them?' asked Jordan.

'Unlikely, my friend. For the same reason as guns. Ignoring the fact that building anything above constant quakes would be a struggle, one who considers himself a God would not bother with creating ancient weapons, and there are not many who wish to build them to fight against the light either.'

'So anyway, are we fighting the trap at Rennes head-on?' asked Matuu, slamming his fist into his palm. 'It's gotta be a trap.'

'Perhaps it would be wiser to take suggestions from a wider audience,' said Nicholas. 'Any suggestions? Zachenne?'

'We should head south-east,' said Zachenne. 'Away from Rennes. Head straight for Aerkin. It seems he will have something waiting for us wherever we go, so we should go to him.'

Nicholas folded his arms as the group murmured in agreement. 'I contest. Kate is heading for the Ruins. Does her companionship mean nothing?'

The group sat without a spoken word for a moment, leaving the insects to dominate with their boundless cries and calls.

'We won't make it in time for her,' said Zachenne. 'Unfortunate, but logical. We cut our losses and hope she stays alive.'

'You say it as if it is paper we are wasting, not lives.'

'Remember, you chose to leave the boy behind. Home is likely in danger, and we didn't go back. We should do the same in this situation. Kate chose to leave, and it will be her choice again to find us.'

Nicholas dropped his half-eaten apple on the floor. 'This is different. Kate is our key, and if we leave her, we may as well fight blindfolded.'

'Our chances are also crippled by your decision to leave your suit. It surely can't be one rule here and one rule there?'

Nicholas stood, looming over the group, with the shadows of firelight swaying across his face. He composed himself. 'We needed a backup plan. I know, in my heart, I have given us our best fighting chance.'

'We need to find Iris,' said Matuu. 'And get our hands on that juicy weapon.'

'It's too late for that,' said Jordan. 'We shouldn't waste all our time and energy looking for people now they know we're here.' Other voices followed, and the group began to bicker amongst themselves.

'I didn't get to bury my brother!' roared Emitai, silencing the others. 'Just shut up, all of you, shut up. All I hear is we must go forward and find this and do that, but what are we even fighting for if we can't take the time to bury the ones we love?' Emitai paced away from the group. 'He's just there, laying on a beach. And we had to leave him for the dogs. Where's the respect in that? Is that what I tell my ma when she asks where he is?

'I couldn't stay there, defenceless on my own. And I can't go back now. Instead, I just have to follow and keep moving with all of you clueless idiots. And when someone else gets lost, you'll leave them behind too. Again and again, and when there's only one of you left, I hope they're able to gather the strength they need to fight on knowing the rest got left behind because I wouldn't be able to.'

Heads in the group started bowing in the corners of Nicholas's vision as he kept his gaze solely on Zachenne.

'This is war,' said Zachenne to Emitai. 'I'm sorry.'

'No, you're not,' replied Emitai.

'We should have buried our companions,' said Nicholas. 'Our family.' He turned to Zachenne. 'I am not perfect, and I will make mistakes. Today I made another. But Kate is our family, and we cannot leave her.'

'I hope you understand my words are from an honest heart and in no assessment of you,' said Zachenne.

'Yes. As always. Although, our intentions should require assessment every now and again.' Nicholas walked over to Emitai, further from the fire and into darkness. He put his hands on Emitai's shoulders. 'I am so sorry, my friend. We live in a world where the shadows reign supreme, but it is the darkness deep inside us that holds our biggest mistakes and fears. I hope you can forgive me.' Nicholas received no response. 'Come. Tell us stories of Denis or sit and reflect in silence. We will listen either way.'

Emitai eventually followed Nicholas back. He did indeed choose to stay silent. Nicholas hung his head and began to think. No. Mindless thoughts would not help now.

'We should return,' blurted Nicholas. 'Perhaps not all of us, but I can return to bury our fallen family.'

'No,' said Emitai. 'Don't be stupid. It's too late. It's dark. There are far more beasts in the Mainland now, and they lurk everywhere at night. Denis won't be there.' Emitai slid his hood up over his head and slouched against a tree.

'I understand your decision, Nicholas,' said Zachenne, returning the conversation to tactics. 'If it is final, then we head for the Ruins of Rennes. We might find Kate. We might find Iris. We might even find Aerkin. But we'll do it together.'

'Together,' nodded Nicholas, looking at Emitai.

The group gloomed as the night wore on. Some had fallen asleep, some kept watch, and the others in limbo sat around the fire. Nicholas kept quiet, whistling a tune, listening to his group as he always did once the sky dimmed.

'Where are you from?' asked Jordan to Emitai.

'I told you already,' Emitai replied. 'North Mainland.'

'No, I mean *where*, where. Before the Worldshift. What country? Mine used to be called England, where you found us. Matuu's from New Zealand.'

'Was on holiday when it happened,' said Matuu, eating a fistful of apples the size of strawberries, spitting the pips out. 'Family trip. One way ticket for the price of two.'

'And Serr…we don't know. But my money's always been on Eastern Europe.'

'Nah. Keep telling you it's South Africa. That accent is unmistakeable.'

'They spoke English there, numpty.'

Serr shook her head, looking perplexed.

'We moved around a lot,' said Emitai. 'Sudan. Turkey. France. I don't remember where we were born. It doesn't matter.'

'Yeah, it does,' said Matuu. It tells you a lot about yourself and your herit—'

'Trust me. It *doesn't* matter.' Emitai took leave and found a quiet spot to rest in the shadows. Nicholas noticed the whistling tune in his head becoming louder, signifying that a conversation starter was required.

'How is your arm?' Nicholas asked Jordan.

'He's acting like a baby,' said Matuu. 'He watched me eat my body weight in fruit and didn't say a thing.'

'Arm's fine.' uttered Jordan, lowering his head. 'Can't wait to finally take on a real fight.'

Matuu tutted. 'It's okay to say you're not finding this easy.'

'It's just a small wound. I'll be fine. And it was a rough night on the boat. I feel like I haven't slept in days.'

'Maybe we should find a way to remove that bullet. It could get worse.'

'No, it's fine. *Leave it,*' snapped a stubborn Jordan.

Matuu huffed in dismission. 'Can't say I didn't try.' He left his seat to find a place to lay down and rest.

Jordan turned his attention towards Serr. 'Hey.' He smirked towards her, followed by raised eyebrows. She rubbed his arm in return and promptly followed Matuu for rest. 'Oh, everyone just leave then. Was it something I said?'

'If you would like to talk, I am still here,' said Nicholas, offering his companion an ear. He leant towards Jordan to comfort him. 'Desolation breeds despair.'

Jordan sat with his bloodshot eyes wide open, staring into the floor. He did not respond to Nicholas, unusual and worrisome. Today, the group had shown signs of splintering; Nicholas could not let it crack.

*

The deep hours into the night brought terrors and trepidation to those still awake keeping guard. Those who ventured in dreams tossed and turned, as the negative cloud of emotions over their group felt more solemn than the rain. Thankfully, when energised, their gloves would abate their shivering in the crisp wind.

Nicholas and three of the Marshals were awake still. His internal whistling had faded, and thoughts began to pop in and out of his head. Visions of Iris and Aerkin would come and go. Screams and shouts. He rocked back and forth through the theta zone of sleep, with only the faint barks and howls through the trees keeping him tied to reality. No sound was overly concerning until an enormous roar exploded through the camp.

'What was that?' asked one of the Marshals.

'Everyone up,' said another, scampering to his feet.

Another ferocious roar rumbled the camp, bringing everyone sharply to their feet. A further roar could be heard from the opposite side. Matuu burst into camp from beyond the trees, pulling his trousers up. 'Bears!'

Emitai scampered to the middle. 'Bears? They're huge! Be careful.'

Nicholas ignited his gloves and approached the trees. Others copied him. He could only see darkness beyond the plant life until the dark body of a hairy beast came into focus. Its size entranced Nicholas, twice as big as any bear he had ever known to exist. He swung his glowing hand from left to right to see the full size of the creature. Another roar. He caught a glimpse of its face, saliva swinging and swaying from the rabid beast's long teeth. The eyes reflected a demonic, bleeding shade of red as if rabidly searching for flesh to chew.

The bears approached aggressively but turned away from the light as it shone into their blood-lusting eyes. A sleuth of bears now surrounded the group, attempting to enter at any point not spread with light. The trees swayed against the weight of these monsters as one toppled inwards. The sound of snapping wood, bark, and branch filled the camp as the tree, and its many flowing branches, collapsed into the centre, thundering and smothering the group.

'Bears, be gone!' shouted Nicholas.

The group continued to shine their light, having regained their footing. They would be fine so long as they could hold the perimeter. One of the Tarios fired a bolt, causing a roar to erupt through the air. They were ferocious but, like any animal, wary of harm. The rustling and roars dissipated. They eventually decided the feast was not worth the failure; they retreated into the night.

'Is everyone okay?' asked Zachenne as the group checked everyone was safe; they were.

Nicholas could not remember a creature like this before. Not polar, nor grizzly. These seemed to be a new species. 'It has been twenty years,' he said. 'Only twenty. They could not have grown so much in that time. Evolution would mutate creatures over thousands and millions of years, but this…this is strange.'

'That's the scariest thing I've ever seen,' said Jordan, trembling.

'It is not the bears themselves that are scary,' said Nicholas. 'It is the science behind them I fear.'

'They were ten times the size of me,' said Matuu, panting. 'Worthy opponents.'

Jordan found himself in the middle of the group, unable to ignite his glove. Emitai stood by him. The two dragged themselves into helping Nicholas and two Tarios remove the fallen tree from camp.

Thundering skies replaced the bears' roars. Perhaps the lightning made its way south from where Kate would likely sleep that night. Nicholas, now fully alert, slouched on a tree opposite Emitai, murmuring Kate's name repeatedly.

'Did you mean it?' said Emitai. 'When you said you weren't coming back?'

'Yes.' Nicholas dropped his head back onto the rough tree bark. 'I have accepted my fate, and I do not wish to think past seeing him again. Clairvoyance is a voidance of reality, and all that leaves me with is a chance. And that chance is sleeping rough somewhere to the north this night.'

'Is she really that special? Can she kill *him*?'

'She is special. She is a full house, my friend. The problem is we are fighting a royal flush.' Nicholas received a blank stare to his old gambling reference. 'She will be fine. I fear for her state of mind rather than her body. Ever since she was a girl, she would display an innate ability to look after herself. I have had to adapt to this new world, but she has grown in it. I would never agree that one is born to do something, but this is as close as it gets.'

Emitai bowed his head, retreating into silence again.

'I don't suppose you and your brother encountered many bears on your way to us?' asked Nicholas.

'Yes, one, well two. Bastilig kept one chained up, so I heard. The other attacked us one night, but Denis fought it off with fire. Denis would always protect me.'

Nicholas recognised the defeated posture of a staunch man still heavily mourning the loss of family. 'Tell me something about Denis.'

'I was just thinking about the way I found him. He was in a bad way. Iris rescued me from Hell, but I could only think of one thing to do, and that was to find and free Denis. That was my only condition before delivering her message. So she agreed to do it and took me to the outskirts of Aerkin's temple. It was the biggest structure I'd ever seen, sitting amongst the mountains. I didn't know walls could stand so tall above the quakes, but somehow they did.'

Emitai looked down and picked up a ball of dry mud. He rolled it between his palms.

'So, then we found him. Iris fought a few soldiers off before others could see; it seemed easy for her. Maybe too easy. But when I saw Denis and finally held him in my arms, that's when I realised I wasn't the one saving him; he was saving me. I felt from that moment I wanted to live on. I wanted to try and make a difference. Before then, part of me just wanted to escape and forget about Iris. But I couldn't. We had to deliver that message at all costs.'

Emitai crushed the ball of mud in his hands. It crumbled through his fingers. 'He saved me, but I couldn't save him. And for that, I feel angry. I won't go home, I will fight by your side, and Aerkin's temple will fall.' Emitai turned to Nicholas, painted resolutely. 'After all this time, he still takes our families away. He still controls our lives.'

'I know the burning feeling inside you,' said Nicholas. 'I also know nothing I could say would make you not want to fight. The vengeance may well fuel you to the very end. And to that, I say, we are with you to the very end, my friend,' said Nicholas.

'I'm with you, friend,' said Matuu, peering over.

'I'm with you, my friend,' added Zachenne.

One by one, the group repeated the same sentiment to Emitai.

'Funny,' said Nicholas with a loose smile. 'The only one in the group without the light is the one whose courage shines brightest.'

Nicholas peered over at Jordan, impressed, leaning forward and hanging onto Emitai's heartfelt words. Jordan opened his mouth to talk but let out a sigh and slouched back. His face fell with refrain. However, he was able to turn to Matuu.

'Hey, sorry we scared the bears off,' said Jordan. 'Were they your cousins?'

Matuu frowned but let out a soft chuckle as the others laughed. 'Speaking of scared, you'll need a change of underwear.'

The light-hearted bickering continued as Zachenne leant his head to Nicholas. 'What do we think of the boy's chances back home?'

'True, we must not forget he is a part of this family too,' said Nicholas, opening his speech to the group. 'I raise my proverbial glass, but far, far away, to Arun.' He paused and hummed to himself. 'The new bearer of the suit. The Guardian of the Hill…For now, Cole and Tej will be taking care of him.'

'Maybe Tej has killed him with his homemade brew,' said one of the Guards.

'Oh!' said another Guard. 'I could go for one of Cole's breakfast baps right about now.'

'Is that what you call them?' said Jordan.

'Tej calls them his bedtime baps!' joked Matuu.

The group continued their bellowing banter as the mood of the group lightened. Nicholas hadn't seen them joyous since they rode away from the Hill singing their merry songs. This brought a smile to his face momentarily.

'It's a lot to ask of a scavenger,' said Zachenne, returning to his original query. 'He has a lot to learn and no time to learn it in.'

Nicholas's smile grew bigger still. 'I have a feeling that suits him just fine.'

CHAPTER TWENTY

TOGETHER STRONGER: PART I

Arun and Malorie continued west through the day, seeking a path or field they would recognise to lead them home. Overflowing rivers blocked a direct route, and all they had to navigate the hills was guile and a rickety compass. Puddles rippled amongst the grass as the trees swayed, but the two travellers would be motionless if it weren't for the trotting of the horse beneath them.

The two had only muttered a handful of sentences since leaving the farm; they directed their attention to arriving home as soon as possible. However, one giant hurdle presented itself in their path in the form of a gaping chasm in the Earth that blocked them in all forward directions. A light mist poured out of the crack to the surrounding field. To the left, ruins lay where a house may have stood once. A rope bridge dangled on the right, rickety, with unevenly shaped planks and one rope thicker than the other, frayed on both sides. But it connected end to end.

'This might be our only way,' said Arun, breaking the silence.

'Can't we go around?' asked Malorie. 'It can't go on forever. Else we would have come past it.'

'There's no way of knowing how far it stretches. We can't afford to go back in case they've grabbed a horse and tried to follow us.'

'Yeah.' Malorie jumped off the horse and looked down. 'It's hard not to make footprints in all the rain. It's great for when I'm tracking an animal. Even small animals. But I guess I never thought something would be tracking me.' She raced away promptly.

'Where are you going?'

'I want to check the bridge. Be nice to her.'

Arun was left alone on a horse for the first time in his life and could only think to pat it. 'There, there. Good job, horsey. Turn right.' The horse turned to the left. Great, the first horse he rides, and it's deaf.

'We can't take the horse over the bridge,' shouted Malorie. 'She's far too big. And…there's one more thing.'

The horse walked in its own direction, unimpressed with Arun's feeble commands. Arun tried to scamper off but caught his foot in the stirrup. Splash—he fell to the puddled grass, back first. No more horses from now on. He trudged over to Malorie to check the bridge's condition and heard a strange rumbling increasing in volume. A breeze of warm air flowed past Arun's arms. The bridge was far worse than it looked from afar—some of the planks were barely tied. Any weight would surely topple them. However, it was beneath the bridge that caused the bigger concern. Arun looked down.

'No. Way.' Arun stared into a deep fissure of fast-flowing lava, deep down as if the crack had opened to the Earth's core. It wasn't mist emanating; it was smoke. Despite the depth, Arun's face began to feel the harsh touch of heat. 'Maybe there's a way around.'

'No, you were right,' said Malorie. 'They could be near. Wait here.' She galloped back to the horse as if she were one of its kind before releasing the saddle. 'Shoo! Go, horsey. Run.' She clapped her hands and attempted to push the horse away. The horse turned its head and bowed for a mouthful of grass, unmoved by the noise. Arun hurried over as she continued to clap, removing a glove. Without warning, he laid a thunderous clap of his own against the horse's hip, causing it to sidestep and turn away, huffing in displeasure.

'Hey!' yelped Malorie.

'It's for its own good,' said Arun, watching the horse slowly trot away. 'Now, come on.'

The two approached the fissure again, despite a huff from Malorie. It reached deep enough that the fall would probably kill them before they felt their skin burn. Something to be positive about. As Arun looked down once more, Malorie caught his eye by continuing on, not breaking her stride as she reached the bridge.

'Wait!' Arun reached out, feeling ever more protective of the young girl.

'I'll go first,' said Malorie. 'I'm smaller and lighter…and faster…and brighter.'

Arun paused to process her rhyme. 'Yeah, but it's dangerous; I should test it out first.'

'Nonsense,' said Malorie, stretching her leg to the first plank. She hadn't given Arun a second to stop her. He scampered over.

'Woah! Aren't you scared? Take your time. Maybe hold onto me. Or we can go back?'

Malorie moved her hands forward along the rope. 'I'm scared of the things behind us. Going forward is all we have. The worst thing here is that I'll go for a hot swim.'

'That's not funny.' Arun held onto the rope. That would help, right? He watched as Malorie took another couple of steps with her hands stretched up wide to reach the ropes. How was she not afraid of heights? Or being burnt alive? 'Careful, careful! Right foot then left!'

'I know how to walk. It's not that bad even. Maybe we can both fit on?' Malorie took another few confident looking steps. Although that confidence soon vanished as one of the planks gave way and began its long, dwindling journey to ashes.

'Girl!' shouted Arun as she clung on.

'I'm okay. I'm okay!' Malorie ignored Arun and continued, holding tighter but taking shorter, faster steps.

Arun could only watch as another plank gave way. Nobody must have used the bridge in quite some time if Malorie's weight tested it. 'Okay good effort, come back now. We'll go around.' He kept watch as Malorie ignored his concerns, and with an enormous sigh of relief, he witnessed Malorie jump to the other side.

'Okay, your turn, it wasn't too bad!' shouted Malorie over the wind and steam. 'Mind the gaps!'

Arun took one step, feeling the plank beneath him bend and creak. Although he moved with far more caution than usual, a clumsy boy attempting careful footing must be a sight to see. It took him seconds before he could release his other foot from safe ground. His body tensed up, his muscles tightened, and he took another step as the wind tried to sway his nerves. Don't look down. Don't look down.

With his many mistakes behind him, Arun felt the muscles in his hand warming up, and his gloves energised around them. His instinctual cling to safety created a panic within him. He grasped tighter—big mistake. The already frayed rope began to burn in his glowing palm as the wind toppled him. He flung himself back, still holding on, shredding the rope in his palms. He missed a plank, getting his foot stuck between two, releasing his hold.

Malorie screamed in the background. Snap—the rope on Arun's left broke as he pulled himself up. Arun's time was up. Another plank broke as the second rope shredded in his palm. Arun leapt to the first plank as another disappeared. With one deep breath, he launched back to safe ground, back to square one.

'Don't do that to me!' yelled Malorie across the chasm. 'Dummy! What do we do now?'

All that remained of the should-be-bridge were the two lower ropes and the assortment of planks and gaps between them. Great. There was no hope now. Arun looked up into the distance from which they came to see a new tower of smoke rising. There was no way out. He had to search for ideas in the depths of his scavenger cunning.

'Can you crawl over?' Malorie continued to yell.

Crawling did propose an idea for Arun. In his early youth, he tied ropes between walls and attempted tightrope walking to keep himself entertained. The wind and spattering rain against his face warned him the weather was not on his side. But he felt he could use the standing ropes and planks to his advantage.

'Hold on, I need to find a board to sit on,' said Arun, although probably not loud enough to be audible to Malorie, more an instruction for himself. He rushed away, scampering to find any kind of board he could sit on in the nearby ruins. The planks on the bridge were wide, so he hoped he'd be able to spread his weight and cross safely.

Arun lifted one brick, then exhausted himself lifting a heavy concrete slab. Looking back at the pile, he realised he could perhaps smash through the slabs if he ignited his gloves. He tensed his hand, brought the light to his glove, and chopped a block of cemented brick wall in half as if his hand were an axe. Incredible!

'Hurry up!' yelled Malorie.

Right. Arun pulled away more debris and searched under every bit of rubble he could lift. His frantic search ended as he found a large, rotting wooden board beneath the rubble. He brought it back to the bridge and placed it on the two lower ropes. The remaining planks were fixed in place under the ropes, so the wooden board should slide right across. Easy, right?

'That's not going to work; it's too windy!' Malorie continued to yell her opinions across the chasm to no avail. Nothing would stop Arun now. He mumbled words of encouragement to himself as he couldn't find the energy to yell back across to Malorie. 'Your balance is good, don't worry. Keep the centre of your body as close to the centre of the ropes as possible. You can do this. Centre of body. Centre of ropes.'

Arun placed his hands onto the makeshift platform and immediately felt the warm, pressing wind attack from along the chasm. He waited for a calmer break in the wind to climb on, and as it came, he slid forward on all fours and prepared to pull himself forward with the ropes.

'Take your gloves off!' shouted Malorie.

Good advice. Arun slid his gloves into his pocket. He pulled himself and the platform forward and kept his balance well. The rope felt tightened and sturdy, although the real challenge would be in the middle section. He pulled himself forward again slowly. He rocked side to side and reached the middle, vigorously holding firm.

Arun's head swung with the platform, nervously looking back and forth to check his balance. Any direction but down. His forehead and underarms became drenched, although he wasn't sure if it was the heat from below or the fear in his gut producing it.

Eventually, he inched towards the end, and Malorie grabbed his arms and pulled him onto the ground. 'Thanks, girl. I never wanna do that again,' Arun collapsed in exhaustion.

'Your gloves fell out!' yelled Malorie in his ear.

Arun jumped inside himself and plunged through his pocket. They weren't there. He crawled back to the chasm, finally able to look down again, frantically checking all directions. 'I can't see them! They're gone! No! Please, no!'

'Oh, here they are,' said Malorie, dangling them in her hand. Arun turned to see a horrible grin across her face. 'It's a lesson my dad taught me. It reminds me to be more careful.'

Arun's face dropped, his teeth clenched, and his fingers dug into the mud. It had not been a day for joking, and he still couldn't shake the image of the knights behind him. He sat staring at her as she tossed the gloves his way.

'Let's go,' said Malorie. 'There's more smoke in the distance. They're following the hoofprints.'

Arun lent a glance behind him. The tall tower of smoke had darkened and thickened but was still far in the distance. Arun burnt the bottom ropes, collapsing the remaining planks, and rose like the smoke. He begrudgingly followed and caught up to her. 'You know, practical jokes don't work so well when murderers are chasing you.'

'It wasn't a joke,' said Malorie, checking her compass for directions. 'It was a lesson. Without those gloves, you'd be helpless.'

'I don't need a lesson from a girl, girl. And anyway, I wouldn't have dropped them.' He stopped and held Malorie back by the shoulder. 'Don't ever do that again.'

'But you were scared when I told you. So you knew there was a chance you dropped them. Don't leave anything up to chance; that's what my dad taught me.'

'Did your dad teach you how to be insufferable too?'

'Did yours?'

Arun scoffed and ended the conversation, picking up his walking pace again.

'Sorry, I didn't mean that,' said Malorie. Arun heard her scurrying after him. 'I've never lost anything. I remember one time I dropped a bag of conkers. It was special. I spent ages drawing my family into each conker for my dad's birthmonth. I wanted to give it as a present. But I couldn't find it anywhere. I searched for days. But then I found it under some branches.'

'Amazing. You should be a storyteller,' replied Arun. At least scavengers would leave each other alone. Malorie the mosquito. Perfect name.

'I'm just saying. I didn't lose it because I never gave up looking. I don't think you could ever lose something you care about. You'd keep looking. Even if it took you a lifetime. So I doubt you would have lost your gloves. Just… misplaced them.'

'Misplaced them into the fiery pits of Earth. Sure. Great lesson.' Arun had managed to render Malorie silent again as they strolled onto an open field from beneath the trees. He recognised the remains of a building beside a path ahead, from when they first journeyed; they were ten minutes from home. They turned to each other in relief, smiles across their face, and burst into a sprint towards familiarity.

*

Nearing three days away from the Hill, Arun and Malorie turned right at the Hill fence and ran straight towards the cottage. Arun spotted Mr and Mrs

Trellock sitting by the cottage window, and they both sprinted out to greet the two youngsters as they saw them approaching the cottage door.

'Malorie! We were worried sick!' blubbered Mrs Trellock.

'Don't you ever do that to us again, sweetie. I thought you were lost to the wind,' said Mr Trellock. The two parents grasped her and squeezed her breath away.

'You,' said Mrs Trellock, turning to Arun, huffing in distress. 'What did you do with her? Why did you take her?' She darted towards Arun aggressively, almost touching his nose with her own.

'No, Mum,' said Malorie. 'I followed him. He saved me and brought me back.'

Arun squinted at Malorie. So much for her parents saying she could come. Judging by their sprint when they saw her, they must have been sitting in the cottage worrying day and night for her return after fruitless searches. Mr Trellock gave him a suspicious look.

'Well. If that's true, and she's okay, then this overly-protective father's gratitude belongs to you,' said Mr Trellock.

'Don't sweat it,' replied Arun. 'I had no choice but to bring her back safely. I don't leave anything up to chance.'

'That's exactly what I say! Great-o!'

Cole appeared, bursting through the cottage door, closely followed by Tej. 'What's all this commotion?'

'Malorie!' beamed Tej, 'There you are.'

The remaining Hillfolk were back together, happy and hugging, apart from Arun.

'Hey, listen,' said Arun. 'We saw these people, Nicholas's notes call them the Aerkin Disciples or Aerkin Knights, and they're here.'

Tej gasped. 'The Aerkin Knights? Here, near the Hill?'

'We've come from a farm a few hours away. They saw us, though.'

Gasps turned to stutters, the group unable to believe what they were hearing. Mrs Trellock crumbled down and placed her hands on Malorie's cheeks, inspecting her health. Arun needn't explain the chaos they could bring if they found the Hill.

'How?' asked Cole. 'How are they 'ere? Are you sure it was them?'

'Certain,' said Arun. 'There were five of them, and they had masks on, and…and they had these weapons of red light. They were going place to place, slaughtering innocent people and burning shelters.'

Cole pressed her hand to her lips with a slight inhale.

'And the others?' asked Tej. 'Nicholas? Kate? Did you see them?'

'I dunno. I don't think they're coming back,' said Arun. 'It feels like they knew we'd be in danger, though. Nicholas's notebook explains everything.'

'Come on, let's talk about this inside,' said Cole. She turned to Arun with a whisper. 'Thank you. She's just a girl.' She kissed him on the cheek. 'You're a good lad.'

Yeah. Sure.

The warmth of the cottage fuelled by the fireplace welcomed Arun home, and he duly picked the table closest to it, where he'd sat that first morning, and removed his damp cloak. As he sat down, Malorie opened the notebook on the relevant page and put it on the table for all to see, proceeding to read. Arun's gaze darted across the Hillfolk. None looked up.

After having absorbed all the information Arun and Malorie had previously read, Cole slumped back into her chair with a perilous look on her face whilst Tej sank his head into his hands. Cole closed the notebook gracefully, sealing the stories shut. Arun continued observing the others, waiting for an idea to be sprung.

'Okay then. I'll get the shovels.' Cole stood, leaving the notebook behind on the table. 'Tej, love, set up a perimeter schedule. Arun, there's barbed wire and bear traps behind the study hut. Bring them to the bottom of the Hill.'

'Do what now?' asked Arun.

'We need to be proactive. They could be 'ere in a day or a week. It's time to knuckle down.' Cole stomped towards the back of the cottage.

'What d'you mean knuckle down? We need to leave. Should we head for the Mainland?'

'Mainland?' laughed Tej. 'Cole's right, fella. This is our land, and we'll protect it no matter what.'

Arun stood in disbelief. The famous saying was that a scavenger always runs, and that was his full intention. 'You can't be serious. Nicholas left the suit with me. I'm plan B; I can't just wait here to be killed.'

'We 'ave the same fear,' said Cole. 'Consider others. We've thought about this for many years and there are traps we can put in place. We 'ave gloves, and we 'ave the suit. We'll do everything we can to defend.'

'You haven't seen them have you?'

'No,' murmured Cole, with a concerned look creeping on her face.

'The way they looked at me. The way their head tilted whilst the rest of their body stayed motionless and stiff. There didn't seem to be anything human about them apart from their shape. And the weapons they held; they had this dark red energy like the purest blood you've ever seen, frantically dancing like flames. I went numb just looking at them, let alone fighting them. We have to run.'

'We stay and fight for our home,' said Tej in a sharp retort. 'Though I wouldn't expect a Tosser to know what a home is.'

Arun paused open-mouthed. Cole winced at Tej's words, but they'd already left his mouth and couldn't be retrieved. Without bothering to grab his cloak, Arun headed for the door.

'Arun, together we're stronger,' said Cole. 'Please don't go.'

'Nah. I'm leaving.' Arun turned as he opened the door. 'I'm sorry you're getting used to hearing that, but I'm not a pig with an apple in its mouth just waiting to be eaten.'

'Why are you running, Arun?'

'It's my nature.' Arun began to turn but jolted as he looked down towards Malorie. A tear fell from her cheek, although she didn't say a word. A burning sensation rose inside him. He breathed heavily through his nose and clenched his jaw, trying not to show the numbness and fear that returned to his body. But he couldn't help feeling partly responsible for this; he couldn't help but care. He turned to leave but stopped himself again.

'Go. Run away again,' said Tej. 'A deer can shed its antlers, but it can't shed its heart.'

Arun placed his hands on the grain of the door, the same as when he found out the others had left him. He remembered that feeling; he couldn't do the same to Malorie. He ignored Tej's obscurity and looked down at her. That damn girl. 'Let's get to work then,' he said reluctantly, leaving the cottage.

CHAPTER TWENTY-ONE

TOGETHER STRONGER: PART II

Opening the door to his hut, Arun could see nothing had changed, not to his surprise. He thought he might have missed the bed more, but he still hadn't fully gotten used to it after a lifetime of sleeping hard.

Arun stepped back out onto the Hill under the dry skies, and his gaze grazed the land, appreciating its beauty as if he had stepped onto it for the first time. Somehow the greens seemed greener, and the trees grew wider, trapping and hiding the group in this little bubble of utopia. He hadn't felt it was home before, but now returning to it, it started to feel much more comforting than the chaotic world outside. Though, as a little girl sprinted towards him, he realised it wasn't the Hill itself he was comforted by. It was the people.

'I'm glad you're not running away,' wailed Malorie. 'I knew you wouldn't leave me.' She grabbed his waist and held it tight.

'Wouldn't be a good friend if I did,' said Arun.

'Friend?' Malorie leaned back and looked up at him, beaming. 'My parents said you're a brave person and would save the Hill with them. They're going to get their gloves and practise. You should practise with them. Can I watch?'

Arun would usually zone out when Malorie spoke in short bursts, but this time he smiled down on her, holding onto every word. 'Okay then, let's start getting ready.'

As Malorie began to lead Arun away, he stopped her. 'Hey girl, just so we're clear, I've only ever stolen something that was stolen in the first place. I've never taken something that someone truly owned.'

'Okay.' She didn't add another word and turned to continue towards her family hut, where her parents prepared their gloves and her brother lay sleeping.

'Ah, little man, lend me your ear,' said Mr Trellock as Arun entered. 'This is one of Nicholas's first pair of gloves. They hold a zig-zag pattern, a little harsh on the eye if you ask me. Bah! But he made them for me many, many years ago, and I haven't worn them in many more. It's been—'

'More than ten years now,' said Mrs Trellock.

'Right-o! So forgive me if I'm a bit rusty.' Mr Trellock had a slight limp as he walked and was coughing intermittently. 'But I think that makes three of us. Oh, and I do hope Malorie wasn't much trouble.'

'No,' said Arun. She was. 'Although she's not exactly how I imagined a young girl to be.' Arun's words brought a smile that split her face as her heels bounced on the spot.

'She's a clever one—like her mother. Excitable too. Children only think about the now, not about the future. Oh, what a blessing. But she's certainly not like any children before the Worldshift, that's for sure. New world, new people.' Mr Trellock winced whilst putting his boots on before examining Arun head to toe. 'So, you've mastered the suit, little man?'

Little? 'Well. I was hoping you'd have some information on it. Maybe you saw Nicholas use it or saw what it could do. All I seem to be able to do is make myself glow, and then I get tired. And I can't use the boots yet.'

'Right-o. Come, let's head to the field. Malorie, sweetie, please tell Cole where we are and to shout "Excelsior" if they need us.'

'But I wanted to watch!' sobbed Malorie.

'Malorie...'

'Yes, sir.' Malorie sprinted out of the hut. So that's how you got her to quieten down. That and…well, the other thing that hopefully wouldn't happen again any time soon.

The three light-wielders headed for the fields beyond the Hill.

*

Arun swung one ignited blade to the left, then the right, each blocked by Mr Trellock.

'Don't go easy on me,' said Mr Trellock. 'My eyes are still sharp!' He held both hands up, lightly glowing, meeting Arun's blade wherever it fell. 'How about your left arm?'

Arun felt less confidence in his weaker arm, but at least the light carried no weight to slow him down. He ignited his left, with his right arm beginning to feel the burn.

'Good,' said Mr Trellock. 'You'll soon be able to switch up your arms as you fight. Igniting and extinguishing at the right moments can aid your performance.'

Arun continued to swing, easing the disconcerting feeling of attacking an elder man with a chaotic weapon of light. A bolt of light then hurtled forward, shot from afar beside the warriors, crashing against Arun's blade and throwing his outstretched arm out wide. The light moved too fast for him to react, so Mrs Trellock must have been practising her aim on moving targets. Would have been nice if she'd warned him beforehand.

'Focus,' said Mr Trellock, pulling Arun's attention back.

Arun extinguished his remaining blade. 'Okay. Hold on. My arms are sore.'

The long afternoon was coming to an end. It took a while for the Trellocks to get used to their gloves again and remind their muscles of their memories, but once they were able to glow, they looked formidable once more.

'Does it feel like it used to?' asked Arun, massaging his hands.

'I'm breathing the weight of the world,' replied Mr Trellock, panting between each word. 'My physical shape isn't what it used to be before we had children. Shame-o. But the gloves are fine. My wife has Tarios gloves, her namesake, so it means she can stay further back and fire bolts of light at them. Easy for some. I need to get a little closer, move a little more, and make sure these limbs have life left still. I mean, look at my hips, for goodness' sake—they're jelly.'

'Aren't you scared?'

Mr Trellock tilted his head to the sky, hands on his jellied hips. 'Let me see. I'll put it this way: hunting is difficult because everything we try to eat is fearful of us. If they didn't fear us, it would be an easy catch every single time.'

Arun understood why Malorie quoted her father so much. He possessed a comforting voice as soft as wool and spoke well, despite the exhaustion, as if he knew the answer to all life's mysteries. Mrs Trellock, however, held a timid posture, though being aware she needed to defend her home and children perhaps plagued her mind.

'So, you wanted to ask about the suit,' said Mr Trellock. 'Do you want to show me what you can do with it?'

'Sure.' Arun obliged and clenched every muscle in his body. He glowed but managed to hold steady, lifting his arms into a fighting stance unlike before. This lasted only a few seconds as the energy drained from him, and he fell to the ground.

'Right-o,' said Mr Trellock. 'So everything apart from the boots, and you're holding for a few seconds. I have some advice for you.'

Arun regained his energy far quicker this time around and returned to his feet, albeit dazed.

'You don't need to hold that glow for a long time,' said Mr Trellock, pulling Arun's arms forward, again with the damn yanking. 'Your hands and your feet: these are your weapons. Your suit, however, glows for protection—nothing more, nothing less. Nicholas would use it in training, but only in short bursts when being attacked. You need to tense different muscles at different times. Attack and defence. Use what's necessary. You've probably guessed that if you hold everything for too long, your energy diminishes, and you need to recover. Not so clever-o.

'Nicholas donned that suit for a long time before giving it up. It took a lot from him over such a long period. If he hasn't told you his age, you'd be surprised to know he's a lot younger than you might think. He says the suit damaged his cells, reducing their ability to divide at an increasingly alarming rate; his bones ached, his muscles weakened, and getting out of bed became a task. You have to use it sparingly.'

What? Damaged cells? Use sparingly? Nicholas's note read itself aloud; the suit would take from him as much as it gave. Kate's words took over, asking him to control his muscles. Until this moment, Arun hadn't fully understood how he should use his body. Surely he had to just tense and fight? No, it was all about calm control. He looked into his hands, his eyes widened, and the light inside his head flicked on. He needed to be the master of the gloves and not the other way around. For the first time since awakening as a Hill prisoner, Arun felt confident in his understanding of the gloves. An extension of his body. Of course!

Mr Trellock walked past Arun with a cheeky grin to match Arun's. 'You should have come to me sooner, little man.'

*

The three continued to train before the darkness set in, with Arun working on his muscle timing and control. He felt more energised and quicker in his reactions. It wasn't perfect, but his confidence had him believe he'd become a warrior of the light. As he trained, he remembered fights he had been in back at his old town. There were times he'd fought off multiple scavengers at once, and he pictured them as the Aerkin Knights. He still felt the fear and adrenaline of fighting against the odds, but it was a fight he never backed down from.

The three returned to find Cole and Malorie preparing piles of foliage at the bottom of the Hill, next to a line of barbed wire. They'd piled loose soil beside a shallow, trench-like hole in the ground.

'Malorie, sweetie, let's eat,' said Mr Trellock, limping into their hut. Mrs Trellock followed, still wearing her timidness. Arun sent a wave to Malorie in return for a vigorous, double-handed one.

Arun stumbled into the cottage, parched and in desperate need of water, feeling light as if in flight. Tej sat on a table alone, staring into his hands. This was the first time Arun had seen him wear gloves. More importantly, a jug rested on the table, so Arun wasted no time dashing over and guzzling what remained.

'How did it go?' asked Tej.

Arun slammed the jug down, wiped his mouth, and slumped into the chair opposite before realising it wasn't water swelling in his cheeks but warm beer. He bravely swallowed, wanting to spit it out, but his level of thirst prevented this. 'Training is tiring, but it's great. I'm getting better.' Arun squirmed with the strong, pungent liquid sliding down his throat.

'Sorry about what I said before,' mumbled Tej, still staring into the gloves he'd retrieved from Nicholas's room. 'I tried again. As hard as I could, of course. I just can't get these damn things to work.'

'Don't you have anything else to fight with?'

'My mind is all I have.' Tej grabbed the jug and swigged from it. He slurred his words, and his head toppled as if his neck was as wide as a needle. 'My mind allows me to dream. I'm happiest in my dreams, where I roam the world of cities and sunshine still. Oh, Brighton Beach, bring me back.'

Awkward. Arun allowed a moment of silence to spread, unsure how to deal with Tej's state of mind. 'So...how old is Nicholas?'

Tej's arms flailed. 'Ah, Nicholas. Leaving us to die. What a great man. Ten out of ten. Hides his books from us so I can't learn anything. Keeps bloody knives.'

'Knives?'

'For all we know, he could be a pirate. Yes! Do you know what pirates are? They take and give nothing back!'

'He gave me this suit. And he didn't leave us to die. The suit is here so we can defend ourselves. He's a hero.'

'Oh, yes. The suit! The magical suit. It turns this lowly scavenger into a hero, slaying all before him as he kisses the girl and rides off into the sunset.' Tej slammed his hands on the table and rose from his seat. 'Why would anyone want to be like their hero? Here's some advice: be your own damn person.'

'Don't be angry at me just because you're a failure.' Arun shot up to meet Tej's gaze.

Tej ripped his gloves off and threw them at Arun. 'Take that back. You're just lucky. It must be those gloves, something special about them.' He stormed over to Arun, reaching out for his gloves. Arun grabbed Tej's wrists and pushed him back. He fell to the floor against the wall, where he remained, lifting up his hands to look at them in disappointment.

'Don't blame the beer. You're tormented.' Arun shook his head. His annoyance mixed with pity for a man who simply wanted to use and learn about dark energy, but couldn't.

Tej's eyes glared through his palms with a menacing look across his face, his top lip quivering.

'Intruders are 'ere!' came a shout from Cole at the bottom of the Hill. 'Intruders!' The cry jerked Arun and Tej from their stare, and Arun hurried outside with Tej dizzily stumbling behind. Malorie and her family were all outside, watching intently. Arun looked down the Hill, and although it was nearly dark, he could just about make out recognisable figures. The group of menacing men and women, scavengers from his old home.

'They're friends!' shouted Arun as the scavengers littered the Hill. 'Well, not *friends* friends, but scavengers, the lot of them.'

'Dearie me, mind the hole!' shouted Cole, waving her arms. 'Don't step near the soil! Go around. Around!'

The scavengers carried bags and bricks, metal and muck. Anything they could bring from town was on their person. Some dragged along crafted weapons, splattered with blood from previous fights. One man limped, heavily injured, with fresh wounds covering his torn clothes and skin. A woman wincing in pain bore no visible scars but held her right shoulder in place. Another, for some reason, had a ripped plastic bag on his head, dragging his legs along. Most of the scavengers were in a frightful way.

'Arun, you been hiding up here now, then?' laughed one of the group, grabbing Arun by the back of his head. 'Better not be any Hillfolk nearby. Where be our lodging, boy?'

'Starving! Food. Me. Mouth. Where?' shouted another in Cole's face with his arms stretched out wide. He looked to be Arun's age.

Cole looked on in disgust as the scavengers walked around aimlessly on the grass, inspecting anything they came across. 'Excuse me? What are you all doing here?'

'Arun boy, left us a little message, didn't he,' said the scruffiest of all the scavengers. 'Come to the Hill. Danger, danger! It took us hours and hours to find here, so where's your food? Come on, honey.'

Arun recognised only half of the arrivals. Fifteen of them stormed the Hill. He looked towards the back and saw a man limping at the rear of the group. Gasp—'Shark. How's he alive?'

'Never mind how,' snapped Cole. 'What message? Where're all these Tossers coming from?'

'Well, here's the thing. I wanted them to be safe. And also help us fight if we were attacked.'

'What are a bunch of Tossers going to do? Apart from eat everything we 'ave?'

Arun turned to the cottage to see Tej greeting the new arrivals. He cheered them on, offering high-fives as they bundled inside. If beer could make Tej respect scavengers, maybe that was the truer cosmic power.

'Please,' said Arun to Cole, 'we can help each other.'

Cole looked at Arun with scepticism in her eyes. She flung her arms out wide and huffed.

'They'll be a pain,' said Arun. 'But I also know they'll be helpful. They'll dig deeper than any can dig and fight until they can't stand.'

'Hello, little lady,' whispered Shark in a creepy tone as he walked past Malorie and Arun. He lifted his hand to wave, or at least half a wave. Malorie ran to her father.

'They're charming,' said Cole. 'But what choice do we 'ave? Your first job is to get them out of the cottage and prepare for any attack. The knights could be 'ere soon. We need everyone focused.' Arun and Cole turned to the cottage to see Tej stumbling into the wall face first. What a man.

*

Hours had passed in the cottage, and the raucous scavengers hadn't lifted a finger so far, apart from raising bottles of beer together. The fireplace kept the cold winds of the night at bay.

Arun returned from a toilet break, readying himself to head to sleep. He made his way over to Cole to say goodnight, knowing the others would be keeping watch until morning.

'And then I kicked him in the head so hard his nose changed shape!' shouted one of the scavengers as the others roared in laughter.

'So much for getting them out the cottage,' grumbled Cole.

'Sorry, I tried,' said Arun. 'They're not used to walking long distances. They're worn down.'

'They're interesting; that's what they are. Are you sure you're one of them?'

Arun smiled. He wanted to laugh but fought the urge. 'Yeah, it's not the beer, sadly. They're always like that,'

'I 'oped they'd be a little more anxious, 'elping us with preparation. You know, to fight.' Arun followed Cole's gaze to two scavengers pushing each other and raising their voices. 'Not each other, though.'

'About that—'

'Speech! Speech, boy,' said a scavenger, calling Arun over.

'Thanks, but I have nothing to say,' said Arun. 'I'm going to bed.'

'Speech! Speech!' cried the group.

'Get on it, boy, this is our first night here,' said a scavenger. 'You dragged us up. Give us some sort of introduction.'

Arun met the stares of life's luckless dwellers and offered a reluctant fist pump, given the troubles that may lie ahead. He'd told these scavengers to journey to the Hill to seek solace, but with the Hill in potential danger, he may have made matters worse for them. He moved towards the front of the room, where he could see them all. Only the Trellock family were absent.

'I brought you all here for safety, and you'll have already seen what's happening across our land. You've probably already seen those responsible. I have. Five figures in black cloaks and grey armour. They're the Aerkin Knights, and they're searching for us. I can't say they won't come here, so we all have to stick together and prepare to fight. Alright?'

The faces of the scavengers started to drop. Arun could see Shark in particular, whose face sank in terror.

'You don't have to fight. You can run. But I know we can beat those knights if we stay. I learnt today that together we're stronger, and I don't doubt that we can pull together and destroy them. We have special weapons, skill, and heart.'

'What weapons?' murmured a voice.

'The only thing we needed was numbers, and we have that now. We can stop them from destroying other towns and lives. We can all be heroes! Come on!' Arun's animated fist roared into the air.

The scavengers looked around at each other. All were quiet, apart from a few mumbles and groans. Several of them upped and left the cottage without saying a word, whilst others stayed to sit quietly contemplating, turning their backs to Arun.

Arun could only watch. Tej sat in the corner, bobbing his head and raising his jug in the air, overcome with dizzy joy. Cole, on the other side of the room, simply nodded to Arun. He felt deflated but held his head high and left the cottage to return to his small hut on the Hill.

Shoes off, gloves on, and Arun shuffled into bed. His candle flickered near the end of its life. He watched the hair on his arms rise from goosebumps, feeling restless, desiring to talk to someone about his thoughts. He checked under his bed, for wishful thinking had him believe Malorie would be hiding under it and would launch into a series of useless stories and questions. She wasn't, and Arun returned his head to his hands. He stared at the ceiling, awaiting sleep to take him, but his thoughts prevented a swift departure from this day. With time though, the candle's flame petered out, and with it took Arun's sight.

*

'Focus,' said Nicholas.

A familiar hill of candles glowed behind Nicholas's bushy face and a pair of cloaked arms that stretched out to Arun's head as he opened his eyes. No, he knew this weightless feeling: this was Kate's body once more. He couldn't move her eyes as they fixated on Nicholas, but the dark hut illuminated her peripheral as clearly as Arun remembered, almost too real. Another dream, another dance with that strange sleeping paralysis. Arun instinctively struggled to gain control of Kate's body, his fingers twitching back in his bed. No luck.

How was this happening? Why Kate? Why now? Arun's mind flicked through their moments on the Hill like pages in a book. His imprisonment. His first lesson in the study hut. The night under the peeking stars, when their hands touched with a surge of energy passing through his body—that final moment alongside her. Wait. Could that be it? It didn't feel like burning muscle at the time but rather a soft, tingling sensation he hadn't felt since. But how?

'Focus, Kate,' repeated Nicholas. His face didn't appear aged as usual, with a hint of brown spreading across his beard, but his eyes maintained that deep, piercing stare of his. 'Picture as much as you can. Their hair colour. Their clothes. Their skin. Your mother's eyes. Your father's hands. Any thing or any moment. Focus.'

A blue glow surrounded Arun's vision, emanating from Nicholas's gloved hands pressed against Kate's temples. Various thoughts came crashing into Arun's mind. A shoe shop. A woman's hand. These were not thoughts nor memories Arun recognised. He shrieked internally, unable to tense a single muscle in her body, bound to her as her thoughts traversed through sadness and joy, loss and love.

Kate began to scream, but Nicholas refused to let go.

'No, Kate,' said Nicholas. 'Don't lose it!'

'Let go of her!' shouted Arun through Kate's hardened jaw, feeling her anguish through him as her entire body stiffened. The blue light engulfed his vision, the voices and screams faded, and he felt his body fly weightlessly back before his vision turned to darkness.

'Nothing,' whispered Kate.

'Not even a face?' asked Nicholas.

'No. I saw nothing.'

Arun opened his eyes once more to a strange feeling: his own eyes had opened. The paralysis escaped him, leaving a cold wooden floor stretched beneath his back. He held his palms out above him, still inside the candlelit hut, with his vision slightly shrouded. He leaned upright, taking in the soft voices as they returned.

'You are putting a barrier up that I cannot break down,' said Nicholas. 'We shall try again tomorrow.'

'No,' snapped Kate. 'It's not going to work. It'll never work.'

Arun lifted himself and walked closer to the figures, sat across from each other with their knees to the floorboards. He examined every detail in their bodies, aware he stood stuck in a dream, unable to wake, not knowing why his mind had chosen to present this moment for him.

Nicholas lent Kate a hand that floated to the floor as she got up. She walked towards the door before stopping. She looked as if she had one final thought to share with Nicholas as the shroud in Arun's eyes began to darken. Kate turned, not to Nicholas but Arun. Her eyes widened, startling him, as the rest of her body slowly turned towards him.

'Kate,' uttered Arun, unsure of what else to say. Arun's sight faded just as Kate moved closer.

'The door,' said Kate, as the world turned dark, and Arun returned to a thoughtless sleep.

CHAPTER TWENTY-TWO

THE JOURNEY EAST

The splashing droplets of morning rain surrounded Kate's ears, bringing the painful truth that she'd have to travel the day having not slept. A long yawn pushed her stiff neck from the rough, scratching tree bark, bringing her to a stretch that threw her to her feet. The pair of sleepless scavengers nearby had hung around all night until the morning. They seemed asleep at first, but one flashed an open eye directly at Kate. All it would take was a thief with cold hands to spoil her journey. She could leave no time for carelessness. She mounted her steed and set off east.

It would be an exhausting journey, as each trot of Kate's horse jolted her aching spine like a beating drum. She had to hurry, though, to meet the group. Plucking up enough courage in her bones, she leaned forward and urged a gallop in her four-legged friend.

The next hour brought the same scenery, although thankfully less rainfall. One muddy, green field would end, and another would begin, over and over, like cycling through an eternal loop of deja vu. If it weren't for the horse's constant jolting, Kate's head would have dragged her body down to the side of the road into a deep sleep. Anything to escape the monotonicity.

Kate eventually found a row of bushes scattered with food, far more diverse in colour and size than the food back home. She couldn't see any standard berries or plums. Instead, the small fruits dominating the bushes were pale shades of red. One bite of a firm red and orange circular fruit brought Kate's lips to freeze and turn inwards. A sour tang similar to biting into an unripe orange filled her mouth, but a pinched nose allowed her to fill her now pea-sized stomach. She gambled on finding tastier food ahead, choosing to leave the sour bush fruit behind.

Midday arrived, and boredom had struck Kate's mind. She was on the edge of collapse, starved of sleep as her belly rumbled once more. She felt a sharp sting running down her injured arm and used her remaining energy to investigate the wound. Shades of deep and light purple ringed around the dried blood, despite the small opening. Her fingertips graced the top layer of skin, causing her to wince. It had to be a filthy, rusty tool, didn't it? At least a blade of light was a clean cut. An infected arm would only get worse with time, but this is where her medical experience ended, and all she could do was hope.

Kate drifted in and out of an active state of mind, her blinking reduced to a turtle's pace. Each time her eyes reopened, they'd pull together again—until they opened to a new vision. A dark, thunderous sky appeared, shouting above red weapons of light that violently crusaded through a village. Kate blinked, and the momentary vision disappeared. She shook her head of the dizzying flash, back to the endless horizon of peaceful, green fields.

Kate's eyes were now wide awake, but her body needed rest. Unfortunately, rest would not be afforded to her, as another settlement of ruins presented itself on the horizon. She rode the muddy path into the ruins with caution, looking around for potential supplies or hostile Mainlanders. Even an enemy may be able to reaffirm that she journeyed in the right direction.

'Hello?' yelled Kate from atop her steed. A moment of silence passed. Kate searched her mind for any Mainland words Nicholas had taught her. 'Bolheil? Hello?'

Not one second later, an old lady ambled out from a three-walled, roofless brick structure in the distance. She hunched with one arm holding her back.

Kate had never seen someone so frail and old before. The stories she must have.

'Hallo!' yelled the old lady in return.

Kate assumed a safe environment welcomed her, but her eyes stretched wide open, scanning all directions with extra caution given yesterday's events. She approached the old lady and dismounted, keeping her arms crossed and her hands under her cloak to hide her gloves. Trust nobody.

'Hi, do you know if east is that way?' asked Kate, looking to the hills.

'Da, is more accurate if you go little left,' replied the old lady in broken speech, with a thick nasal tone, pointing her hand slightly to the left of Kate's gaze.

Kate's nostrils flared with the old lady's pungent body odour. Dried mud covered her body head to toe, similar to Kate's face, and small twigs and bush leaf nestled in her thin, flowing grey hair. The only thing Kate feared for were her senses.

'Thanks,' said Kate. 'Thought you might not speak my language by your accent.'

'Da. Not fluent. Enough. Glad you understand. Need food for journey?'

The hospitality surprised Kate. 'Really? You have enough to spare? Sure, thank you.' She rattled off polite pleasantries as her stomach roared, joining the conversation. She'd do anything for good food right now.

'Da. Come, follow. Uma cognis pon geheim.' The woman waved Kate on, switching between languages. The two walked beside the roofless building. Their slight footprints ruptured the wall; small pieces crumbled from a newly formed crack. This structure wouldn't last another year in its state.

Kate stood beside two slanted, wooden doors on the floor with a torch burning beside them, with two foreign words painted over. 'Have you always lived here? You know, before?'

'Before? Fifty years. Five, zero. Long, long time.' The old lady bent as far as she could, struggling to open the first door, as Kate rushed to help with the second. 'Earthquake not good for building above ground, but below seeming be fine. Funny world.'

The old lady cackled to herself and grabbed the torch. She took one slow step down, minding the wet stone slab, and another, struggling down, eventually reaching the shadows. Kate moved to join her but stopped in hesitation. She peered into the tunnel of darkness as the torchlight dissipated, cautious of where it would lead. A glance at her gloves reaffirmed her confidence, though, and the chance to eat good food couldn't go amiss. She shook the worries from her head and followed.

Walking a dark, long, and narrow passageway, Kate soon found herself in a broadening open space with a long wooden table in the far corner, stretching out along both sides. The air was still, icy cold, caressing her skin. Sharp exhales brought a cloud of heat to the air, ambushed by the instant cold. The light flickered against the weak stone walls that had somehow managed to stay together. Some stones were entirely out of place, a touch away from falling out.

The woman placed the torch on the wall by the passageway as Kate keenly watched every step she took. She walked over to the table and pulled a long cloth towards her with mounds of vegetables spread across. These were far more familiar to Kate than the wild fruits before. Carrots, potatoes, and mini cucumbers sent Kate's saliva into overdrive.

'So much food in world now,' said the woman. 'I once was poor. No money. No food. No space. No bed. Now so much food. So much space. I live no worries. Sosinon i retnis. Prellundis Aerkin.'

Kate's fingers curled, and her lips pressed together in anguish upon hearing that phrase. However, it did take a slightly different meaning now, coming from an old lady and not a crazed preacher. Perhaps she could offer some answers instead of an open hand. 'What does that phrase mean?' asked Kate.

'Prellundis Aerkin? Praise. No judgement. Always Aerkin. One true God.'

Kate smirked. 'Global mass murder should probably be judged.'

'No. Nature happy. Animals happy. Trees happy. Plants happy when sun return. Before? Everything unhappy. Humans always selfish. Now all equal.'

The old lady was blunt in her judgement, but Kate had always thought jarringly along these lines. Kate's gaze fell to the ground; her goal was to kill

Aerkin, and nothing would change that. However, she'd always been grateful for the world she found herself in, and the journey through these fruitful lands and swarming seas only strengthened this belief.

'My mentor seems to think we're all suffering,' said Kate. 'I'm happy with how beautiful the world is. I guess I thought, maybe, it was much worse out there. Maybe the Mainland was famished, and there were no animals or trees. But it's like home. A bit muddier, maybe, but still. Remove all the rubble of the cities, and it's still a beautiful world.'

'Da, da.' The old lady handed the vegetables over to Kate, who removed her hands from her cloak and took hold of the gift. The old lady smirked. The outside wind swirled and brought the wooden doors to crash shut behind them, leaving only the torchlight illuminating the two within the shadows.

'How can I thank you?' asked Kate. 'What's your name?'

The old lady paused for a moment and laughed. 'Is okay. You needing to eat lots of food.'

Kate chuckled in return for the first time in a while.

'So, what bringing you here?' asked the old lady, running her hand along the table and returning to the vegetable mound.

Kate cradled the food in her arms, considering the truthful answer. 'With a group of travellers. On a bit of a journey.'

'Da. So travellers. Not family? Not friend?'

'As close to friends as we can be. Don't always get along.'

'Group is hard. People always wanting different thing. What you want?'

'We want to travel far into the Mainland, and—'

'No, what *you* want?'

Kate couldn't remember being asked this question before and released a short sigh. She'd lived her life intending to free the land and live a life where she didn't have to feel hidden each day. She bowed her head. This had always been Nicholas's purpose, and he drilled it into Kate. This was her entire life, but she had to unravel what she truly wanted out of this. What purpose did she have?

'I...I don't...' Kate's mind tore in two as she turned away to the dark corridor. The darkness swayed, and a recognisable voice echoed. Away from Nicholas's guidance, she felt happiest in her memories. The memory of holding her mother's hand in a shoe shop. The memory of being sat next to Iris as the songbirds swooped through the moors. She fought a selfish yearning rising inside her that pulled her towards finding Iris and escaping to a peaceful pasture.

She didn't know where her current path led. None of Nicholas's promises of finding memories or doors had come to pass. Who's to say he wasn't right about their journey, too? He could be dragging them to their deaths along a reckless path of vengeance. Had Nicholas been right about anything? The thoughts scattered in her mind, yet they all pointed to one thing. 'I just want to feel loved.'

Kate turned back but froze. A chipped knife appeared pressed to her throat, and her eyes snapped open. She stared at the blade, blunted but could still cut an artery.

'Don't do anything silly,' said the old lady, placing her free hand on Kate's long gloves. She ripped them off with one smooth backwards swipe. As she did, Kate back-stepped away from the knife, releasing the food to the floor. The old lady thrust the blade forward, but Kate had retreated far enough.

'You asked my name,' the old lady croaked. 'My name is Rillen.'

Kate's eyes pondered at what her ears had told her, snapping out of her fearful gaze. Rillen. That name. Perhaps it sounded similar by coincidence. No. It was definitely the same name.

'Met someone by that name yesterday,' said Kate, displaying calm, with her palms held forward in the air, choosing not to back away further.

'Indeed you did, and you still have your gloves.' replied Rillen, her language now elegantly strung together, unbroken by foreign tongue. 'Don't worry. I'll succeed where they failed.'

'Try me.' Kate's eyebrows strained together along with her eyes. Each blink felt heavy. Her stomach rumbled, still fighting her hunger and sleep deprivation despite being alert to this woman's altered mannerisms. Regardless, she could not leave without the gloves. Even if it meant losing her life with them.

'We Rillen are the eyes and ears of Aerkin's land. We do what we must to bring the light back. Do you understand? Now go. Leave.'

'Already killed one Rillen. Don't make me kill you too.'

'I was warned your evil kind would bring death.' Rillen was no longer hunched or withering. 'Even to a poor, frail old woman.'

Kate's aggression turned to a confused scoff. 'We're not the evil ones.' Rillen sent a cautionary swipe through the air as the last word left her lips.

'Stay back, thief. Leave now and never return.' Rillen looked at the gloves as she inched closer to the torchlight. It was as if they illuminated and sparkled in her eyes.

'You're making a huge mistake,' warned Kate, solid as a statue. 'You can't use them. You don't know what they can do.'

'Da. I do. And I know you do too. It must be intoxicating, no? Seeing your memories as clear as if they were now. Reliving the highs. *Changing the lows.* Oh, to think how your mind could not be your own, how you could retrieve the memories of others. Living. Or dead.' Rillen stared deeper into the gloves. 'But no. You can't control it. Only he can. I must return them to their rightful owner, and he will look upon me with great pride and glory. I will be rewarded, da, me, with a golden palace to bathe in.' She moved a step closer, thrusting the knife aimlessly once more, pushing Kate back into the corridor shadows. 'You have no option but to run. He is giving you one last chance.'

'He doesn't get to decide. He's not here.'

'I told you. We are his eyes and ears. He can see you and hear you as clearly as I can. His whispers are in my head. He knows your ruthlessness—how you drove your dagger through a poor boy crying for his father's help. Tut, tut.' Rillen smiled in a dazed wonder, running her fingers through the gloves.

Kate's stomach lifted. She couldn't believe it. How could Rillen have known? She inched back further into darkness as the torchlight flickered behind Rillen, eclipsing the light from her body as if she were an encroaching demon.

'You…people. You're not normal.' Kate was lost for thoughtful words.

'He's thankful that I've taken the gloves. He's…he's saying that I'm his favourite child. Thank you, Aerkin! Riches beyond any coin. Yes, Aerkin! Yes! I will be one with him. Immortal souls. One! Eternal!'

Kate's exhaustion tightened her eyes. Her head pounded, and her limbs ached. But losing her gloves drove an adrenaline spike through her body that took control of her. As the woman pushed forward, lost in the glory of the gloves and her own voice, Kate raised her foot high from the shadows and kicked the knife from Rillen's hands. She wrestled Rillen to the ground back down the corridor and into light, grabbing her throat; Rillen could only fight back by pushing her hands into Kate's face. Kate didn't budge, strangling Rillen, pushing her thumbs down into the centre of Rillen's throat with all her body weight. Kate's merciless eyes peered through Rillen's stretched fingertips, without blinking, staring at her as her struggle eased and her life ended.

Kate winced as the pain returned to her injured arm from her tensed grip; it snapped her out of her fury. She removed herself from the lifeless body beneath and slid her gloves back on in a panicked state, as if she were naked without them on. She stormed down the dark hallway with her gloves leading the way. She reached the bending wooden timbers above her and smashed through the door with her ignited fists, without care for what could await. She didn't return to gather the gifted food; she wasn't thinking straight.

Outside, Kate spotted an older man a dozen metres away, sweeping the floor with a rusty rake; he must have closed the door. A mistake? No. She knew what the man would see: a stranger leaving the basement with glowing gloves and blood stained clothes from the day before. Kate strode directly towards him. The man hesitated in fear, stumbling, and dropped his rake.

Without thinking, Kate drove a dagger of light through his heart, taking no chances nor considering what threat or help he offered. His mouth stretched as wide as it could, releasing a whimper as his hands reactively shook in mid-air. He fell to his knees and into Kate's legs.

Kate's head and heart pounded as she looked around, finding no one else to pierce by blade. There wasn't a moment to stand still; she strode to her horse before others could appear and curse their own lives. Before climbing on, she looked towards a tree with a patch of grass beneath it. It looked like the perfect place to rest. Kate's body craved it, but her fluctuating adrenaline masked her tired mind. Did she kill a frightened and unarmed man? No, it was too risky. It was the right thing to do. Wasn't it? It could have been the man with the baby all over again—no need to take that risk.

Kate stumbled to the patch of grass and knelt beside it. She pinched her nostrils as hard as she could, turning her nose red. She wasn't here to rest. She took two handfuls of mud and smeared it over the already dried mud on her cheeks and forehead.

Jumping on the horse and throwing away her thoughts, Kate escaped east by instruction and took to the fields again.

*

The late afternoon brought rain and thunder, and Kate made her way to shelter in woodland beside her travelled path. Rillen: what did it all mean? Her mind exhausted its thoughts, and her eyes could no longer push against gravity to stay open as she searched for a dry patch beside a tree. She collapsed her back into its solid splintering wood, not feeling a thing, and begged her body to fall into a deep sleep. The only thing keeping her inert body awake were the images of the eyes of each Rillen as their lives slipped away.

*

Cracking raindrops. Cold brisk air. No more trees. Riding atop a horse, Kate looked down to see Iris's gloves yet again. She held onto Malorie in a strange environment she didn't recognise. What was Malorie doing here? Kate's vision was pulled to her right towards a crooked farmhouse, where three masked warriors stood staring deep into her as if reading her thoughts.

As fast as the dream had stirred, it sank to a roar of thunder filling the skies, jolting Kate's eyes open. It was night; she must have fallen asleep without a moment's thought. She found her bearings, searching around for the farmhouse, but instead found herself laying against a tree. She instantly panicked, having wasted time away from continuing her journey. Was the group waiting for her already, perhaps? Her stomach ached and shrivelled, and the thin streaks of mud that didn't wash away had dried on her face. She wouldn't be able to travel far, if at all, in the pitch dark. The dream she'd awoken from faded into the back of her memory as she slumped past her horse.

Her stomach lacked the energy to rumble, and her arm felt too numb to notice. All Kate could think to do was to walk out to the pouring skies, lift her head to the heavens, and let the rain fall into her open mouth.

CHAPTER TWENTY-THREE

A NEW LEADER

ADE 13—*Another year of minor food resurgence brings a recruitment drive. Those on the Hill search for more people capable of wielding light. Hope continues to grow. More varied food brings a sliver of strength back to humanity.*

Large herbivores such as horses, deer, and cows are seen roaming in fields, as opposed to rare sightings. Life's determination to survive against all odds is a truly remarkable thing.

Kate is growing up fast. Ever so fast.

ADE 14—*After calming weather patterns over the years, an increase in thunderstorms begins. It becomes dangerous to venture far. Towns and cities of sorts are avoided at all costs, apart from the scavengers that are too scared to leave. Food growth begins to improve. The fruit on the bushes is small and bitter, but the carrots, potatoes and such that grow underground are huge and flavourful wherever shields of trees can prevent waterlogging.*

ADE 15—*I gain connections with those travelling across the lands still. They bring grave news. The 'Aerkinism Era' truly begins, and the new religion begins to spread. Shrines emanate from the centre of the Mainland, making their way north. They praise this so-called God of dark energy that glows like fire and* reigns three hundred metres tall. The one 'searching for those who stole the sun'. If only they knew.

A Hill warrior, Iris, goes missing and is feared dead during a meetup. Her gloves are lost, but plenty more have now been made, with fifteen pairs now worn on the Hill. The day will soon come when we no longer need to hide.

*

'We, the fine returners,
    Of summer sand below,
    Our feet and toes where the south wind blows,
    Oh, where we'd rather go?
    We, of no surrender,
    Ride far beyond despite,
    These stormy nights that attest our mights,
    Oh, where we'd rather fight?'

The voices of the Marshals belted across the flatlands, drowning out the songbirds as they scurried across trees in the afternoon breeze. Whilst keeping the mood light, Nicholas and the group continued their strenuous walk towards the Ruins of Rennes.

'I penned that song a long time ago for them, so it is a welcome surprise to hear it once more,' said Nicholas, walking alongside Jordan, sheltered in the centre of the group. 'It seemed like an interesting juxtaposition at the time.'

'I don't know what that means,' replied Jordan, kicking the mud in front of him.

Nicholas carried on without reply, simultaneously whistling the group's song instead. Behind the joyous tune, his thoughts were threatening to break through his mind. *Nicholas,* his mind whispered. The tune faded. But as it did, and as his mind's song quietened, the bears by the shore entered his thoughts. *The bears, Nicholas.* Their size and eyes were unlike any species of bear before the Worldshift. This was not a simple case of mutation. Not a slight change. They did not grow an extra toe nor grow more prominent ears. The red eyes held the answer: they were engineered weapons, and they must belong to Aerkin.

Nicholas's pondering thoughts diminished as his darting eyes caught Jordan's scrutinising stare. 'Ah. What's the time?' Nicholas checked his watch.

'Uh, you decided we don't use time,' said Jordan, concern etched across his face. 'Does that thing even work anymore?'

'Yes, sorry. I glance at it occasionally.' Nicholas blinked fiercely. 'Bears. No, sorry. The watch. I remember the feeling of seeing six in the morning and feeling dread. Glancing at it in the evening and realising it was time to send my daughter to bed. The ambivalence of weekdays and the exuberance of weekends. An entire life dictated by numbers. Truly amazing how life can change. Time was one of humanity's most fascinating inventions, but in reality, it is simply the movement of order to disorder. A decay; hence where we find ourselves now.'

'I can barely remember time. Except for my parents telling me I was late for school. Again.'

'Too busy styling your hair, I presume?' Nicholas examined Jordan's solemn mood; his left arm grasped his right.

'I should warn you, Jordan, a world without hospitals means even the slightest of wounds gives me cause for concern.' Nicholas's words had little effect on Jordan. 'Kate would have you believe this world is perfect now. Without doctors or medicine. We can only hope that an infection will not spread, and your arm will begin to heal. Are you too stubborn to cauterise the wound? I mean, burn the skin. A bullet to the arm could soon be fatal.'

Jordan's eyes popped out, staring a hole through Nicholas.

'No. Sorry, of course not. Extremely unlikely. Bears. What? No. Perhaps we should take your mind off these troubles.' Nicholas observed the significant contrast of the singing Marshals against the lonely wandering Emitai further ahead, again blinking fiercely to compose his state of mind. 'Ah, yes. I would like to assign you a slightly different task along this journey, Jordan, concerning our new friend in mourning.'

Jordan looked concerned about many a thing. 'Uh…am I not doing well?'

'Jordan, you will find you have many redeeming qualities. Masking your pain and disappointment is not one of them. You do not have to display the qualities you think other people will like in you. You have to show the ones you like for yourself.'

Not the quickest in retort, Jordan fluttered his eyelids with a frown.

Nicholas continued, wary of his audience. 'Challenges like this can bring out the best and worst in us.' He paused, given his statement concerned himself, too. 'It can also bring out who we truly are. I think your ego and your belief in yourself is, perhaps, for show. Where I think you would benefit greatly is to take a protégé, someone like Emitai, under your wings.'

'What would that prove?' said Jordan, with a slight tone of rejection.

'I believe in helping someone, you would feel good about your abilities and maintain that fierce confidence of yours, in addition to ridding yourself of negative thoughts. It would help you to think more about the fate of someone who would struggle more than you. Teaching is not a one-way street. It can often help both sides to grow.'

Jordan held his head high, pursing his lips together. 'He doesn't have gloves, though, so what am I teaching him?'

'He'll do fine without. There's much more to us than our gloves.' Nicholas acknowledged Jordan's continuing stares. 'Listen, my friend. Courage goes a long way, and that young man has a Hill-sized basket full of it. The most important thing is how he is coping and making sure he has kept his courage. Otherwise, a weapon will do him no good. Perhaps it is too soon for Emitai to be concentrating on courting friendship. But I think we owe it to him to try.'

Nicholas fell back in his comfort zone, applying his wisdom. It was in turmoil and under attack that he lacked experience. And such turmoil unlocked his mind. *Nicholas.* The calm walk allowed him to push these thoughts, and the thoughts of the bears, into the back of his mind once again. The others still sang, and he whistled along with them, leaving Jordan to run ahead and catch up with Emitai.

A tall, displaced road sign soon appeared in the misted distance. It bore an old icon for a train station, hiding behind a blood-stained symbol smeared on seemingly by hand. It consisted of a circle, which contained a sphere at the top. A line ran from the sphere to the bottom, and four lines spread away.

'That is Aerkin's symbol,' said Nicholas to the group. 'A weapon firing down on the ground. It does not settle the nerves.'

'No it isn't,' said Jordan. 'Looks like a flower with long blades of grass.' The others walked on without word. 'What? It does.'

'So everything is Aerkin's now?' asked Matuu, trailing behind and wheezing. 'Are we walking the Aerkin path between the Aerkin trees?'

'Your misplaced sincerity aside, I am afraid so. Everything in this land is his by default.' Nicholas turned to his bag and retrieved his map. 'There is a railway running by the river that leads directly to Rennes. We need to find the tracks from hereon. Keep watch.'

The day's scenery stagnated, and the legs of many grew heavy. Nicholas observed the group as always, looking ahead to see Jordan and Emitai walking together with their heads turned in opposite directions. Matuu and Serr were behind, also silent apart from the occasional clapping of their hands as they played a game of walking slaps. Songs no longer ambushed Nicholas's ears either. 'This day is doppeling along,' drawled Nicholas. He often used the term doppeling to describe a day that seemed to drag longer the later it got. He also used the term when timeless time flew by. His tone would dictate which version he meant.

A rest and a meal followed. Nicholas huffed; his knees needed this more than any. Moanings of tired legs not used to long travel interjected patches of silence until an unexpected wisp of light shot through the group. A sharp, zapping sound brought Nicholas to life as the light travelled across the grass and caught a squirrel's head, blasting it clean off. Nicholas led a wave of heads, turning to face the front of the group.

Zachenne stood tall with his arms akimbo. 'A snack.'

'A snack would be a pack of Grain Waves,' said Matuu. 'I'd give anything for a pack of honey mustard—no—sour cream and chives.'

'How'd you get his head from there?' asked Emitai, eyes stretched. Zachenne stood twenty metres away from the lifeless rodent at the group's tail.

'Archery: six years. Tarios training: fourteen years.' Zachenne gave a nod—one of the Tarios took to retrieve the meal.

'Right,' said Emitai. 'And *Tarios* is?'

'A name for our group, our gloves, and the name of the woman I love. A beautiful and brilliant archer.'

'Is she dead?' Emitai's tone suggested he feared the worst, the norm for anyone asking such a question.

Zachenne adjusted his gloves, head held high. 'Worse. Married to someone who could give her what I couldn't. Children.' Zachenne whistled a signal for his group and walked ahead once more.

'It's best to leave the questioning there,' whispered Nicholas to Emitai before leading the others to their feet. 'I believe that's our cue.'

Nicholas caught up to Zachenne, ahead of the now strolling pack, to have a private word. 'We have enjoyed a safe passage so far, but it is all a bit too quiet; it feels unsettling to me.'

'This land is vast,' replied Zachenne. 'He can't be everywhere. It makes sense that the danger lies on the shores and what remains of the villages and towns.'

Nicholas hummed in agreement. 'You still appear to have no fear when faced with peril, unlike me.'

'Don't beat yourself up. It comes at a price when you feel nothing else.' Zachenne stared straight ahead, not activating a single muscle in his face.

A fleeting thought made its way into Nicholas's head. 'I would prefer for you to lead our group forward from now on.'

Zachenne lifted an eyebrow as the other dipped, pitching his voice slightly higher. 'Excuse me?'

'Yes, sorry, that appeared from thin air. I mean to say…my decision making under pressure has been questionable. My thoughts are troubling me. I believe it is in the group's best interest for me to humbly step down, as I feel we would fare better under improved leadership, leaving me to offer wisdom, advice, and caution, perhaps still.'

'Nicholas…' replied Zachenne, his lips unsure of where to rest. 'You have led us all these years.'

'Yet you have a propensity for leadership, given your career. I am afraid I do not. I spent the early years of my life a timid physicist, after all. In fact, I am not sure why I did not suggest it sooner.' Nicholas placed his hand on the left of his chest. 'I can feel it, my friend. The drumming of my heart. Whenever I think he might be near. I pause for too long, and it will only grow more difficult. I will stick to my main task but leading the others must be yours.'

Zachenne stopped in motion, searching for words. Nicholas granted him a moment with an arm around his shoulders.

'I can't,' uttered Zachenne softly. 'I refuse.'

'If you would prefer me to be as blunt as you usually are, I will be. You know I will not return after I confront Aerkin. Changing leadership is inevitable. It would be wiser if we did it to give you experience now rather than later. This is who you were born to be.'

'I've been a leader before, and remember how that turned out. Besides, I'd assumed we wouldn't require leadership after this journey. There would be no need to fight once our task is complete.'

'Humans will always require leadership.'

Zachenne looked resigned to appeal this time, head bowed. 'I will do what I can. Thank you.'

'Look at that. Back in your natural role. It seems you do have emotions, after all.' Nicholas chuckled softly. 'That is settled then. I suppose one comfort this new world gives us is the return of courage and guile defining our leaders, not greed and falsities. I will follow you every step of the way, my friend.'

A peaceful transition of leadership had passed. Before the moment could be appreciated, arguing voices from far ahead interrupted the past and present leaders. Nicholas recognised the voices of Jordan and Emitai and scurried to reach them.

'Easy for you to say with those gloves on!' shouted Emitai.

'Don't take your anger out on me, little man,' replied Jordan, arms folded.

'What's going on?' Nicholas stepped between the two.

'He called me weak.' Emitai strained his eyes at Jordan and threw his hands in the air. 'He said I have no chance against anyone if I choose to fight. I can fight!' Nicholas's arm stretched across Emitai to hold him back.

'He took it the wrong way; he's being pathetic,' said Jordan.

'Pathetic? You try losing someone you care about! You try going through what I did. You don't know anything, but you still feel free to judge. How sad a life that must be!'

'I do!' shouted Jordan. 'I know loss! And I care about Serr and how she makes me feel. I care about Matuu, and if he ever thinks I'm insulting him. I care about Nicholas. I care about the group. Even the kid back home. And I care that you lost your brother and how you're feeling. I just don't know how to express any of it.'

'These are just empty words from a man who hasn't finished being a boy.' Emitai turned his back and continued his march along the puddled path.

Nicholas offered his arm around Jordan's shoulders. Jordan declined the offer with a huff of his breath and walked on.

'I'm looking forward to dealing with this,' said Zachenne, approaching Nicholas with the Tarios nearby. 'Or can emotional conflict still fall under your remit?'

Nicholas smirked. 'You will find it is most rewarding if you do, though take my words with a fistful of salt.'

With the majority of the group still halted, Nicholas took the opportunity to silence the murmurs and speak to the group in unison. He cleared his throat and raised his voice. 'I would like to hijack this moment if I may.

'I have had the pleasure of leading you all for many years. I have watched you all grow and helped you all to do so in one way or another. I believe that has been my great strength, the proof being before my very eyes. You are the men and women that have chosen to fight for the future's children. I look at all of you, at all your varied backgrounds and your different journeys here, and I could not be prouder.

'So, this is where I must abdicate and where Zachenne must take the reins. My greatest weaknesses will become clearer in the days and weeks ahead, and they will not be allowed to affect you all. But I will still be here, lending my ear and waffling into yours.'

Although Nicholas had only handed over decision-making power, the words he pulled from the depth of his heart sent a lump into the back of his throat. He searched the faces of his followers, sensing a mix of confusion and sorrow. He felt a strong bond with every single one of his companions.

The group members raised a gloved hand high one by one, clenching their fists, until no right arm was left to dangle. Nicholas had not seen this gesture before nor heard it spoken of. It appeared spontaneous, but every one of them looked around and seemed to understand its meaning, as did Nicholas. The bond could not be stronger. The Guards and the Marshals, despite having fallen companions, sent smiles and nods Nicholas's way.

As the evening reached its end, the group stumbled across an old railway, which Nicholas had marked on his map. The overgrowth covering the tracks lay reasonably stable, but much of the metal had snapped or distorted, weaving between the polka-dot puddles of rain. Overgrown trees lined the way and provided cover for the group from all angles. The tracks stretched endlessly into the distance as if they would never end. Above the tracks, a sharp bolt of light ignited and faded instantly, brightening a patch of cloud for a second. A satellite, perhaps; a message passed down from those who came before. They were becoming rarer with each passing year. He often wondered if the universal space stations were still in orbit and if bodies of abandoned astronauts were frozen in forgotten time, trapped in the white planet's grasp.

'This is it,' said Nicholas, looking back beneath the clouds. 'It should be about two nights' sleep along this path.'

'What do you think awaits us?' asked Zachenne. 'Iris?'

'It could be nothing. It could be war. I am not sure, but surely a surprise awaits,' Nicholas watched as Zachenne marshalled the group forward, embracing his new leadership, and his eyes glazed over. His mind emptied. *Nicholas. Be careful. He's coming for you.*

Nicholas followed, fighting his mind at the rear of the group as the train tracks directed them to the Ruins of Rennes.

CHAPTER TWENTY-FOUR

THE RUINS OF RENNES

*A*DE 16—*The Mainland Temple construction is rumoured to be complete or near complete. Thunder-snowstorms meet with lava from the mountain volcanoes. Not much else is known about what lies in or around the temple.*

I make contact with people further south to gain information on the Mainland. I set up secret routes and connections. There is word of a new virus spreading: the Dengtu. It is carried by a resurgence of mosquitoes in some areas and can be fatal. It has not made its way off the Mainland as far as we know.

ADE 17—I travel to the Mainland for the first time in seventeen years to make further contacts. Unfortunately, I am spotted by a suspicious group of five individuals in the distance. Dark energy does not affect them, one of which can block my beam. Aerkin is making weapons. It is clear now; Aerkin is still searching for me and must want me alive. I escape.

Kate is surpassing all my expectations of her. She has produced light with a yellowish tint with a density to break through my blue light. If her trajectory continues, she will be the one to bring Aerkin down. What a woman she is becoming.

ADE 20—Goodness. It has been a few years since I have felt the need to return to this notebook; I have been a little busy. Where to begin? Peaceful years continued with constant rainfall. We are still plagued with thunderstorms and quakes, but overall the weather and temperature is improving year on year. The Hill now grows plenty of food and trades with local individuals (Indies) for information. Meetings, jobs, and routines; life is beginning to have a touch of normality, dare I say.

The Mainlanders believe I am hiding on the coast or have travelled by boat. Aerkin does not know where I grew up, so I need not worry about hiding here. He may soon expand his presence to the Home Isles. And with no news of the Aerkin Knights, I feel this year is simply the calm before the…oh. The horses need feeding. I knew I forgot something. Should not be writing this down.

*

Two dry nights had passed without incident on the railway to Rennes, apart from a scattering of quakes that brought the feeling of the trains running once more. It had been a welcome treat for the group to enjoy calmer days after the previous two. Nicholas worried the railway would offer the group up to all sorts of scouts, onlookers, and beasts, but this did not seem to be the case. The only visible encounters came with harmless survivors who would flee and hide with the sight of the travelling ensemble. They seemed to have no religious affiliation, no connection with war, nor hate. Perhaps they could not afford the trouble; they were living in desolated peace.

One whole week after leaving the Hill, the group had reached the outskirts of Rennes. The greys of concrete chaos replaced the greens of the trees. The outskirts alone felt more extensive than any city they ventured to back home. This city looked to once hold a stadium and a university—technical marvels of the past.

A fetid scent of rotting corpses hit the group. Stepping between fallen power cables, the group soon found themselves stepping between decomposed bodies, most of which were skeletons, but some had only lay resting for a year or under. Flies emerged as the dominant population here. With luck, this spot would be isolated and would not carry through to the city.

'Disgusting,' uttered Jordan. 'This is a graveyard,'

'The Earth is a graveyard,' replied Zachenne.

Nicholas did not know what to expect here. Aerkin's familiar red symbols were apparent wherever a large slab of concrete lay, painted across the graffiti of old, undoubtedly spelling trouble in some form. As Zachenne led the group forward, Jordan joined Nicholas and Emitai, looking eager to restart his task. Nicholas prepared to play peacemaker, given the friendship of his company could only be described as non-existent.

'What about your light beam?' asked Emitai, continuing from a string of dark energy questions from earlier. 'Can you use it to destroy a whole army?'

'It becomes a matter of control over chaos,' replied Nicholas. 'Presume there are one hundred men in front of me wishing to kill me, in a straight line, with nothing behind them. I could take their lives instantly, yes. That brings a moral dilemma, however. Should any living being be able to take the lives of so many, let alone in such a short time?'

'But you'd be helping end a war and save lives.'

'Precisely the dilemma, my friend. Saving lives by killing lives. How many must be saved for how many to die? What serves the greater good? What is the greater good? It is a point of view for us all to consider. I could save one life by killing one thousand, all based on *my* good point of view.'

'Sure, I get it. There's good and bad. But Aerkin's army is pure evil.'

'Your brother was in that army. Was he evil? I thought you and your brother believed that evil could not be born, only manifested?'

Emitai looked pensive, stepping between broken train track planks. 'He said that, not me.'

'How did Iris free you?' Jordan joined the conversation whilst kicking a rock along the floor.

'With her hands,' replied Emitai.

'I believe Jordan speaks with sincerity, my new friend,' said Nicholas. 'Though his half-hearted demeanour would have you think otherwise.' Nicholas aimed a stern look Jordan's way.

Emitai dismissed Nicholas's comment with a shake of the head. 'So would you use your light if they attacked us now?'

Nicholas scanned the environment. 'It depends. There is a lot of debris around, and my light would destroy most of everything in front of it. The repercussions were minimal at sea, but I would have to consider what damage that would cause on land. If it is easier for the Tarios to pick the attackers off, I would wait.'

'Waiting could mean someone dies.'

'Being careless could mean someone dies.'

Emitai shook his head again without reply. He kept his pensive stance and walked in silence, seemingly pretending to admire the tortured scenery. His thoughts looked to consume him. He eventually responded to Jordan's question. 'It was luck. There were eight of us, and Iris saved only me. I was in the closest cage to the door. The other seven must still be there, living in torment.

'I don't know how she got in; my mind is still blurred by how fast it all happened. Klasa wasn't there—the woman who kept us. The cages had locks and bars, and that's it. It was degrading. Whenever my brother defended evil, it never made sense.' Emitai's speech softened with the tightness that crushes one's throat. 'She wasn't red behind the eyes. She didn't look damaged or tortured. She looked just like a normal person but seemed to enjoy being evil.

'She had a…metal thing…with that glove material of yours. It sat around her waist. It had eight solid arms leading out to each of us, out of her reach. We surrounded her like a human shield, attached by metal braces. She made us practise defending ourselves—defending her, with shields and metal chopped and filed into swords. If one of us slipped up, she would push down on the metal, and red light would burn into all our skin.'

Emitai lifted his top to show a wide ring of red skin circling his back. Nicholas held his breath and felt Jordan do likewise. 'What's the need for this kind of device?' continued Emitai. 'Who thinks of such a thing? No matter her story or reasons, there's no excuse for becoming that. I tried so hard not to think about it. With my brother, I'd just pretend to be a stupid kid again. Pretend it never happened. But without him now, it's stuck with me.'

Nicholas's voice deepened. 'It is with great apology that I say, despite once thinking you a fool, you have done remarkably well to get here. The wounds you bear are….' Nicholas would seldom struggle for words mid-sentence nor end in underwhelming fashion. Emitai's words had cracked him. 'Such strength, without the cheap confidence that a weapon like ours can give, I have never seen before.'

Jordan looked as if he had hung on to every word Emitai said. 'Hey, mate. Did you want to try on one of my gloves at some point? It probably won't fit or work. But it's worth a try.'

'Sure,' replied Emitai, his head returning to the scenery again after a transient smile.

The group walked on as fallen bridge debris frequented the path, slowing their navigation over rocky ground. It would not be long before they spotted peering eyes through the debris and heard scampering footsteps around every corner. A strange clicking sound became apparent from a loose wall beside the tracks. A hand appeared around the side and ushered the travellers to come closer.

Zachenne turned to Nicholas from the front, who offered raised eyebrows suggestively in return. Zachenne halted the group and proceeded alone, his head darting from side to side.

'I don't think we should be talking to people,' whispered Jordan. 'This isn't a good idea.'

Reaching the wall, Zachenne appeared to be in deep discussion with the unknown entity. The group watched on as their new leader bravely stood on his own, assessing the danger. Moments passed, and Zachenne finally moved, turning around to return to the group.

'She uttered the name "Iris",' said Zachenne in earshot. 'I don't find that name to hold much secrecy anymore, but she said there's a trap up ahead for Iris's friends. She recognised us by description. We're to follow her instead, to an underground location.'

'Nope, not gonna happen,' said Jordan. 'An underground location? In the dark? This sounds like the real trap.'

'On the contrary, my friend,' said Nicholas, beaming. 'A promising situation, I promise you. It has seemed so far that hostiles desire to make themselves known. It is the ones that choose to hide that pique my interest. Zachenne?'

Zachenne scanned the Hillfolk faces. 'I've decided my first change as leader is to leave major decisions to a vote. We'll do a show of hands. Those against following strangers into the dark underground, raise your hand.'

The group raised their hands instantly and almost unanimously.

'Very well,' said Nicholas. 'You proceed above ground. I will investigate our new friend. I have a gut feeling that our path lies here…I hope.'

'Excuse me?' said Zachenne, remaining stoic. 'You'd stray from us just based on a hopeful feeling?'

'Yes. It is the best feeling we can have at this moment. Just as I planted the tree at the top of the Hill; it may never grow tall, the sun may never shine on it, and it may never create shade or bear fruit, but I still planted it out of the hope it brings.'

'Nicholas, we can't separate.' Zachenne crossed his arms. 'The group has voted: we move on.'

Nicholas preferred not to argue with ex-military. 'Agreed. You have leadership over the group. However, I did not give you leadership over me. I will no doubt be following your path very shortly.' Nicholas veered off the tracks and walked back to the woman behind the wall. Nicholas knew he could not be stopped, but he assumed the group would change their minds and follow as he kept his smile.

'What happened to "I'll follow you every step of the way"?' Zachenne raised his voice after Nicholas had paced halfway. 'Every move you've made since we left the Hill has been the opposite of what I expected from you. Now how do you expect us to trust in this plan if this is your behaviour?'

Nicholas stopped and matched Zachenne's raised tone. 'I have never asked you to trust in my plan. I have asked you to trust in me. Even when the plan changes, or if you think it will fail, you must understand that every choice I have made as a leader and continue to make as a man is for the betterment of you all.' Nicholas returned in his march towards the mysterious woman.

'Fine.' Zachenne's tone sounded dismissive. 'We honour the vote and move on. I trust we will see you soon.'

Nicholas did not turn his neck to see the group's reaction as Zachenne's words faded but felt a strange pit in his stomach, for he now journeyed on his own. His mind opened up again as his whistling tune disappeared. Thoughts came rushing out. *You're alone now, Nicholas.* For all the work he had done leading the group here, for them to follow someone else's path for the first timeless time felt disconcerting. But it was his decision, after all. He hoped they would not falter under new leadership. *Is your instinct right, Nicholas?* Yes. He believed to be right in trusting this woman and strolled over to the pair of peering eyes.

'Hello. I am willing to follow if you have news,' said Nicholas.

'Quick, down. We must go down,' whimpered the woman, waving her hands vigorously. Her bright ginger hair mixed with muted browns, like scratched copper, tied in a ponytail. Her tank top looked just as dirty, and the cold weather made it a strange choice of attire, whilst her energetic movements defied the heavy bags under her eyes. 'They watch. Their eyes see all. Come quick. No mosquito. No Dengtu. Safe with us.'

Nicholas. Run. Nicholas held his thoughts at bay and trusted the scruffy woman, who led him down an alleyway constructed by mounds of rubble on either side. A restaurant sign for coffee poked out of the rubble on one side, and a decayed shop mannequin protruded from the other. It only took a few minutes of crouching and tiptoeing for them to reach a large concrete slab on the floor. It looked like any other piece of rubble, but three patterned taps from the woman brought it to rise on one side.

'Crawl, quick,' said the woman. 'Others coming?'

'No, just me.' Although Nicholas placed trust in her, this seemed far too reckless. The small gap offered no light, and for all he knew, it could drop into a room full of red-eyed bears. Those cursed bears again, filtering into his mind.

'Go, go,' ushered the woman again.

'After you,' insisted Nicholas. He refused to move, bringing a scowling glare from the woman, who dropped to the floor and proceeded to crawl under. Nicholas had no option now and reduced his aged knees to the stones and into the dark.

Nicholas found himself inside a cramped sloping tunnel. The muddy, unlit walls prevented a steady grip, but he followed the echoing murmurs of the woman ahead regardless. It did not take too long for him to spot a glistening of light. He reached level ground by sliding through another small gap and opened his eyes to the sewers beneath the city. Torchlight sparkled off large puddles of water dotted throughout the disused system.

As Nicholas slowly examined the environment, the woman walked away, heading out of view around a bend. The path to his left had collapsed through, leading to a dead-end consisting of piles of sheets and a group of scruffy men sleeping. More people lay awake along the other side of the tunnel, some talking and others playing a throwing game against the curved wall with various materials. They spoke a mix of French and other languages, and Nicholas could not catch a word.

Nicholas rushed ahead to find the woman bending over a pile of dry sheets that held a baby. It looked a few months old by Nicholas's understanding and cried as the supposed mother lifted it and placed it against her shoulder.

'Would you kindly lead me to whoever is in charge?' asked Nicholas before tilting his head to the baby. 'And congratulations.'

The woman led the way again, turning left down a narrower tunnel, which opened into a dome lit all around with torches, with tunnels leading off in each direction. A table constructed from loose slabs of concrete stood in the middle, as four women stood around it talking. The woman whistled, walked to the table, and waited as another woman and two men entered. It looked as if they had set up an underground strategy room.

'Iris's warriors have arrived,' the woman announced, calming the cries of her baby. Her voice was less hurried now but deep and stern. 'Things are gonna move *real* fast now.'

'You know for sure?' asked one of the women.

'Yeah. This is probably Nicholas. He fits the description loosely.' She finished her passage in French before sending Nicholas a concerned look.

Nicholas cleared his throat. 'I recently—'

The woman spoke to the others in French again, pointing to Nicholas's gloved hands.

'If I may ask,' said Nicholas, resting his hand on the table, but lifting immediately to the touch of a disgusting, sticky substance clinging to his glove. 'In the interest of trust, how did you find us walking the railway?' All eyes turned to him.

'Iris worked out that you'd come to the west. With the new Bretagne cliffs from Saint-Brieuc to Vannes, your best bet was to arrive at the gold cliff beach at Pénestin, oui? Yes? Following the river to Redon next, then the railroad would lead you up here.'

'Iris always was meticulous.' Nicholas placed his hands on his hips. 'That sounds incredibly accurate despite my limited knowledge of this land. Where is she?'

'She's been taken.' The woman gave Nicholas barely a second to finish his sentence. 'Whoosh. Gone. Days ago, in the middle of the night. They'll be taking her to Aerkin, but there were only eight measly soldiers that'll let their guard down soon enough, and she'll kill them all. Around halfway, there's a large community called the Caldeira. My guess is she'll make her way there. That's where we were going to go when you arrived. To get *the weapon*. All that's left here is a trap awaiting you all, so you best tell your others.'

'I half expected as much. What do I need to tell them exactly?'

'To get them gloves warmed up.' The woman smiled and nodded at Nicholas. He knew all about this confident mentality, which usually resided within him. He must be talking to the leader of these underground rebels.

'So, I think we all agree we need to make our move,' said the woman. 'I'm

Hena with an H. You don't need to remember that. Focus on remembering the paths I show you when we're above ground. We've been told a—'

'Sorry, I rarely interrupt, but we are here to meet someone,' said Nicholas.

'Right. As I said, gone. We'll rid the intruders from Rennes and set off after Iris, deal?'

'No. Apologies, I meant a woman named Kate? Have you seen a lone brown-haired woman wander through here, wearing gloves like ours?'

'I don't know, sorry.' Hena handed her baby over to another sewer dweller.

Nicholas worried for his closest companion but turned his attention back to Iris. 'It is good to see you are as confident in Iris as I am,' said Nicholas with a wry smile.

'She knows what she's doing. As for us, we've been told a monster by the name of Bastilig has been overseeing this trap. Do you know this name?'

Nicholas attempted to rub the sticky substance off his gloves. 'I believe one of my men possesses quite a bit of knowledge of him.'

'Great, well if you need more, Tomas here travelled with them. He came from the Domum Bia and defected when he arrived; he's one of Iris's recruits.'

Hena pointed to a short-haired man sitting in the shadowed corner, wrapping a ribbon of soiled cloth around the bottom half of a long, metal pole with his head down, hiding his face.

'The executioner,' said Tomas, his head unmoved, his voice muted. 'They fuel him with the same red light they fuel all of Domum Bia.'

'Fuel?' Nicholas stepped closer to make sure he heard every soft word spoken.

'The bridge that glides to the entrance, the lights that switch on and off in the towers, the fires that heat the arena—all with this infinite energy source. It's a glimpse of the future, resigned to the past.'

Nicholas at first believed every word, but without the material and technology needed, Aerkin could not harness dark energy for dynamic contraptions and constructions. Impossible. With a simple weapon, trapping light was feasible. But a temple of moving bridges and lights was a dream of twenty years ago. He turned to Hena. 'Do you trust this man?'

'By default. Iris trusts him, and I trust her.' Hena brushed past Nicholas to pick up a spear leaning against the sewer wall.

'I witnessed his birth,' whispered Tomas. 'Bastilig has no weakness. We'll leave him to you.'

'Before, um—' Nicholas unusually faltered in his speech. 'Before we get involved in any war, this Domum Bia you speak of. The logistics of a—'

The conversation halted with the distant sound of a horn above ground. Nicholas's group owned no such instrument, and Hena's blank stare showed the same. They both listened out again, and in several seconds a sharper call from the horn flowed through the sewers.

'There will be time to talk, don't worry. But the horns mean they've spotted your group. We have to go. Tomas, Di, Paul…Allons-y!' Hena, finishing with a flurry of commands in French, waved the others forward. 'Are the rest of yours coming, yeah?'

'I believe they will have continued on the railway,' replied Nicholas.

'Good. We'll meet them in the centre.' Hena set off as the others grabbed weapons and called down the tunnels for others to prepare themselves. Tomas looked suspiciously relaxed as he lifted himself, one hand pocketed, the other holding his pole, his head still down.

Hena hurried Nicholas back out to the main tunnel, where groups of men and women came flooding from numerous side tunnels. All of a sudden, the sewer bustled to life with a crowd of underground warriors.

Hena climbed on a ledge to view all in her presence. She spoke a flurry of different languages to address the crowd before settling on English. 'Women and men of the Mainland uprising, Iris calls upon us. Them Hillfolk warriors from the north are here, and the suit of energy will light the way for us. The Hillfolk and Habitants united as one. They've run us down here for too long, but we will no longer suffer the sewers. Today, we take back everything. The return to the ruins. The rising of Rennes has begun!'

A raucous war cry echoed through the tunnels, men and women banging on the walls and against shields. Nicholas, however, clung to the mentioning of the suit. It would be best not to mention it possessed a new owner, given the hordes of strangers waving spears in his face.

'For Iris! For Rennes!' shouted Hena.

'For Iris! For Rennes!' followed the warriors' eardrum-piercing yells.

'Do you expect all these people to climb through that small shaft?' asked Nicholas.

'We have a passage to a sinkhole in the centre of town,' replied Hena. 'Being spotted is inevitable now.'

They marched. They charged. A stranger wrapped his arm around Nicholas's shoulders and dragged him along the sewer. Nicholas felt lost as the strangers pulled him into a battle he had only just arrived to join. No matter his feelings, and no matter his emerging thoughts, the charge had begun. *Nicholas,* his mind called out. *Nicholas,* to no reply.

CHAPTER TWENTY-FIVE

PERSONA MORTIS: PART I

A horn roared in the distance. Arun opened his eyes. The soft bedsheet beneath his fingertips made way for a dry, hard surface with tiny stones scratching his bare palms. Pairs of feet paced around him whilst his chin hovered close to the ground. The shoes—they were different. Some black, some white, but mostly clean. Trousers stretched upwards on a figure walking by, with no holes or dirt. A lady with a briefcase stormed past. Arun looked up. A young man held a device to his ear, rambling on about "some video that's gone viral". Arun couldn't believe his eyes. The world wasn't broken.

Arun stood, turning his head slowly, watching as the wrecked cars he'd been accustomed to hiding in had burst into life and swept across the untainted road. Buildings stood as they once did, filtering the flow of an abundance of humans that Arun had never seen before. A heavy, smoky smell polluted Arun's nose down to the back of his throat. Either nobody else seemed to mind, or they simply couldn't smell it.

Arun gulped to clear the smoke from his throat and tilted his head back. And there it lay, the beautiful sky. It shone above, with pockets of a shade of pure blue flowing between parted clouds.

'Kate,' shouted a woman's voice. 'Come on.'

The clouds shook. Familiar darkness blighted the blue between them, and just as Arun began to wonder if the sun would show, a dark shroud swallowed the sky and took with it the distant buildings from left to right. Cars drove head-on into nothingness, the road and pavements hurtled towards him, and people, without a hint of irregular movement, disappeared forever.

Arun turned sharply to find a shop door closing. He leapt in as the shroud devoured the world behind him, leaving the shop windows peering into a hazy emptiness.

'Stay inside,' said the woman, with a vibrant, blushing face and bright red lips. 'I'll be two minutes.'

Arun lay crumpled on the floor inside a shoe shop that remained calm from the shroud. A young girl stood in front of him, whose face he instantly recognised from the mole in the middle of her chin. Kate. She must have been three or four years old, fiddling with a toy, lost in her own world. He picked himself up, calm in his movement, so as not to startle anything. A man walked towards the door and walked straight through Arun like a ghost. Kate then looked up. Her eyes focused directly towards Arun's. It was clear she could see him, but could nobody else? The two didn't belong here.

A young Kate pointed towards Arun. She spoke softly, 'Mama. A door.'

Arun glanced behind himself. Nothing but shelves of shoes. He looked down towards his feet, breathing in as he did. His body glowed, a soft white glow.

'Come on, Kate,' said her mother. She held Kate's hand and led her out of the shop, but Kate's focus remained. She reached out for Arun as the shroud outside the shop disappeared and gave way to the returning people and cars once more. No. Arun turned. The shroud had now formed inside the shop. He reached for the entrance door as it closed, and just as it did, he grabbed the handle. But the handle didn't turn. It rather turned to dust in his palm, and the shroud finally engulfed him.

Arun's eyes shot open, bewildered by his state of mind. That dream—it felt so real. Arun had to readjust to his hut. He lay on his bed feeling as if his body had shifted, and his muscles had suddenly contracted after a marathon run. The sounds of the car engines and the chattering all around him continued to ring in his head. It sounded incredible—an industrial orchestra of the old era. But as he gradually snapped back to reality, lifting himself, he couldn't help but think he was beginning to lose his mind.

*

No news of the Aerkin Knights had arrived on another rainy morning on the Hill. Arun found himself where he'd begun, sitting on a creaking wooden chair in Nicholas's dark hut, pondering Nicholas's whereabouts on his travels, puzzling through the recent dreams that felt so real. He'd agreed to keep watch this morning but bought himself five minutes to sit and contemplate. He had so many questions to ask Nicholas still. Yet, as he sat on the creaking chair, kicking his feet, he imagined a life without ever seeing the rest of the Hillfolk again.

A sharp pain ran through Arun's left shoulder, momentarily.

'Arun!' came a recognisable shout from outside, a young girl's voice, sending the pain away.

Arun stepped out of the hut, ambushed by the cold air. Halfway between the hut and the cottage stood Malorie.

'Watch this!' said Malorie before twirling on the spot. She bounced forward, then back, breaking into an elegant dance routine with precision and perfection, surprising Arun. The girl who owned a crossbow and went hunting could dance. She threw her hands into the air wildly, basking in the rain, swinging them back down and laughing with such innocent joy.

Arun fought scavengers much older than himself and built shelters at that age, so it was strange to see a child enjoying herself without a care in the world. He laughed instinctively, more through happiness than humour. He couldn't explain why, watching with intent to remember the moment. The grass calmed as the rain faded, and the trees danced along with Malorie. Only a ray of magical sunshine could make this moment more perfect. For a second, Arun replaced all fear of hateful knights with bliss and joy.

Arun's attention drifted. A glimmer of light. He looked to the blue-leafed tree on his left. Despite Nicholas's note, he'd neglected to look after it so far, but the tree had grown broader and taller since and at least twice as tall. Strangely, all the leaves on the tree faced him. Despite no path leading to the tree, he walked across the grass to take a closer look. As he did, the blue leaves turned, still facing Arun. Not at all unsettling.

The bark felt like any other bark would do—rough and splintering. But the streaks of blue had thickened, about a centimetre wide now, and felt glossy to Arun's gloveless fingers. A soft, pure fragrance surrounded the tree, though it didn't sway nor bear fruit. An alien-like mystery surrounded it.

Arun's unstable focus drifted past the tree to the most mysterious thing on the Hill for him: Kate's hut. He left the tree as Malorie's audience and strolled over to Kate's hut with an eerie air engulfing him. He pushed the door open; he wasn't sure if he'd expected more. It was a simple hut like the others, consisting of a bed, a pile of objects and clothing, and a crooked table resting under the window. Two plants sat on the table, one growing full of volume and full of life; the other brown and wilting. He turned to the bed and spotted a pair of green shoes underneath, too small to belong to her.

'Come on, fella,' said Tej. Arun snapped out of gazing at Kate's bed to spot Tej's head hovering around the door. 'That's a little bit weird, don't you think?'

'I wasn't…' stuttered Arun. 'Never mind.' Tej had already disappeared.

Arun followed Tej to the top of the Hill to begin their patrol. The plan remained: loop around the higher perimeter in shifts to see if they could spot any sign of the knights. A tree branch out of place, a smell of foul-play, anything seen was to be reported.

From the top of the Hill, Arun could see out into the neighbouring fields through the trees. It would seem this way in every direction, except for the bottom, where Cole prepared traps, wiping sweat from her brow. A few of the scavengers dug beside her with bent shovels. Resourceful—Arun's kind.

'How much d'you know about dark energy?' asked Arun, scouting the outer fields once more. The question had burned in him inside Nicholas's hut. Asking Tej seemed the next best thing. 'You know, the science behind it, yadda yadda.'

'Not nothing, not everything,' replied Tej. He rubbed his eyes. 'I know one thing, though. I miss paracetamol.' Arun returned a blank stare. 'It's for hangovers. Anyway, you were saying?'

'Something strange is happening to me. For the past few nights, I've had dreams where I'm in Kate's body.'

Tej scowled. 'Excuse me?'

'No, no, as in I'm Kate, and I'm seeing what she's seeing. One took place on a boat with the others, and then I had a vision I…she was killing people. Lots of people. And then she was with Nicholas, and then there was this blue light that shot me out of her, and she spoke to me.'

'What do your twisted hormonal dreams have to do with dark energy?' dismissed Tej, looking as if all his energy directed to his eyes and not his ears, looking out to the fields. 'Look.' Tej pointed. Arun followed Tej's hand towards a hill near the horizon bearing three towers of smoke, camouflaged by the clouds, rising in close proximity. 'That smoke is probably a few hours back. Nobody has reported them yet.'

'Yeah. I don't like this. I think that's the knights. And that's towards the direction Malorie and I came from.'

'Let's keep an eye on it. They could be heading away from us.' Tej removed his scowl and lent a sympathetic look to Arun. 'You're not a bad kid. You're the opposite of Nicholas. For someone so smart, he never seemed to do too much thinking.'

Uh. Arun scratched the back of his head. That wasn't exactly a compliment, was it?

'So tell me more about the dreams,' said Tej. 'Sorry for calling them hormonal.'

'Well, that's pretty much it,' replied Arun. 'But it feels more real than a dream. When I'm her, I can feel these strange thoughts and emotions that aren't my own. And I remember them vividly, whereas other dreams fade with the day. Is it possible this is really happening? Or has happened? And I'm just watching?'

Tej chortled to himself. 'Science has proven there are many amazing things in these universes. But sorry fella, I highly doubt you're peeking into her mind or dream swapping.'

'Dream swapping?' Arun's head sprang up enthusiastically. 'Is that possible?'

'I just made it up.' Tej smiled, not to Arun's amusement. 'Lighten up. Yeah, you're definitely the opposite of Nicholas. You remind me of myself at your age. A battler, of course, searching for answers.' Tej moved his stare to the towers of smoke. 'If there's something to these dreams, it might be an issue of consciousness of which I have my own theories. What do *you* think consciousness is?'

'Our thoughts? I never thought about it.'

'There are two ways I like to think about it—the first being data. Memories, thoughts, and dreams all created and stored on this enormous computer chip we call a brain. Then one little area in the middle would be your active self. Your consciousness, pushing and pulling data back to all the different parts. Logical, I suppose.

'The second way is much more romantic—a natural phenomenon. Just like dark energy or gravity floating in and around us. And not just us. All animals, all plants. Even planets and galaxies too. Energy, gravity, consciousness: all binding the universes together. Therefore, it's not entirely nonsensical to say it could have bound your consciousness with Kate's. Perhaps it's just in dreams for now, but maybe you could find a way to connect memories and thoughts.'

Tej walked across to a lone oak tree, narrow but branching out tall. He rested his hand against it. 'Think of how you'd tether yourself with ordinary matter. You'd use a rope and tie yourself to someone else, let's say. Could you do the equivalent with dark energy? It would tie into one of my theories: that we're all simply twigs on the same tree. For now, you could have found another twig, but what if you were able to tether yourself to a branch? Or the trunk? Or even the roots? That could be what this all is. We're all part of the tree of life.' Tej ended his lecture by peeling off a piece of bark and allowing it to tumble to the grass.

'Nicholas went a step further. He said, before the Worldshift, telescopes discovered the light from other universes. He thinks each universe is exactly the same but owned by a single consciousness. Perhaps you've seen Kate's universe.

'Or. You could simply just admit to yourself and me that your tired mind and lustful heart are aching for her return.' Tej whistled, put his hands on his heart, and swivelled around before throwing his head back with a blissful sounding sigh.

Arun huffed, still concerned about being compared to Tej. They couldn't be more different. Arun turned to the hills again and paused. 'Weren't there only three lines of smoke before?'

Tej escaped his twirl and joined Arun. The newly rising tower puffed into the sky, closer in view than the others. The two looked at each other without saying a word; this wasn't the time for a discussion.

'Playtime is over,' said Tej as he turned. They brought an end to their patrol and hurried back to the group to share the news. Tej made his way to Cole, splitting from Arun as he diverted to the Trellock's hut to inform Malorie. Rushing down and out of breath, Arun knocked on the door three times. Abrupt, sharp, and heavy. 'Hello? Te-lue? Anyone there?'

Silence—no answer, Another three knocks brought the same reply. Where could they be? This wasn't the time to go for a family stroll. What to do now?

*

Arun spent the next few hours training on his own. He was becoming familiar with the suit, boots aside, and charging his light at regular intervals. He could throw an energised punch in one swift move and ignite his body to protect himself, blocking his face with the other hand before extending a sidekick. He extensively extended his foot in a wild groan, almost begging it to ignite, but it didn't. How he could do with Nicholas and Kate right now.

Arun sat on the damp grass, exhausted from anguish rather than exercise.

He pounded the ground with both fists beside him, sending the strong, woody smell of burnt grass up to meet him. He rested his head in his hands, still glowing, and he groaned into a shattering scream. The gloves: they burnt his temples. Not in a harmful way, but with a warm contraction.

Arun could feel his arms twitching, attempting to pull away beyond his control as if they had their own master. His hands swept forward in his mind, throwing swords of light through the air. He couldn't understand it; he could only feel it. This almost felt like muscle memory. Was it from the gloves?

Arun shot up and brought a Linai sword to his glove. His arms wanted to move before his brain could send instruction. He threw his arm back, then forward again, twisting and flicking his wrist and releasing his grasp on the sword. It spun ahead, but only for a second did it remain before fading. How did he know how to do that?

Bewilderment filled Arun. He swung again and again, each time failing to replicate his previous motion. His thoughts regained control and his muscles relaxed. No. Don't disappear. He fought his body, grabbing his biceps, placing his hands back on his head, doing anything to bring his arms to life again. Nothing seemed to work, but the feeling of anguish disappeared, even if for a moment with the muscles' memories. Yes, Arun was definitely losing his mind.

*

After finishing his training, Arun returned to the Hill to spend the rest of the afternoon helping Cole and the scavengers. Some had spent most of the day resting in huts or on the grass whilst others roamed around. The few that remained helped Cole with her digging. Arun walked towards Cole.

'Stay where you are!' shouted Cole, placing twigs over a hole. 'Don't move forward, don't move right. Take three steps back and 'ead towards me. You're between the bear traps!

Arun navigated the makeshift minefield, thankfully not at his peril. Perhaps these traps would work after all. 'What if they come from another direction?'

'When we finish 'ere, we'll do the top as well. It's unlikely they will as if they come 'ere they'll be following the paths that lead to the bottom of the Hill. A few of your Tosser friends are digging near the stables where another path leads. They're digging so much there'll be no ground left if they carry on.'

'Yeah, they don't like to be called that. But I guess the more holes, the better.'

'Yes, I know, sausage.' Cole picked up a shovel from the ground and handed it to Arun. 'The plan is simple. The 'oles we'll cover with twigs and foliage, with barbed wire laid at the bottom; it's rusted, but it'll do. We trap them in confined spaces where their weapons will be less effective, buy some time, and attack from above, so long as the camouflage 'olds up against the rain. We only had three bear traps, so we've surrounded the 'oles to catch them above ground. Your…friends…can act as a lure and bring the knights towards the traps and can attack with whatever debris they have. Once they're trapped, Rachel, Malorie's mum, can pick them off at a distance, whilst you and Sam, her dad, go in to finish the job. Me and Tej will stay around the cottage with the children. Sound like a plan?'

Would this work? Even if not, Arun couldn't think of any better traps. Restricting the use of their weapons was the best thing to do. 'Sounds like a plan.'

'Great! One last thing, take a look at this cutie I found.' Cole handed Arun a small piece of smooth but crumpled paper with a light layer of dirt over it.

'What's this?' asked Arun, looking at a photo of a young girl with a smart dress on. It looked a little bit like…

'Kate! Well, she looks three years old 'ere. Found it when I was digging. She must 'ave lost it when she first arrived. Or buried it. Either way, keep it for when she gets back.' Cole winked at Arun. 'So, are you going to 'elp, or stand here talking?'

Both. 'Where are the Trellocks?' Arun placed the photo in his pocket and began a half-hearted attempt at digging. He was more used to using his hands, not these fancy tools. However, his mind was firmly placed with Malorie's whereabouts and wondered if Mr Trellock would help unravel his flying sword mystery.

'I believe they're organising something for the children if—'

'If?' interrupted Arun.

'I'm just saying, it must be 'ard to 'ave children in this world.'

'Did you and Tej ever think to?' With his eyes fixed on Cole, Arun simply pushed the shovel into the same patch of loose ground without moving the soil.

'Yes, we thought about it.' Cole paused her deadly decorating. Arun followed her pensive stare to a small stream of water rushing along the bottom of the Hill. 'There were times we wanted to try, but Nicholas would remind us that bringing up a child wouldn't be a good idea in this world. The Trellocks thought otherwise. Well, before the Trellocks became the Trellocks, Rachel arrived with Zachenne, but any 'opes they had of 'aving kids was dashed. Zachenne chose to follow Nicholas's ideals, and Rachel…oh, now you've got me wittering on. Anyway, we've planned on getting married. We're probably the first people to do so after the Worldshift, so that's something. We deserve a bit of joy. But kids…it's too late for us now.'

'Why too late?'

'Your books didn't tell you much about making babies, did they?' Cole stood straight, her forehead sweating. 'We had thirty other 'ungry mouths to feed. That's always been our role 'ere. And then we watched them grow up and leave the Hill as strong men and women. In a way, we've been parents after all.'

'Did you mean to find any of them? Or me? Did you know I'd find the gloves?' asked Arun.

'When I said "stand 'ere talking or 'elp me", that wasn't a real choice.' Cole sported a cheeky smile on her face. She swooped beside Arun and wrapped her arms around him. 'All that matters is that you're 'ere now.' She grabbed his shovel and pushed it into Arun's chest. Her smile beamed, the same as always.

Arun heeded Cole's words and thrust his shovel into the ground with the others. It looked as if the other holes were deep enough to fall into but not deep enough to stop anyone from getting back out. They needed to be bigger. It would buy them time, at best. But if only or two knights fell, there'd still be enough of them to overwhelm the Hill. There had to be a way to stop them all at once.

'That's it!' blurted Arun mid-thought. 'They want Nicholas, right? We just have to tell them he's not here. We can tell them to search the place if they really want. We'll tell them the truth—that he's gone to the Mainland.'

Cole huffed, though it wasn't clear if it was prompted by Arun's idea or the fact he'd stopped digging again. 'Sausage, I don't think they're 'ere to talk.'

'But we just have to be strong. If they get past the defences, then we have gloves. They won't want a needless fight and to risk dying for nothing.'

'Tell you what—you keep digging, and you can say whatever you want to them when they're down there. Deal?'

Arun nodded and returned his shovel to the ground. Now then, on with thinking of something to say to a band of ruthless killers.

*

Evening came with a furious rainstorm, and Arun spent his time amongst many of the scavengers in the dimly lit cottage. They sat discussing weaponry and tactics for any potential arrival. The scavengers stuck true to their nature, not considering tactics or traps but instead choosing their weapon and hiding place. Many had scrap metal from old cars and buildings; others had bags of debris to throw. Shark, understandably the quietest, suggested hiding and chose no weapon.

One of the scavengers decided to sing a song to liven the cold, misty air.
'The boy took down a hundred bricks, but the house it didn't fall,
And the menacing men across the hill, returned the bricks to the wall.
So the boy took down two hundred bricks, from the walls at either side,
And the menacing men across the hill, returned the bricks out wide.
Now the boy knew any brick he took, wou-n't stay down very long,
The house would stay forever still, rebuilding tall and strong,
But the boy took down a hundred bricks, from the bottom all around,
And the house without foundation fell, crumb-ling all the way down.'

'Who's goin' round tearin' down houses?' asked one. 'That don't make no sense.'

'There ain't no houses no more!' shouted another.

'Aren't we in one?'

'It's about solving your problems, stupid,' said the singer. 'It's like, 'cause your problems are a house. And the bottom problem is, uh, the floor, and you gotta look below, and not the top.'

'Are you brain-dead or sumfin?'

'We're all brain-dead!' The scavengers roared and cheered in unison.

Arun turned to Cole and Tej, who chose to sit on their own, holding hands around a collection of candles. The wood in the fireplace lay brown and cold that evening, and the two watched the cold shrouds of air cover the other's face before spreading into the dark. They giggled and stared into each other's eyes, enjoying one another's company. It must be a nice feeling to find a partner in this world.

Arun sat by the window. He could imagine the holes struggling to stay covered in the rain as the Hill directed slivers of water towards the small stream at the bottom. It might be the case that each day they'd have to rebuild their traps. Exhausting.

As candlelight flickered atop it, Arun stared into the table, wondering about the absent Trellocks. Perhaps Cole's vague explanation meant they had simply vanished to take the children somewhere safe. It would make no sense, but what did Arun know of having children? It was not uncommon for the adult scavengers to abandon him unexpectedly when trouble arose in his teenage years. A scavenger always runs.

Looking at the window again, Arun watched as each raindrop searched for a partner before joining and journeying to the bottom pane, picking up other passengers on the way. Arun saw the reflection of a boy, turning into a man, who'd begun a wild journey, but only a dozen days ago, he knew nothing other than to sit in his shelter, reading his books.

The bickering faded. The giggles simmered to a stop. Beyond Arun's reflection and the journeying rain, his worst fears emerged. The lenses in his eyes thinned as he looked to the bottom of the Hill. Five soaked figures stood still. It was not too dark into the night that they were shadows but not light enough to make out their details. Arun's heart stopped a moment before beating into overdrive. His stomach lifted. It could only have been *them*.

Arun turned in shock to Cole and Tej, who caught his sharp reaction. He could almost feel the colour in his face go amiss. He tried to speak, but his lips trembled. Cole and Tej rushed over to the window. Arun saw it in their faces—his imagination hadn't been unleashed. The Aerkin Knights had arrived on Berkley Hill.

CHAPTER TWENTY-SIX

PERSONA MORTIS: PART II

Each of the Aerkin Knights ignited their light, one by one, spreading the red glow through the rain, illuminating their surroundings. Their masks and armour reflected red, fading to dark. One knight held a whip with radiant red light slithering to the floor: the Scourge Knight. The second held a long inward curved handle of a double-headed axe, with light replacing what would be blades: the Axe Knight. On the other side, a figure held a chain that led to a sizeable, unstable orb of light: the Mace Knight. The fourth had light stemming from a small handle to a point, like a long glowing red sword: the Sword Knight.

The middle figure wasn't as tall as the others and held an unlit object about the size of a head. He stepped forward and removed his hood on what looked like a sleeveless cloak. This had to be the Unknown Knight. Arun could make out faint markings on the mask in the red glow. These soon disappeared as the figure's head ignited, seemingly bursting into burning flame, imploding in on itself instead of spreading with the wind. No markings remained, no facial expressions, just a pure glow of vibrant shades of smouldering and crackling red against the dark, voided air. The entire length of his arms followed with the same furious light.

Still, they stood in their place, examining the Hill. There was no doubt the knights had seen Arun and the others as candlelight reflected off the cottage windows. They had to move.

'Weapons, now!' shouted Cole, running to the back of the cottage. 'Tossers, lure them to the traps! Tej, where're the Trellocks? Arun, follow!'

Arun stood still, but Tej yanked him out of his skin and followed Cole as the scavengers hurried out of the cottage, carrying what they could.

'No sign of the Trellocks.' Tej began putting on his gloves as the three hid behind the cottage.

'Don't be stupid!' whispered Cole in a thunderous tone, looking at Tej's hands. 'Don't you dare, Tehjin! Stick to the plan!'

Arun peeked around the corner as the scavengers burst out from the cottage, shouting and yelling. They held firm, and the knights didn't move, their masked faces firmly facing uphill.

'Wait for it, wait for it,' whispered Cole, looking away from the knights.

A minute of fearful standoff had passed, with the scavengers still goading the knights with insults. The Unknown Knight lowered his hands, illuminating the traps and foliage that the rain had passed through. He placed his glowing red hand onto a bushy object, which sprang shut, locking the knight's hand in a bear trap.

'What's 'appening?' said Cole, now trembling onto Arun.

The teeth in the trap had bent, not pierced. The knight simply lifted the trap and threw it back down the hill, ripping its teeth from his ignited arm. The rain and the mighty red light defeated the Hill's efforts, and one by one, the knights moved forward over the holes with unerring footsteps. The first line of defence had failed.

Arun watched as the knights began their incline, ignoring the bait of diversion holes leading towards the other bear traps. Scavengers greeted them with howls, and Arun attempted to run out to join them, but Tej held him back.

'Wait,' instructed Tej.

'The plan,' argued Arun. 'It's time! I know they're not trapped, but we have to fight together. They'll die!'

'They're not trapped?' said Cole. 'Somebody tell me what's 'appening!'

'Wait,' said Tej. 'We've already failed. Not even one of them is caught. You should run.' Arun had no option as Tej tightened his hold on him, pulling him back from the knight's view. 'We need to protect you now. Arun, go!'

Arun fought Tej's grip and peeked around the corner again to see the scavengers launching material. Two of the knights simply sidestepped the projectiles and another two destroyed objects with swift swipes of their weapon. They reached the scavengers, who launched into the knights with metal poles and scrap material. The knights cut through the metal as cleanly as the rain cut through the air.

'Arun!' hissed Tej. 'Get away from here. Run away!'

Arun could only watch on as the shards, spears, and whips of red light crashed down on the scavengers one by one, scoring them to the ground. The hurt scavengers tried to crawl away. Some couldn't; their limbs had been sliced off. Arun had seen enough. He escaped Tej's restraint.

'Nicholas isn't here!' Arun screamed at the top of his lungs, his voice cracking through fear and regret. 'Leave now. Or…prepare to die.'

His bravery was foolish, but it drew the attention of the knights. The remaining scavengers were simply tossed and batted aside. Agonising whimpers and screams covered the ground as the bodies illuminated in a red glow. The knights seemed uninterested in wasting time slaying them as they lay; a purpose grew within their stares as they moved towards Arun.

Arun stood his ground, not knowing his next move. He had a plan of what to say, but he couldn't remember it. He froze. He wasn't sure if the knights had seen his gloves and his armour in the evening mist. They seemed at first to be alien, but the Unknown Knight halted the others and stepped forward to reveal his humanity.

'Your gloves,' said the knight, in a deep, muffled tone from behind the mask. Raindrops in the air vibrated as they carried his voice.

'Yeah, I'm glad we agree they're mine,' replied Arun. His words emitted confidence and strength, but his heart thumped, blood cells stampeding in a herd. His legs shook and felt light beneath him, barely holding him up.

'For now.' The knight took a step forward. Didn't they care that Nicholas wasn't here? Were they looking for something else? Arun turned his head to a blue light in the trees, hovering in mid-air, frazzling yet still. Suddenly, the light fired at great speed towards the Unknown Knight. He held out his arm and blocked the bolt with his energised hand, the blue light shattering in his palm.

Another bolt launched, and another. The bolts fired towards different knights as they dodged and blocked each one. Mr Trellock stormed out from the trees as Mrs Trellock paced, firing bolt after bolt, not letting a second go by without light filling the air. The Scourge Knight began a menacing walk towards Mr Trellock, who hobbled in a hurry towards the centre of the Hill.

'Arun, run!' shouted Mr Trellock. 'It's too late!'

No. Arun ignited his gloves, drawing the attention of the other knights. He backed away slowly as the Axe Knight approached him. Some scavengers began to rise, but the knights kicked them back down in an instant. To his right, Mr Trellock attempted to launch himself into the knight with a weapon, but the knight's whip struck the side of his leg and brought him to the ground. Where were his gloves?

Arun focused back on the Axe Knight, who stalked close. His training would have to pay off now. Adrenaline pumped every inch of his body. He brought his hands together and pulled them apart again, igniting the sharp, blue Linai swords curving from his palms. When his hands had reached as far as they could stretch, he flicked his wrists and grabbed hold of the light, raising the glowing swords in front of him.

He glanced to the right again and saw the Scourge Knight avoid another bolt. The knight struck Mrs Trellock across the face with his whip. Arun felt alone, but that was not a new feeling for him. He held firm and took a deep breath. The knight raised his axe and moved to strike Arun. As he did, Tej leapt in front of him, holding his gloved hands up, ignited blue, blocking the blow of the axe. However, the concentrated red light was too strong, and it shattered Tej's shield, shooting him to the ground.

'Tehjin!' screamed Cole, frantically sprinting out from her cover and dashing between Arun and the knight to check on her fallen partner. Through his anguish, Tej looked at his hands in wonder.

Arun, enraged at Tej's fall and protective of Cole, strained every muscle in his body. His suit ignited along with his swords. He stood in front of the axe-wielding knight, wholly energised, apart from his boots.

'Wait,' demanded the Unknown Knight, loud enough for the others to hear. The Axe Knight stopped his attack and froze before Arun.

Arun couldn't hold his glow much longer. He extinguished all but his gloves, begging his arms to take control, to no avail. Out of breath, he charged at the Axe Knight, swinging one Linai from left to right, over the ducking knight's head, and the other from right to left. The knight blocked effortlessly with his axe and swung once more.

'Wait!' the Unknown Knight bellowed, stopping the Axe Knight in his swing. 'This is the suit.'

'He's too young,' croaked the Axe Knight, in a similarly deep, vibrating voice.

'No wounds. Concur.'

'Concur,' replied the rest of the knights in unison, all with that same deep voice.

The Axe Knight moved his weapon to the floor above Cole and Tej before turning his masked head to face Arun. The suit stopped them, but why? Did they think he was Nicholas? Arun had no choice, as he looked down on the two, to fade his weapons.

'Companionship. Weakness,' said the Unknown Knight. 'Come to me. Hulius Uma.'

The Scourge Knight distracted Arun for a moment by walking into the trees. Arun's body froze again, wondering if Malorie hid in the darkness. 'Hey whippy, everyone's here,' goaded Arun, but the knight ignored him.

The Unknown Knight approached Arun with little motion. His head and arms were still ablaze with dark energy. It was the most frightening sight Arun had witnessed in any moment or dream in his life. It was as if a demon from a fantasy world in one of his books now controlled his fate.

'Who are you?' asked the Unknown Knight as Arun approached him. 'Where is Servington?'

'I'm the Guardian of the Hill.' Arun clenched his fists and his jaw. 'Nicholas is gone. It's just me now. I have his suit. Let the others go, and we can talk.'

The light in the Unknown Knight's arms faded. 'Brave. Barbaric. There is nothing more to say.' He knocked Arun to the floor with one punch, as fast as light, and the world went dark.

*

Screams and shouts scattered in the distance. Arun's eyes were barely open. They closed again, seemingly for a while.

*

This familiar setting once more. The shoe shop, a young Kate, and the faint buzzing of shroud surrounding the building. Arun looked up to see Kate pointing at him again.

'Mama. A door.'

'Come on, Kate.' And just like that, Kate's mother began to lead her out the shop once more. Think, Arun. Why did he see this? What did it mean? She reached out for him again. She was moving too fast. What does it all mean, damnit? Don't go. Stop—

'Kate!'

Arun's voice paused the shroud.

The faint buzz stopped.

Arun noticed the eyes, all peering his way. Kate, her mum, the man behind the desk, the two young men, the older woman, all looking at Arun. Still, lifeless, not a single hair swaying, not a single breath taken. But then there was Kate, still breathing, free within Arun's mind. Her hand slipped from the woman, allowing her to push forward, step by step, her eyes white with the reflection of Arun. Only it wasn't Arun as she inched closer, looking up at him. Her eyes showed a door, whiter than white, sparkling as bright as the sun surely would have.

'There's no handle,' said Kate.

'What?' Arun searched his torso, pinching his skin and prodding his body. 'What do I do?'

'Open, silly.'

Arun's head began to ache. He reached for his forehead, running his fingers over that throbbing red wound, swelling in the centre just as when he woke up on the Hill. Wait. The Hill. The Knights. Was he still there?

Kate continued to stare but resumed her soft pacing walk forward towards Arun. Before he could stop her, she passed into him. He twisted, looking behind and back in front. She vanished, and the shroud began to buzz once more. No. Not yet. As the air turned black, sparkling, fizzing multi-coloured lights consumed Arun's vision as if he had rubbed his waking eyes. The lights slowly congregated into sparkling balls of white light. Before Arun could make sense of it, the lights faded away and left him with Kate's departing voice. Though it wasn't her innocent voice as a young child anymore; it was her deep, familiar voice, and it said only one word.

'Te-lue.'

*

A painful headache pounded Arun's skull as the blur in his vision rescinded. Kate? The door? How long had he been out? Crackle—a distant noise simmered but without screams. His hands pressed together behind his back, kneeling on the floor. His fingers were cold and wet; they'd taken his gloves. The world was now painted a hint of red and orange. He focused. The colours were real, and so was the crackling that reached his ears. The huts were ablaze. Arun scanned the Hill, and every single hut, including the cottage, threw fire to the sky.

Arun stared at the burning Hill, still recovering his senses, before becoming fully aware of what had taken place away from his dream. He let out an exhaustive scream which energised his suit for a second before falling limp. Two large hands grasped Arun's shoulders from behind, firmly, keeping Arun in place.

Arun scanned for signs of life. He saw scavengers, Mr and Mrs Trellock, Cole, and Tej, all lined up on their knees across the Hill, through the fire and rain. Arun was hopeless; he thought this would be where his end happened.

'Let me go!' yelled a childish voice from the trees. Arun groaned. The Scourge Knight emerged, carrying Malorie's brother George in his arms. Mr and Mrs Trellock yelled out for him, and the knight threw the child down in front of them in obligation. However, Malorie was nowhere to be seen in Arun's frantic search.

'Prellundis Aerkin,' chanted the knights. They surrounded the hostages halfway up the Hill, their bodies shaking in the fire's glimmer.

The Unknown Knight cleared his throat. 'Pick one.'

Arun wheezed, watching as the Axe Knight paced behind the Hill's hostages. His eyes glanced in different directions, not knowing who or what to focus on.

'You have five seconds. Pick one to die. They will all die if you don't.'

'No, I can't!' screamed Arun. 'I won't do it!' Arun frantically tried to escape, but he only had enough room to wiggle, anxiously pulling on every muscle in his body.

'Four. Three.'

'Stop! I'll tell you anything. I'll give you everything!'

'Two. One.'

'Shark!...Shark.' Arun held his head low, clenching every muscle in his face. The rest of his body felt numb. It was the only name he could think of. It came instinctively, helplessly.

'See, boy. Nothing is yours. Not even choice.' The Unknown Knight signalled to the others. 'Execute them all.'

'No!' Arun lost all breath. He glanced over to Cole and Tej. Time slowed down.

Tej grabbed Cole's hand and looked into her eyes. 'To end this journey by your side is all I could have asked for, my love.'

'Til death do us part,' said Cole.

The Trellocks held their boy in their arms.

The Axe Knight and the Sword Knight ignited their weapons, raised them, and slaughtered Mr and Mrs Trellock. Screams were instantly silenced. Arun closed his eyes in anguish, but he could hear his friends and allies' rolling heads tumbling towards the bottom of the Hill. One by one, they fell. The rolling heads against the soft, wet grass tortured his ears. Each bouncing roll grew louder and louder before fading behind him. One brushed past his thigh on the way down. He opened his mouth in agony but didn't make a sound. Tears flowed down his cheeks, but the rain washed them away. His eyes remained shut. A writhing cry left his mouth as the knights concluded their punishment. No more rolling could be heard, just the crackling of wood.

'Make it quick,' groaned Arun. 'Please.'

'No,' replied the Unknown Knight. 'You belong to Aerkin.'

Arun cried through his teeth as strings of saliva dripped out. He was distraught yet rabid. He had no control over his body.

'This Persona Mortis is yours to bear,' said the Unknown Knight. 'As it is also ours.' He signalled for another knight to pick up the object he'd carried here. It was a mask, much like the ones they were wearing but in keeping with a slightly altered face. Arun didn't have his mind about him to make sense of it, but it was solid metal. It sank around his head, encapsulating him. Arun's tears continued to fall as they lowered it down, but fury consumed his face, enraged in pure anger and despair. His eyes vanished. His quivering lip soon joined, disappearing behind the metal. Narrow openings to his eyes now hid an otherwise unrecognisable face.

Another knight brought over a large key, and they inserted it into the back of the mask. They turned the key several times, tightening the mask's grip around Arun's head. The knight removed the key, broke it, and threw the pieces into the puddled mud.

'The Persona Mortis holds a painful reminder,' said the Unknown Knight slowly and concisely. 'You will remember yours, as we did ours, until you are strong enough to wield a weapon of Aerkin. Only then you will be an Aerkin Disciple.'

As the Unknown Knight released Arun's shoulders, Arun fell to the puddled ground in a heap. His stomach turned, and all he wanted was for the rain to carry him to the stream and far away.

'You will concur,' warned the Unknown Knight, bending on one knee to talk to Arun. 'It will hurt more if you do not.' He lifted Arun by his arms and held the back of his neck like a lion to its cub.

The Unknown Knight forced Arun through the fence at the bottom of the Hill as the fires roared into the night sky behind him. Arun chose not to look down, to avoid the sight of familiar faces looking back at him, questioning his role as the Guardian of the Hill. Faces he'd known for a week, others he'd known for years. Gone. Nothing could have prepared him for this sinking feeling: the ultimate failure.

The flames continued to burn in Arun's truncated vision through the mask's slit as timbers from the cottage cracked and collapsed inwards. Behind stood the tree; its leaves emitted a faint blue glow to fight the onslaught of red.

The knights led Arun away on the path from home. Just as he began his journey on the Hill, he ended it the same way: a prisoner. There were no perks this time. Nothing. Abandoned by Nicholas, Arun's new journey rested with Aerkin.

CHAPTER TWENTY-SEVEN

THE ROUSING OF RENNES

Rennes came alive again. Warriors of the sewers spread onto the streets like an overflowing drain as Nicholas, twisting and turning, fell towards the middle of the pack. He guessed two hundred bellowing warriors surrounded him.

'Can you call for your group?' asked Hena, approaching Nicholas from the head of the swarm. 'Don't worry about being quiet—we're prepared to fight.'

There existed only one way to send word: Nicholas launched a beaconing beam of light into the air that any friend or foe nearby would see. It faded before reaching the clouds, with splashes of blue light falling away. He turned his attention back to the group with the signal sent, and they marched forward through the rocky street terrain.

'Up ahead is where most of those monsters patrol,' said Hena. 'When the path reaches the end, it splits left and right. I believe they have camps set up in each direction.'

The settlers had cleared wide paths in the rubble, and cracked roads led the way as they once would have for the bustling city. No building stood tall, but the rubble created concrete mounds that blocked their views from each angle. The Habitants continued forward, taking Hena's lead through the rubble streets to the city centre. Scraps of metal armour bumped and bashed against each other, a clanging wave echoing through the streets.

Another blow of the horn permeated the crumbled streets, raging on, not allowing for the clear and crisp cold air to settle. The warriors looked all around, unable to sense the direction of the horn. Furthermore, two horns at varying pitches seemed to answer the call of the first beyond the debris.

'Nicholas!' shouted Zachenne from behind. He and the others were fast approaching. They would have been unaware of the nature of these new warriors. Before Nicholas could call back, a wall of rubble exploded ferociously ahead of the Habitants, propelling rubble into them, crashing against arms and armour.

'Hold!' shouted Hena as the Habitants raised their armour and weapons. Nicholas fell back, returning to his arriving crew.

'They are with Iris's uprising,' said Nicholas. 'There is a trap for us.'

'I can see that,' said Zachenne. The duo turned to watch enemies emerging above the mounds of debris ahead of the Habitants. The hostile roars were weak and shrill individually but grew louder in unison. More trickled over the exploded wreckage waving shields, spears, and sticks. They were similar in attire, almost uniformed, with scrap metals bound together around the chest and shoulders for armour, splattered and coated in blood-red markings and paints. Some had loosely fitting helmets to match. Underneath it all, however, they were men and women, just like the Hillfolk, but with the look of blinded anger.

The Tarios reacted first, firing over the heads of the Habitants, slaying those appearing past the hill of rubble. They ran to the mounds parallel, taking higher ground for their aim. Enemies with luck drove past the bolts and the mound, and they charged at the Habitants, screaming, enraged. The Hillfolk remained behind the Habitants as the battle birthed.

'Defence. Two lines. Wide.' Zachenne ushered the group into formation, a two-line perimeter facing each direction. 'Where are Iris and Kate?'

'Iris is on her way to Aerkin,' said Nicholas. 'I am not sure how or why. And Kate…nowhere.'

'It's not wise to become entangled here without them. We must head in Iris's path to Aerkin.'

'We cannot leave these people to die.'

Rubble tumbled down the mounds to the left and right of the path, ahead of the Tarios. Rising enemies came into view over the concrete hills, now surrounding the Habitants from three sides. The group had to engage, no matter their wish.

'Every day, we stray further from our task,' warned Zachenne, staring at Nicholas with an etched concern. 'You expect me to lead so that I'm the one bearing our casualties. That's if you don't kill us all.' A glimmer of anger almost broke through his jaw. His lips trembled. He turned to the group and announced with a tone of reluctance, 'Enemies surrounding. Prepare your light!'

The group ignited their gloves in their entirety. They marched forward to join the Habitants, surrounding and protecting them from the sides at the back, but they couldn't find clear passage to the front. More enemies bundled over the rubble, a stream of chaos, as objects were hurled from above into the Habitants crowd.

Nicholas watched on, his arms resting by his side, as Serr leapt into a frenzied assault on any enemies that breached to the left. The Marshals followed close by. Serr's shield made way for a barrage of ferocious kicks and screams, breaking through metal with ease. The enemies changed their tactic. They leapt in great numbers from the higher ground of the rubble to the Marshals below, crashing into them with disregard for their own bodies. A swarm unleashed.

On the other side, Matuu led a charge, bulldozing forward, arms first. His gloves created sparse clouds of light that ravaged incoming enemies, warming their skin and blinding their view. His light lacked the density of others, but anything travelling at speed through it would be ravaged. Launched spears decelerated in the energised shroud before they could pierce him, floating to the ground like a feather with a decayed surface.

'We need help!' yelled Hena. Nicholas rushed over without hesitation, storming past Zachenne. In his scurried looks around, he spotted Emitai following close behind. Jordan, in turn, was following Emitai. The three made their way through the Habitants, with Nicholas leading their charge to the front.

Weapons and debris were flying, clashing between the throws and swings of soldiers and warriors that had never before seen war. Bodies around Nicholas fell from both sides as the sound of agonising screams echoed all around. Blood sprayed across the concrete wherever he looked. Nicholas felt helpless. He could not fire a beam of light as the two sides of war mixed in battle. Instead, he could only ignite his gloves to block any incoming strikes.

'Emitai, what are you doing here?' shouted Nicholas, scrambling to help the Habitants.

'I don't know, I don't know, I don't know,' mumbled Emitai repeatedly, finding himself surrounded by clashing weapons and shouting fighters. His hands crossed his hunched torso as his head swung side to side. From behind, a hostile woman came charging towards the unarmed Emitai, raising a bar of metal to strike him. He was out of reach from Nicholas, but Jordan leapt forward before impact, smashing the woman to the ground and saving Emitai.

Nicholas turned back to the Hillfolk, finding his warriors having no troubles dealing with the assault. He trusted them enough to leave them to fight; it was the Habitants he worried about. He spotted Hena, swivelling her spear around her head, before knocking a man to the floor and stabbing another through a gap in their armour. Her warriors, however, were not faring as well, being beaten down and not returning to their feet. The rubble of concrete was fast becoming layered with the rubble of bodies.

Jordan and Emitai continued to flank Nicholas in safety.

'Use your gloves,' said Emitai.

'My arm is hurt. I can't fire it right now,' replied Jordan.

'What about your other arm?'

'I never bothered training it. I can just defend.'

A soldier attempted to take out Jordan from behind. As Nicholas ignited his gloves, Emitai charged Jordan out of harm's way, returning the earlier favour, leaving Nicholas to hammer down his fist and slay the soldier.

Another horn blasted in the distance. It belted out a haunting, stretched tune, and the enemies fell back instantly. The Tarios continued to pick off as many as possible as the remaining Hillfolk rushed over to join Nicholas at the battlefront.

'We need to move,' said Zachenne to Nicholas. 'There's a main road that looks to lead directly south. We need you to stay with us.'

'Any Hillfolk injuries?' asked a panicked Nicholas.

'None, but we—'

The horn sounded again, louder. A trembling rippled through the debris. The concrete mounds continued to crumble but without foes. The group edged forward, scouting as one organism with hundreds of eyes. They reached the junction. The tremble now pounded on eardrums. A barricade of hostiles came into view down a wide path to the right, marching towards the group. They filled the path left to right, spilling up onto the rubble on each side.

Hena whistled to the others. The path to the left held another army of marching soldiers. Enemies on either side flanked the group as the hostile swarm from both camps emerged in their entirety. There seemed to be no end to the amount of them, and they far outnumbered the united group in the middle.

Nicholas stepped forward to the path on the right, staring down the fast-approaching enemies.

'Take the other side.' Nicholas gestured to those in his group nearest to him. Zachenne mumbled disapproval under his breath, but Nicholas stood firm regardless. 'I will take care of these. Go!'

As Nicholas began to turn, Emitai uttered the name, 'Bastilig.' A warrior, much taller than those around him, cleared a path in the middle of the marching crowd. Black armour covered what could be seen of him, bar a wide slit in the front of his mask where his eyes peered through. Nicholas could almost sense a disturbed air around this monstrous man.

Jordan took Emitai's frozen hand, and the two retreated behind Nicholas's view.

The charge of warriors filled Nicholas's ears as he stood motionless. The enemies ahead pushed closer, bearing their tongues through their broken teeth. Nicholas drew his hands together. He stood in silent anguish for a moment, aware he was about to bring the end to many lives without much effort. Nobody should ever be able to have this power. *You have no choice, Nicholas.* He stood firm against his will to protect the lives of those behind him. Bastilig, and these followers, must die.

The enemies launched into a sprint, spear and sword above heads, all focused on Nicholas. Timeless time seemed to pass much slower than usual. Nicholas's hands trembled. *You can do it, Nicholas.* The charge ahead bore down on him, with the war cries merging into one solid sound passing through him. *Take them. Take them all.*

Nicholas ignited his beam. With brutal accuracy, he fired from left to right. The giant beam of bright, blue light powered through all in its way. He watched in agony as the voices in front of him rose and dipped in an instant. These were his gloves, his weapons. He had come too far down this path to stop at the first sign of his destruction. He could not stop the thoughts flowing out of his mind as he decimated a crowd of his own species in front of him. *For the greater good, Nicholas.* He could not help but feel a disturbing resemblance to Aerkin.

Nicholas extinguished his beam and stood breathlessly at the path in front of him. He expected to be horrified by the sight before him, but not much remained to look upon. His beam contained an unfathomable power, so powerful it had disintegrated anything in his front arc. Loose metal and rubble collapsed amongst severed body parts, but he could see little blood. It was clean. Too clean. He had transformed into a harrowing magician performing his final act. Nicholas had always known what his gloves were capable of, but he didn't quite know what he could expect to witness in its aftermath. He looked to his hands. His gloves were immaculate, shimmering white, innocently angelic as if they knew nothing of the carnage they caused.

The last piece of falling material settled, where a large glow of red light frazzled. It took the shape of a large shield, ahead of a row of distant soldiers hobbling, out of reach of the beam. Slowly, the red light faded, and Nicholas looked upon Bastilig crouching, with his forearms raised ahead of him. He stood, relaxing his arms, staring directly at Nicholas.

Bastilig flicked his hands into motion. Soldiers behind him that had ducked to avoid Nicholas's beam unfolded. Bastilig drew no concern for them, pacing towards Nicholas once more.

'Run. Leave this area,' shouted Nicholas, sensing Emitai and Jordan remained close. 'Now!' he yelled at the top of his voice. After a moment, footsteps scattered away. Further back, the sound of battle cries raged on, with the Hillfolk and Habitants still at war. The swords and spears that were no doubt lashing from left to right had no impact on Nicholas's mind. The danger lay in front. He clenched his fists to face Aerkin's chosen warrior.

Bastilig drew closer. His black armour was not entirely black, for a red chasm of glowing light sat in the middle of his chest, like the Earth opening up to the volcanic core below. Red lines resembling veins on the underside of a leaf spread from the chasm to every edge of his suit, one running up one side of his mask. *Run, Nicholas.* Bastilig approached Nicholas with little urgency and stopped when he came within earshot.

'You must be the one Aerkin seeks,' said Bastilig in a rasping tone. His voice was not deep, but it strained and stretched as if his vocal cords had twisted a knot. He held the top of his chest as he spoke.

Nicholas was in no mood for discussion after the destruction he had caused. He lit up his gloves again, and Bastilig, in turn, ignited his armoured hands a deep red. He approached Nicholas with menacing intent and swung to grab his neck. Missing, he swung again; this time, his hand was caught in flight. Nicholas's inferior blue glow could only hold a second, and Bastilig clenched his hand into an unlit fist and knocked Nicholas to the floor.

'You're lucky he wants you unharmed,' screeched Bastilig, standing over Nicholas. 'Submit to me.'

'I do not grant him that pleasure.' Nicholas kicked Bastilig in the shin to no avail. Nicholas rolled back, impressively for his aged body, and reignited his gloves. Again, Bastilig swung for his neck, looking to grab him but not take his head off. Nicholas ducked and swiftly moved around Bastilig.

Nicholas tried to ignite his beam and catch Bastilig from behind, but Bastilig turned and shielded himself. Nicholas's beam crashed into the red shield at close range. Most of his blue light collapsed into the red as if being sucked into a black hole, with sharp streams of light managing to escape at the sides. The red light continued to absorb with an infinite will, but Nicholas did not stop, despite his growing screams. Above the light and in the distance, Nicholas saw the blurred outline of the continuing battle behind Bastilig.

The stalemate roared on, and Nicholas showed no signs of breaking, crunching his teeth agonisingly together. Bastilig stood calm as if holding back a child. The stalemate had to break. Bastilig released a frustrated groan, breaking his shield and rolling out the way. Nicholas lowered his arms. His beam fizzled out, but before he could stop, it had carried forward and down into the ground. Ahead, a gaping line separated the concrete path, embering and melting concrete. Nicholas could see the line stretched far forward to the opposing battle, continuing through the crowd. He looked ahead in horror. Before he could process his devastation, Bastilig struck Nicholas in the back of the head with an unlit hand and knocked him to the ground.

Get up, Nicholas. Kill the bastard. The clouds descended to Nicholas's mind. He could barely move nor make sense of anything. He squinted to make out Bastilig's masked face occluding his eyes from the daylight. No white or pupil resided; Bastilig's eyes were wholly blood red.

'I can see why you'd want to fight,' said Bastilig. He turned his head and winced in pain, releasing a screech from the back of his throat. He struggled to speak and placed his hand near his neck once more. 'This is just the tip of our army. You won't get close to Aerkin. So come with me, and your people will live.'

Nicholas tried to lift his arms, but Bastilig dug his hands into the pit of

Nicholas's elbows and let out another awful screech.

Bastilig's eyes met those of Nicholas. 'He wants you to know…you'll suffer greatly for your sin.'

'I need my suit,' uttered a dazed Nicholas through broken breath. He struggled to keep his head off the ground. *The suit, Nicholas. You need it.*

'Listen to me, old man. He will watch you as you burn alive. It's only fair. Then the world will be free of you both.' Bastilig proceeded to laugh before the laugh turned to a cough.

'Nicholas!' screamed a faint voice from the battle. Bastilig looked up. A Marshal came launching into him. Bastilig blocked, eradicating the Marshal's blue light in a stream of red. He knocked the Marshal down with a swipe of his arm. Nicholas turned his blurring vision to his fallen comrade. *Get up.* Bastilig towered over the Marshal, grabbed his hair with one hand, and with the other, brutally smashed his ignited fist straight through the Marshal's skull. Nicholas looked on as Bastilig returned his focus.

'You're coming with me.' Bastilig grabbed Nicholas by his hair.

'He's not going anywhere,' said another voice from behind Bastilig. Nicholas looked past the masked maniac and saw a blurry figure. He focused as intently as he could.

'Kate!' he screamed.

Bastilig released Nicholas and raised himself to meet the returning warrior. 'Run along, little girl.'

Nicholas looked on in agony. He couldn't bear her following the same fate as the Marshal. Kate had no words to offer, nor did she look to Nicholas. All she offered was her ignited gloves; one shone blue, her other shone yellow. She burst forward, swiping as fast as she could. Bastilig blocked and launched his fists towards Kate. She screamed in anger, avoiding the attack. She was too fast and attempted to stab Bastilig, but he blocked it as the tip of the dagger graced his chest. The yellow dagger did not deplete as fast as the blue light, though, causing Bastilig's head to tilt.

A roar of enemy soldiers arrived as Bastilig's remaining fighters stormed towards Kate. On the other side, however, the Habitants and Hillfolk could be heard storming forward, presumably having claimed victory.

Nicholas held his breath as Bastilig looked into Kate's fearless eyes. 'You'll regret this.'

Kate grimaced. 'Regrets are for the weak.'

Bastilig pushed her back before escaping behind his stampeding soldiers.

Kate slashed one soldier down, and another, spraying blood through their flayed armour. Bolts from the Tarios flew beside her and pierced incoming targets. The hostiles were not overwhelming in number but enough of a distraction for Bastilig to trudge away out of view. Kate made a final sweep of enemy bodies, dismissing them with a look of ease. The last body fell as the Hillfolk and Habitants arrived in number. Nicholas looked to the end of the path where Bastilig disappeared. Kate did not give chase, however, and instead lent Nicholas her first glance since her return.

Nicholas rose to his feet, dizzy but aware, with the help of Jordan. He looked around at the destruction as the warriors cheered and chanted at the victory. For a moment, in his dazed state, he imagined the city as it once stood.

'Nicholas, you okay?' asked Kate.

Nicholas looked towards Kate. He heard her question, but it had travelled to him as the voice of a small girl. She had asked the same question many years ago when she was new to the Hill. She saw him writing a poem to his daughter with a tear in his eye. It was memorable for him, as Kate was the same age as his daughter at that time. He looked upon her and made a promise to himself to always take care of her.

'Nicholas?' repeated Kate.

'You are so beautiful to me,' said Nicholas. 'You always have been. I cannot let you leave my side again. I love you.'

Nicholas looked into her eyes; one blue, one yellow. 'I will always protect you, my dear Kate. There is nothing inside me now but the certainty of your success.' Nicholas fell faint into the arms of two warriors. He felt a damp patch on the back of his head and examined his fingertips to find the red spill of war.

Nicholas was still aware through blurred eyes, enough to spot a creature pacing from behind the debris mound at the end of the path: a bear, bigger than the ones he had encountered in the forest. It was hard to tell by the distance as armour surrounded its body and head, but it was undoubtedly a monstrous creation. Atop sat Bastilig, returning the victors' stares. As quickly as he appeared, he had vanished.

'Hill warriors,' said Hena, arriving. 'Now's no time to stand around. Iris's plan is in full motion. We've suffered many losses, you have suffered two yourself, and the rain is coming within the hour. We need to take care of the bodies before then, mourn, and then rest. Tomorrow we move to the Caldeira.'

Nicholas stumbled back to balance and greeted Hena.

'Your weapon. It's...' stuttered Hena. 'It's reckless. We should talk.' Hena looked through Nicholas's cloak and would have noticed no suit of armour; instead, a plain cotton shirt. Hena parted from him with a stare, to lend an arm to members of her group. 'Don't waste any time, Hill warriors.'

Nicholas bowed his head in anguish before picking up on her previous words. 'Who have we lost?'

'Zachenne,' replied one of the Tarios. 'He saw the beam coming. He pushed me out of the way and...he saved me.'

Nicholas turned his pounding head in shock and scrambled to the other side of the junction, tripping over himself and debris, stumbling past Hena. He carried himself alongside the deeply burnt line through the ground that his beam had created, and eventually, it reached its end, where he found the group's fallen leader. The beam had taken part of his body, but his wavy, silver hair and distinct facial features were pristinely laying in peace to one side.

Nicholas fell to his knees, knowing his reckless weapon had done precisely what he feared it would do. *What have you done, Nicholas?* He looked back along the path of the beam, seeing other body parts and carved weapons beside its path. Enemies and allies alike. He lacked control at that moment, and his consequences lay around him. The others arrived to help with the bodies and to put an arm around Nicholas. Nobody said a word by his side, but he knew their thoughts.

Nicholas looked to Kate, strolling past the remains of battle in a carefree manner, failing to acknowledge Zachenne. 'What do we do now?'

'We bury the bodies and prepare for tomorrow,' said Nicholas mournfully, still fixated on the ground. 'That is what he would have ordered.'

Before the rain fell, the Tarios laid their fallen leader into the ground, finding an open grassland area away from the concrete. Nicholas oversaw, but not much was said; indeed, no discussion of leadership going forward took place. That was best saved for later. Beside him, the Habitants laid their fallen warriors. It would have been easier to use the Hillfolk's light to dig, but out of respect for the hard work the fallen warriors had put in, they insisted on digging the holes.

One of the Habitant women spoke with the final throw of dirt. 'If this is how sombre a victory feels, then I wonder why we even fight.'

*

That night, the Habitants and Hillfolk sat underground, with the stormy rains pouring overhead and a small stream of water passing through the middle of the main tunnel. The groups mostly sat together throughout the tunnels, making new acquaintances and sharing stories. One could not debate that those who sat alone had lost someone dear, such as Emitai did. Matuu, Jordan, and Serr chose to entertain Hena before Jordan made himself aware of those around him, leaving his old friends to join Emitai. He had a small amount of Hill bread left, which he offered to his new companion. Emitai rejected it but asked Jordan to stay. The two smiled.

A gloomy Nicholas watched events unfold to one side of the tunnel. The returning Kate appeared and took a seat beside him.

'Are you well?' asked Kate.

Nicholas sighed. 'I fear I have strayed so far from my comfort zone that my blood has turned blue. Did you not hear our scathing review? I wield a reckless weapon, thus making me a reckless man.'

'The woman, Hena, said they'd have suffered greater if it wasn't for you.'

'I killed Zachenne. And we must all suffer with that. If I carry on along this path, I will be responsible for more of our deaths.'

'Feeling sorry for yourself won't help anyone. You need to be stronger than that, for everyone.' Kate collected berries in her hand from a folded napkin. Her words carried more strength and sternness than several days ago.

'You seem to have fared well. Did you have a smooth ride here? No injuries?'

'Made a couple of friends,' said Kate.

Nicholas sensed the meaning behind her words and chose not to question her further. 'Iris is heading for Aerkin.'

'Yeah, Hena filled me in.' Kate handed the berries to Nicholas. 'Eat. The days ahead will be long.'

The berries were soft and discoloured to one side. Nicholas had no appetite before, nor did he now. 'I need you to take the lead for that trip. I am weak and need to take care of my head.'

'I don't—'

'Kate. Please. You will do just fine.'

Kate zoned out momentarily. She seemed as if she were a world away since returning. The colour change in her eye, the void expressions, no more nervously pinching her nose. She replaced a blood-soaked cloth from the back of Nicholas's head with the napkin from the berries. 'Sure. Whatever you ask. I owe you.'

'You owe me nothing.'

Kate placed her hand on Nicholas's aged, bearded face. 'I do. I can see her. My mama. When I close my eyes now. It worked! I don't know how you did it but it finally worked! She's in a shoe shop holding my hand, and she bought me a pair in my favourite colour but didn't show me until we got home. Until now, all I'd been able to remember were the shoes. But now she's there, smiling down at me. Bright red lips, wearing makeup, real makeup and not mud. She's as beautiful as I remember her.

'I was riding…nowhere, and that's when I saw it. The door. The void. The orbs. All of it! It hit me as if I was in a dream.'

Nicholas sat confused, unsure how to feel. Kate had found the door but not with his help. Perhaps she was mistaken.

'Thought you'd be a lot more excited that I mentioned finding a door,' said Kate, her eyebrows pinched. 'You must be exhausted. But I wanted to tell you—you were right about everything. I should have listened to you. The door, the orbs. I can hear her call my name; it's so beautiful. I feel her, and it's all thanks to you. I'm sorry. I'm so, so sorry. I won't leave your side or doubt you again.'

Kate hugged Nicholas tighter than she'd ever done. 'I love you too,' she whispered. She returned to his vision with a smile, distant-eyed again. 'Get some rest, okay? We'll talk later. I'm sure you have a thousand questions.' She promptly turned and walked away on her own, gliding past the tunnel bend. Nicholas's faint smile from her words was replaced with a pensive stare. Returning memories? Nicholas knew the power that dark energy could impose on the mind. *The door, Nicholas.* He sat, wondering, calling upon lost thoughts, aimlessly looking around.

Surrounding Nicholas, the atmosphere in the sewer brought familiar sights. The sewer lay a land away from the Hill in appearance and distance, but the people were the same. Some were silently mournful, yet some were full of life, boisterous in song. Nicholas looked to his wrist to find a pane of broken glass and two bent fingers, one missing; his precious watch, the link between old time and new, had perished.

Nicholas closed his eyes. Kate's story disappeared. The atmosphere disappeared. Zachenne's face disappeared. No whistling tune came to mind, and no murmurs dictated his presence. His head cleared out all distractions, something that hadn't happened in many years, to rid himself of his mistakes. But with it came the unlocking of the section of his consciousness that dark energy had shrouded. A whisper. *Nicholas.* His thoughts had been threatening to escape these last few days, having been pushed back for so long. This journey— it had been too much. His head ached and pulsated, pulling torturous tales from his reticent mind. *You can hear clearly, now.* The sewer chatter diffused. Nicholas could no longer hide from his thoughts; they had returned.

His heart beat faster. *How could you, Nicholas?* Richard, no. *They still scream my name. It's in your hands, Nicholas.* Why? Please, thoughts. Be gone. *They burned alive. They called my name.* They did no such thing. *You burnt my house. You burnt my family. They screamed as you watched, Nicholas.* No. *You'll pay for what you did to me.*

Plague him no more, thoughts. The suit: it was foolish to allow him to possess it. All these years. His heart threatened to burst out of his chest. The footsteps. The drumming thuds inside his ears. *You need your suit back. I know you do.* He had no other choice. Those around would never comprehend. *You'll lead them all to their deaths.* The forgotten feeling of regret pained him. It had pained him for twenty long years. Please, thoughts, never return to him. *You need your suit back from me.* Stop. *Come get it!* Stop!

Nicholas opened his eyes. He sat by the cold sewer wall, silent, tortured by repressed thoughts and the dormant voice that now raged in his mind. His face remained motionless despite the battle he fought inside. No clenching jaw, nor a shaking hand, not even a blinking eye. All that came to light, as Nicholas sat still, was a single, falling tear.

CHAPTER TWENTY-EIGHT

END

Morning arrived, and the sewers of Rennes emptied of life for the last time. Kate stood by herself, basking in what was as close to a beautiful day as could be. The white of the sky spread east to west, unusually without a single dark cloud in sight, and the day only brought a gentle breeze to the gathering of Habitants and Hillfolk. They carried bags of food in one hand and weapons in the other; it would be all they needed.

'What now?' asked Emitai.

'I know which direction they've taken Iris,' said Hena. 'She'll most likely be at the Caldeira community. It's heavily protected. We would have joined them sooner if it was safe to leave here in large numbers, but we had no choice. Iris has your weapon there.'

'More walking?' asked Matuu. 'Do we at least have a name for ourselves so I can make up a song on the way?'

'Good question,' said Hena, her baby strapped to her chest. 'We have come back, to return this world to what it once was. We are Revenirs.'

'Magnifique,' said Jordan.

Hena pointed. 'Straight ahead for now, that way. For many, *many* days. Everyone ready?' Kate followed Hena's gaze down the rocky path ahead.

'Nicholas, are you leading us?' asked Jordan, as a roadblock of newly named Revenirs stretched across the path.

Kate jumped atop her horse and turned to Nicholas. He needn't say a word, nor had he done all morning. He was unusually quiet and could only offer a nod to her. She took a moment to look out at the path ahead and rode out to the front of the group. She turned back to meet familiar faces and new ones. No smiles could be seen above the tightly wrapped cloth and cloak that kept bodies warm, only uninspired faces and dropped heads. She knew exactly what Nicholas would do in this moment.

Kate spoke loud and clear. 'I know some of you have just lost friends and family. We all know that feeling, all too well. The feeling of pain and hurt, and giving up. But that's how he wins. It's not what he does with his mind that matters, but what he does to ours. I won't give him that control over me and neither will you. I'll take back the feeling of pain so it's mine to feel, so that it's my emotion, and so that I'm the only one that gets to rule my own head. I'll show him everything I have and I'll hold nothing back. My strengths. My weaknesses. All whilst I'm plunging my dagger though the tip of his thick, demented skull!'

She ignited her yellow blade and thrust it to the sky, shimmering bright as if the sun had returned. The Hillfolk, all but Nicholas cheered instantly, confident in their companion. Even the few remaining bowed heads that didn't speak her language looked up to the blade. The response prompted the deafening cheers of all others that followed with a rising orchestra of clattering metal. Kate looked across the animated crowd. This felt somehow natural. Her calling. This is who she was always destined to become, and that moment had arrived. The leader of a rousing revolution.

A stoic calmness descended over Kate, above the city roars, as the crowd began to march past her. The same calmness that graced her the night before. She glanced into the distance, with nothing in focus, only a haze over the horizon. The air was without breeze for a brief moment as her skin turned to ice.

That's when she heard the call again.

Kate.

A white light opened her eyes. Orbs of white light in a vast, infinite darkness surrounded her. In every direction, far in the distance, a few leaps away. The orbs pulsated softly, emitting a faint hum that caressed her ears. She scanned the orbs, for they all contained objects in suspended movement within their glow. One could be seen rotating clearly in the light to her left. Not an object—a hand. These were human bodies, caught in spheres of light, connected by thin, white rays to one another. She was no different, floating in her own sphere of light, connected to two others; a pair of faint dots in the distance. Her hair flowed far longer than it ever had, stretching down the length of her spine, and her left shoulder was clean and unwounded on her unclothed body. It felt so real. It *was* real.

Kate remembered every step in the shoe shop as if it had only just happened, as recent as the memory of the streets of Rennes, only this time she didn't leave the shop with her mother. In her new memory, a door closed behind her: the one that called her name, the one that led her here. Her memories began to fight one another. Old reality crashed with new. Her second mind had truly awoken, and one overwhelming feeling came to her as she stared deep into the infinite network of trapped bodies beyond—she was more alive than living.

Kate continued her examination of the orb realm, simultaneously with the familiar world of ordinary matter; green grasses and rocky roads, the Revenir bodies marching around her and ahead. She tapped her horse to trot forward, an ethereal smile across her well-rested face replacing the mud that masked her from the world. Despite the mysteries that surrounded her in her new mind, the path in front of her had never been clearer. The path to Iris. The path to healing the world.

She rode.

APPENDIX ONE

THE GLOVE DIRECTORY BY NICHOLAS SEVERINGTON

All gloves known to exist thus far.

Dark Energy gloves are created using two compositions of Falkum, and in one case, three. These are ridge, mantle, and Elast. The different properties of each allow dark energy to be captured and manipulated based on the material's shape and size.

When charged, an arrangement of small, raised bumps on one side of the Falkum material can pass through to the other side. When charged with Falkum, dark energy reflects visible light on the electromagnetic spectrum to humans but has also been detected with higher frequencies.

*

The Pegasus Gloves—*Matuu*. Requires large hands and fingers and thumbs pushed together with no gap. On the right glove, the ridge of the front glove forms a Fibonacci-like pattern. The back of the glove consists of mantle with hundreds of raised ridge dots. The left is almost solely ridge, with a circle of mantle in the palm.

The user must ignite and spin hands with the glove's pattern to generate a smooth flow of energy. The user can use the right hand solely to create a wind-like effect. The longer a spin is generated, the faster the wind becomes. Alternatively, the right hand can be spun above the open left palm, focusing the energy to the point and creating a tornado of light.

*

The Diamond Gloves—*Serr.* Requires fingers to be spread out wide. The fronts consist mostly of mantle, apart from a solid ridge inner palm, and the backs are solely ridge.

The user must spread their fingers, creating a large surface area for dark energy to be held. Hands can stay still or move, and light will emanate outwards on a flat plane. If fingers are slightly forward or slightly back, the light will bend. Can be used as a shield to protect a vast area, and held for as long as the user can tense.

*

The First Gloves—*Location unknown.* Distribution of ridge and mantle forgotten. Original prototype gloves required an electrical current to be passed through. Gloves would attract static charge and release visible electricity. Can be activated with human energy or electricity.

Usage unknown, presumed unstable.

*

The Fractal Gloves—*Samuel.* Requires fingers to be spread and protruded in a curved shape. The front and back of the gloves contain small twisting zig-zag patterns that all lead to the fingertips.

The user must press wrists together and open hands and fingers akin to a vase or bowl. Light will emanate in a tree-like fractal, growing and splitting off to form thinner roots in mostly forward directions. Initially spreads quickly, but the longer the user holds it, the slower it gets as more light paths are generated. Caution is recommended when directing the light, as it can pierce the ground if aimed low or held out for too long. Energy is initially sparse, allowing gentle movement of hands without moving the light. Becomes denser further along its path as energy collects.

*

The Guard Gloves—*Guards*. Requires muscular arms and fists to be closed. The ridge is on the inside of the fingers and thumbs, and the top of the palms. The rest of the hand is mantle. The gloves stretch down the forearms, close to the elbows, with the front consisting solely of ridge and the back mantle, from wrist downwards.

The user must close both fists. In attack mode, the hands and forearms of the user will glow thick with light. In defence, the forearms should be held together in front of the body to create a much thicker barrier of light. This protects the upper body and head. Crouching gives near-full front protection.

*

The Hadron Gloves—*Jordan*. Requires powerful muscle to work efficiently. On the right glove, the back and front are mostly ridge, with lines of mantle running to the front, where they all reach a single point in the middle of the palm. The left glove consists solely of mantle on the back of the glove, apart from the fingers. The fingers are entirely ridge on both sides, as is the palm.

The user must propel their right hand forward with speed and power. This throws a bullet of light at great speed and distance. It can travel further than the eye can see if used with great power and accuracy. To defend, the user uses their left hand, clenching their fist and facing their palm towards them. The back of the hand creates a small thick surface to act as a shield.

*

The Hercules Gloves—*Nicholas*. Requires experience and specific hand placement. The right glove is made entirely of mantle, and the left is mantle on the front and ridge on the back.

The user must place left hand behind the right, both facing forward, crisscrossed and interlocked at the thumbs. Ensure left fingertips overlap the right hand and press inwards. Curve the right hand inwards. The thumbs should be aligned and leave no gap. The hands can then be domed and faced outwards, with the left hand pressed down against the back of the right to create a beam of light. The beam reaches far before dissipating, and can destroy all in its path, ground included. If the hand placement is slightly off, the beam will spread uncontrollably. Use with severe caution.

*

The Linai Gloves—*Iris*. Requires rapid wrist movement. The front and back of the gloves have mantle lines leading from the fingers, thumbs, and sides into a coin-sized circle in the palm. Two straight lines leading out from either side of the circle are thicker than most. Most lines reach the top of the circle to generate a curve and sharpness to the light. The rest is ridge.

The user must hold their palm out to create a sharp, curved sword of light. Once it has reached the desired length, the user must then snap their wrist inwards and grab hold of the light. Slow movement leads to dissipated light. Placing the little finger under first will prevent the light swinging down. Users with experience can then swing the blade back with the thumb, so it emanates from the left of the palm, rather than the right, and also propel swords forward if enough momentum is generated.

*

The Marshal Gloves—*Marshals*. Requires fast and robust hand movement and fists to be closed. The gloves are mostly ridge apart from striped mantle lines running down along the front and back of the fingers and hands.

The user must clench their fist to use traditional boxing combat with light covering the entire hand. With an open hand, the user can emanate non-fatal bladed light with a swipe of their arm, but the light does not reach far. Useful for close combat only.

*

The Tarios Gloves—*Tarios*. Requires steady arms and flat, straight palms. The gloves consist of an integrated malleable Falkum composite material around the wrist: Elast. This can be stretched along the forearm and down to the shoulder with enough strength. The back of the gloves are entirely ridge. The front of the gloves have a slightly sloping mantle line descending from the palm to the wrist, but is otherwise ridge.

The user must hold either arm straight out, and with the other, pull back the wrist Elast. This creates a bolt of light that, when released, fires in a fast, straight line. The bolt is only as big as the distance pulled back, and will fire further if longer. If the palm is not entirely straight, the bolt can fire off aim or dissipate sooner.

*

The Twin Dagger Gloves—*Kate*. Requires rapid wrist movement. The front of the gloves have mantle lines leading from the fingers and thumbs into a thin vertical line in the palm. Two straight lines leading out from either side of the circle are thicker than most. The back is solely ridge. The gloves stretch down the forearms, close to the elbows, with the front consisting solely of ridge and the back mantle, from wrist downwards.

The user must pinch all fingers and thumbs together on each hand. With light emanating from the palm, the user must widen their fingers as the light pushes through, creating a sharp point. This differs from The Linai Gloves in that the blade is flat rather than tubular.

APPENDIX TWO

LANGUAGE OF THE MAINLAND

Known terms and words in use on the Mainland, by Nicholas Servington. A compilation of information and interrogation, and a little guesswork.

*

bastil—execute.
bolheil—hello, general greeting, pleasantry.
beunfowl—help, under threat, threat spotted.
besin—only, alone.
cogni—know, knowledge.
da—yes.
dachi—nature that roams the day.
entin—everything, all.
ental—others.
feli—happy, joy, good.
fortuna—fate.
geheim—hide, secret, secrecy.
hue—light.
hulia—daughter, woman of.

hulius—son, son of.
i—will, will happen.
kisa—rain.
kisarya—storm, heavy rain.
imun—rise, up.
medin—submit, submit to, surrender.
mortis—death, to die.
nachi—nature that roams the night.
persona—mask, identity.
pon—you, your (possessive).
prellundis—praise without judgement.
rillen—senses, to sense, extend.
retnis—live, alive.
slusha—listen, hear, be quiet.
sosinon—the hidden sun, the hidden light.
Uma/uma—one, the One, I, singular.
viande—meat, animal meat, human meat.
vilintrus—intruder, unwelcome.
zeuthor—thunder, thunderstorm.

ABOUT THE AUTHOR

A.T. Southorn began life in Hertfordshire, UK, before moving to London. A keen programmer, astronomer, and short-story writer, he has brought his imagination to life in the first of a science-fiction trilogy.

For updates on upcoming work, please visit his website:
www.atsouthorn.com

You can also connect with him on social media:
www.instagram.com/atsouthorn

Lightning Source UK Ltd.
Milton Keynes UK
UKHW040257290122
397844UK00001B/15